'Trust me.' Damien stood and ... ...
the same way ·· ... ɔɔ ·

'All right.' Savannah lowered her hand into his and he pulled her up from the stool, closing the space between them. Savannah's breath caught in her chest. He brushed a strand of hair off her face, his finger leaving a line of heat across her cheek. If they hadn't been surrounded by people, she would have thought he was about to kiss her. Or maybe he *was* about to kiss her. Right here, in front of everyone.

***

Courtney stared at Brett, feeling like she could get lost in his green eyes. Then she realised what she was thinking and she looked away, shaking the thought from her head. They would be stepsiblings soon. She couldn't help her reaction to him, but it wasn't appropriate.

Brett tried to say something, but the music drowned out his voice.

'What?' Courtney screamed, leaning towards him and cupping a hand around her ear. Her hand brushed against his shoulder and the contact made her stomach flip.

'Want to get out of here?' he asked.

***

'So, what did you do last night?' Courtney asked Peyton as they passed the show. 'I didn't hear you get back.'

'Just hung out with a friend.' Peyton replayed the night in her mind. After the fireworks at Myst, Oliver had said he was sick of his father watching his every move, so they'd gone to another club. The drinks had flowed all night, so everything was hazy, but they couldn't keep their hands off each other. Since Oliver lived with his parents and Peyton lived with her sisters, Oliver had the brilliant idea of getting a room.

She smiled at the memory of what had happened once they got there.

Michelle Madow has visited Las Vegas every year since she was fifteen years old and was inspired to write *The Secret Diamond Sisters* while walking through the beautiful Wynn Hotel. She grew up in the suburbs of Baltimore, then went to Rollins College in Winter Park, Florida. She wrote her first novel, *Remembrance,* in her third year of college, which she later went on to self-publish as book one of the Transcend Time Saga. She wrote *The Secret Diamond Sisters* in the year following graduation and is so happy to finally share it with the world!

Michelle lives in Boca Raton, Florida, where she is writing more novels for young adults. She loves reading, spending time with family and friends, travelling, shopping, sunshine, Disney fairy tales and Broadway musicals. She loves connecting with readers online, so be sure to follow her on Facebook (Michelle Madow), Twitter (@MichelleMadow) and Instagram (@MichelleMadow).

THE
SECRET
DIAMOND
SISTERS

MICHELLE MADOW

Published in Great Britain 2014
by MIRA Ink, an imprint of Harlequin (UK) Limited,
Eton House, 18-24 Paradise Road,
Richmond, Surrey, TW9 1SR

© 2014 Michelle Madow

ISBN 978 1 848 45287 9
eBook ISBN: 978 1 472 05500 2

47-0314

Harlequin (UK) Limited's policy is to use papers that are natural, renewable and recyclable products and made from wood grown in sustainable forests. The logging and manufacturing processes conform to the legal environmental regulations of the country of origin.

Printed and bound by
CPI Group (UK) Ltd, Croydon, CR0 4YY

To Brent Taylor,
for believing in this book from the beginning

www.campusbuzz.com

First Post :)
Posted on Sunday 07/03 at 12:51 AM

It's about time campusbuzz got a high school forum. I'm sure we'll have lots to talk about. We're young, we're beautiful, and Vegas is our personal playground. But let's save the whole "who's the hottest girl/guy in the school" stuff for later (although I fully expect to be mentioned in that discussion), because I just discovered something *much* better to talk about.

You know how the school started building a new (and much needed) gym in the beginning of summer? It's going to be named the Diamond Sports Center. And yes, by "Diamond" I mean Adrian Diamond, the owner of the new Diamond Hotel and Casino, along with a bunch of other hotels on the Strip.

An anonymous source told me that three new girls with the last name of Diamond will be starting at the Goodman School in the fall. My guess is they're somehow related to Adrian and the school let them in because of the money he gave for the gym. Makes sense, right?

Except that I checked online and couldn't find anything about Adrian Diamond having a daughter—let alone three of them!

Anyone got any info?

1: Posted on Sunday 07/03 at 01:31 AM

the internet says nothing about adrian diamond having

any kids. sounds like your "sources" don't know what they're talking about. maybe you can find something on facebook?

2: Posted on Sunday 07/03 at 01:47 AM
Facebook's got over 165,000 people on it with the last name Diamond. Dumb idea.

3: Posted on Sunday 07/03 at 06:20 PM
i don't go to goodman but my mom works at the diamond and said their getting a 3 bedroom condo on the top floor ready for some "special guests" who will be staying there for an extended period of time...

4: Posted on Sunday 07/03 at 06:40 PM
Poster #3—interesting to know. But you should consider applying to Goodman. If you manage to get in, then you can learn the difference between "their" and "they're." Just a suggestion :)

chapter 1: *Savannah*

"You're definitely coming to the movies with us tonight, right?" Savannah's best friend, Evie, asked as Savannah got out of the car. "And sleeping over again?"

"Of course." Savannah shared a conspiratorial smile with Evie, knowing that "movies" was code for pretending to walk into the theater while Evie's mom was watching, then having Evie's current boy toy pick them up and drive them to the unsupervised party five minutes away. They could only stay at the party for three hours, but it was better than not going.

"Thanks for driving me home from volleyball, Mrs. Brown," she said, waving to Evie's mom. She was always glad Mrs. Brown didn't mind dropping her off, because Evie was the only friend of hers who had seen where she lived. If the other girls on the volleyball team saw the ramshackle apartment building where she lived with her mom and two older sisters that looked more like a run-down motel than a home, they would probably laugh about it behind her back.

"It's no problem, Savannah," Mrs. Brown said from the driver's seat. She had the same strawberry-blond hair as her daughter, and the two could almost pass as sisters. "Are you sure you don't want me to pick you up tonight?"

"I'll get one of my sisters to drop me off." She didn't want to make Mrs. Brown come out of her way twice in one day. It was already more than enough that Evie's mom drove her home every day after practice during volleyball season, and that she didn't mind when Savannah stayed the night for two or three days at a time over the summer.

Anyway, her sisters owed her after making her come home now, when she was supposed to have stayed the rest of the day at Evie's before they went out for the night. Life would be so much easier once she got her license. Of course, she would have to figure out how to borrow Peyton's car. Convincing her sister would be difficult, because Peyton had saved up for years for that beat-up piece of crap whose engine sounded like it could die any day, but the possibility was better than nothing.

"See you soon, S!" Evie called as her mom pulled away from the curb.

"Bye, E," Savannah replied, and they both made the sign-language letter for *C* with their hands. Savannah and Evie called themselves S.E.C., which stood for the "Savannah/ Evie Club," and the letter *C* was their special symbol. "See you tonight!"

She walked down the sidewalk to the door with the peeling blue paint, wondering what was up. Her sisters never made her come home when she had plans, but Courtney's voice on the phone had sounded so strained that Savannah knew something was wrong.

She let herself inside and found Peyton and Courtney standing around the stained kitchen table, their grandma and a man

Savannah didn't recognize sitting in the two chairs. He wore a fancy brown suit that probably cost more than everything in Savannah's wardrobe combined, and his expression was so solemn that he looked like he was at a funeral. Her grandma and sisters looked equally upset.

"What's going on?" Savannah dropped her sleepover bag on the cracked linoleum floor. She hadn't been home since yesterday morning, and had an awful feeling this had to do with the one person who wasn't here—her mom.

"Hi, sweetie." Grandma always looked younger than her seventy-so years, but her eyes were so sad right now that her age shined through. "Sorry for making you come home early. I wouldn't have asked unless it was serious."

"Where's Mom?" Savannah swallowed and leaned against the arm of the living room couch, expecting the worst. Her mom had always drunk a lot, but after she'd lost her job as a secretary last year, she had spiraled out of control. Her sisters tried to shield Savannah from seeing what went on, but Savannah wasn't stupid. She knew her mom was drinking all day, so much that she got physically sick at night and in the morning, and that she couldn't hold on to a hostess or waitress job for longer than two months. They could barely keep enough food in the house anymore, since Mom blew all the grocery money on alcohol.

"That's what we needed you here to discuss," the man cut in. He looked like he would fit in better in a fancy office building than their crappy apartment in Fairfield, California.

"Who's he?" Savannah asked Grandma.

"This is Mr. Webster," Grandma said. "He's a lawyer who works for your father."

"What?" Savannah's heart pounded. That couldn't be true. Savannah had always been warned that her father was dangerous, that he didn't want anything to do with her and her sisters. She hated that he felt that way, but it was how her life had always been, so she'd accepted it and moved on. "Am I missing something?"

"We all are." Peyton's eyes blazed. "We've been lied to for our entire lives."

That was becoming clear to Savannah, but it was Courtney who caught her up on what had happened while she had been having a sleepover at Evie's.

"Last night, Mom was pulled over for drunk driving on her way to work," Courtney said, somehow managing to stay calm as she relayed the story. "They brought her to the station, and she lost her license and job." Was that the fifth or sixth job she'd lost in the past year? Savannah had lost count. "I called Grandma to get Mom out of the station, and then…" Courtney shrugged and looked at Grandma, as if she wanted her to continue.

"I hoped your mom would be able to keep a job and get her life back on track, but enough is enough," Grandma said in her matter-of-fact manner. "I know it's never been easy living with her, but I've seen what the three of you have gone through in the past year, and I can't sit back and watch anymore. I would take you in myself if I didn't have so much on my hands with your Aunt Sophie's chemo treatments." Her chin quivered at the mention of her twin, who had been staying with Grandma in her one-bedroom apartment since her cancer diagnosis a few months ago. "So I did the only thing I could think to do—I called your father for backup."

Savannah couldn't believe she was hearing this right. "But our father wants nothing to do with us." She turned to her sisters for support, but Peyton looked angry enough to shoot fire from her eyes, and Courtney's expression was blank, as though she was fighting to hold on to an inkling of control.

"Mr. Diamond has been aware of your living situation, and was about to take action himself when your grandmother called him," Mr. Webster said. "He made some calls last night and arranged for your mother to receive inpatient treatment at a rehabilitation facility in Arizona. She was flown there this morning and is settling in, but the facility has given strict orders that your mom not contact anyone from outside until her doctors feel she is healthy enough to do so. They hope she'll be ready to switch to outpatient status in a few weeks, but they warned it could be longer."

Savannah's head spun. How had all this happened while she had been having a sleepover at Evie's, gossiping about which girls at school they wanted to try to become friends with next year and what guys they thought were hot, while experimenting with daring makeup looks?

"You didn't let me say goodbye?" She looked at her sisters, unable to believe they could betray her like that.

"None of us were able to say goodbye." Courtney came over and wrapped an arm around Savannah's shoulders. "Mom didn't want us to see her like that. She said it would be easier this way, and you know she hates goodbyes. We just need to focus on being thankful she's finally getting the treatment she needs."

"She was probably ashamed, and afraid we would ask her questions she wasn't ready to answer," Peyton said. "And she would have been right."

"But with Mom not here, where are we supposed to go?" Savannah wiped away a tear that had slid down her cheek. She was grateful her mom was getting help, but they still needed

her around. Sure, she wasn't always the best at taking care of
them, but she was all they had.

"You know I love you and your sisters, and would be
happy for you to live with me if there were no other options," Grandma said. "But you deserve more than sleeping on the couch and air mattresses in the living room, and
I worry about the stress the changes would cause Aunt Sophie. Luckily, your father has generously offered for you to
move in with him."

"Are you serious?" Savannah didn't believe this. She and
her sisters had never met their father. And now he was of-
fering for them to *move in* with him? "Why now? I thought
it wasn't safe for us to be around him? And where does he
even live?"

Mr. Webster was the one to answer. "Mr. Diamond asked
me to provide as little information as possible, because he
wants to personally answer your questions, but I can assure
you that your safety is his top priority. He's sending a driver
to pick you up tomorrow morning who will take you to the
airport. I know this is short notice to give you girls to pack,
but do what you can and Mr. Diamond will arrange for the
rest of your belongings to be brought to your new accommo-
dations at a later date."

A plane. Which meant if it took her mom longer than a few
weeks to get better, Savannah would start her sophomore year
at a new school, with people she'd never met. How was she
going to break this to Evie? And how would she get through
school without her best friend by her side?

"What if we don't want to go?" Peyton crossed her arms
and glared at Mr. Webster. "I'm almost eighteen, you know.
I should have a say in this." Peyton's birthday was in March,

which hardly made her "almost eighteen," but Savannah kept her mouth shut.

"As it is now, you're still a minor, so you have no choice," Mr. Webster said. "With your mother unfit, it is in your father's rights to insist you live under his care. You will pack your bags and be ready to leave by ten o'clock tomorrow morning."

"What about the apartment?" Courtney asked. "What will happen to it while we're gone?"

"Mr. Diamond will make sure it's maintained," Mr. Webster said. "I'm sorry to throw this on you all at once. I know this won't be easy for the three of you, but he will answer all your questions when you arrive. Now, I imagine you need time to pack. Is there anything more you want to ask?"

"I think you have it covered, Mr. Webster." Grandma spoke for them. "Now if you wouldn't mind, I would like some time with my granddaughters."

"Of course." He nodded and let himself out.

"You can't expect us to do this," Peyton said to Grandma once he was gone. "All my life you've said our father is dangerous and he doesn't want us around. Now we're expected to forget all that and move in with him? I won't do it. I refuse."

"Your mother has her reasons for wanting to distance herself from your father, and while being around him can be dangerous for those close to him, he's not a bad man," Grandma said. "He'll explain it all to you once he meets you. Just remember that your mother loved him once, and while it won't be easy, I hope the three of you can find it in your hearts to give him a chance. Can you promise to do that? For me?"

When she put it like that, it was impossible to say no. "Okay." Savannah nodded, trying to swallow away the lump in her throat. "I'll try."

Her cell phone buzzed in her pocket, and she took it out to check the text. It was from Evie.

Any luck convincing one of your sisters to drive you tonight?

Savannah stared blankly at the beat-up flip phone. The plans she'd made with Evie less than an hour ago felt like they'd happened in another life. She couldn't wrap her mind around what she'd just learned, let alone tell someone else, even if that someone was her best friend.

Can't go tonight. Something big happened. Not ready to talk about it yet but I'll call you when I am <3

She pressed Send, then dropped her phone in her bag, not wanting to look at it again that night.

The next morning, they lugged their bags outside and tearfully hugged Grandma goodbye. The stretch limo that pulled up in front of their apartment looked foreign amongst the beat-up cars lining their street, and the sight of it sent Savannah's ideas of who her father was out the window. He couldn't be a homeless drugged-out loser if he'd sent a *limo* to pick them up.

As of last night, the most expensive car Savannah had ever been in was the Volkswagen Jetta Evie's mom drove when she brought them home from volleyball practice or to the mall. Now, she climbed into the sleek limo, her fingers grazing the soft leather of the wraparound seat. Lights lined the ceiling, and there was a wooden minibar across from the long side of the seat, an open bottle of champagne chilling in the ice bucket and three glasses on display. The label on the champagne read Dom Pérignon, and while Savannah had never tasted Dom before, she recognized it as a pricey drink from the television shows she watched.

She wasn't hugely into drinking, because she'd seen first-hand how destructive alcohol could be, but she wasn't a prude, either. She didn't want to be "that lame girl" at the party who refused to drink. And now she had the opportunity to taste Dom Pérignon! Her friends would be so envious when they found out. It was the sort of drink she imagined she would get to try if her dreams ever came true and she became a famous pop star. One glass wouldn't be the end of the world.

"Don't even think about it," Courtney warned as Savannah reached for the bottle.

"But it's Dom Pérignon." Savannah hated when Courtney tried to boss her around. They were only eleven months apart, but Courtney was so responsible all the time. It made the gap feel wider. "It's probably hundreds of dollars for this bottle. We have to try it."

"I'm not trying anything *he* buys for us." Peyton scrunched her nose and plugged her headphones into her ears.

Knowing Courtney wouldn't physically stop her for fear of making a mess, Savannah poured herself a glass and took a sip, the tiny bubbles gliding down her throat. Dom Pérignon was better than anything she'd ever tasted. But there *was* that little voice in the back of her head, warning her that drinking in the morning was something her mom would do. Savannah cleared this up with her conscience by reminding herself that if her mom were here, she would finish the bottle. Savannah was only having one glass, and only to taste it.

She felt so sophisticated with her drink, and wished she'd worn something dressier than the dark jeans and pink tunic top she'd bought at Forever 21 a few weeks ago. She'd thought it looked good when she'd put it on this morning, but she hardly looked like the type of person who arrived at the airport in a limo.

But there was nothing she could do about it now.

She looked at Courtney and Peyton, sitting in the front-facing seat, and wondered how they didn't share her amazement that they were in the back of a *limo*. Courtney's long blond hair had dried into natural waves—the kind Savannah wished she had—and she was staring out the window, her chin balanced in her hand as she watched the scenery. She kept biting her thumbnail—a giveaway that she was nervous, which made Savannah feel on-edge, too. Courtney never had a problem handling everything thrown her way—school, keeping the apartment clean, taking extra shifts at work to pay the bills and making sure Savannah got her homework done. While the bossiness got annoying sometimes, Savannah didn't know what she would do without her.

Peyton slumped in her seat, her headphones plugged into her ears and huge dark sunglasses covering her eyes. She had pulled the hood of her black terry-cloth jacket over her head midway through the ride, and her long, light brown hair with the occasional streak of blue fell over her shoulders. Savannah hated the blue streaks. Why her sister would *want* to look like a freak was beyond her. Not that Peyton would listen to Savannah's opinion.

Getting the vibe that neither of her sisters felt like talking, Savannah looked out the window. They drove past some small run-down apartment buildings and entered the highway. They passed by tons of vineyards, the grape vines bright green and alive under the hot July sun. Where were they heading? Last she'd heard, her father lived in Las Vegas, but it had been fifteen years since her mother had left him—right after she got pregnant with Savannah. He could be anywhere now.

It wasn't like he'd bothered to contact them. They didn't even know his first name. Savannah always assumed he was incapable of taking care of them, but if he could afford a limo, why hadn't he made an effort to get to know his own daughters? To acknowledge their existence? He was only interested in them now because he had no other choice. Savannah's eyes watered as she realized again how alone she and her sisters were, and she took a sip of champagne to force away the tears. She and her sisters had plenty of differences, but at least no matter what was coming next, they would have each other.

Courtney must have noticed how Savannah had tensed up, because she looked at her and forced a smile. "How does it taste?" she asked, motioning to the champagne.

"It's good," Savannah replied. "Are you sure you don't want some? We probably won't have an opportunity to taste something as expensive as this ever again." She took another sip, relishing the citrusy taste. She'd bet the champagne cost more than the Longchamp bag Evie had just gotten for her birthday. Savannah wished she had a phone that could send picture texts, so she could show Evie and some of the other girls from the team what she was drinking. They would be so jealous.

"I'm sure." Courtney shook her head. "It's first thing in the morning, and the champagne isn't even ours."

Savannah shrugged at Courtney's goody-goody attitude and looked over at Peyton, who was lost in iPod land and ignoring her.

Savannah decided to change that. She lifted the half-filled glass to her lips and threw her head back, taking a large gulp. It fizzed going down her throat, the liquid swirling in her stomach as it made its way down.

"Getting drunk first thing in the morning?" Peyton removed one of her earbuds and dropped it onto her lap. "You'll end up like Mom."

"Is that necessary?" The harshness in Courtney's usually calm voice took Savannah by surprise. "Mom messed up, but she tried. Don't be so hard on her. But Peyton's right," she said, refocusing on Savannah. "You shouldn't be drinking— not after everything with Mom. I know you think she doesn't care about what you do, but she wouldn't want you to repeat her mistakes."

"I'm not like Mom," Savannah insisted. "I only wanted a glass. I mean, it's Dom Pérignon. Do you know how many people would *kill* to try this? Besides, Mom would have finished the bottle by now."

"She would have," Peyton agreed—which surprised Savannah, because Peyton never agreed with anything she said. "Which made it real easy for our nonexistent father to take us away from home without giving us any say."

"The nonexistent father who she led us to believe was a homeless drug addict," Savannah said. "Which he clearly isn't. Not if he can afford all this. I know it's a long shot, but maybe…"

"Don't tell me you're wishing he's that big-time hotel owner again," Peyton said. "Just because he rented a limo to get us doesn't mean anything. He wasted all this money trying to impress us, and it won't make me like him after he ignored us for our whole lives. Besides, you know there are seventy-five people with the last name of Diamond in Las Vegas—"

"And twenty thousand in America." Savannah cut her off, imitating her sister's superior tone. "I know this. You've told me a million times. But it would be cool if he was."

Okay, it would be more than cool if her father was *the* Adrian Diamond—the one who owned numerous hotels in

Las Vegas and had more money than Savannah could imagine. The life she could have then would be beyond her wildest dreams.

It would be like living in a Las Vegas fairy tale.

"I wouldn't even *want* him to be our father," Peyton continued. "Who the hell goes fifteen years without talking to their daughters and then suddenly wants custody?"

"Our dad," Courtney said, her voice tight. "But Mom needs to be in rehab. After all the years we tried and failed to convince her to get help, she's finally there, and I'm glad she's getting treatment. Just think—in a few months, Mom will be better. And in the meantime, maybe our father won't be that bad."

"Are you sure you didn't have any champagne while I was sleeping?" Peyton snickered and plugged her earbud back in.

Courtney opened her mouth as if she wanted to retaliate, but of course she didn't. Arguing with Peyton was pointless. Peyton never listened to anyone.

"Maybe you're right," Savannah said to Courtney. "He did send a limo. He wouldn't have done that if he didn't care about us."

"Yeah." Courtney frowned, her forehead creasing in thought.

Savannah didn't like seeing her so worried. She wasn't used to feeling like she had to take care of her sisters. Usually it was the other way around. Her throat tightened, and while she wanted to say something comforting, she had no idea what would help. Instead, she looked out the long window in front of her, the sun lighting up the cloudless California day. The limo exited the highway and passed a large sign announcing their arrival at Napa Valley Airport. There were barely any other cars around, and the airport was small. Only a few boxy buildings and planes were up ahead, and beyond that, the rolling hills of the vineyards in the countryside.

"Is it just me, or does this place seem deserted?" Savannah asked.

"Napa Valley is a *private* airport," Courtney said. "I don't think they have commercial flights."

"No commercial flights?" Savannah repeated. Because if the airport didn't have commercial flights, they only had private ones. And that would mean…

Savannah's stomach swooped at the possibility, and she leaned closer to the window. Could her guess about their father be right?

The road widened, and her heart thumped as they approached the buildings. The limo drove past a few planes—some small, some large—and came to a stop.

Towering in front of them was the biggest private jet of them all, the gold lettering along the side spelling three distinct words:

Diamond Resorts Worldwide.

Adrian Diamond was their father.

chapter 2: *Courtney*

No way.

Courtney stepped out of the limo and stared at the jet. If this plane was for them, sent by their father…then Savannah was right. Courtney had always dismissed her younger sister's fairy-tale notion that the infamous hotel owner Adrian Diamond could be their father, never considering that Savannah *could* be right. But unless the limo driver had accidentally picked them up instead of three other Diamond sisters living in a run-down apartment in Fairfield, California—this jet was for them.

Not believing what she was seeing, Courtney examined Savannah's reaction. Her younger sister had frozen, her mouth dropped open. A breeze blew some of her dark blond hair across her forehead, and she pushed it behind her ears, her eyes fixed on the jet. Courtney would have laughed if she didn't feel as astonished herself.

"Are you the Diamond sisters?" A low voice belonging to

a large man in a white suit pulled Courtney out of the shock. His black hair had been slicked back with enough oil to fuel the plane, and he had one of those square jaws she associated with football players.

She would have assumed he was their father, but his dark features bore no resemblance to their own.

"Yes." Courtney looked him in the eye and stood straighter. "I'm Courtney. This is Peyton and Savannah."

"I'm Captain Rogers." He held out a strong hand in greeting. Courtney shook it, then quickly dropped her arm back to her side. "I'll be taking care of you today."

So he wasn't their father. Adrian Diamond must have more important things to do with his time than pick his daughters up himself.

Not that Courtney expected much from the man who hadn't spoken to them in fifteen years. She didn't want to jump to conclusions, but he had some major explaining to do when they met. Courtney didn't know how she was going to handle that. What could he say to make it okay that he'd disappeared from their lives? There was no good reason for that, especially for someone as well-off as Adrian Diamond. What could have happened for him to want nothing to do with her or her sisters? For him to have abandoned them?

Her head spun, and realizing her breaths had become shallow, she forced herself to inhale deep and gain control of the situation. She would handle this like she handled everything—one step at a time. There had to be a logical reason why Adrian Diamond hadn't been involved in the lives of his three daughters.

But as much as Courtney hated to admit it, they could have used his support. If he'd helped them out growing up—just a little bit—she had no idea how different her life would be.

She hadn't minded getting a job to help her family, but if she'd had more time to focus on her studies instead of having to pick up extra shifts to pay bills, her grades and practice SATs would have been better. They weren't bad—she had a 3.76 GPA and her practice test scores were above the 90th percentile—but with more time to study, she could have improved.

Courtney wrapped her arms around herself and looked up at the plane. All she could do now was focus on meeting her father. Peyton was so angry, and Savannah was so hopeful, that neither of them could approach this rationally. Her sisters needed her to be the one in charge.

"So do we just…get on?" Peyton pointed her thumb at the entrance steps to the plane, which were surrounded by security guards.

The captain laughed. "If you're ready to depart, then yes. You can 'just get on.'"

"And the plane is going where?" Courtney asked.

"Las Vegas," he answered.

"Vegas!" Savannah clapped her hands. "I knew it!"

Seeing a movement in her peripheral vision, Courtney glanced at the van with their luggage, which had followed the limo to the airport. Three men of varying ages had already opened the back doors and were unloading it. They didn't have much to worry about—only six duffels between the three of them, and Savannah's beat-up guitar. Last night, Grandma had helped them pack all their stuff from the bedroom the three of them shared.

The captain motioned toward the jet as if he was saying "all aboard" with his hand. Savannah bolted for the stairs, her hair flying behind her. Courtney followed, and she heard Peyton stomping behind.

Courtney couldn't believe this was happening. A private plane? Maybe she was dreaming. Savannah's ideas about their father being *the* Adrian Diamond must have invaded her subconscious. But while Courtney had vivid dreams, they were nothing like this. She felt the cold metal of the railing against her hand when she walked up the steps, and smelled the warmth of summer as it blew through the air. If her mom could see them now, she wouldn't believe it.

Then Courtney realized her mom *would* believe it. Because her mom had known who their father was, and she'd never told Courtney or her sisters. Even Peyton had been too young when they'd moved to remember him. Their mom had always said she didn't want the girls growing up in the dangerous environment their father lived in, and left it at that. The divorce papers for the short marriage had gone through right after Savannah was born, and their mother had always refused to discuss him, other than to say that his lifestyle wasn't appropriate for raising children. It had been her decision, but Courtney figured if he'd wanted them around, he would have done something about it. He hadn't, so she'd done her best not to think about him. Getting upset about the past accomplished nothing.

So what made him care now? Courtney couldn't ignore what was right in front of her—their father was a powerful man. If he'd wanted to be in their lives, he could have made it happen.

But she shouldn't jump to conclusions. She would sort out her feelings when she was able to hear the responses to her questions from her father himself.

Courtney reached the top of the stairs and stepped through the door. The jet was unlike anything she could have imagined. It looked like a fancy living room; the tubular shape and the windows along the walls were the only hints that they were in a plane. Down the aisle were four cream-colored seats, two on each side facing each other, and farther back against the walls were matching leather sofas. There was even a dining area at the end, with a dark brown wooden table and four chairs. Every inch of wood shined like it had been coated with layers of gloss, and the cream leather of the seats and sofas looked and smelled brand-new. It was as though they were the first people to ever step inside.

Courtney had only seen planes in movies, and those were commercial ones. She'd had no idea they could be like *this*.

She had never felt so out of place, and she didn't know what she was supposed to do next.

Savannah jumped onto one of the couches and sprawled across it, apparently not sharing Courtney's discomfort. "This is awesome!" she said, stretching her arms above her head. "Can you believe this is happening? Limos, private planes... It doesn't seem real."

"And moving to a city where we know no one, to meet a father who hasn't spoken to us in fifteen years," Courtney reminded her, sitting on the sofa across from Savannah.

"Maybe he has a good reason," Savannah said hopefully.

Peyton slumped into the couch with Courtney and leaned against the opposite armrest. Her torn black tights, jean shorts with the pockets hanging out of the bottom and gray striped T-shirt were out of place here, but she didn't look a bit uncomfortable.

"Don't be naive," Peyton said, popping a piece of gum into her mouth. "This is nice and all, but don't let it blind you to how our father ignored us for our whole lives. If you act impressed by his money when you meet him, he'll think it means you forgive him. And I sure as hell don't. It actually makes me angrier. If he has all this money, we wouldn't have been a burden to him. He should have reached out to us before now. The only reason he didn't is because he doesn't give a shit about us."

"We should remember what Grandma told us and listen to what he has to say," Courtney said, although she'd had the same worries herself. "We have to hear his side, even though it's hard to imagine what good excuse he could have."

"Because he *can't* have one," Peyton sneered. "It's impossible."

"Nothing's impossible," Savannah shot back. "Stop being so negative."

"I'm not being negative." Peyton rolled her eyes. "Just realistic."

"So you're not going to give him a chance?"

"He doesn't deserve one," Peyton replied. "And if you'd stop freaking out because 'Omigod, we're in a private jet!' then maybe you'd see that."

Courtney looked back and forth between the two of them. If they were going to be like this when they met their father, it was going to be disastrous. Luckily a flight attendant asked them if they wanted any drinks before Savannah and Peyton could argue any more.

The captain made sure they were ready to go, and Courtney moved to a window seat, pressing her forehead against the glass. She tapped her nails against the armrest as the plane sped up, and her stomach flipped as they rose into the sky, the world below shrinking to resemble a clay model. Everything was so small that she felt like she could reach down and pluck a truck right off the road.

She still felt like she was in a dream. Less than a week ago, she was working extra shifts at Starbucks to help her mom pay rent and make sure they had enough groceries for the week.

Now she was flying in a private plane to Vegas, about to meet the father she'd never known.

Things like this didn't happen in real life.

But they were happening in hers.

Chapter 3: *Peyton*

Even Peyton had to admit that the Las Vegas Strip was impressive from above. The mishmash of buildings along both sides of the wide street looked like it had been dropped randomly in the endless brown desert, and no two hotels looked similar. There was a shiny black pyramid, a medieval castle, matching gold-plated towers, a massive green building that reflected the sunlight and a tall one at the end that looked like the Seattle Space Needle, just to name a few.

Peyton wondered which one was her father's.

Her father. Adrian Diamond. The owner of Diamond Resorts Worldwide.

It was completely unreal.

And it pissed Peyton off.

She clenched her fists, pressing her fingernails into her palms to release some of the anger. Someone who made zero effort to get to know his daughters had to be a horrible person. Peyton didn't blame her mother for not accepting charity from him. Not after he married her, only for her to find out four years—and three children—later that his life was "too dangerous" to have a family and he didn't want them around anymore. It was way messed up.

No, Peyton didn't blame her mother at all. She admired her for it. Her mother had raised them to the best of her ability—until the constant drinking came into the picture. She'd always had an alcohol problem, but it had gotten way worse when she'd lost her secretary job a year ago. Then Peyton had had to watch her mom come home drunk every night, usually with a sleazy guy she'd picked up at a bar. She'd wanted to move out and get her own apartment—especially after one of her mom's boyfriends kept hitting on her and trying to touch her. Peyton had told him to back off and threatened to call the cops on him if he laid a finger on her or her sisters. That had stopped him from going too far, but she'd shuddered whenever he'd looked at her, and she'd warned her sisters to never be alone with him. She'd tried to tell her mom what was going on, but her mother had just called her a slut and said she was asking for it by leading him on. Peyton couldn't have been happier when her mom had discovered he was cheating with a young bartender and told him to get lost.

She wouldn't have been able to get her own apartment anyway, because no one would rent to a seventeen-year-old, and while she didn't get along with her sisters all the time, she could never leave Courtney and Savannah to handle their mother and her boyfriends alone. They needed her—especially Savannah, who didn't know how bad things were. With Courtney always at work and Savannah at sports practice or out with her friends, it was up to Peyton to do damage control, pouring her mom's alcohol down the sink and helping her sober up before the other two got home. Her mother yelled at her, calling her a bitch and a slut, but Peyton didn't care. She'd learned not to take the name-calling personally, and whipping her mom into shape and cleaning the apartment before her sisters got home was her responsibility. Courtney did her part by taking extra shifts at work to pay the bills, and Savannah was too young and naive to have to deal with it.

But with her mom continuing to go downhill, Peyton couldn't have kept it up for much longer. Maybe Adrian Diamond really did care that their living situation had gone down the tubes.

But she doubted it.

The plane landed, and another limo pulled onto the tarmac to pick them up. After thanking the captain and saying goodbye, Peyton and her sisters got into the backseat and headed off to wherever they were going.

Guess it would have been too inconvenient for their father to come to the airport to greet the daughters he hadn't seen since they were babies. Peyton clenched her jaw, grinding her molars together. It was just more proof he didn't care about them.

Add it to the overflowing list.

The airport was close to the Vegas Strip, and while Peyton didn't want to like the place where her asshole of a father lived, she couldn't help admiring the hotels as the limo drove by. Some were themed like cities—New York, Paris, Venice—while others were shiny and glitzy. One had a gigantic fountain in front of it, the bursts of water dancing to a classical number coming from invisible outdoor speakers. A crowd had gathered around the railing to watch. Even the Denny's sign was surrounded by flashing lights. Everyone walking along the sidewalk was laughing and having fun, a lot of them sipping colorful drinks that were two feet tall. It was only the afternoon, but that didn't seem to stop anyone from starting to party.

Or maybe they were continuing the party from the night before.

Finally the limo pulled up to two crescent-shaped gold-plated buildings standing side by side, stretching high into the sky. They had to be the tallest buildings on the Strip. Lighter shades of gold lined the tops and bottoms of every floor, eventually stopping to leave a wide space for swirling cursive writing on the top. Peyton held her hand over her forehead to shield the sunlight, squinting to make out the words. The farther building said The Diamond Hotel, and the closer one The Diamond Residences.

"Wow." Savannah pressed her hand against the window as they pulled into the circular drive of the Residences. Limos and luxury sedans lined the curb, and wide columns surrounded the golden double doors. Two men in white suits flanked the entrance, their hands clasped in front of them, their hair gelled back so they looked nearly identical. Beside each of them stood pedestals with arrogant sphinxlike gold lions.

Peyton had never seen anything like it.

The limo stopped in front of the entrance, and one of the men opened the door on Peyton's side. She stepped out into the stifling desert heat and breathed in the stale dry air, focusing on her physical discomfort to hide her astonishment at her surroundings. She wanted to look pissed at her father, not like she was reveling in the energy of Las Vegas.

Before she could take another step, an elderly man—also in a white suit—approached them. He had wrinkled skin, wispy gray hair, and thin lips that looked like they were permanently pressed together. Surely he couldn't be their father.

Peyton didn't think Adrian Diamond would be so…old. Then she caught sight of the gold badge pinned to his suit. Unless Adrian had changed his name to Bernard, this man wasn't him.

Peyton exhaled and crossed her arms. Her father hadn't bothered to meet them at the airport *or* the hotel. This was not a good start to whatever relationship Adrian Diamond planned on having with them.

If he planned on having a relationship with them at all, which she was starting to seriously doubt.

"Peyton, Courtney and Savannah Diamond?" Bernard asked, giving them a once-over. His lips pressed tighter together when he looked at Peyton. There were only four blue streaks in her hair—and they didn't stand out much—but Peyton still got the feeling he disapproved. He probably wasn't a fan of the Hot Topic bracelet collection up her arm, either. She shot a nasty look back at him, and he looked away, nose in the air. Hopefully everyone in Vegas wasn't this stuck-up.

Courtney stepped forward and told him he had their identities correct. Trust Courtney to take the lead. Most people assumed that because Peyton was oldest, that made her the most responsible of the three.

How wrong they were.

"It's nice to finally meet you," Bernard said. "Mr. Diamond sends his apologies for not being able to greet you himself."

"Sure he does," Peyton muttered.

Her hostility only threw Bernard for a second. "I imagine you're tired after your travels and would like to get situated in your condo," he said, plastering a smile on his thin lips and motioning to the giant gold doors. "Please follow me."

"What about our bags?" Courtney pointed to where their stuff was being unloaded from the car behind them.

"Don't worry about your luggage—the bellhops will bring

it up for you." He turned on the heel of his polished black shoe and led them to the entrance, where two men pulled the doors open for them, and Peyton took her first step inside the Diamond Residences.

She wasn't sure what she had expected, but it was nothing like this. The inside of the building was magnificent to the point of being otherworldly, and it took her breath away. Marble diamond-shaped tiles lined the floor, with an occasional colorful mosaic design forming the shapes of different gems. There was greenery everywhere, brilliant ferns and trees lit up with white lights surrounding the wide path that led from the entrance to a circular bar in the center of the lobby where people milled around drinking cocktails. Just past the bar, Peyton could make out gaming tables and slot machines. Groups of people dressed in everything from bathing suit cover-ups to expensive dresses walked around, holding pool bags, drinks and shopping bags, smiling and chatting animatedly. The energy was contagious, and Peyton's veins buzzed as she took in everything around her, but she concentrated on maintaining her outer appearance of boredom. She refused to like *anything* her father had created.

"The Residences Tower and the Hotel Tower are connected by a hallway, so while you'll live in the Residences, you can go back and forth to the hotel as you please," Bernard said, his mouth barely moving as he spoke. "Would you like a tour first, or should I show you to your condo?"

"We'll go to the condo," Peyton said before Courtney had time to speak. Savannah pouted, but Peyton ignored her. She didn't want to clue in Bernard that she cared. There would be time for exploring alone later.

"If you change your mind, let me know and I'll be happy to show you around," Bernard said, leading them down the tree-lined path to the casino. The casino played a song of its own—slot machines dinging, chips clacking as the dealer passed them out to the players at the tables, and the chatter of people throwing down money with the hope of hitting it big. There was a faint smell of cigarette smoke, but the casino must have a great ventilation system, because it wasn't overpowering like the smoke in the Indian casino Peyton had gone to once with her friends in San Fran. Some of the machines even spoke in happy, cartoon-sounding voices, asking people to give the game a try or coaxing them to continue playing. It was a carnival for adults. The red carpet was new and plushy, and waitresses with model bodies wearing tight, low-cut gold dresses walked around delivering drinks. A person could get lost for days in a place like this.

Peyton caught sight of a sign saying Main Elevators, but Bernard continued past it.

"I thought we were going to the condo?" she asked.

"Yes." He didn't look at her as he continued on. "There are separate elevators for those living on the top ten floors. Follow me."

Special elevators. Top ten floors. Peyton felt farther away from home than ever. Everyone walking around the hotel was dressed up like they were headed somewhere special—even the bathing suit cover-ups people wore looked designer—and Peyton had never felt more out of place. She wasn't going to change for anyone, though, so she would have to act like she didn't notice. She never let not fitting in bother her at home, and that wasn't going to be different now. Instead, she would see it as standing out. The thought gave her a rush of empowerment.

Once inside the elevator, Bernard stuck a shiny gold key card into a slot above the buttons and pushed Floor 75—the highest one. No wonder they needed separate elevators. They would have to constantly stop for people to get off and on otherwise.

"Here are your keys," Bernard told them, pulling identical cards out of his pocket and handing them out. Diamond Residences was printed on them in the same swirling font Peyton had seen at the top of the building. She mumbled, "Thanks," and shoved hers into the back pocket of her shorts.

When they reached floor 75, the elevator doors opened, and Bernard motioned them to exit before him. This hallway had thick ruby carpeting, and the paneled walls were topaz and white. Crystal chandeliers hung from above, and classical music played from invisible speakers, providing a calm atmosphere very different from the excitement below.

Bernard led the way, and Peyton and her sisters followed. "As you can see, there's an exclusive gym here for the use of everyone living in the penthouses," he told them, motioning to the right. "Inside are the highest-quality machines available. We also have outstanding trainers on staff who will happily work with you personally, and group fitness classes that take place in the main gym downstairs."

Peyton looked through the glass windows that separated the hall from the gym. She never went to the gym at home. Savannah went enough for both of them, especially during sports season. Inside on an elliptical cross-trainer was a girl with straight hair so dark it was almost black. She looked around Peyton's or Courtney's age. Her oval-shaped face, tanned skin and cat-shaped eyes made her look like a snobby movie star. Next to her was a tall tanned guy with brown hair and dark eyes. He was cute. More than cute—he was way hotter than her own boyfriend of the month, Mike.

The thought of Mike reminded Peyton of the phone call

she would have to make in the next few days to break up with him. He had to know it was coming. It was no secret that Peyton never stayed with a guy for longer than a few months, and she didn't want to do the long-distance thing.

Trusting a guy in a different city only meant trouble.

Trying not to think about Mike, Peyton gave the guy working out a seductive smile. He either didn't see her, or he ignored her, instead smiling at Savannah. Jerk. Savannah wrapped her arms around herself and lowered her eyes, her cheeks turning pink.

Apparently he wasn't into Peyton's look. Not like it bothered Peyton. There were other guys out there.

Then the dark-haired girl turned to the guy, said something to him, and laughed.

Peyton shook her head and kept walking. She had no interest in hanging out with judgmental bitches. And yes, she was referring to both the girl *and* the guy.

Bernard led them to the end of the hallway and stopped at a golden double-door entrance to insert the key card into the slot. "Welcome to your new home," he said, pushing the door open and waving them inside.

Chapter 4: *Madison*

Madison Lockhart didn't like the Diamond sisters already.

At least, she assumed they were the girls who had just passed by the gym. It wasn't every day that three girls who looked alike walked around the top floor. They had to be Adrian Diamond's daughters.

And her parents wanted her to be friends with them. *So* not happening. One of them looked like a total freak who had come straight off a Cirque du Soleil stage, with blue streaks in her hair, goth bracelets up her arm and so much black eyeliner that she could be on the set of *Cleopatra*. The petite one looked like she was trying to be fashionable but was failing miserably, and the tallest one looked like she had just rolled out of bed.

"Two of them are hot," Damien said from the elliptical next to her.

Madison tried not to show her irritation. "I didn't know you were into blondes," she said smoothly.

"You're right. I do prefer brunettes," Damien said with a

sly grin. "But seeing as my favorite brunette always has her sights elsewhere, I've gotta have my fun, too."

"And you think those girls look fun?" Madison rolled her eyes. "Whatever."

Damien smirked. "Are you…jealous?"

"No." Jealous because Damien thought those girls were hot? Yeah, right. "But the one with the blue streaks seemed like she liked you. Maybe you should go for her."

"The little one was more my type," Damien answered. "And she looked the most innocent. Which makes her the most interesting."

"Whatever," Madison said again, focusing on the screen in front of her. She'd burned 150 calories working out, and she'd eaten about 400 so far that day, which equaled a net of 250. If she was careful during dinner she should be able to stay under her maximum calorie goal of 800 a day. She would have to watch what she drank tonight, as well. Alcohol had calories, too—about 100 calories per glass of wine, to be exact. Not that Madison liked being wasted. Acting like an idiot and doing things she would regret wasn't her style.

She upped the incline of her workout, the muscles in her legs burning, and grabbed the bottle of ice water in her cup holder to take a sip. Damien watched her every movement. Their flirting was always playful, but Madison suspected if she wanted to take their friendship to the next level, he would jump on the opportunity. He was probably saying that stuff about the Diamond sisters to make her jealous.

The explanation satisfied Madison. No way would she let his comments affect her. Besides, at least having Damien around didn't make her feel as terrible about Brett Carmel's rejection a few weeks ago.

Her feelings for Brett didn't make any sense. Her friends

thought he was a major loser. They were right, but ever since she'd tutored him in biology last semester, she'd known he was different. His deep forest-green eyes always made him appear to be thinking about something important, and while she would never admit it to anyone, she was intrigued by the way he blew off everyone at Goodman to hang out with his public-school friends. He was always talking about an indie movie or local band they were going to see—activities that Madison's friends would never dream of attending. It was like a foreign world, and hearing Brett talk about it made her curious about what it would be like to not worry about being photographed in the same outfit in too short a time span, or to not feel like she had to constantly entertain the people around her. She had mastered maintaining a perfect balance of being exciting, funny, charming, confident, inclusive to her friends, and exclusive to those who couldn't keep up with them. She loved having that control, but it did get exhausting at times.

Before meeting Brett, she never would have considered going for an outsider like him. But the way he'd looked at her two weeks ago at Myst when they'd made out for practically the entire night—it was like he'd really cared about her. Like he'd thought there was a possibility of more between them.

Then again, he'd been drinking that night. The next day he'd told her he wasn't interested in her as more than a friend, since they had too many differences to make it work, and that they should go back to the way things were before.

Too bad Madison didn't agree. How could he ignore the chemistry between them? His resistance only made her want him more, and he would be at Myst tonight, so Madison would find a way to capture his attention.

Energized by her determination, she picked up her speed

on the elliptical. She'd never had a problem getting guys to notice her. Why should it be different with Brett?

"Madison?" Damien's voice snapped her out of her thoughts.

She tried to push Brett from her mind. "Yeah?" she said, doing her best to look cheery.

"You seem upset. What's going on?" Damien's face softened, and Madison's heart twisted in guilt. Why couldn't she want him instead of Brett?

"Nothing." She smiled and shook her head, making sure to appear untroubled. "Just figuring out what to wear to the Fourth of July party tonight."

"Very deep thoughts." Damien chuckled, his eyes roaming up and down her body. "You'll look great in whatever you pick. You could wear what you're wearing now and you would still be the hottest girl there."

Madison glanced at her gym clothes and scrunched her perfect ski-slope nose in a way she knew looked cute. Okay, she was more than aware that the tight black shorts and pink sports bra showed off her curves. And she totally wore stuff like that when she worked out with Damien because she liked catching him admiring her. But she would never wear it to a party—especially not one at Myst. She needed to stand out in a good way. No guy she was interested in had ever turned her down, and she wouldn't let Brett be the first.

Damien slowed his machine and came to a stop.

"Ending your workout early?" she asked.

He picked up a towel and wiped sweat from his forehead, messing up his dark hair. "The Diamond sisters are most likely in their condo right now," he said. "I might as well stop by and introduce myself. See if they want a tour of the building…"

Madison's grip tightened around the handles of the elliptical. Why was she getting upset about Damien's interest in those girls? Damien went from girl to girl all the time, and she had never given it a second thought. No matter what girl he was with, he'd made it clear he would drop them if Madison wanted to take their friendship to the next level. Which she didn't. So she had nothing to be jealous about.

But something about those Diamond girls bothered her.

"Want to come with me?" Damien asked. "I'm sure they'd love to meet you." He shot her the smile that made most girls fall all over him, but Madison wouldn't be falling all over Damien anytime soon. Or ever.

"No, thanks." She brushed off the invitation, acting like she didn't care. She *shouldn't* care. She was prettier than those girls, and he was only trying to make her jealous. So much for her mom telling her to be welcoming to them. It technically wasn't fair to dislike someone before meeting them, but Madison didn't want to get to know the Diamond girls, and she wasn't going to pretend otherwise. "I have fifteen minutes left on my workout. Then I have to get ready for tonight. You're still coming to dinner with our friends before the party, right?"

"Our friends" was the term coined by Madison for anyone important at Goodman—at least when the people in her group used it.

Damien swung the towel around his neck, a mischievous glint in his eyes as he backed up to the doors. "Wouldn't miss it for the world."

www.campusbuzz.com

Fourth of July party at Myst
Posted on Monday 07/04 at 03:40 PM

If you're like me, then you're going to the Fourth of July party at Myst tonight. With access to the VIP floor on the third level, obvii. (But the pool on the first floor is always fun. Especially with the caves that you can swim into if you want some private time with one other person, if you know what I mean).

Basically, if you go to Goodman, you should be there tonight. Everyone else will be.

Cya in a few!

1: Posted on Monday 07/04 at 04:06 PM

I think the new girls will be there tonight, too. The Diamond sisters. Rumor has it they arrived in the Diamond Jet this afternoon and were seen in the hotel lobby gazing around the place like they've never seen a casino in their life.

2: Posted on Monday 07/04 at 04:32 PM

That's cause they're from some hick town. They're probably losers. Don't get too excited about them.

3: Posted on Monday 07/04 at 05:40 PM

hick town or not, i hear they're HOT!!!!

chapter 5: *Savannah*

Is this actually *happening?*

That was the first thing Savannah thought when she stepped through the golden double doors into the condo. *Her* condo. Her breath caught in her chest at the realization that this was where she would be living for the rest of the summer. It was unreal; a palace in the sky, the type of place Savannah saw in magazines but never imagined seeing in real life, let alone living in. Marble floors, mirrored walls, shining tables, sunlight streaming through the floor-to-ceiling windows overlooking the bustling Strip—and that was just what she could see from the entrance.

That, and a round glass-topped table in the middle of the foyer with a crystal bowl on it. Inside the bowl was a note surrounded by three black credit cards, like petals on a flower.

"Mr. Diamond left a message for you." Bernard motioned toward the bowl. "If you don't need anything else, I'll be going back downstairs. Your luggage will be up shortly, and there's a butler button on your phone if you need to reach me. I'm happy to assist you in any way necessary."

Bernard was their *butler?* This was beyond awesome. She wasn't sure why she would need to call a butler, but she would have to find a reason to do so soon. Something that cool couldn't go unused.

"Okay," Savannah said, pretending to be the type of person who called butlers all the time. She didn't want him to think she was unsophisticated. "Will do! Thanks, Bernard."

The second Bernard left, Savannah hurried to the table, snatched up the envelope and opened it. This was the first piece of communication they'd ever had from their father. Her heart pounded. Of course, she was more looking forward to meeting him in person, but this was better than nothing.

Her sisters gathered around her, and she unfolded the letter, admiring the elegant script and reading out loud:

"Dear Peyton, Courtney and Savannah,

"I'm sorry I wasn't able to greet you upon your arrival. I had an urgent meeting, and I don't know how long it's going to run. I will be by as soon as it is over.

"We will be going to dinner tonight at 7:30 p.m. before the Fourth of July party at Myst in the hotel, so please use this time to get ready. I am sure you have much unpacking and settling in to do. In case you need to reach me, my personal cell number is (702) 555-2688. I live next door in condo 7500, so this one is your own. I hope you find it to your liking.

"Sincerely,

"Adrian Diamond

"PS: The credit cards are yours. Feel free to use them for whatever you would like."

Savannah frowned and placed the letter down on the table. It wasn't the warm greeting she'd hoped for, but at least he'd promised he would be by soon. Her head spun at the notion that she would be meeting her father today—and that he was *the* Adrian Diamond. This had to be a dream, or a parallel universe, or *something* fantastical. If it were a dream, she was determined to enjoy it until she woke up.

Noticing the black American Express cards again, she picked up the one with her name on its bottom-left corner. Was this for real? She'd heard of these before, because famous people had them, and now she was holding one with *her* name on it. The card was cool against her skin, like it was made out of metal instead of plastic, and it was thick and heavy, so it didn't bend like a normal credit card. Would it even slide through a swipe machine? She hit it against her palm, surprised by the echo of the metal. Rock-solid, it felt indestructible.

"I wonder what the limit is on these," Courtney mused, picking up hers and examining the back.

"Limit?" Savannah threw her hair over her shoulder and held the card up higher, admiring how it gleamed under the light. "We flew here on a private jet. I doubt there's a limit."

Courtney pressed her lips together, as if Savannah had said something wrong. "Maybe not, but no matter what the limit is, it's not our money. We'll ask Adrian about our budget once he gets here."

Leave it to Courtney to suck the fun out of the situation. If she couldn't see the possibilities in an unlimited credit card, maybe Peyton could. But Peyton's blue eyes looked like they were about to burst into flames.

"All it takes is a stupid credit card and a dumb letter, and you've forgotten how Adrian has ignored us until now." Peyton stomped to a small trash can and dropped her card inside. It hit the metal with a resounding clang. "He hasn't even bothered to meet us yet. I won't take his bribe money—I have more dignity than that."

Whatever that meant. Savannah exhaled, rescued the card from the trash (luckily it was the only thing in there) and slid it in her back pocket so Peyton couldn't try to toss it again. Peyton and Courtney were bringing everything down. She wished Evie were here. Unlike Courtney and Peyton, Evie would see the potential in what she could buy with an unlimited credit card.

Savannah ran her thumbs over the raised lettering on her card's metallic surface, amazed she was seeing *her name* on a *black American Express.* In his letter, Adrian had said they could use the credit cards for whatever they wanted, and Savannah planned on doing just that. Finally she could get her boring, dark blond hair highlighted, and maybe get extensions to make it thicker and prettier than Courtney's. She could buy pigmented high-quality makeup instead of the cheap chalky stuff from the drugstore, expensive clothing from the department stores she walked through when she went to the mall but could never afford, designer sunglasses and shoes.... The list went on. She could already see herself walking down the Las Vegas Strip like a movie star or a pop singer. Everyone would stare at her as she walked by.... It would be incredible. She could also get a quality guitar to replace the beat up one with the warped neck she had now that went out of tune all the time—one with solid wood to give it rich, resonant sound, and better action to make it easier to play—like a Taylor or a Martin. Maybe she would get both, for the fun of it. Or start a collection. A new guitar could be the push she needed to bring her music to the next level.

This would be the start of a new, better Savannah Diamond.

She couldn't wait to get home once her mom was better and see the reactions from the girls on the volleyball team, and from the guys in school. Finally, Savannah would be noticed.

Then she remembered the idea she'd had while reading Adrian's note.

Gripping the card, Savannah rushed down the hallway. Her sisters hurried behind her, Courtney asking where she was off to so fast. The two doors on the left were close together, and she opened both of them.

Both bedrooms were the same size, so they weren't what she was looking for. She rushed back down the hallway and through the living area, past a sleek wooden dining set, cream-colored armchairs, a sofa in front of a gigantic flat-screen television and an eating area near the granite-countertopped kitchen. Then she arrived at the carved white-wooden double doors at the far end of the condo.

Savannah flung open the doors and raised a fist in victory. The huge bedroom had floor-to-ceiling windows overlooking the Strip, allowing beams of sunlight to stream inside, and it was enormous—bigger than the entire apartment she'd shared with her mom and sisters in Fairfield. She ran across the plush carpeting and jumped onto the king-size bed, the white comforter cushioning her fall, so soft that she sank right into it. She stretched her arms over her head and leaned back into the mountain of pillows stacked in front of the headboard. A white vanity backed against the wall—perfect for doing makeup—and across from the bed stood a glass table with two cream-colored chairs facing a flat-screen television. Mirrors separated by white wooden panels covered the interior walls, and Savannah looked over her shoulder to smile at her reflection.

"I guess you're claiming this room?" Courtney asked from the doorway.

Savannah sank deeper into the pillows, enjoying the feeling of the silk against her skin. "I found it first," she declared, staring dreamily up at the ceiling. A crystal chandelier hung in the center, the lights sparkling everywhere, and Savannah felt like a modern princess. Still, she checked to see if Courtney looked upset. Savannah wanted to keep this room—and she had a feeling her sisters would let her—but she didn't want Courtney to be unhappy about it. Most people didn't know when Courtney was mad, since she didn't scream or lose her temper, but Savannah could always tell because she got withdrawn and more polite than usual.

"I don't mind," Courtney assured her, and Savannah could tell by her genuine tone that she honestly wasn't upset. "I don't have enough stuff to fill one of the other rooms up, let alone this one. And each room has a private bathroom."

"Private bathrooms?" Savannah's eyes widened. "Finally! Now I won't get yelled at to hurry up in the morning."

"I never yell at you," Courtney said.

"Peyton does," Savannah said, thinking of how Peyton banged on the door of the shared bathroom in their apartment and screamed at her to get out when she wasn't halfway done getting ready. "But now she won't have to."

Peyton joined Courtney in the doorway. "I only yell because you use my makeup," she said, leaning against the wall and snapping her gum. "Not that it matters, since I plan on getting out of here as soon as I can, but you can have this room. None of us need this much space. We won't have enough stuff to fill the smaller rooms, let alone this one."

Savannah ignored Peyton's comment about "getting out of here"—it was just Peyton being stubborn, and Grandma had made it clear they had to stay with their father until Mom was better. She felt guilty for rushing to claim the master bedroom knowing her sisters would have given it to her if she'd asked, but the doorbell rang before she could apologize.

She sat up quickly, the world blurring. Was it Adrian? His note said he wouldn't be done with his meeting until they finished unpacking, but maybe the meeting hadn't taken as long as he'd expected. Her stomach flipped, and she looked at her sisters in panic. Could they be about to meet their father? Was she *ready* to meet her father? She had no idea what she was supposed to do, or what she should say. She wished more than anything her mom or grandma were there to help.

"We should get that." Courtney's face paled, her voice so calm that Savannah knew she must be freaking out inside. At least the three of them had each other. They would get through this together.

"What joy," Peyton huffed, and rolled her eyes. "We get to meet the jerk who screwed us—and Mom—over for our whole lives. This will be enlightening." Her sarcasm made it clear she thought it would be anything but.

"We should at least listen to what he has to say," Savannah said, standing up and straightening her shirt. Her body tingled with nerves to the point that she felt like her blood was about to burst out of her skin. Needing to do something with her hands, she ran them through her hair to brush out the tangles. She could do this. Satisfied with her reflection, she marched past her sisters and pulled the front door open.

Standing in front of her was the hot guy she'd seen at the gym. His dark brown hair was messed up in a sexy "just finished working out" way, his black T-shirt clung to his defined abs and his tanned skin glowed as if he spent every day lounging around a pool.

Savannah's arm dropped to her side, and she stared up at him, speechless. What was he doing here? She'd never had a superhot guy show up at her doorstep. She had no idea what to say to him. If Evie were here, she would come up with something perfect. But she would also take the attention away from Savannah. The tough part about having Evie as a best friend was that they always liked the same guys. And then the guys liked Evie more than Savannah, so Savannah got stuck with the second choice.

This move to Vegas might be the perfect chance to break away from Evie's shadow. Could Savannah become a different—improved—version of herself just from *wanting* to?

She wouldn't know if she didn't try.

"Who are you?" Peyton narrowed her eyes at the guy and snapped her gum. Of course she had to steal the attention by talking to the hot guy first.

"Damien Sanders," he replied, barely looking at Peyton before turning back to Savannah. Her heart jumped—maybe all wasn't lost. "I live on the floor below yours, and noticed you walking by while I was working out in the gym. I didn't know if you knew anyone here yet, so I figured I would stop over and introduce myself."

Wow. Not only was he hot, but he was supernice, too.

"No, we don't know anyone here yet," Savannah answered, her words coming out faster than she intended. Evie said she always knew when Savannah was nervous because she turned into a talking chipmunk. She took a breath and forced herself to slow down. "Except for you now. We just got here today—we moved here to stay with our dad for a while. I'm Savannah."

Damien leaned lazily against the door frame. "So you're the infamous Diamond sisters?"

"Infamous?" Savannah asked. "I'm one of the Diamond sisters, but I didn't know we were infamous."

"I'm kidding." He laughed. "There's just been some talk about you three, and everyone's been curious to meet you."

"Oh, okay." Savannah knew Adrian Diamond was well-known, but she hadn't realized that meant people would talk about her and her sisters, too. "Who's everyone?"

"Just some of us who go to the Goodman School," he said. "A few of us live here and in nearby condos. Your dad made a donation for the school's new sports center, and the talk is you'll be attending in the fall."

Savannah had hoped her mom would get better before the end of summer so she wouldn't have to start her sophomore year with total strangers. She bit her lower lip, trying to figure out how to reply in a way that wouldn't make her sound clueless. "We haven't talked with our dad about school yet."

Well, they hadn't talked to their dad at all yet, but Damien didn't have to know that. And Savannah hadn't realized that donations—or any payments—were necessary to go to school. At Fairfield High, new kids just signed up on their first day.

"Too bad," Damien said. "You'll have to let me know when you find out. But you'll be at the Fourth of July party at Myst tonight, right?"

"Yes." Savannah breathed a sigh of relief at the mention of something she knew a little bit about. That was the place Adrian had mentioned in his note. "Have you been there before?"

"Been there before…" He repeated her question, lingering on every syllable. "Of course I've been there before. It's the hottest new club on the Strip. And it's the best, just like everything else at the Diamond."

"Then I can't wait to check it out tonight," she said, proud of how cool and collected she sounded. Maybe just *being* in Vegas would shape her into the Savannah Diamond she dreamed of becoming. Perhaps a talent agent would discover her, and then her dreams of being a pop star would come true.

"You'll have fun." He sounded confident, like it was impossible for her to not enjoy herself. "A bunch of us are going to dinner before the party. You three should come."

"We can't." Peyton crossed her arms and glared at Damien, as if he were doing something to seriously piss her off. What was her problem?

Damien ignored her and turned back to Savannah.

"We already have dinner plans with our dad," Savannah explained, the word *dad* feeling alien coming from her lips. "Otherwise I would go. But we'll be at Myst afterwards."

"I'll find you there, then," he said. "My friends and I will be on the third floor—it's VIP—but I'm sure that's where you'll be, too."

"Right." Savannah tried to act unfazed, even though she'd never been VIP for anything before. But obviously they would be VIP here, since Adrian—their dad—owned the building. Well, buildings. "Does the club let everyone in? I'm not eighteen yet, so I hope that won't be a problem.…"

"Not eighteen?" Damien faked disbelief in a fun, joking way to let her know he'd already figured that out. "Really?"

"Really." Savannah laughed. "I'm fifteen."

"And the rest of you?" He looked at Courtney and Peyton.

"Sixteen," Courtney answered, sounding like she wanted to be anywhere but here. Savannah wished she could at least pretend to be interested.

"And you?" he asked Peyton.

"Nineteen," she lied, crossing her arms and giving Damien a stare of death, as if she were daring him to contradict her.

Damien didn't bother. Instead he looked back at Savannah, his eyes gleaming with the knowledge that Peyton was lying.

Savannah couldn't believe the attention he was giving her. "She's seventeen," she whispered conspiratorially.

"Same as me," Damien said. "But thanks for the honesty. I like that in a girl." He paused to let the words sink in, and continued, "You're supposed to be over twenty-one to get into the club, but if you're on the VIP list they won't bother you. Which you will be."

"Okay." Savannah couldn't stop smiling. Being around Damien made her feel like she'd downed a venti cappuccino. "I'll see you tonight, then."

"It was nice meeting you." Damien flashed her one last grin before turning to walk down the hall. Savannah thought he was going to leave it at that, but then he called over his shoulder, "I'll see you tonight."

She waved to him and closed the door. After it was shut she leaned against it and smiled, her heart beating so fast that she could float away from happiness. He was the hottest guy she'd ever met—and it seemed like he was interested in *her*. Not Courtney, who was tall and gorgeous even when she didn't wear makeup, or Peyton, who was fearless and not afraid to speak her mind. She might have even sounded sophisticated when she talked to him, as if hot guys invited her to VIP parties at trendy nightclubs all the time.

The day couldn't get more amazing than this.

chapter 6: *Courtney*

A bellboy had dropped off their bags after they'd finished talking to Damien, and Courtney now stood in front of the full-length mirror in her room, frowning. What should she wear when meeting her father? Her jeans and T-shirts didn't fit in with everything she'd seen in Vegas so far, which was loud, flashy and sparkly. Meaning the opposite of Courtney. She had only three dresses—the ones she wore to church before her mom had started drinking so much that she was too hungover on Sunday morning to drive them. Hopefully one of those would be acceptable to wear to dinner. The nicest restaurants she'd been to were Applebee's and Macaroni Grill, and she suspected the ones in the Diamond were a few steps above those.

She took off the flowery blue dress and replaced it with a pink one that had white lace on the top and bottom. She normally wore this dress with a jacket, and the spaghetti straps made it the most revealing one she owned even though it fell two inches above her knee.

Would it be acceptable to wear to a fancy dinner and a club in Las Vegas? She had no idea. But she did know that her flip-flops weren't going to fly. Flip-flops were pretty much all she owned, though. She was already taller than most of the guys in her grade, so wearing heels made her feel like a clumsy giraffe. Then there was the practical issue that heels *hurt*. It didn't make sense to wear shoes that blistered her feet when flip-flops were a more comfortable solution.

She studied her reflection and sighed. No way did she look ready to go to a fancy dinner. She needed Savannah's help. Savannah studied fashion magazines and was great at finding similar-looking items for practical prices.

She headed to Savannah's room for advice, amazed at the magnificence of the condo as she walked through it. Was this real? She felt like an intruder, unable to shake the feeling that the actual person who lived there would walk in at any second and ask her what she thought she was doing snooping around somewhere she didn't belong.

In their apartment in California, the furniture had been crammed together, the rooms dark and dreary. Here, the windows overlooking the Las Vegas Strip let in tons of sun, the ceilings were fifteen feet high and everything inside sparkled like it was brand-new. It was so airy and spacious, with furniture that looked too expensive to use without worrying about messing it up. She couldn't believe she would be living here. That she *was* living here.

Then she realized she was acting like Savannah—so enamored with their new life that she could forget everything she'd left behind. Hopefully their mother was doing well in rehab. Her throat tightened at the thought. She missed the days before her mom had started drinking all the time. She remembered one Saturday night in particular, when their mom had stayed up with them for hours watching a DVD of Savannah's favorite CW television show. They'd ordered in pizza, and their mom had used her curling iron to style their hair, pinning them into elaborate updos they could have worn to prom.

Their mom had always drunk more than other people's parents, but before she'd lost her job, she'd managed to go a few days at a time without getting trashed. That's when they would have fun nights like that, when they felt like a normal family. But that had stopped in the past year. As their mom's drinking spiraled, it had made her look sick on the outside, too—she'd gained weight, her eyes, which used to be bright blue, became glassy and bloodshot with puffy dark circles beneath them, the skin on her face had turned wrinkly and red and her dark blond hair had become dull and limp. As hard as it was, Courtney knew rehab was the best choice. Once their mom got better, they would have that other woman in their lives all the time—the one who watched TV with them and fixed their hair like they were about to attend a magnificent ball. If that were possible, it was worth enduring a few weeks, or even months, in Las Vegas.

Courtney blinked away tears and knocked on Savannah's door. The radio blared from inside, and Savannah was singing along, as if she didn't have a care in the world. She had a beautiful voice—it was too bad she was terrified to sing in public. Her dreams of being a famous singer would never come true if she didn't get over her stage fright. But no matter how much Courtney encouraged her by complimenting her talent, Savannah insisted she was only saying those things because she was her sister.

"Come in!" Savannah yelled, lowering the volume as Courtney walked inside.

Savannah stood in front of the mirrored wall, admiring the flowy aqua dress she had on, which was short enough to be a long shirt. The high waistband reminded Courtney of the style popular in the Regency era, and the V-neckline dropped low, but not so low that it looked inappropriate on a fifteen-year-old. Not that Savannah had much in the upper region to show off.

"Hey," Savannah said, as she attempted to tease her hair. "I wish we had time to go shopping before dinner—I had the hardest time picking out what to wear tonight. I can't wait to get a new wardrobe."

"What about the stuff you like?" Courtney asked. "You're not going to get rid of it, are you?"

"I'll find stuff I like better." Savannah plucked a tube of pink lip gloss from her vanity and leaned closer to the mirror to apply it. "Now that we can buy what we want, it doesn't make sense to shop at big discount stores anymore. It'll be great to get real designer clothes instead of imitations."

Courtney didn't like how Savannah was so willing to leave her old life behind. "I can help you go through your clothes so you can decide what to keep," she suggested, since Savannah wouldn't get through such a meticulous task without Courtney sitting by her side to keep her focused. "Then we'll find the local Goodwill and donate what you don't want."

"Good idea," Savannah said. "Let's go shopping this week, and when we're done you can help me sort through my stuff."

Courtney nodded, although she hoped Savannah wasn't going to go too crazy with buying things. Then she remembered why she was here. "Do you think this looks okay?"

she asked, motioning to her dress. "I usually wear it with a sweater."

Savannah stepped back and examined Courtney's outfit, raising her index finger to her chin like this was the most important assessment in the world. "It's fine, and you definitely don't need the sweater," she finally said. "We're going to dinner in Vegas—not church at home. And flip-flops? Really? Please tell me you weren't actually thinking of wearing those. I'll find something else." She ran to Courtney's room, coming back a minute later holding the pair of shiny white pumps she'd forced Courtney to buy at a clearance sale at Payless last year. Courtney had tossed them into the back of her closet, so they were still brand-new. "These would be much better."

Courtney put them on and looked into the mirror. She hated the extra height, but Savannah was right. The white pumps transformed the dress. "I guess it does make a big difference," she said, practicing walking a few unsteady steps. Hopefully her feet wouldn't be covered in blisters by the end of the night.

"More than that!" Savannah insisted. "It makes you look like a supermodel. Anyway, what'd you think of Damien? He's hot, right?"

Courtney shivered at the memory of the conversation they'd had with him earlier. They hadn't talked with him for long, but she'd gotten a bad vibe from him. He seemed too… smooth. It was rare for someone that attractive and overconfident to have good intentions. Courtney wasn't an expert with guys—she'd never had a boyfriend—but the way he'd eyed Savannah when he'd mentioned seeing her tonight unnerved her. She didn't want Savannah getting in over her head with him.

"He's attractive," she said. "But you need to be careful. The guys here aren't like the ones in Fairfield."

"What do you mean?" Savannah asked.

"There's just something about him I don't trust."

"Well, I thought he seemed nice." Savannah picked up her straightener from the vanity and ran it through her hair. "And you don't know him, so it isn't fair of you to judge him."

"It's just a vibe I got," Courtney said.

"You and your vibes." Savannah rolled her eyes. "But he seemed into me, right?"

"He was giving you more attention than Peyton or me," she said truthfully.

"Good," Savannah said. "I thought so, too, but I wanted to make sure. I hope he doesn't have a girlfriend. But it didn't seem like it from the way he was talking to us. I mean, he was practically asking me out. Don't you think?"

The doorbell rang before Courtney could respond. She'd have to deal with Savannah's infatuation with Damien later—preferably after she gathered more evidence of how he was not the type of guy that Savannah, or any girl with self-respect, should swoon over.

"Omigod." Savannah dropped the straightener down on the vanity, her eyes wide as she looked at Courtney in the mirror. "That has to be him."

Courtney's stomach swirled, the morning's anxiety returning. She wrapped her arms around herself and took a few deep breaths to calm down. It didn't work. She felt more nervous than ever.

"You ready?" she asked.

Savannah nodded, and together, they gathered enough courage to walk out of the room. Courtney wanted to grab her sister's hand for support, but she didn't want to seem like she couldn't handle the situation and was panicking about meeting her father.

Her father. It sounded so strange.

Peyton walked into the foyer at the same time as Courtney and Savannah. She was wearing one of her signature "going out" outfits—a short leather skirt, a tight black tank and stiletto knee-high boots. Normally Courtney would suggest she put on a jacket to make the outfit less provocative, but now they had something bigger to worry about. The three of them looked at each other, and Courtney knew the wide-eyed anxiety and straight-lipped worry on her sisters' faces were mirrored on her own. Their lives were about to change forever, and she didn't feel close to ready.

She stepped forward to open the door, but the handle moved before she got a chance, and it swung open.

A man walked through, and there was no doubt he was their father. His medium blond hair was clean-cut, and his eyes were the same blue as theirs. And he was tall. The navy suit he wore and his strong, high cheekbones made him look like an aristocrat from an old movie who knew what he wanted and the right way to get it.

"Peyton, Courtney, and Savannah," he said, looking at each of them as he said their names. "Did I get it right?"

Courtney nodded, unsure how to reply. "Hi" felt too casual. Her mouth went dry, and she swallowed again, trying to think of something to say.

"You all look just like your pictures." He glanced at the table in the foyer and ran his fingers over the glass surface. "I see you got your credit cards. Good. Have fun with them, but don't do anything too extreme." He walked through the foyer, his black leather shoes tapping against the marble floor. "I'm Adrian Diamond." He cleared his throat. "Your father. Although I suppose you've figured that out already." He laughed, but it wasn't enough to take away the heavy awkwardness in the air. "Welcome to your new home. I trust everything is to your liking?"

Courtney had a million things she wanted to say to him, but she felt useless. It was like the world was spinning out of control, and she couldn't figure out how to make it steady again.

"We did get our credit cards." Peyton stared him down. "And then I threw mine in the trash."

"Really?" Adrian actually chuckled, even though Peyton was still giving him a hate-glare. "Why would you do that?"

"She didn't really throw it in the trash," Savannah chimed in. "Well, she did, but nothing else was in there and I rescued it."

"Good to know." He still had an amused smile on his face, which Courtney guessed wasn't the reaction Peyton had been expecting. "If you don't want your credit card, that's your choice—I don't mind if you toss it in the back of a drawer in your room—but they can't be thrown away due to security reasons."

Peyton set her jaw and didn't respond.

"It was kind of you to give them to us." It was the best thing Courtney could think to add to the conversation. "We'll use them as responsibly as possible, and only for emergencies."

"That's very mature of you, Courtney," he said, and while she shouldn't have wanted to earn the respect of the man who had abandoned her and her sisters, she felt proud of his approval. "But you can use your credit card for whatever you'd like—as long as you don't do anything too extreme, like buy a yacht or charter the jet around the world. You'll have to ask permission before doing anything like that. But most everything else—shopping, food, spa days or whatever else you want—is fair game."

Courtney wrapped her arms around her stomach, unable to

meet his eyes. She knew she should thank him, but this huge gift made her feel as if all the money she'd worked for around the clock over the years meant nothing now. All that time she'd slaved away mixing coffee drinks for minimum wage felt demeaned knowing that Adrian could have just handed her an unlimited credit card. A lump formed in her throat at the thought that it had all been for nothing, and she swallowed it away. That work *wasn't* for nothing. She'd earned that money through her own means to help out her family. She would always be proud of that.

"So I can get a designer tote bag for school?" Savannah asked. Courtney wanted to tell her not to take Adrian's generosity for granted, but she was glad the attention had shifted from her. "And designer sunglasses, and clothes and shoes?"

He smiled at her enthusiasm. "I know someone who will be more than happy to shop with you for whatever's going to be popular next season," he said, a knowing glint in his eyes. "But aside from that, we have a lot to discuss. I was sorry to hear about your mother." He paused and glanced out the window, his thoughts seeming far away, as if he were remembering a time long past. Then he refocused and returned his gaze to Courtney and her sisters. "I didn't know just how rough this past year has been on the three of you until your grandmother informed me. I'm sorry you had to go through what you did."

"Why did you wait until now to do something?" Peyton crossed her arms and narrowed her eyes at him.

"I knew things were bad, but I wasn't made aware of the extent of it until your grandmother called me," he said. "After the divorce your mother forbade her to contact me, but I suppose that, given the circumstances, she decided to take charge. She always was a spirited one. I suppose that's where you get it from."

"I don't mean months ago." Peyton ignored his semi-compliment. "I mean for our whole lives. We didn't know if you were alive until now! And now we find out that you're...." She paused, as if searching for the right words to describe him. "Well, that you're *you*."

"Mom always said you were bad news.... She let us think you were a homeless drug dealer or something," Savannah added. "Why would she want to keep us away from all of this?" She motioned around the condo to show what she meant.

"Your mother never approved of the three of you growing up in this environment," Adrian said thoughtfully. "And I didn't disagree with her. The Las Vegas Strip is not the... safest place to raise children."

"Couldn't you have moved?" Courtney finally found her voice. "So you could be near us?"

"No." He shook his head. "It's best for my business if I live here."

"And your business is more important than your daughters," Peyton said.

"Some parts of my business are dangerous no matter where I live, especially for those close to me," he said with what Courtney could have sworn was resentment. "But we're already ten minutes late for our dinner reservation, so I'll go more into detail about that once we're seated. You three have arrived on a very important day. Not only is tonight the Fourth of July party at Myst, but today I had a meeting with a colleague regarding a proposal for a beneficial partnership." He paused to look them over again. "You're all ready to leave?"

Courtney nodded along with her sisters and tried to smile. Didn't Adrian care about sitting down with them privately so they could get to know each other? To explain why he'd ignored their existence for their entire lives? Instead, they were going straight out to dinner. Yes, he'd said he would explain more to them once they got to the restaurant, but Courtney hadn't expected that discussion to take place somewhere so public. The thought of being on display like that took away any semblance of an appetite she'd had until now.

But maybe she was thinking about it wrong. Maybe he thought taking them out to dinner would be considerate. Which, she supposed, it was.

"Good," he said. "We have a private room, so we'll be able to talk without other people listening. I also have two people who I want you to meet. They've been looking forward to this, so I would appreciate it if you were on your best behavior."

They hadn't been here a day yet and he was already going to introduce them to people? Courtney felt nauseated at the prospect. What if she said something wrong and made a fool of herself?

"I know you might feel out of your element," he said, "but please roll with it, and remember that I'll answer any questions later."

He looked at the three of them again and walked to the doors, leaving them no choice but to follow his lead.

Chapter 7: *Peyton*

None of them spoke as Adrian led the way down the hall.

Peyton hadn't expected him to bombard them with bear hugs, but she wasn't prepared for him to be so formal. He was treating them like they were a business deal instead of his own daughters. He'd even *laughed* about her throwing the credit card in the trash. What was up with that?

After a silent, uncomfortable elevator ride, Adrian escorted them through the casino to a balconied area with two escalators curving around to the floor below. Peyton felt like she'd been dropped into an alternate universe. Huge chandeliers hung from a high circular ceiling—she guessed there were ten of them in all. They were different shapes and colors, most of them red, orange and yellow. It was like being in a cavern, with chandeliers instead of stalactites. But despite it being beautiful, Peyton made sure to look bored and uninterested. The last thing she wanted was for Adrian to think she was happy to be here.

At the bottom of the escalator, Adrian walked through an archway with the words *Five Diamond Steakhouse* in cursive on the top. Peyton had never been to a restaurant this fancy. White cloths covered the tables, and silk drapes fell over parts of the burgundy walls. Bronze chandeliers that looked like hanging lamps dropped down from the ceiling, their golden glow bringing the restaurant to life. Not that it needed it. Every table was occupied with people engaged in lively conversation.

The host spotted Adrian and hurried to the four of them. "Good evening, Mr. Diamond," he said, bowing his head like Adrian was a king. "Your table is ready."

Most of the people dining looked up at Adrian as he walked by, whispering and pointing as he passed. How many of them knew he was the owner of the hotel? Even if they didn't, Adrian had an air about him that announced he was someone important. He greeted people as they passed, shaking hands, smiling and joking like he was best friends with everyone. Peyton could see why people liked him. Why couldn't he act this friendly around his own daughters?

She supposed it made sense, though—dealing with teenagers wasn't part of his job description, but making hotel guests happy was.

His "regular table" was in the back of the restaurant in the private room he'd mentioned, and the two people he'd warned them about were already seated. One of them was a guy who appeared to be around Peyton's age, and while he wasn't as obviously good-looking as Damien, he was attractive. His face was round, and his green eyes had a faraway look, like he was trying to distance himself from the world. He was underdressed in a T-shirt and a black hoodie, but his mom must not have cared enough to tell him to change.

At least Peyton was 99 percent sure that the woman sitting next to him was his mom. She had a young-looking face, with the same high cheekbones as the boy. She'd pulled her hair back in a bun, and the strand of large pearls around her neck gave her a regal appearance. Adrian smiled when he saw her, his eyes becoming soft and loving.

Who was this woman, and why was Adrian looking at her like she was more valuable than any diamond in the world?

"Girls," Adrian said, "this is my fiancée, Rebecca Carmel, and her son, Brett. They'll be joining us for dinner this evening."

Fiancée? Peyton looked at the woman in disbelief.

Rebecca softly cleared her throat and shifted in her seat. She straightened her silverware, and Adrian rested a hand on her shoulder. Peyton couldn't blame her for being nervous. This was an awkward situation, and Rebecca was now front and center.

"You have a *fiancée?*" Peyton finally said to Adrian, not caring that the doors to their private room were still open. "And you didn't think it was important to tell us this first?"

"I didn't want you to have any preconceived ideas about Rebecca before meeting her," Adrian said calmly. He motioned to the doors, and the host closed them as he left their room. "Plus, I thought this conversation might be easier for the three of you with a mother figure around."

"We already have a mother." Peyton crossed her arms, standing her ground. "We don't need another one."

"Maybe we should do this another time...." Rebecca reached for her handbag, and she looked so uncomfortable that Peyton felt a little guilty for being outwardly mean to her.

"No." Adrian put his hand on top of hers and slid into the

seat at the head of the table, looking at her in what seemed like desperation. "It will be best for all of us if you stay."

Peyton couldn't believe it. Adrian seemed calm and collected, like he could handle anything. But could he actually be so nervous to be around them that he needed Rebecca there for emotional support?

Her stomach rumbled; the restaurant smelled like fresh bread and perfectly cooked steak, and she hadn't eaten since breakfast. She took the seat next to Brett, which was as far away from Adrian as possible.

She placed her napkin on her lap and looked at her silverware in confusion. Why did she need two forks and two knives? And why was the spoon so small and above the plate?

"Start at the outside and work in," Brett whispered to her. "And don't touch the spoon until dessert."

"Thanks." Apparently she'd looked as confused as she'd felt.

Adrian ordered a bottle of champagne after they went through the introductions. No one mentioned that they were underage, and the waiter didn't care. Brett didn't seem fazed, either. Peyton accepted a glass—she was nothing like her mom and could handle her alcohol just fine—and Savannah got one, too. Courtney gave Savannah a warning look and said she was fine with water.

Peyton wondered if Courtney would ever let loose and have fun. They weren't at home anymore—they were as far from it as possible. Not geographically, obviously, but Vegas couldn't have been more different from Fairfield if it tried. Peyton wasn't going to let Vegas change *her,* since she was fine just as she was, but it might not hurt Courtney to live a little.

"I hear you three will be attending Goodman in the fall," Rebecca said, playing with her pearl necklace as she waited for an answer.

A pit of dread formed in Peyton's stomach. She recognized the name of the school Damien had mentioned, but she wouldn't be in Vegas long enough for school to start. Their mom had to get better before September.

If it ended up taking longer and she and her sisters had to do a few weeks at Goodman, no one had told them yet. Anyway, what was the big deal about the school? It wasn't like they had an option where they would go. How different could this Goodman place be from Fairfield High?

"Yes," Adrian said. "After I informed the headmaster that I would make a generous contribution toward the new sports center, I mentioned my three daughters were moving to town and hadn't picked a school yet. Coincidentally, Goodman had three spots waiting to be filled."

"How wonderful." Rebecca beamed. Peyton wasn't sure if she was fake or trying really hard to get them to like her. Judging by how nervous she seemed, she suspected it was the latter. "It's the best school in the state. Brett goes there. He'll be a junior in the fall, so he'll be in Courtney's year. He can introduce you to the other students this summer so you'll know people once school begins."

"Because you know how much I hang out with the prep school crew," Brett said. Rebecca gave him a look that said, *Stop being so insolent,* but Brett just smiled and took a sip of water.

"Back up a second," Peyton said. "Isn't it too early to worry about school?"

"I know no one wants to think about going back to school when it's only the beginning of July, but this was late notice," Adrian said. "Their deadline for applications is January. Luckily for the three of you, they were able to make an exception."

"That's not what I mean." Peyton clenched her fists, angry

at how he played head games with his words. "If Mom's better in a few weeks, by September we'll be back home and at Fairfield High. We shouldn't think about school here until we know when she'll be out of that place."

"Oh." Rebecca's face crumpled, and she looked at Adrian in question. "They don't know yet?"

"Know what?" Courtney asked softly.

"I would have said something earlier, but my meeting ran late and we had to hurry to dinner," Adrian said. "Plus, I thought your grandmother would have told you herself before you left...."

"Well, apparently she didn't." Peyton couldn't take this anymore. "So spit it out."

Adrian took a sip of water and cleared his throat. "Your mother is in an extremely difficult, stressful point in her life," he said, looking seriously at each of them. "Once she's released from inpatient treatment, she'll have many struggles ahead while getting her life back on track. I've purchased your grandmother a larger house—she wasn't happy about it, but she eventually accepted—and your mom will move in with her once she's released. This way she'll have your grandmother's support while recovering. So until the end of the next school year, the three of you will be living here, with me."

Peyton slammed her hands down on the table. "You've got to be kidding me," she said. "This is going to be my senior year. It's the last year I'll have with my friends before we graduate. And now you're saying I'll have to spend it *here,* with total strangers? No way is that happening." She checked to see if her sisters were just as pissed. Courtney's face had gone white—she seemed shocked, not angry—and Savannah had the nerve to look excited. What the hell was wrong with them? Didn't they also want to go home?

"You'll be staying here for the next year." Adrian didn't flinch. "It's in your mother's best interest. I understand you're missing home, but I hope you want to do whatever you can to help her recover. She needs to focus on herself in the upcoming months, and that's going to be easiest for her if she doesn't have to worry about taking care of anyone else."

Peyton pressed her lips together, her breaths coming fast. Way for him to make them feel like an unwanted burden.

"But won't Mom want us around?" Savannah asked with tears in her eyes. Peyton didn't want to see her cry, but at least this was better than her being excited about staying in Vegas.

"Once she begins outpatient treatment, you'll be able to visit her," Adrian said. Then he got very still, as if what he was about to say was hard for him. "But, while I know this might be difficult for you to believe right now, you're here because I want you to be here, too."

Peyton leaned back and crossed her arms. No way would she believe that crap.

At the same time, she wanted her mom to get better, and she refused to do anything that might send her spiraling. If staying in Vegas for the year was what it took, she would tough it out and get through it. But she wouldn't make it easy for Adrian. He hadn't wanted them in his life until now, and she wasn't about to smile and forgive him.

"Fine," she said. "But Goodman isn't a *private* school, is it?"

"Of course it is," Adrian said. "Where else would you go?"

"Public school." Peyton said the obvious response. "Like we always have."

"The Goodman School is the best in the state," Adrian said, like that should be reason enough.

"It might be," Peyton replied. "But we don't need a fancy private school. We've been in public school our whole lives, and it's never been a problem." No one said anything, so she looked at her sisters for backup. "Right?" she said, expecting support. She wouldn't fit in with the people who went to private school, and she didn't want to. They were probably a bunch of stuck-up snobs.

"I don't know, Peyton," Courtney said carefully. "It will look better on college applications if we go to a school like Goodman."

"They have a one-hundred percent college acceptance rate," Rebecca said proudly. "Last year a fourth of the graduating class went to an Ivy League or similar level school."

"I'm not going to college." Peyton smirked. "So there goes that one hundred percent."

Worry flitted across Rebecca's face, but Adrian didn't look concerned. "We'll see." He sounded so superior, as if he knew something Peyton didn't. It made her want to hit something.

Instead she looked at Courtney, betrayed by her sister's reaction. "You never mentioned wanting to go to private school before," she said.

Courtney looked down at the tablecloth. "That's because it was never an option."

Peyton looked at Savannah for support, but her normally talkative sister didn't say a word. Was she the only one who hated the idea of going to school with overprivileged snobs who would have nothing in common with her?

"I'm not going to Goodman." Peyton stood her ground. "I'll go to the local public school instead."

"How about we compromise?" Adrian said. "You'll start at Goodman in the fall. If after three months it's as awful as you imagine, we can discuss other options."

Peyton thought about it. "One month," she countered.

"Two months and you have a deal," Adrian said, with a hint of a smile.

"Fine." Peyton nodded. "Two months." She was going to hate it no matter what, but at least being there for two months was better than the entire year.

Nobody said anything for a few seconds, and Peyton felt like she could cut the tension in the air with a steak knife. Finally the waiter walked through the French doors that led to their private dining room, a bottle of champagne in his hand. Thank God. Peyton didn't think she could stand one more moment of sitting there with no clue what to say. It was ironic, really. She had so much she wanted to know, but no idea how to start asking her questions. Continuing to talk about their family drama in front of Brett and Rebecca would make dinner more awkward than it already was.

Then Peyton realized what she'd thought. Was she worried that something wouldn't be *appropriate* to bring up at dinner? The pompous atmosphere of the hotel must be getting to her. Time to change that. She could tell attention made Rebecca uncomfortable, so she might as well start there.

"So," she started, looking at Rebecca. "How did you two meet? I'm sure our father would have told us, but since he hasn't bothered to be in our lives until now, we haven't had much time to talk." She folded her hands over the table, as though she couldn't wait to hear the answer to her question.

"Well…" Rebecca lifted her hand to her necklace, looking at Adrian for help.

"Rebecca and I were high-school sweethearts," Adrian said, his voice confident and strong. He reached for one of Rebecca's hands and squeezed it. She smiled gratefully at him, and he continued. "But we didn't go to the same college—she stayed local, while I went to the University of Pennsylvania—

and our lives went in different directions. We were in other relationships when I returned to Las Vegas after graduation to invest in my first hotel. Recently we both became single again, and fate brought us back together."

"How interesting." Peyton lifted her glass as though making a toast, threw her head back and took a large gulp.

Rebecca reached back to touch her bun, as if a sprayed strand might be out of place. Peyton felt guilty for making Rebecca feel uneasy. She seemed nice, and it did sound like Adrian loved her. It wasn't her fault that he was a crappy, non-existent father who was trying to act like he hadn't overlooked his daughters for their entire lives. The funny thing was, if Adrian and Rebecca were in high school together, that made Rebecca almost ten years older than Peyton's mother, even though she looked much younger. All that drinking could really age a person.

"Yes," Adrian said. "But please don't mention the engagement to anyone. We plan on announcing it at the grand opening on Saturday night."

Peyton looked at the packed dining room. "The hotel looks open to me."

"This is the soft opening," Adrian explained. "Doors opened for both the hotel and residences a month ago, and the time since then has been a test to make sure everything is running smoothly. This way we can work out any kinks ahead of time, so we know nothing will go wrong on the night of the grand opening."

"Sounds efficient." Peyton skimmed over the menu as Rebecca ordered her food, zeroing in on the most expensive dish on the menu. Maine lobster—seventy dollars. Perfect. That would do a good job pissing Adrian off. She wasn't sure if she liked lobster, or how one person could eat seventy dollars' worth of food in one sitting, but she would find out tonight.

"A fine choice," Adrian said after she ordered. "I'll have the same. You girls should consider it, as well," he said, looking at Courtney and Savannah. "It's said we have the best lobster on the Strip."

Savannah found it on the menu, and her eyes bulged. "I guess I'll have the lobster, too," she said, closing the menu and handing it to the waiter.

He turned to Courtney next. "The lobster for you, as well?"

"I'm sure it's delicious, but I'm a vegetarian," Courtney explained. "I'll have a Caesar salad, lightly dressed."

Adrian had asked for a taste of everything for appetizers since "the girls should try it all," which meant the waiter brought out two three-tiered stands of plates, each one full of food, like the appetizer version of a wedding cake. It was outrageously fancy, with pieces of what appeared to be seafood displayed like art instead of something to eat. Some of the food was still in the shells, and some had been drizzled with orange, yellow and green sauces. This was a far cry from the nachos and wings Peyton and her friends usually got at chain restaurants. She had no idea where to start.

Adrian picked up a shell with a slimy white slug-looking thing on top of it, lifted it to his mouth and tipped it downwards so the slug-thing slid out. He chewed and swallowed. "Oysters on the half-shell," he said, motioning to the display. "Delicious."

Curious, Peyton picked one up and lifted it to her mouth. It jiggled in the shell, all lumpy and gross. And it smelled salty, like the ocean. She wrinkled her nose. But she couldn't back out now, no matter how nasty it looked.

Following Adrian, she tipped the shell toward her mouth

and let the oyster slide out, holding her breath so the smell wouldn't overwhelm her.

It didn't only look like a slug, it tasted like one, too. Not that Peyton had tasted a slug before, but it was what she thought one would taste like if she had. She forced it down her throat, her eyes watering as she tried not to gag. Once she swallowed, she placed the shell back on her plate and chugged water to get the salty taste out of her mouth.

Those were supposed to be a *delicacy?* What were these people thinking?

"I suppose oysters aren't to your taste?" Adrian asked. The corner of his lips twitched up, and he dabbed the side of his mouth with his napkin.

"That was disgusting," she said, still trying to get the taste out of her mouth. She used the fork and knife closest to her plate for the rest of the appetizers—the ones that according to Brett were for the main course—but if anyone noticed, they didn't say anything.

Next came the main course. Two and a half pounds wasn't a huge amount of lobster, especially for being seventy dollars' worth of food on a single plate. That much money could have fed her family for two weeks.

Savannah and Courtney had involved themselves in a conversation with Rebecca, so Peyton turned to Brett with a brilliant idea—flirt with her future stepbrother. That would surely piss Adrian off. "So, Brett," Peyton started, using her mini-fork to get some lobster out of the claw. "Do you live here, too?"

"In the Diamond?" He cut into his steak and took a bite.

Peyton nodded. What did he think she meant—Las Vegas?

"Yeah," he answered. "Mom and Adrian share a condo, so I have one to myself. It's pretty sweet."

"You have your own condo?" Peyton leaned closer to him. "You should show it to me sometime. Does it have a Jacuzzi?"

He said yes, and took another bite of his steak.

"We have a Jacuzzi in ours, too." She batted her eyelashes conspiringly. "You should come over sometime and christen it with me."

Okay, that was overkill, even for her. But at least it'd gotten a raised eyebrow from Adrian.

"Maybe." Brett shifted away from her and focused on his food. She could tell she'd made him uncomfortable, and he didn't say anything more.

She scooted back in her seat and took another bite of lobster. Brett was a total bore.

He turned to Courtney and asked if she'd thought about what colleges she wanted to apply to, since they were both going to be juniors and junior year was when the honor students worried about that stuff. Peyton, on the other hand, meant it when she said she wasn't going to college. She wanted to get out of boring, stuffy classrooms and into the real world as soon as possible. If she ever changed her mind, she could just sign up for the community college in Fairfield.

But, of course, Courtney perked up at the mention of college plans. "Stanford," she answered shyly. "What about you?"

"UCLA," he said. "I've wanted to go there since middle school. They have great courses for people interested in careers in the movie industry, so I'm taking an Intro to Film class this summer at UNLV to get ahead and show I'll be serious about my major."

"Wow." Courtney looked impressed. "I want to be an English major, because I love reading and think I would like working in publishing, but I hadn't thought of taking a summer course. I've just been focusing on my grades and SAT scores so I can hopefully get a scholarship."

"I've been working on the SAT this summer, too," he said. "I have a tutor who comes to my condo twice a week, and he teaches me all these great techniques on how to 'outsmart standardized tests.' Maybe you could join in on our sessions."

"I would like that." Courtney smiled.

Brett would rather study for the SAT with Courtney than lounge in the Jacuzzi with Peyton? Whatever. She was stuck listening to their nerd-tastic conversation through the rest of the main course, and while she loved her sister and all, it was unbelievable how long Courtney could talk about school. To make it worse, the lobster wasn't even that amazing. She would have much preferred a cheeseburger.

The busboy cleared the plates once everyone finished their meals, and the waiter approached their table again. "Dessert, coffee or tea?" he asked.

Adrian whispered to Rebecca, then turned to the waiter. "Coffee, please," he ordered. "Black." Then he looked at Peyton and her sisters. "Would you all care for anything?"

Savannah passed, Courtney ordered tea and Peyton got a coffee. The waiter turned to Rebecca next.

"Actually, Brett and I will be leaving now," Rebecca said, placing her napkin down on the table.

Brett seemed confused for a second, but then he understood. After the waiter left they said their goodbyes, leaving the three of them alone with Adrian.

"Girls," Adrian said. "I suppose we have a lot to discuss."

That was the understatement of the past fifteen years.

"Why did you wait so long to contact us?" Peyton broke the ice.

"Has your mom ever told you why she left Las Vegas and moved back to Fairfield?" Adrian asked.

"All she's told us was that she didn't want us growing up around your kind of lifestyle," Courtney said softly.

"And she was right," Adrian said. "As I mentioned earlier, this life has its dangers."

"What kind of dangers?" Peyton asked. Adrian Diamond had the world in the palm of his hand. What could be so bad that it would keep him away from his daughters?

"I'll tell you now, but please listen without interrupting," Adrian said. "You can ask questions when I'm finished." The three of them said okay, and he continued, "There's no easy way to say this, so I'm just going to tell you flat-out. When you were a baby, Courtney, you were kidnapped and held for ransom when your nanny was taking you out for a walk. He took the nanny's life and said you would be next if I didn't meet his demands. Luckily I was able to negotiate with him, and he returned you safely. Your mother and I were lucky to get you back, but it could have been worse, and we both knew it. Your mother was traumatized at the thought of what could have happened. She was already pregnant with Savannah at the time, and after such a scare, we agreed it was best for the three of you to live under the radar until you were mature enough to handle yourselves in this kind of environment. We also agreed it would be best for you to not have a connection to me, since that was what put your life in danger in the first place."

Courtney dropped her teacup onto the plate, the clank of the china filling the room. Peyton had never seen her normally composed sister so speechless. Her heart pounded at the danger Courtney had been in, and more so at the possibility of what *could* have happened if Adrian hadn't successfully negotiated with the kidnapper.

"No, Mom never mentioned that to us," Peyton said, since Courtney clearly wasn't ready to say anything herself. She didn't know what she had expected Adrian to say, but it wasn't that. And if their mom had never told them about something so important, what else could she be hiding?

Peyton couldn't imagine the possibilities.

"Wow," Courtney finally managed to say. She blinked a few times, then took another sip of tea, as though it could help her organize her thoughts. "Peyton's right—she never told us that. But I guess it explains why my baby book was never as detailed as Peyton's or Savannah's."

"What do you mean?" Adrian looked alarmed.

"Just that, with the kidnapping, Mom must have been so stressed that she forgot to update it," Courtney explained. "And since we moved after it happened…she must not have had time to keep on top of it. Right?"

"Of course." Adrian stirred his coffee, even though he was drinking it black. He looked so sad, like he was remembering something painful that he didn't want to think about.

It was a lot to take in. On one hand, Peyton understood how scary something like that would be, and why he would feel like he was a danger to them. On the other, he was their *father*. He could have involved himself in some part of their lives, even if he couldn't live in the same city.

"You could have visited," Savannah said. "Without anyone finding out. It would have been good to know you cared about us a little."

"I know," Adrian said. "I made a mistake. After what happened, I threw myself into my work. Your mother didn't want you to have anything to do with me, and I couldn't blame her." His eyes were glassy, as if he was genuinely upset things had turned out the way they had. Maybe he really *did* want to get to know them now. "Your grandmother never agreed, but it was your mother's decision. And it was a decision I supported. I wanted to give her money to help raise the three of you, but she refused it, claiming she could take care of her family without my help. Instead, I had it put in trusts for when you're older."

A trust fund? Peyton didn't know how to wrap her mind around that. "If living in Vegas is really that risky for us, then why are we safe here now?" she asked. "Yeah, we're not babies anymore, but we're not exactly trained in fending off kidnappers."

"You will be kept secure at all times," Adrian said. "I promise you that. I've hired professionals to protect you. You won't even know they exist."

"If our lives are in danger, why did you wait until now to hire them to protect us?" Peyton asked.

"The men I hire are the best," Adrian said. "I've had guards keeping tabs on you for your whole lives. They dressed modestly while guarding you in California—their usual uniforms would stand out too much there—but now they've returned to their formal attire. I believe it's time I introduced them to you." He typed something on his phone. Immediately, three men stepped into the private dining room.

They were all tall, built and wearing matching black suits with Bluetooth cords attached into their right ears. But while they all wore the same outfit, they varied greatly in age. One was older, with gray hair and skin beginning to wrinkle, another looked to be a little younger than Adrian, but with dark hair and sharper features. The last one could barely be older than Peyton herself. With his blond hair cut nearly to his scalp and a sculpted body, he could easily pass for a senior on a high school football team. Surely he couldn't have the same amount of experience as the men beside him.

"Girls, I want you to meet Carl, Teddy and Jackson," Adrian said, pointing to each man as he said his name.

Carl was the oldest, Teddy was the one who looked Adrian's age and Jackson was the youngest. Even his name sounded fitting for a football player. His hazel eyes met Peyton's, his gaze strong and confident, which sent her stomach flipping. How old was he? He had to be older than her, but she doubted he could be more than twenty-five.

"It's nice to meet you," Courtney said, and Peyton had to press her lips together to stop from laughing. It always amused her how Courtney remained polite in the strangest situations.

"They have each been assigned to one of you personally," Adrian said. "Carl is in charge of Savannah, Teddy is in charge of Courtney, and Jackson is in charge of Peyton. They will keep tabs on your whereabouts. They will remain invisible to you as much as possible, but since security in Vegas requires higher measures than Fairfield, you will notice their presence at times. They've been staying under the radar today since you were unaware of them and they didn't want to scare you, but from now on when you leave your condo they will be in the hall, and they will accompany you in the elevators. Apart from those instances, they will mostly go unnoticed by you. This will be an adjustment, but go about your lives the same as you did before you were aware of their presence. They are not babysitters, so they will not tell me anything about your personal lives unless it is necessary for your safety."

Adrian dismissed the bodyguards, and Peyton gave Jackson one last small smile before he left. He probably wasn't allowed to show much emotion, especially in front of Adrian, but she thought he smiled back. While she didn't love the idea of someone trailing her every move, Jackson was hot enough that it didn't bother her. Maybe he even had a fun side. It would be worth finding out.

"My bodyguard can't be much older than I am," Peyton said, hoping Adrian would reveal his age.

"Jackson is young, but he is one of the best at what he does," Adrian said. "He will do an excellent job keeping you safe at all times."

Peyton was disappointed he didn't give her an exact age, but it wasn't a problem. Jackson would be trailing her every move. She would have many opportunities to discover that fact on her own.

"As I mentioned earlier, you'll live here for a year and go to Goodman," Adrian said. Peyton crossed her arms, and he added, "Or another school, if after two months at Goodman you decide it isn't to your liking. When the year is up, you can choose where you want to go from there. I will support your decisions, as long as they are sensible. There are some rules, though." He looked each of them in the eyes before continuing. "Since it's summer, you don't have a curfew— your bodyguards will keep you safe at all times—but I expect you to come home at night. Once school begins you'll have a curfew, but we'll discuss specifics later. I also don't mind if you have a glass of wine with dinner, or a casual drink with friends. Despite your mother's struggles, I allow this because it's the way I was raised. I believe if I prohibit you from drinking, you'll do it secretly anyway and go overboard with it, as many people your age are known to do. But if you're caught being irresponsible with alcohol to the point where you embarrass yourself publicly, that will end."

He paused to let that sink in, then continued, "As I told

you in the condo earlier, I have no problem with you using your credit cards to buy what you please. I encourage it, since I doubt you had the privilege to do so in your previous circumstances—but there's a catch. You may not do anything that will result in bad press for our family. We all know of some infamous hotel heiresses—no need to name names—whom I've had to bar from my properties for…inappropriate behavior. It's in your best interests to remain under the radar. Use your judgment and act wisely, because gossip pages *will* talk about what you do. People will take pictures of you and post them on the internet. I don't want any negative attention brought to our family. If that happens, your credit card privileges will be severely limited, and you will have an early curfew. Do you understand?"

Peyton nodded, just so he would drop the subject. She was sick of listening to this lecture. She ignored the rules at home, especially since her mom didn't follow through with punishments, and she would continue doing whatever she wanted here, no matter what boundaries Adrian tried to place on her. She hadn't needed an unlimited credit card in Fairfield, and she wasn't about to become dependent on one now. Plus, no one even knew who they were.

Yet.

Adrian looked straight at Peyton, making her feel uneasy. "No negative press also means no flirting with your future stepbrother," he said. "That line is not to be crossed."

"I wasn't flirting with him," Peyton protested, glad Adrian hadn't caught her eyeing up Jackson. She didn't want him trying to put an end to that before it had a chance to begin. "He looked bored and I was being friendly. It wasn't anything more."

Adrian didn't appear to believe her, but he dismissed the

topic. "I'm glad we discussed that, but we need to go to the club. Some of your future classmates will be there. Brett will introduce you to them." He finished his coffee and continued, "I'm sorry we didn't have more time to get to know each other since your arrival. Things have been busy around here, and while I wish the timing was better, there will be plenty of opportunity for all that in a few days, after the grand opening for the hotel and residences on Saturday night."

At that, he stood up to leave the steakhouse. It was time to go to Myst.

Chapter 8: *Madison*

Madison Lockhart loved Myst. It was the most extravagant nightclub in Vegas, with its three-story waterfall cascading from the ceiling into the lagoon on the first floor. She sat with her friends in a semicircular booth on the VIP level, waiting for international DJ superstar David Guetta to hit the stage. A few people danced on the elevated lit-up platform—mainly adults who had already had a few drinks. Normally Myst drew a younger crowd, but this Fourth of July party was a special event. The fireworks show was rumored to be better than the one at Caesars Palace, and would be choreographed to David Guetta's music. Madison couldn't wait to see it.

She watched her parents step onto the floor and dance with each other. This was one of the few nights they both weren't working, which was rare since her dad was the lead neurosurgeon at Sunrise Hospital and Medical Center—the best hospital in the state—where her mom also worked as an anesthesiologist. Nights when they looked this relaxed didn't happen often.

They waved her up to join them, but Madison shook her head. That so wasn't happening.

"I think your parents want you to dance with them," Oliver Prescott joked from his seat next to her.

Madison rolled her eyes. She and Oliver had been best friends since elementary school, but whenever she looked at him now she was reminded of how much he'd changed in the past year. Oliver had always been good-looking, but he'd started working out over the past few months, and it showed. Every inch of his body was more defined. He'd also grown his hair out during their sophomore year, and while it wasn't long, it looked much better than the shaved look he'd tried to pull off when they were freshmen. It brought out his dark eyes. And one thing Oliver knew how to do was use his eyes. He had the "look at a girl and make her melt" technique down perfectly. He could get any girl he wanted, and he knew it. But it didn't matter who they were—students at UNLV or celebrities—Oliver never kept his attention on one girl for long.

Madison hoped he wouldn't be like Damien and set his sights on the Diamond girls. That would piss her off. But while Oliver and Damien had a lot in common, Damien liked the emotional game—dating and making girls fall head over heels for him—whereas for Oliver, it was about the physical conquests. But it had never been like that between them. She wouldn't want to risk messing up their friendship, even if she thought she could trust him in a relationship. He had also been on a gambling spree this summer, but as the son of one of the wealthiest hotel owners in Vegas, at least he could afford it.

Oliver scooted closer to her, tilting his head in concern. "Is something wrong?" he asked softly.

Why had everyone been asking her that recently? First Damien, and now Oliver. It was seriously irritating.

"Nothing's wrong." She brushed off the question and poured herself a glass of champagne from the bottle that came with their table. Screw the calories—she needed to relax. She would make it up tomorrow by eating less and adding more time to her workout. "Why would it be?"

Before Oliver could answer, Damien slid into the booth and swung his arm around Madison's shoulders. His skin radiated heat, like he'd been dancing. "You look amazing," he said, his face inches from hers. He smelled like vodka and orange juice, and Madison wondered how much he'd had.

"Thanks," Madison said, glad she'd chosen the Shoshanna dress. She loved wearing black—not only was it slimming, but it looked best on her. This particular dress was sleeveless, so it showed off her defined collarbones, and it was short without being *too* short, falling to midthigh. Plus, most of the other girls were wearing red, white or blue dresses, so hers stood out.

Oliver shifted in his seat next to her, and he said something to their friend Larissa. Oliver and Larissa had an "agreement"—friends with benefits, or something like that. Madison suspected that Larissa felt more for Oliver than she let on, but he didn't take her seriously. Which was good, since Oliver and Larissa would make a terrible couple. He deserved someone who would challenge him, and Larissa wasn't that person.

"You look good, too," Madison told Damien. It wasn't a lie. Most girls at the party would have killed to be sitting so close to him. "I like this." She brought her hand up to the thin leather necklace he had on, allowing her fingers to linger across his skin. "Is it new?"

His breathing slowed at her touch, and Madison curved her lips into a small smile. "I've had it for a while," he said, bringing his hand up to rest on top of hers. "But since you like it I'll make sure to wear it more often."

Not wanting to stay like that for too long—she liked occasional contact with Damien, but she didn't want to lead him on *too* much—she brought her hand back down to her lap and scanned the room for one person in particular.

It didn't take long to spot Brett Carmel sitting at the bar by himself. He never was the most social guy on the planet—which was why he was so mysterious to her.

"I'm sick of this champagne," Madison announced, placing her glass down on the table. "I'm getting something else."

Damien let her out of the booth, his eyes following her every movement. "Do you want me to go with you?"

"I'm fine." She glanced at the bar to make sure Brett was still there. He was. "I'll be back in a minute."

She sauntered across the club, feeling heads turn, enjoying the rush from the attention. Brett didn't notice her until she slid into the seat next to him.

"Is this seat taken?" she asked, rotating the stool to face him.

"Nope." He looked straight ahead and took a swig from his bottle of beer. His lack of excitement to see her disheartened her, but she wouldn't give up. Maybe he was just having a bad day.

She pointed at his drink. "Didn't they offer you a glass for that?" Not many people ordered beer on the VIP level, but the bartender should have served it in a classier way.

"It tastes better from the bottle." He drank from it again, looking behind him like he was searching for someone who *wasn't* Madison. What was his problem? Most guys would be thrilled if she gave them the time of day, and Brett had the nerve to act indifferent.

Her confidence waned. Why was Brett so disinterested in

her? She might not have a reputation for being the friendliest girl at school, but she wasn't cruel or slutty. Definitely not slutty. She wasn't going to whore herself out to any guy who wanted her (which was a lot of them), so she would be patient until she met someone she wanted to be with. There had been times when Madison had contemplated giving up the hope of romance and losing her virginity to a friend. Oliver would probably be on board if she asked. But she held out hope that her first time would be special—with someone she loved, who loved her in return.

"So…" she said to Brett, trying to figure out how to continue the conversation. "I haven't seen you here recently."

"That's because I haven't been here recently."

"Oh." He wasn't making this not-awkward thing easy. "Why'd you change your mind and come tonight?"

"I was forced."

Madison didn't know how to respond, so she ordered a glass of Meursault Chardonnay from the bartender. He carded her and scanned the fake ID Oliver had gotten through a connection for everyone in their group of friends, giving it back to her once it came through okay. The ID was top-notch and hadn't failed her yet.

Madison lifted the glass to her nose and inhaled. Meursault was her favorite—full and buttery, with a finish of honey. It might mean another 100 fewer calories that she could have tomorrow, but she needed the liquid confidence. She swirled it around and tasted it. "This is delicious." She savored the sweet aftertaste and held it out to Brett, leaning closer so he got a good look at her cleavage. "It's my favorite wine. Want to try it?"

He rested an elbow on top of the bar and rubbed the corners of his eyes. "Not really." He sighed, and looked at her with what might be pity. "Madison," he said her name extra carefully. "If you're looking for a repeat of two weeks ago, I already told you we're not right for each other. Summer makes it easy to forget how you and your friends ignore me around school, but if that's not going to change, then we're never going to happen."

"It could change," Madison said. "Your mom is dating Adrian Diamond, so now it will be easy for you to fit in with my friends. If I tell them to accept you, they will."

"You don't get it." Brett looked sad, and a little frustrated. "I like you, Madison, because you're smart and determined, but I don't want to change who I am to fit in with your friends. I have my own friends, who like me for who I am and who I have things in common with. If you want, you could hang out with us for a change."

He'd invited her before. It had always been tempting, but then her friends had pointed out there was a can't-miss-it party coming up and how Madison had to be there. Spending time with her friends was always fun, and she never wanted to turn down an invitation from them, but sometimes the constant partying got repetitive. Would she enjoy herself at the places Brett invited her, too?

"I don't know, Brett," she said honestly. Because if her friends found out she was hanging out with those weirdos Brett spent time with outside of school, they would give her hell for it. They wouldn't understand her interest in him. Which made sense, since she could barely understand it herself.

"Okay," he said. "Then I'm not sure what else you want from me."

Madison frowned. *To know why you're so disinterested in me,* she thought, taking another sip of wine to maintain her composure. She refused to let Brett see how much his lack of interest hurt her. "I was getting a drink, saw you here, and wanted to say hi. Is that so bad?"

"Have you told Nick about what happened between us yet?" Brett asked, ignoring her question.

Madison jolted back at the mention of her ex. "No," she answered, not wanting to think about how she broke up with Nick a day after she'd made out with Brett. Nick hadn't said it directly, but she knew he didn't buy her reason that her feelings for him had faded. And while she didn't regret what happened with Brett, she hated that she'd cheated on Nick. He was a good guy. He deserved someone better than her. Someone who loved him more than she ever had—or would.

"You should keep it that way." Brett took another swig of beer. "I wouldn't want to be responsible for getting between you two."

"I wouldn't take back what happened between us," she said calmly, despite her growing frustration that she would never get through to him. She tightened her grip on her wineglass and took another sip, willing herself not to snap. "Besides, you didn't think 'we weren't right for each other' when you kissed me."

"Look, Madison, I'm really sorry for leading you on," Brett said, and her head pounded with dread about whatever he was about to say next. "But I had too much to drink that night. I wasn't thinking straight. Like I said earlier, we have nothing in common, and we hang out with different people. The two of us together would never work."

"And like *I* said earlier, that's no problem at all," Madison said. "If I vouched for you, my friends would welcome you into our group." She crossed her legs in his direction and smiled, hopeful he would see it her way. Because if this was really Brett's biggest qualm about making it work between

them, it was easily solvable. It would be as simple as him inviting her and her friends over to his condo tonight for an
after-party once David Guetta finished DJ-ing.

Brett looked at the table where Madison had been sitting
with Damien and the rest of them. "I know you're close with
that group, but I have my own friends, and I prefer hanging
out with them."

"You mean the ones who go to public school?" Madison
asked. He could do so much better than those losers.

"Yep," Brett said. "They're good, down-to-earth people
who like me for me, not because my mom's dating Adrian
Diamond. Anyway, why are you so worried about this? Every
guy at school loves you. Until this summer, you didn't know
I existed."

"I tutored you in bio last semester," Madison said. "I knew
you existed. And I always thought we got along well."

"We did," Brett agreed. "But only during the tutoring sessions. If your friends were around, you pretended you didn't
know me."

"That's not true," Madison said, even though it was. She remembered one time when Brett had said hi to her in the hall,
and Larissa had asked how she knew the loser who slummed
it with the public-school kids. Madison had laughed and
explained how she was tutoring him, and it was funny he
thought that meant they were friends. Then she'd felt terrible
for being mean and switched the subject.

"It *is* true," Brett said. "But besides all that, I'm interested
in someone else."

He had his choice between her and someone else, and he
was choosing the other person? This hadn't happened to her
since she had lost twenty-five pounds in the summer before
eighth grade. Tears filled her eyes, and she swallowed to make

them go away. She should leave now. Get up and go back to join her friends. Damien would be happy to see her.

Maybe if Brett saw her with Damien it would make him jealous.

She shook the thought away. Flirting with Damien was fun, but he was one of her closest friends, and hurting him like Brett had hurt her wouldn't be fair. And who was to say Damien wouldn't get sick of her like he did with every girl he dated? Maybe the only reason he was interested in her was because she didn't fall all over him like the rest of them.

Madison was about to get up and say "bye" to Brett when she spotted Adrian Diamond and his three daughters walking into the club. The girls looked like total hicks. The little one was wearing an aqua dress that resembled a cheap Halloween-store costume, the tall blonde looked like she was going to church in Kansas in her silly pink sundress and the one with the freaky blue streaks might as well have come straight from the trailer park in a short black skirt that was obviously fake leather. The matching knee-high boots and excessive eyeliner made it worse.

They would never fit in here in a million years.

"Adrian Diamond's daughters," Madison said in distaste. "Have you met them yet?"

"Yep." Brett didn't look at her when he answered; instead he focused on the Diamond girl with wavy blond hair—the tall one in the stupid pink sundress. To make things more scandalous, she recognized Brett's wistful look as he stared at the Diamond girl. Heated jealousy filled her lungs, which was ridiculous, because that twig of a girl had nothing on Madison. But it sure seemed like Brett had a crush on his.... What was the right term for the daughter of your mother's boyfriend?

Whatever it was, the way he was looking at her shouldn't be legal.

"They definitely don't look like they're from around here." Madison rested an elbow on the bar and held her wineglass in front of her.

Brett plunked down his empty beer bottle, and Madison jumped at the loud clang. "I'm going to say hi to them," he said. "Have fun tonight."

He stood up before Madison could reply. What had she done to make him so uninterested in her? Maybe she could have been nicer to him around school, but they always got along when she tutored him. And two weeks ago, when he'd kissed her, she knew he'd wanted her as much as she'd wanted him. Now he'd left her sitting at a bar by herself. It didn't make sense.

Her eyes filled again, and she stared into her glass, refusing to turn around and watch Brett greet those girls. Seeing that would be too painful. Instead, she swallowed away the tears and took another sip of wine, closing her eyes as it traveled down her body, pretending it could cool down all the jealousy and anger she was feeling. She made herself breathe steadily, like she did in yoga class when they were getting rid of their stresses from the day. Inhale positive energy, exhale negative.

Nearly a minute passed until she started feeling like herself again. And she needed to stop sulking. Brett had made it clear he wasn't interested, and while that hurt, she wasn't going to be pathetic about it.

She lifted her shoulders, stood up and straightened her dress. The club had grown crowded while she'd been talking to Brett. Colored spotlights darted around the room like they were dancing to the thumping music, and dry ice hovered an inch or so over the dance floor, flowing over the edges.

Madison surveyed who was sitting where, every muscle in her body tightening when she caught sight of the one person she had hoped wouldn't show up.

Nick Gordon sat a few booths down from the one she was sharing with Damien, Oliver and the rest of their friends. His blond curly hair shined under the flashing lights, and he laughed at something someone said, the same genuine grin on his face that she'd grown used to seeing since they'd started dating in March. His table was full of football players, volley-ball girls and cheerleaders from Goodman. Madison couldn't handle more than five minutes around most of the cheerlead-ers—they were such wannabes with their bleached hair and orange skin from tanning salons. She did know a lot of the football players, though, since Nick was the quarterback. Dur-ing the three months they'd dated, he'd insisted she go to some of the lame suburban house parties thrown by his friends. She hadn't had a bad time—Nick was always good company—but they belonged in different crowds. It was part of the reason why the two of them didn't work out.

But there were a few events on the Strip that he—or anyone else that mattered—wouldn't miss, and David Guetta playing the first Fourth of July party at Myst was one of them.

She would have to avoid him. She didn't have any hard feelings, but seeing how pained he looked every time they'd spoken since the breakup made her want to sink into the floor and disappear.

Now that she thought about it, that wasn't a bad idea. Not in the literal sense, obviously, but she could go down to the second floor for a bit. And she knew just the person to join her.

Luckily for Madison, the table where her friends were sit-ting was close to the bar, so she wouldn't have to pass Nick and his crowd on the way there. She downed the rest of her wine and marched over to the booth. She fought off an initial bout of nausea—Meursault wasn't meant to be chugged—but it was soon replaced by the pleasant buzz of alcohol. Her head tingled with giddiness, and as she walked she arranged her hair in front of her shoulders in a way she knew looked hot, smiling knowingly at the guys who watched her.

Damien and Oliver stared at her as she approached. After reaching them she placed her hand on the back of the booth to steady herself, trying to make the movement coy instead of an attempt to appear not as tipsy as she was.

Damien scooted out of the booth and stood up, motioning her to go in. "Welcome back," he said. "Who was that you were talking to?"

"Some loser from school." Madison rolled her eyes. "He was at the bar by himself and started talking to me." Damien couldn't find out how badly she was just rejected. It was humiliating enough that she knew; everyone else knowing would make it a million times worse. "It took me a few minutes to escape."

"How kind of you to consider his feelings," Damien said, his tone laced with sarcasm.

"And what have the two of you been up to?" she asked.

"Just making a bet." Oliver rubbed his hands together and smirked. "Damien will owe me a grand by the end of the summer."

"Really?" Madison raised an eyebrow at Damien. "Why's that?"

"Oliver said he could easily hook up with all three Diamond sisters before school starts up," Damien said. "And I bet he couldn't. Especially since the youngest one already has it bad for me."

"You guys are disgusting." Madison pretended she didn't

care, but the mention of those girls made her blood boil. She didn't want to discuss them for any longer than necessary.

Trying to be subtle, she peeked over Damien's shoulder to see what Nick and his friends were up to. Luckily, her ex seemed too involved in chatting with the people at his table to have noticed her yet.

"Come with me." She reached past Damien for Oliver's hand and grasped it in her own, pulling him closer. He seemed surprised. Then a crooked smile spread over his face, showing the dimple on his right cheek.

"Where are you dragging me, Mads?" he asked, although she could tell he was having fun. He kept his hand in hers, staying seated as he waited for her answer.

"The second floor." She leaned down and whispered conspiratorially, "I want to dance."

"Let's dance, then." He gripped her hand tighter and slid out of the seat, pulling her close when he stood up. His body pressed hard against hers, and he grinned at her before raising his arm in the air, allowing her to twirl underneath. She laughed, loving how her flowing dress spun out with the movement. He held his other arm around the curve of her back, pulling her close and resting his forehead against hers.

"Come on," she said, leading him to the spiral steps. Not letting go of Oliver's hand, she peered over her shoulder to see what was going on at the table they'd vacated.

Damien had taken her seat in the booth. He was talking with Larissa and pouring himself another drink. He looked up at Madison, and she expected him to say something snarky about how she should have asked him to dance instead of Oliver, but he just lifted his glass in a silent toast. She could have sworn she saw a hint of jealousy in his eyes. But she shook away the thought, amused it had crossed her mind. Damien jealous of her dancing with Oliver? Please. Oliver was the last person Damien should worry about.

A few people greeted her and Oliver as they walked through the VIP floor, and she said hi in return, even to the people she didn't recognize. As they neared Nick's table, she gripped Oliver's hand tighter, pulling him closer.

He rested his head against hers and whispered in her ear, "So, I'm guessing the little show over there was for Nick's benefit?"

"No." She kept her eyes focused on Oliver's. "I was just having fun."

He raised an eyebrow. "You never were good at lying."

"That's not true." Her lips parted in pretend shock. "I'm just not good at lying to *you*."

"Should I take that as a compliment?" He seemed amused.

Then Madison made the mistake of peeking in Nick's direction. When her eyes met his, he looked like someone had punched him in the stomach. Madison leaned into Oliver for support. If she hadn't spotted Nick on the slopes in Deer Valley over spring break, then none of this would have happened. Dating him had been a stupid idea in the first place, but she'd enjoyed the time they spent together. He was sweet and kind. And after that week in Deer Valley, they'd made their relationship work for the rest of the school year.

Until Madison had screwed it up.

Nick lifted his arm like he was about to wave to her, but she looked away from him before he had a chance. "Come on," she said to Oliver, pulling him with her to the steps leading downstairs, where she could lose herself in the music and forget about the huge mess she'd somehow managed to create.

www.campusbuzz.com

Red Rock Overlook
Posted on Monday 07/04 at 6:01 PM

You all keep talking about Myst, but who wants to go there for Fourth of July? Myst sucks. The only people who look like they're having fun there are wasted beyond oblivion.

Red Rock Overlook is better for Fourth of July if you ask me. The fireworks beat anything on the Strip, they're over beautiful natural scenery, and you get to watch them with a chill group of people. Best of all, it's FREE. I don't know about the rest of you, but that's where I'm gonna be tonight.

1: Posted on Monday 07/04 at 6:23 PM

red rock overlook? are you serious? who the hell goes there?

oh wait, that would be losers. are the public school kids trolling our board?

2: Posted on Monday 07/04 at 6:47 PM

Whoever posted this either doesn't have a good enough fake ID to get into Myst or isn't on the VIP list. Because otherwise they would know how dumb they sound. Anyone who's been to Myst knows it beats sitting in the mountains in the killer summer heat.

3: Posted on Monday 07/04 at 7:42 PM

you all are so dumb. who cares about the "coolest" place to watch fireworks?

4: Posted on Monday 07/04 at 7:57 PM

Apparently you, since you replied to this post. Now it's time to get ready for tonight. Myst or Red Rocks?

The answer should be obvious. I'll see those of you who *matter* later.

chapter 9: *Savannah*

Myst was unlike anything Savannah had ever seen. It was a tropical wonderland. There was even a *waterfall* inside. Savannah had never seen a real waterfall, but this one had to be more beautiful than anything created by nature. Lights shined behind it, making it look like something from another world. She wanted to run up to the balcony, lean over it and watch the water cascade from the top floor into the lagoon. But Adrian led her and her sisters inside the club—directly through the VIP entrance on the third floor—and she didn't want to embarrass him by looking like a ten-year-old at a candy store.

After all, she was a hotel heiress now. People here saw places like this all the time, and she wanted to appear as worldly as the rest of them. Not many people got to start their life over; it was the perfect opportunity to reinvent herself.

From now on, she was no longer Savannah Diamond, small-town girl who was overshadowed by her prettier, funnier best friend, and who couldn't keep up with the fashion trends of the girls on the volleyball team. She was Savannah Diamond, daughter of one of the richest hotel owners in the world. She could be more than the wide-eyed girl whose friends thought she needed to get her head out of the clouds. She could be more than Evie's second-best. She could buy the expensive bags and shoes the cool girls flaunted around school, so she wouldn't feel like an outsider. She would finally fit in—more so once she got her new wardrobe, highlights and hair extensions. She could practically feel them cascading down her back already. Maybe she could even forget about that embarrassing moment in eighth grade when she sang at the school talent show and forgot the words to the song, which made everyone think she was an idiot. She had practiced every day for a month, but once she'd gotten up onstage and looked out at everyone watching her, she'd blanked.

She hadn't performed in front of an audience since.

Of course, this Savannah Diamond needed the hottest, most desirable boyfriend by her side. Someone like Damien Sanders. Just thinking about him standing in her doorway, with those deep brown eyes, perfectly messed-up hair and gorgeous smile sent her heart racing.

He'd said he would be here. Now she had to find him.

The elevated dance floor was filled with people her parents' age, so she looked around the edges of the club. The closest booth to her was packed with people who could be in high school, mostly the football player/cheerleader type. A muscular guy poured drinks for everyone, and they all cheered and clapped—except for a blond guy with curly hair who seemed like he was about to cry. Savannah's heart went out to him; he looked like a lost puppy.

But he wasn't her problem. She was on a mission—find Damien. She just hoped Courtney wouldn't feel the need to babysit them. She could tell her sisters didn't like him, but they had to give her more credit sometimes. Savannah was perfectly capable of handling her own life.

Brett walked up to them before Savannah could look around any more. She had always wanted a brother, and she liked Brett from the little bit of conversation they'd had at dinner. He wasn't a big talker, but there was no denying he was cute. Savannah had always imagined that her brother would be good-looking, so he would have good-looking friends to introduce her to. That was the perk of having a brother, right? Peyton would never dream of introducing her guy friends to Savannah (and the freaky guys Peyton hung out with weren't Savannah's type anyway), and Courtney was so busy with school and work that she never hung out with guys at all.

Which gave her an idea—maybe Brett was friends with Damien. Maybe he was *best* friends with Damien, so she would get to see him all the time. That would be perfect. And everything was working out well for Savannah recently, so it was possible.

Adrian let them know he would be with Rebecca and some of their friends, pointing out their table so they could find him if they needed him, and left them in the care of their stepbrother-to-be.

"Hey, Brett," Savannah greeted him, trying extra hard to be friendly. "How's the party been so far?"

"It's all right." He shoved his hands in his back pockets and shrugged. He sounded like he was stuck listening to a lecture at school instead of at the coolest club Savannah had ever been to. Well, the only club she had ever been to. But if she had been to clubs before, she'd still bet Myst would be the best. "To be honest, it's not my scene."

"Oh." Savannah played with the ends of her dress, beginning to doubt he would introduce her to tons of people to-night. But she was still going to try. "So, Adrian said you were going to introduce us to people from Goodman?"

"Well, you've got the sports crowd over there." Brett motioned to the group Savannah had noticed when she'd arrived—the one with the football players, cheerleaders and sad guy with puppy-dog eyes. "Two booths from them are the high-strung, overinvolved kids who run for every position on the SGA. Then, a few more down, are the kids who have endless money and believe they're God's gifts to the universe." He shook his head as he looked at them; clearly he disapproved. "I know your dad said I would introduce you to people from Goodman, but my friends go to public school, and they went somewhere else tonight. Sorry."

Savannah's hopes that Brett would be a cool, fun stepbrother who would introduce her to tons of hot guys disappeared. It looked like she was going to have to find Damien on her own.

"I'm going to get a drink," she decided. "I'll be back in a minute."

Unless she found Damien.

"I'll go with you," Peyton volunteered. "A drink sounds good right now."

"Okay," Savannah said, less than thrilled. At least Courtney was staying with Brett, but Peyton's pleather miniskirt looked cheap compared to the expensive clothes everyone else was wearing. It was too bad her oldest sister shrugged off her fashion advice. Maybe that would change once Peyton realized what everyone in Las Vegas wore, but Savannah doubted it. Peyton never listened to her; she was too headstrong to take advice from anyone. Plus, she thought Savannah was clueless in everything.

Savannah followed Peyton to the bar. She felt the thumping

music—a remix of her favorite song that was constantly played on the radio—vibrating from the floor and traveling up her body. She couldn't wait until David Guetta hit the stage later; she was going to take so many pictures to post on Facebook. Evie and the rest of the girls on the team were going to *flip out* when they saw them. Everything had been so busy since arriving in Vegas, and Evie had texted during dinner to see how she was doing, but this was too much to share in a text message. Savannah had promised to call her tomorrow morning, and she was beyond excited to hear her best friend's reaction.

She and Peyton passed the elevated dance floor, walking through the fog seeping from the sides. It was like a jungle paradise. Then the dark-haired girl she'd seen working out with Damien passed by, hand-in-hand with a guy with brown hair. Whoever that girl was, Savannah got the impression she was always surrounded by hot guys. Sort of like Evie, but multiplied by a thousand. Evie *wished* she could get with guys as hot as Damien and whoever the gym girl was with right now. Which would make it better if something ended up happening with Damien. Evie would be so jealous, especially when she saw the pictures online.

She tried spotting Damien within the groups packed in the booths. The one with the SGA kids was obvious now that Brett had mentioned it—the boys mostly wore plaid shorts with Lacoste polos, the girls in patterned dresses that could only be from Lilly Pulitzer. They looked like the types that joined every club and did well in school. Savannah could see Courtney hanging out with people like that, if she branched out from wearing jeans, T-shirts and flip-flops every day. The move to Vegas might help Courtney lighten up and have more fun. Maybe she would even carve time out of her busy schedule to date a guy.

Crazier things were possible.

Then Savannah spotted Damien in the booth with the kids Brett had referred to as "the ones with endless money who think they're God's gifts to the universe." He was involved in a conversation with a pretty girl with short blond hair, and Savannah stopped in her tracks, her confidence plummeting. The girl laughed about something he said, their heads close together like they were sharing a secret.

This was not good.

"Asshole number one, straight ahead," Peyton said to Savannah.

Savannah glared at her sister. There was no reason for Peyton to be mean, but the two of them had different tastes in guys. Savannah had good taste—she liked guys who played sports and actually had friends—while Peyton liked losers who partied so hard they nearly failed out of school. Which meant if Peyton didn't like Damien, he was perfect for Savannah.

"I thought he was nice," Savannah said. "We should say hi. He told us he wanted to hang out tonight when we talked earlier."

"He said he wanted to hang out with *you*," Peyton corrected her. "And now he's looking at us." She rolled her eyes and pretended to be interested in her chipped black nail polish. "Fantastic."

He waved them over, and Savannah couldn't believe it. Her nerves buzzed, and she drummed her fingers together, full of anticipation for whatever the night had in store.

"I'm off to the bar," Peyton said. "Have fun with your new friend. Try not to get in too much trouble, and make sure he doesn't have a girlfriend first."

Savannah gave her an irritated look. What had happened to

Peyton two years ago had sucked, but that didn't mean every guy was a jerk, as Peyton believed.

"I will," she said, hurrying to the table before Peyton could say any more.

Damien's attention dropped from the short-haired blonde as he watched Savannah approach. She made sure to keep a steady pace and not rush over to him. The new, sophisticated Savannah stayed calm in the presence of hot, popular guys. And whatever happened, she would *slow down* while talking to him. She took a deep breath. She could do this.

"Savannah Diamond," Damien said once she was standing in front of him. "You look beautiful."

"Thanks." Her cheeks flushed at the compliment. She'd never had a guy call her beautiful before.

"So are you joining us or what?" He scooted over to make room for her. "Everyone, this is Savannah Diamond," he said to the group, all of whom watched her as she sat down. "She's one of Adrian Diamond's daughters, and she got here today."

He poured her a glass of champagne and introduced her to everyone. The blonde he was talking to was Larissa, the boy in the middle was Harrison, and she remembered a Kaitlin, a Tiffany and a James, but for the most part they all blended together. Savannah was horrible at remembering names.

"When did you get here?" Damien sipped his drink, a mixed concoction with orange juice.

"A few minutes ago," she answered, embarrassed after she said it. Now he was going to think she'd sought him out right when she'd arrived.

Which she had, but he didn't have to know that.

"I'm glad I snatched you up before anyone else could." He smiled at her lazily, and her doubts disappeared. Of course he wanted to spend time with her tonight. He'd made that clear when he'd stopped by the condo. He wasn't just waiting for someone better to come along—*she* was the one he wanted to be there with. Her heart raced, and she played with her bangle bracelets. Realizing it made her look nervous, she used both hands to hold her glass of champagne to steady them. Hopefully she would live up to his expectations.

But how was Savannah supposed to pretend this glamorous life was what she'd always known? She was from a slummy neighborhood in a town outside San Francisco. These people were going to see right through her, and it was going to be worse than when she'd messed up at the eighth-grade talent show. If Evie were here right now, she would laugh about how Savannah was pretending to be someone who didn't exist.

At the image of Evie laughing at her, tossing back her shiny red hair at Savannah's pathetic attempt at fitting in with these ritzy kids, Savannah made a decision. To Damien and his friends, she was an heiress to a vast hotel fortune. She was going to act like it.

"I'm glad you did, too," she finally said.

"We should do shots to celebrate your first night here," he decided, waving over a waiter. "Eight shots of Don Eduardo Silver." Apparently he wasn't giving her an option—Savannah was doing a shot. The one time she'd tried a shot, when she and Evie had sneaked into her mom's liquor cabinet, she'd hated it. It had burned like crazy and she could only finish half of it. She'd only tried it to appease Evie. Other than that one time, she'd avoided hard alcohol, because that's what alcoholics drank to get wasted. As long as she was only having a glass of wine with dinner, or slowly sipping champagne while hanging with friends, she wasn't concerned about following in her mom's footsteps and going overboard. Hard alcohol, however, was a totally different ball game.

But Savannah wasn't about to argue with Damien. She would stop at one and pretend she didn't mind the taste when it was setting her throat on fire.

"Aren't they going to card us?" she asked, worried about what would happen if anyone asked to see her blatantly underage ID.

"Nope," Damien said. "We have our own table, and I used my fake ID when I checked in, so it's assumed we're all old enough to drink. Oliver will hook you and your sisters up with IDs soon—I'll make sure he gets on it. But as long as you're sitting with us, no one will question you."

The waiter placed the small glasses in front of each person, along with shakers of salt and a glass full of limes. Savannah tried not to think about how much she hated straight liquor. Some of the girls licked the spot between their thumb and index finger, and shook salt on it. Savannah wasn't sure why, but Larissa handed her the salt, and she followed their lead.

"To Savannah Diamond!" Damien said, raising his shot in the air. Everyone else did the same, and Savannah lifted her drink to complete the circle.

It seemed silly to toast out loud to herself, so instead she thought silently, *To everything working out the way I want with Damien*. The other girls licked the salt off their hands and took their shots. Savannah imitated them, holding her breath so the taste wouldn't overpower her, and thankfully managed to choke it all down. It had the burn that was inevitable with hard alcohol, but it wasn't as bad as she remembered. Everyone sucked on a slice of lime after their shot, so Savannah did the same. Hopefully no one could tell this was her first time doing this shot-taking ritual.

She placed her empty glass next to Damien's. "That wasn't bad," she told him. "Thanks."

"Don't worry about it." He grinned. "I'm always up for te-quila shots. But back to you—how are you liking your first night in Sin City?"

"I love it here," she gushed, the warmness of the shot re-laxing her nerves. "Myst is amazing. I had no idea it would be so…big."

"And this is only a small part of it," he said. "What do you say we explore? I'll give you the grand tour."

Savannah took a sharp breath and smiled back at him. The tequila gods had heard her private toast and were granting her wish. "That sounds fun."

"I'm going to show Savannah around the club," Damien told everyone at the table. "We'll see you all in a bit."

Savannah said it was nice to meet everyone, and stood with Damien. "Where to first?" she asked.

"Let's start with the first floor." He wrapped an arm around her waist and directed her around the dance floor. His skin felt warm where it touched her back. "The waterfall drops into a lagoon, and it's open for swimming. It's pretty fun."

"There's swimming in the club?" Savannah had never heard of such a thing.

"You'll see." He led her to a wrought-iron staircase that twisted to the lower floors, taking her hand in his. Her heart did somersaults from his touch, and she was glad the dim lights hid the flush that was surely heating her cheeks.

"I didn't bring a bathing suit," she said, trying to be out-wardly cool and not obsess over how *he was holding her hand*. "I didn't realize there would be swimming."

"Don't worry about it," he said. "There's a store downstairs that sells them, and a locker room where you can change. You can charge it to your room."

When they stepped onto the first floor, Savannah couldn't

believe her eyes. The lagoon was the size of a basketball court, with mist floating up where the waterfall collided with the surface. White cabanas with romantic drapes lined the sides of the pool, and people lounged on the cushioned seats, talking animatedly and holding colorful drinks.

"What do you think?" Damien whispered in her ear, pulling her closer to him.

"It's amazing," she answered, watching a big group of people dancing in the pool. They looked like they were having tons of fun. "I had no idea places like this existed."

"So let's stop looking around and join the party." He motioned to the store and locker rooms. "I'll meet you right here after we change, okay?"

"Okay," she said, trying not to let her excitement show too much as she made her way inside. Once she was out of his sight, she pumped her fist in the air and did a small victory spin, smiling at her reflection in the mirror. It was only the beginning of the night, and it was already better than she could have ever imagined.

Savannah turned the key of the locker where she'd stashed her dress. The bikini she'd picked was white with stitched, dark blue designs, and showed off her thin stomach. It would be more flattering if her boobs were bigger, but at least she wasn't completely flat. Hopefully her makeup would survive. If she'd known she would be swimming, she would have worn waterproof mascara.

She left the locker room, and when she saw Damien in his swim trunks it took her a second to process that he was waiting for her and not some other girl. His body was as perfect as she'd imagined; tanned and toned, and the blue spotlights dancing around the room reflected off his dark eyes. A few girls walking into the locker room checked him out, but he didn't notice. He only had eyes for her.

"And I thought you couldn't look any more beautiful than you did earlier." He took her hands in his and held her at arms' length, his gaze lingering over every inch of her body.

Savannah shifted uncomfortably. Guys had hit on her before, but they were always her age, so scrawny and awkward that they never made her nervous. They looked like little kids compared to Damien, who resembled a Greek god.

"You don't take compliments very well, do you?" Damien asked.

"It's not that," she said. "I can take compliments. Just not…" She wanted to say "Just not from guys like you," but she didn't want to sound uncool. "Just not very often."

"If you keep walking around like that you'd better get used to it, because there'll be no escaping it." He squeezed her hands and pulled her closer. "You ready to go swimming?"

Savannah looked at the people in the lagoon. Most of them were dancing in the center, the lights on the bottom of the pool illuminating them in an unearthly glow. Then she noticed a bunch of people congregated around what seemed to be a bar.

"Is that a bar in the pool?" she asked.

Damien gave her hands another gentle squeeze. "Yes," he answered. "It's a swim-up bar. You've never seen one before?"

"No." Savannah shook her head and watched the bartender serve a girl a drink. It would have been normal, except the girl was sitting on a stool immersed in the water. "Places like this don't exist in Fairfield."

She almost smacked her forehead for saying that out loud. Wasn't she supposed to be the new, sophisticated Savannah? But with the warmth of the drinks and Damien's hands wrapped around hers, she felt like she didn't have to pretend to be someone she wasn't.

Someone she wasn't yet, she corrected herself. After adjusting to life in Vegas, she would leave Fairfield and who she'd been when she'd lived there in the past—where it belonged.

"Are you ready for your first swim-up bar experience?" Damien asked once they reached the edge of the lagoon.

She breathed in the smell of chlorine and dipped her toes in to test the temperature. "It's warm," she said, immersing her foot farther to make sure she wasn't imagining it. "Like a bath."

"Yeah," Damien said, lowering himself into the water. "This is the Diamond Hotel. They want to keep people happy, and I doubt people would enjoy swimming in cold water."

"Although most of them look too drunk to notice." Savannah followed Damien into the pool, the water reaching her hips. It enveloped her skin like a blanket, and she unwrapped her arms from around her stomach, swirling her fingers across the warm surface. She'd never thought pool water could be anything but freezing. If the local pool in Fairfield had been like this, she would have gone much more often.

"To the swim-up bar?" Damien asked, holding out a hand. Savannah briefly thought about what Courtney had said about him earlier, how she thought he was an arrogant player. Her sister couldn't have been more wrong. Damien had been nothing but welcoming since she'd arrived.

He wrapped his other arm around her to make sure she didn't lose her footing, and led her to two empty stools at the bar. She sat down, the water lapping just over her belly button, and watched Damien take the seat next to her.

His knee rested against the side of her leg, and Savannah's heart pounded faster. "Another round of tequila shots, or a glass of champagne?" he asked. "Or whatever else you want. I'm sure they'll have it."

"Just a Cherry Coke," Savannah said, since her head already felt tingly from the champagne and tequila shot she'd had earlier. She didn't want to get wasted. She'd seen how out of control her mom got when she'd had too much, and she wasn't going to let that happen to her.

Damien charged the drinks to his room—a Cherry Coke for Savannah, a vodka tonic for himself—and raised his glass. "Your turn to decide what to toast to," he teased, watching her expectantly.

"To…new beginnings," she decided, clinking her glass against Damien's.

"New beginnings." He brought his glass to his lips and took a sip. "So…" he said. "What was the town like where you grew up?"

"I thought we were toasting to new beginnings?"

"We are," he said. "But I want to get to know you. It's okay if you don't want to talk about it, though."

"No." Savannah moved closer to Damien, and his knee pressed harder into her leg, sending another jolt of warmth through her body and making it hard to think straight. He'd barely broken contact with her since she'd found him in the club. "It's just that Fairfield isn't anything special. It's a small town in California—nothing happens there. At least not anything like this." She looked around the club to let him know what she meant. "The most exciting dances we had were at school. I thought they were fun then, but I guess they were pretty lame compared to this."

After she finished speaking, she realized how not cool she sounded. She used to think high school dances were fun? What a moron. She couldn't believe Damien was still talking to her—he probably thought she was a complete loser. Was he only flirting with her so he could make fun of her to his friends later? Some of the volleyball girls had laughed at her behind her back for "trying too hard" to be friends with them, and she didn't want a repeat of that with Damien's friends. It would be so embarrassing.

"Why'd you wait so long to decide to move here?" he asked, sounding genuinely interested in her answer. Maybe he *wasn't* talking to her just to make fun of her.

Savannah couldn't help but laugh at his question.

His expression twisted into confusion. "Why's that funny?"

"I didn't exactly 'decide' to move here," she began. She wanted to tell him the truth, but she also didn't want to tell him about her mom being in rehab. She'd never told any of her friends—except Evie—about her mom's drinking problem. She didn't want Damien to feel sorry for her, or worse, think badly of her because of it. "My mom had some…stuff happen, so my sisters and I couldn't stay with her anymore," she said. "We didn't even know where we would be going until this morning. You see, our dad hadn't spoken to us for a while until this afternoon."

"And by 'for a while,' you mean…"

"The last time he spoke to my sisters was before I was born." She shrugged, trying to stay lighthearted and keep the sadness from her voice, but that was impossible. "So I guess by 'a while,' I mean 'never.' He might have had some contact with my mom, but she never told us. She didn't want to take any of his money. Also, he said it was dangerous for us here, just because we're his daughters."

Damien nodded. "I guess that makes sense," he said. "Something pretty bad must have happened for him to feel it was safer for you to not have him in your life."

"Yeah," Savannah said, although she didn't want to mention what Adrian had told them at dinner about Courtney. That felt too personal. "But what about you?" she asked, trying to move the focus away from her and her messed-up family life.

"What about me?"

"You said you were seventeen," Savannah said. "So you're going to be a senior next year?"

"Yep," he said. "And I can't wait. Senior year will be the best."

"What's Goodman like?" she asked. "Adrian told us at dinner that we'd be starting there in the fall, and I feel like it's going to be really different from Fairfield High."

"Is Fairfield High a public school?"

Savannah nodded. She hadn't said much when Peyton made a big deal at dinner about not wanting to go to private school, because Damien went to Goodman and any place he went was good for her. But she was nervous. What if private school was too hard for her? She wasn't as smart as Courtney, the genius of the family, but Savannah knew she wasn't stupid. Unfortunately she cracked under pressure, whether taking tests or being onstage. It would be awful if she struggled at Goodman and everyone thought she was dumb.

"It will definitely be different," Damien said. "But I'm sure you'll be fine. Anyway, we have two months before school starts, so let's worry about that later. Do you want to see something cool?"

"Cooler than this?" she asked.

"Trust me." He stood and held out his hand the same way he'd done earlier.

"All right." She lowered her hand into his, and he pulled her up from the stool, closing the space between them. Savannah's breath caught in her chest at the realization of how close they were standing. He brushed a strand of hair off her face, his finger leaving a line of heat across her cheek. If they hadn't been surrounded by people, she would have thought he was about to kiss her. Or maybe he *was* about to kiss her. Right here, in front of everyone.

She wasn't sure how she felt about other people watching such a private moment—especially if it was going to be her first kiss with Damien. Wouldn't that make it less special than if it was just the two of them?

"Follow me," he instructed, apparently deciding not to kiss her. Savannah's heart dropped, and she wondered if she'd done something wrong, but dismissed the thought. Wasn't she just thinking about how she *didn't* want him to kiss her right there? Her emotions must be going haywire.

They made their way to the opposite side of the pool, where walls that looked like the outsides of caves converged to form an entrance leading into a dimly lit path. It reminded Savannah of the scene from *Phantom of the Opera* when the Phantom leads Christine through the underground lake. Courtney had made her watch that movie with her a hundred times.

"Is that a cavern?" she asked Damien.

"It is." His features were darker in the dim light, the shadows dancing off his face making him look dangerous, like an underwater god. "Want to explore?"

"Yes," Savannah agreed wholeheartedly. Not only was Damien hot *and* nice, but he had a romantic side, too. This night couldn't get any more perfect.

Damien's hand remained strong around hers as they headed into the cavern. It smelled damp inside, the constant dripping of water creating a relaxing soundscape in the background. Savannah ran her other hand along the walls—they were bumpy and rough, like real rocks. Every three feet or so, the wall would veer into a narrow pathway. Damien peeked inside each one, and finally stopped at one of the openings so far down that Savannah could no longer see where they'd entered.

"Ladies first," he said, and Savannah stepped inside. The small pathway led to a room the size of an aboveground hot tub. In the back a love seat dipped under the water, with what looked like cushions on the bottom.

Surely this was the place where Damien would kiss her for the first time. Why else would he have brought her here?

Suddenly she realized how nervous she was—her throat felt tight, and sometime when they were walking, every muscle in her body had tensed. She needed to relax. She'd kissed guys before. Not many, but a few, at some of the parties she and Evie had snuck out to attend. And, okay, most of them were from Truth or Dare, or Spin the Bottle. But the technical aspect of kissing was still the same, right?

Except that her whole body hadn't been shaking before she'd kissed those other guys. And they'd all looked like young boys next to Damien, who was older, more experienced and had chosen *her* out of all the girls he could be with right now.

Why had he singled her out? And what was she doing pretending to be someone she wasn't, thinking she could reinvent herself in one night? Soon Damien would see through her to the inexperienced almost-sophomore from a run-down town that she was.

Calm down, she told herself. Her muscles relaxed, and she looked back over at Damien. Then Courtney's warning popped into her mind. Yes, he seemed nice, but how well did Savannah really know him?

She tried not to overthink it. She was here with him now, and she was happy. Well, if happy was the same as being so nervous that she was glad she was standing in water or else she might have fallen over, then, yeah.

Damien sank into the love seat and pulled Savannah down next to him. Her heart thumped so loudly it was amazing he couldn't hear it. She was aware of every place where her skin touched his—the side of her leg, his arm around her back and her shoulder resting against his chest. She was surprised she wasn't shaking. Her experience with guys stopped at second base (and that had happened only once), but a guy like Damien had probably gone far with girls…maybe even all the way. What was he expecting of her?

"You seem tense." Damien traced small circles against Savannah's back. His touch felt good, and she willed her muscles to relax.

"I'm not," she lied, trying to sound smooth and confident. "This has been the best night ever."

"Good," he said, closing the space between them. His lips were warm against hers, full and perfect. He kissed her softly at first, his other hand caressing her cheek. Then his kisses became more urgent, as though he had been waiting for this moment all night. He pulled her onto his lap and Savannah wrapped her arms around his neck, her fingers weaving through his thick, soft hair. Her blood pumped faster, heat rising within her as their bodies pressed closer together, like they couldn't get enough of each other.

His lips traveled down to her neck, and Savannah tilted her head back, her heart pounding so fast it would be impossible for him not to feel it. Then his lips returned to hers and she kissed him back with more force than before. She never wanted their time together to end. Lost in the feelings and emotions coursing through her body, she was only vaguely aware of his hand traveling away from her back until his fingers cupped her breast, the thin material of her bathing suit the only barrier between his skin and hers.

What if he thought her boobs were too small? Her barely B-cups were probably anthills compared to the girls he'd been with before. And this bathing suit didn't have padding! Savannah wished she'd thought about that before, except it would have been awkward if he went to feel her up and it was only stuffing. But he kept rubbing his fingers over her breast, and he didn't seem dissatisfied, so she refocused on kissing him.

He lowered his hand, so gradually that she wasn't aware of anything but his touch. Then he slid his fingers between her stomach and the bottom of her bathing suit, going further down until he touched her where no one had ever touched her before.

Savannah gasped and jolted backward, breaking off the kiss that had been so urgent a second earlier.

"Are you okay?" he asked slowly, his voice low and hoarse.

"I'm fine," Savannah answered too quickly to be believable. She readjusted in his lap, relieved when he removed his hand from her bathing suit bottom and wrapped it around her waist. "It's only that I just met you today, and…well, this is all a little fast for me."

If he didn't think she was inexperienced before, he was definitely going to think so now.

Damien closed his eyes and rested his head against the wall, breathing so steadily that Savannah suspected he was trying to contain irritation. She should have relaxed and gone along with it. It wasn't like he was trying to have sex with her—or, he hadn't tried to go that far *yet*.

Then again, maybe she was overreacting. He didn't think she would do that with a guy she'd just met, right? The only girls she knew who had had sex were juniors and seniors on the volleyball team. Even Evie had only been to third base so far, and she'd only done it once. But maybe the girls in Las Vegas—even the ones who weren't sophomores yet—would have sex on the first date.

If this was even a date.

It took everything in her not to bury her face in her hands and cry. She felt humiliated, and she had no idea what to do. Other girls who lived in Vegas would probably love to have Damien's attention, and her inexperience had blown it.

After a few long seconds he looked back at her, his eyes soft again, like he hadn't been annoyed less than a minute ago. "What do you want to do, then?" he asked slowly.

Savannah was glad he'd cooled off, but then his jaw muscles tightened, like he was still trying to contain his anger. Disappointment surged through her body, along with a twinge of guilt. She shouldn't feel guilty, because this wasn't her fault, but she'd screwed things up. If she went back to kissing him, he might try to touch her *there* again. Yes, Damien was hot, but she didn't want him to pressure her into moving faster than she was ready for.

"It's not that I don't like you," she tried to explain, her cheeks turning what was surely a deep shade of pink. "I do. I really do. It's just…this was all so fast…and I didn't realize…" She ran her hands through her hair, unable to look him in the eye. Was he going to make her say it out loud?

"I get it," Damien cut her off. "Do you just want to go back upstairs?"

"Okay." She let out a breath she hadn't realized she was holding and stood up, the cave starting to feel claustrophobic.

Tonight had been great until that moment. Why did she have to screw it up so badly? Damien and his friends would realize that even though Savannah was Adrian Diamond's daughter, she was inexperienced, uncool and always just outside the inner circle, peeking in but never fully accepted.

Now that he knew all that about her, had she ruined her chances with him forever?

chapter 10: *Courtney*

Courtney had never been to a nightclub before, and Myst proved why she'd never had an interest in going to one, even on the under-eighteen nights at the club in San Francisco that Peyton frequented with her friends. Loud music, crowds of people she didn't know, the overpowering smell of alcohol and cigarette smoke—it made it hard to hear her own thoughts. She wanted to run up to the condo, curl up on her bed and read. Maybe she could get some SAT studying done. Her performance on the math section wasn't where it should be, and she needed to work on it if she wanted to qualify for scholarships to good schools.

Then she realized something she hadn't thought about before. Back at home, if she hadn't done well enough in school or on the SAT, she might not have gotten a full scholarship to a good school. Without a scholarship, she couldn't afford to go. But now, knowing her father was Adrian Diamond, money wasn't an issue. If she got into Stanford, she could go, even without a scholarship. Getting a scholarship was still important, because college was expensive and she didn't feel right having anyone give her so much money, but the realization that she didn't *need* one to go was strangely freeing. It was like a pressure had lifted off her chest, and Courtney wasn't sure how to react. She still wanted to get the best grades possible, but now if she didn't do perfectly in school, her future wouldn't be ruined.

Her life had changed in less than a day, and it didn't feel real.

But now wasn't the best time for Courtney to contemplate how the changes in her life would affect her future, because it seemed like she would be stuck at Myst for the rest of the night. She was left standing with Brett, and she felt a little annoyed at her sisters for deserting her so quickly. Savannah was searching for Damien—Courtney hoped she didn't find him—and Peyton was probably looking to meet a guy at the bar.

Courtney wasn't interested in accompanying either of them on their missions.

As for being alone with Brett, Courtney was glad to spend more time with him. She'd enjoyed their conversation at dinner. Peyton and Savannah gave her a hard time about not dating, but whenever she tried to talk with guys in Fairfield about school or discuss the book they were reading in their English class, their eyes had glazed over. But Brett was different; he seemed driven and goal-oriented. It was refreshing to meet someone she could relate to. He was the type of guy she would consider dating—if they weren't about to be step-siblings.

Courtney wished her long-term plans were as solid as Brett's. All she knew was that she wanted to do something with her love of books. There were tons of jobs in the book industry, and while she didn't know which one would be right for her, she was leaning toward editing. She enjoyed helping out at the tutoring center at Fairfield High during her lunch block, even though most people she tutored were only there because their teachers were forcing them. She liked fine-tuning a paper to take it from a rough draft to worthy of turning in for class. It was a concrete example of the improvements that resulted from hard work, and she enjoyed having an important part with helping it get there.

"So, what do you think of Myst?" Brett asked.

"It's…nice," Courtney said, trying not to sound too negative. Anyway, it wasn't a lie. The club was pretty. The waterfall made her feel like she was in a jungle—it would be relaxing if not for the thumping music and crowds of drunk people packing every inch of space.

"You're not the clubbing type, are you?"

"What gave it away?" Courtney laughed.

He studied her, the intensity in his eyes taking her by surprise. "I can tell you like to have real conversations with people, and clubs aren't the place for that. Once David Guetta comes on it'll be impossible to hear over the music. And you're interesting to talk to, so you shouldn't be drowned out. You're also not running to the bar. People who like clubs tend to want a drink in their hand all the time."

He thought she was interesting? Knowing that made her smile. "You're interesting to talk to, too," she said, surprising herself by how forward that sounded. "Dinner would have been awkward for me if you weren't there. This whole situation with Adrian…" She played with her purse, wondering if she should say more.

"It's hard for you, isn't it?" Brett asked, taking a step closer to her. Courtney stared back at him, feeling like she could get lost in his green eyes. Then she realized what she was thinking, and she looked away, shaking the thought from her head.

They would be step-siblings soon. She couldn't help her reaction to him, but it wasn't appropriate.

She felt like she would have to constantly remind herself of that whenever she was around him. Adrian had made it clear while laying down the rules: Courtney would have to control whatever feelings were brewing inside of her toward Brett. Anyway, it was ridiculous she felt this way at all. She'd only known him for a few hours. She couldn't have developed an interest in him in such a short amount of time. Her emotions were just acting strangely because of the sudden move to Las Vegas, and meeting the father she'd never known. Once she woke up tomorrow they would be steady and in control, as they always were.

"Yes, it's a lot to take in." She strained to talk over the loud music. If she had to continue speaking this loudly, she would lose her voice by the end of the night.

The song changed to one that was even louder. Brett tried to say something, but the music drowned him out completely.

"What?" Courtney screamed, leaning toward him and cupping a hand around her ear. Her hand brushed against his shoulder, and the contact made her stomach flip. She didn't mind having to get closer to him to talk, but at this rate, they would never be able to finish their conversation from dinner.

"Want to get out of here?" he asked, so close to her now that she could feel his cool breath on her cheek. "I know a better place to watch the fireworks, and we can actually talk there."

She'd never run off with a guy she'd just met before, but she trusted and felt comfortable around Brett. "Won't Adrian get mad?" she asked. "Not that I don't want to go… I just don't want to get in trouble on my first day here."

"Everyone here wants five minutes with Adrian, so he's busy mingling," Brett said. "If he notices you left, you can tell him you were tired from traveling and weren't in the mood for a club. I don't see how he can get mad."

Courtney examined where Adrian sat with a dark-haired man wearing a suit similar to his own. He did appear occupied with whatever they were discussing. It would be easy to leave, but what if her sisters—mainly Savannah—needed her and she was gone? Savannah had never been to a place like Myst before, and while her younger sister *thought* she would be fine, you never knew with Savannah. Her hopes got crushed so easily.

But Peyton had followed Savannah on her quest for Damien, so Peyton could keep Savannah in check. And the three of them had bodyguards now. Well, apparently they'd *always* had bodyguards, but now she was aware of them. Savannah needed supervision, but her bodyguard would protect her from danger.

Knowing she wasn't responsible for making sure her sisters stayed out of trouble made Courtney feel strangely light, like a weight had been lifted from her chest. Maybe with all these changes, she could focus more on herself and not worry about constantly watching out for her sisters. She could be a normal sixteen-year-old who didn't have to be the caretaker for her entire family.

The thought was refreshing and scary at the same time.

"My bodyguard won't tell on me, will he?" she asked. At dinner Adrian had assured them their bodyguards weren't babysitters, but she wanted to make sure that was the case.

"We're not doing anything that will put you in danger, so he has no reason to tell your father where we're going," he said. "Ever since my mom and Adrian made it public that they were dating, I've had a bodyguard, too. They're good with giving us our privacy and letting us be teenagers, as long as we don't do anything too extreme."

"And going somewhere without letting Adrian know isn't extreme?"

Brett chuckled. "That's tame compared to what some teens in Vegas do. I doubt your bodyguard will think twice about it. We'll let our bodyguards know where we're heading, and they'll follow us to make sure we're safe and that we get home, but that's all. They're not tattletales. They're here to protect us from serious danger. So unless you plan on getting too close to a firework when it goes off tonight, I think we'll be safe."

When he put it like that, it didn't sound so bad. "Okay," she said, happy with her decision once she voiced it, especially since it made Brett smile. "I just need to text my sisters to let them know. Then we can get out of here."

"Thank God." He let out a breath of relief. "The last thing I wanted was to be stuck here all night."

"Couldn't you have left even if I didn't agree to go with you?"

"I could have." He nodded. "But that would mean leaving you alone, and I wouldn't want to do that."

Hearing that took Courtney's breath away. "I would have had my sisters," she told him. "But I wouldn't have wanted you to do that, either."

"Good." He reached out as if to touch her arm, but brought his hand back to his side. She was disappointed that he pulled away, but he'd done the right thing.

Maybe if she kept repeating that she would start to believe it.

Brett's red convertible waited at the front of the hotel when he and Courtney arrived.

"That's your car?" It looked so expensive that Courtney was

afraid to touch it. But she didn't have to, because he opened the door for her.

"Yeah," he said as she slid into the passenger seat. "There's a Lamborghini dealership in the hotel, so Adrian got it for me as a move-in present."

Courtney hadn't gotten a car for her sixteenth birthday—not that she'd expected one, but some people she knew bought them used—and Brett had gotten one just for moving into a new condo. And not just any car. *A Lamborghini*. She couldn't begin to comprehend how expensive it must have been.

And you can probably get one, too, said a small voice in the back of her head. Then she pushed the thought away. Being able to access so much money didn't mean she should abuse the privilege. Her bike had gotten her around just fine in Fairfield. She hadn't been able to bring it with her to Vegas, but she would save up enough money to buy a new one. She'd seen a coffee shop in the Diamond Hotel—this week she would go there and ask about submitting a job application.

Brett slid into the driver's seat and looked over at Courtney. "Are you ready for some real fun?" he asked, his eyes glinting with mischief.

"Anything would be more fun than the club," she answered, laughing.

"You're a cool girl, Courtney," he said as they drove away from the Diamond. The Vegas Strip was beautiful at night—sparkling lights illuminating all of the buildings, the city buzzing with life. "It sounds like the circumstances that brought you and your sisters here sucked, but I'm glad you moved here."

"It's been hard," she said. "Everything here is really different from Fairfield, and this all happened so fast. I hope my sisters are able to handle it okay."

"You feel responsible for them, don't you?"

"Savannah more than Peyton," she said. "Peyton tries to make it seem like she doesn't need anyone, but I know that's not true. And Savannah's always been sheltered. She was my mom's favorite, so Mom never took things out on Savannah as much as she did on me and Peyton."

"Savannah's the favorite?" Brett seemed surprised. "I would have assumed that would be you, with your dedication to school and how you helped out at home."

"I was our mom's least favorite." Courtney laughed, although it came out strained. This wasn't something she normally talked about. "My mom barely bothered to fill out my baby book."

"Huh." Brett furrowed his eyebrows. "That doesn't make sense."

"All my life, my mom's looked at me with…regret." She tried to shrug it off like it wasn't a big deal, even though it had always bothered her. "It's like she wanted more than she got with me. At dinner tonight, when Adrian told my sisters and I about the kidnapping, I thought it would explain why my mom's always been like that. But it doesn't make sense— it seems like she would be grateful I was okay, not resentful. I've tried so hard to do everything right, to not disappoint her, but it's never enough. It's like *I'm* not enough."

"I doubt that's true," Brett said. "My mom told me about what happened to you, and I don't know why your mom did what she did, but it sounds like she wasn't being fair to you. You deserve better than that. I know we only just met, but from what you've told me, you work harder than anyone I know."

"Thanks," Courtney said—Brett's kindness surprised her once again. But she didn't want to talk about her family drama now, especially the kidnapping. It was a lot to process. "So, do you want to tell me where we're going?"

"A better place to watch the fireworks," he answered. "Trust me on this."

"I trust you." It wasn't something she told people often—if ever—but with Brett, she didn't have to think twice about it.

"That's quick," Brett said. "Seeing as we only met three hours ago."

"I get vibes about people," she explained. "And I like you." She looked away from him, surprised at how up-front she'd been about her feelings.

"I like you, too," he said, his voice softer than earlier.

Courtney's cheeks heated up. With Brett, she felt both jittery and comfortable at the same time. She'd never felt this way around anyone. "Can you give me a hint about where we're going?" she asked.

"You don't do well with surprises, do you?"

"Not really," she admitted. "I plan everything in advance."

"This is a surprise you'll like," he promised. "We have about twenty-five more minutes. Think you can handle it?"

"No," Courtney said, only half joking. "You can't just tell me now?"

"Nope." Brett smiled, refusing to budge.

Courtney gave up, since it was clear he wasn't going to give in, and the conversation flowed the rest of the way there. She was happy to forget her family drama for a little while. She discovered Brett would watch any movie (minus chick flicks), so he knew all of Courtney's favorites. Their music tastes were different, but he promised he would make her a playlist, and Courtney wanted to hear the music he enjoyed. Music revealed a lot about a person, and she wanted to know more about Brett.

"I'm not a fan of EDM," he said. "And I take it you're not either, since you didn't mind leaving the club."

"What's EDM?" she asked, unable to hide the alarm from her tone. It sounded like something from *Fifty Shades of Grey*.

"Electronic dance music," he explained. "What'd you think it meant?"

"Nothing." Courtney felt her cheeks heat up. No way was she telling him what had crossed her mind. "But you're right. I'm not very into whatever they were playing at the club."

Soon their surroundings changed to a sprawling desert. The barren mountains stretched out for miles, and while it was hard to tell in the dark, Courtney knew from when she'd flown over them this morning that they were a bright shade of brown that looked almost red.

"The park isn't usually open at night, but they make an exception for Fourth of July," Brett explained as he drove past a sign that said Red Rock Canyon National Conservation Area.

"Since it's a good place to watch the fireworks," Courtney said, quoting what he had said earlier.

"You got it."

A few people were milling around the nearly full parking lot, getting food and beer out of the trunks of their cars. While it was nighttime, it was still hot, and Courtney was glad she was wearing the airy sundress instead of her usual jeans and T-shirt. But she wished she had changed into flip-flops before leaving. She would have to manage in the pumps—or take them off and be barefoot.

At the edge of the parking lot, an expansive area held kids spread out on blankets, drinking and laughing. There must have been hundreds of people there. Some groups had speakers playing music, but nothing so loud that it was as overwhelming as the club. A metal rail guarded the ledge where the ground dropped into a cliff. Below was a basin full of sparsely leaved trees with a stream running through it, and red, jagged mountains lined the horizon. The light of the almost-full moon gave the park a surreal, magical glow.

"Come on." Brett held out his hand, but then pulled it back. "I want to introduce you to my friends."

She didn't blame him for pulling his hand away—it was the right thing to do given their situation—but if he hadn't, she had a feeling she would have taken it. What was happening to her? She'd never been impulsive, but it was like Brett was bringing that unknown side of her to the surface. And she wasn't sure how she felt about that yet.

He led her over to where two girls and a guy sat on a big blue blanket. The guy sat close to one of the girls, and Courtney guessed they were a couple. The other girl sat farther away from them. She looked irritated, and Courtney felt guilty for a second—what if this girl and Brett were an item?—but she brushed the thought away. She couldn't be more than friends with Brett. She was already a disappointment to her mother; she didn't want to disappoint her father by breaking a clearly stated rule.

They went through introductions—the guy and girl who looked like they were together were Scott and Vanessa, and the irritated-looking girl was Dawn. Brett sat down and Courtney sat next to him, leaving a decent amount of space between them.

"Do your friends go to Goodman?" Courtney asked.

"No," Brett said with a small laugh. "They go to Palo Verde—my old public school."

"At dinner tonight, your mom made it sound like you've been going to Goodman forever," Courtney said. "When did you switch?"

"My mom *wishes* I had gone to Goodman forever," Brett said. "But she couldn't justify the expense, since Palo Verde is one of the best public schools in the area, and I liked it there because I've known everyone forever. But once my mom got serious with your dad and we moved into the Diamond, he wouldn't hear of me going to public school any longer, so he convinced Goodman to let me in last January. And by 'convinced' I mean donated a large sum of money to the school."

"Do you not like Goodman?" Courtney asked, surprised. Judging from their conversation at dinner, she'd assumed he would want to be as challenged in school as possible.

"The academics are great," Brett said. "I was behind their curriculum when I started, but that was solved by some hours at the student tutoring center. I appreciate the small class sizes, and I have a better chance at getting into UCLA coming from a school like Goodman, but I still prefer hanging out with my friends from Palo. The kids at Goodman are a little bit..." He paused, as if contemplating how to word it. "Never mind. You'll see once you start."

"They're a little bit what?" Since she would be going there, she wanted to be prepared.

"They're very privileged," he explained. "There are a few scholarship kids per grade because the school is required to have them, but other than them, no one has worked a day in their life. They spend winter break in the tropics, spring break skiing in the Rockies or the Alps and at least two weeks in the summer traveling Europe or another foreign country, if they're not doing an academic or sports program designed for high school students at colleges throughout the world. Their worldview is...skewed. So when I'm not in school I choose to hang out with my friends from Palo, much to my mom's disappointment."

"Wow." Courtney could barely comprehend what he'd just told her. "It does sound really different."

Before he could reply, the girl with the thin brown hair—whom he'd introduced as Dawn—plopped down on the blanket, ending their conversation. "How long will you be in Vegas?" she asked Courtney.

"A year, at the least," Courtney said, repeating what Adrian had told them at dinner, playing with a thread that was coming loose from the blanket. She'd never been away from home, and a year felt like such a long time. She couldn't wrap her mind around it.

"Cool," Dawn said, looking back and forth from Courtney to Brett. "So, your parents are dating, right?"

"They are," Brett confirmed, his tone neutral.

"So that would make you two…"

"Friends," Courtney jumped in, not looking at Brett.

"Right." Dawn didn't look convinced.

Brett moved closer to Courtney, his proximity sending her stomach flipping. She pretended she didn't notice, so that Dawn wouldn't grow more suspicious. "What time are the fireworks starting?" he asked his friends.

"Any minute now," Vanessa said. Dawn scooted toward Vanessa and Scott, and the three of them talked about some band they liked. Courtney was glad to be able to talk with Brett privately again. Well, as privately as they could, given the situation.

She angled her body towards him, wishing they were watching the fireworks alone. But it was better this way for both of them.

"Tell me something about yourself," Brett said, quietly enough so only Courtney could hear. "Something happy."

Courtney searched her mind for what to say. She didn't want

to talk about her past—not with Scott, Vanessa and Dawn there. "I want to travel the world someday. Paris, Rome, New York…" She paused to look up at the sky, taking in the stars twinkling overhead. For her whole life, seeing the world had only been a dream, but now, as Adrian Diamond's daughter, it could be a reality. "I want to see the art in the Louvre and the Met, the ruins in Rome and maybe even an active volcano."

"Rome's pretty cool," Brett replied. "There's so much history there—it's one of my favorite cities in the world."

"*One* of your favorites?" Courtney didn't bother hiding her disbelief. "How many cities have you been to?"

"A few." He rubbed the back of his neck, looking uncomfortable. He had probably been to more cities than he could count on all of his fingers. And toes. "I've never seen an active volcano, though."

"You've never been to Hawaii?"

"Oh, I have," Brett said. "But when we took our private helicopter tour over the Big Island, the volcano was having an off day."

"Poor you." Courtney couldn't stop from laughing. "How did you get to travel so much, though? I thought your mom couldn't afford private school before moving in with Adrian."

"My mom only divorced my dad about two years ago," Brett explained. "He's a lawyer, so we were comfortable enough to go on family vacations. But he went to public school when he was our age, so even though my mom wanted me at private school, he refused to pay for it since the public schools for our neighborhood were some of the best in the state. They bought their house specifically so I could go to those schools."

"I guess that makes sense," Courtney said.

The fireworks started before either of them could say anything more, bursts of light shooting into the desert sky, bigger than any firework show Courtney had seen in Fairfield. It was impossible to ignore the electricity bouncing between the inches of space separating her and Brett, dancing across her skin with each boom overhead. She couldn't stop glancing at him from the corner of her eye. He looked lost in thought, although sometimes she swore she caught him watching her, too. This went on for twenty minutes, and then came the finale— shot after shot of fireworks exploding, without a second's break between them. Some soared into the air like comets and others spread like meteor showers, filling up miles of sky.

When it was over, Courtney was sitting so close to Brett that their arms were an inch from touching.

"How did you like it?" he asked, not making an effort to move away.

"I loved it," she replied. "Thanks for bringing me." Her head felt fuzzy, and she pushed a strand of hair behind her ear, her arm brushing his. She stilled at the touch, and he looked at her with more intensity than he had the entire night.

"Are you two ready to leave?" Dawn destroyed the moment, standing up and brushing invisible dust off her jeans.

Courtney jerked backward, torn out of her trance. If the others hadn't been there, what would have happened between her and Brett? She'd never kissed a guy before, but from the way he was looking at her, she felt like he'd wanted to kiss her. And if he had, she wasn't sure she would have stopped him.

She shook her head at the thought. Courtney had never broken a rule in her life.

Whatever had just occurred between her and Brett could never happen again.

Chapter 11: *Peyton*

Peyton sat at the bar on the VIP floor of Myst, sipping a martini that a random guy had bought her when she'd sat down. She spotted Damien leading Savannah downstairs and decided not to bother them. She had assured Courtney via text message that she would watch out for Savannah, but it's not like they were leaving the *club* together. What trouble could her youngest sister get into in public? They had their bodyguards to keep them from anything too terrible. Peyton only hoped Savannah wouldn't become so infatuated with Damien that she got hurt when it was over. She knew how it felt to be humiliated, and she didn't wish that on anyone, especially her sister.

Now Peyton was left by herself. Screw that. She stirred her drink and took another sip, trying not to think about her mom. Peyton liked to drink, but she wasn't an alcoholic. Alcoholics drank by themselves. Peyton only drank when she was out, and never somewhere unacceptable, like at school.

She'd seen how bad her mom got drinking alone at home, and she never wanted to cross that line.

Her phone buzzed, and she took it out to see Mike's name flashing on the small screen. She frowned and tossed the phone back in her bag. She would have to break up with him sometime, but that conversation couldn't happen in the loud club, and she didn't feel like dealing with him right now.

Instead, she looked around the crowd, trying to see if she could find her bodyguard—Jackson. She hated that he'd been watching her for so long without her knowing, but it was hard to hate it *too* much when Jackson was so hot. There were worse things in life than a gorgeous guy following her everywhere. Adrian had said their bodyguards would always be around, but they wouldn't make their presence known in public. Jackson was doing a good job of that, and the club was dark and packed, making it easy to blend.

Finally, Peyton spotted him. She smiled to herself; tonight was about to get more interesting. He was standing at the corner of the bar, behind a large group of what looked like college students. If he weren't dressed in a suit and tie, he could have easily fit in with them.

Which brought Peyton's biggest question to mind: How old was Jackson, and how had he gotten into this career path at such a young age?

There was only one way to find out.

She picked up her half-empty cocktail and sauntered toward the end of the bar, where Jackson stood watching her. She expected him to move away, since Adrian had said their bodyguards were supposed to give them privacy in public, but he stayed where he was. Probably because with the way Peyton was looking at him, any member of the male species would know she was heading in his direction for one purpose: to talk to him.

Jackson stood straighter and raised an eyebrow, but other than that, his reaction to her approach was neutral. Most guys would smile, lean toward her, ask her how she was enjoying her night or say the dreaded "Do you come here often?" line. She got none of that from him. He glanced at her and swallowed, and Peyton could see his Adam's apple bob in his throat. Still, he said nothing.

She situated herself in the seat closest to him. He was tall as it was, and now that she was sitting, he towered over her. Since he wasn't Mr. Talkative, she took it upon herself to start the conversation.

"Hi," she said, since it was as good of an intro as any.

He straightened, and his gaze met hers, distant and hard. "Is there anything I can do for you, Ms. Diamond?" His voice was strong and steady, as if he calculated each word before speaking it. It fit his looks perfectly.

"Ms. Diamond?" Peyton crinkled her nose and laughed. She was only seventeen. No one had ever called her Ms. before. "That's what people call my mom. My name's Peyton. And you're only, what…three years older than me?"

Jackson cleared his throat. "My age is irrelevant," he said. "I work for your family, and protocol states I should address you formally, since your father is my employer."

Peyton huffed. "And since you work for Adrian, does protocol also state that you should do what his daughters ask?"

"It depends."

"Depends on what?"

"If what you ask directly interferes with my ability to keep you safe," he said, surveying the crowd. "It's my job to protect you no matter what."

Even though he looked like he was her age, the way he was talking to her made it sound like he was in his thirties, speaking to a child. He must have to act like that because of his job. Could she get him to lower his guard around her? It would be tough, but Peyton never turned down a challenge. She thrilled at the thought, crossing her legs in his direction and smiling in a way she knew looked mischievous. This was about to get fun.

"I doubt my asking you to call me by my first name interferes with your ability to keep me safe."

She could have sworn the corner of his lip turned up into a smile, but it disappeared before she could say for sure. "I suppose it doesn't, Peyton," he said.

"Good." She leaned back in her seat and rested an elbow on the bar. "And I'll call you Jackson. That is your first name, right? You're not one of those guys everyone calls by his last name?"

"You have a lot of questions," he said, and this time he smiled for real. "But shouldn't you be spending time with your friends instead of talking to me?"

"I don't have any friends here," Peyton said matter-of-factly. "You're my only one so far."

His expression hardened, but the freckles across his nose kept him from looking like a complete tough guy. "I'm your bodyguard, Peyton, not your friend."

"So you're supposed to watch over me every moment when I'm awake, and we're not supposed to be friends?" Peyton acted more confused than she was. "That doesn't make sense."

"It's my job," he told her. "And I don't plan on losing this job when I've only just started."

"But I thought you all had been looking after me and my sisters for a long time." Now Peyton really *was* confused.

"Carl and Teddy have," Jackson said, his tone still frustratingly formal. "I only started being your bodyguard about seven months ago, after your previous one retired."

"Seven months ago," she repeated, staring into her drink. "That means you saw the worst of it."

"What do you mean?" he asked.

She looked back up at him, surprised at the concern in his eyes. "That was right after my mom started her downward spiral. I mean, she was always pretty bad, but seven months ago…" Peyton thought back to what exactly had been going on at that time. "That's when she lost her first waitressing job and brought home three different guys in one week. It was disgusting."

"Yes." He swallowed. "That's around the time I started."

"You must have thought we were all so pathetic." Peyton kept her home life secret from her friends, and knowing Jackson had seen it made her feel transparent.

"No, I don't." He shook his head. "Not at all. I was impressed with you. I still *am* impressed with you. You're stronger than most people your age."

"Oh, yeah?" Peyton laughed. "Why do you say that?"

"Because I'll never forget what happened with the last guy your mom brought home that week," he said. Peyton's throat tightened, immediately knowing which one he meant. "The one who brought the drugs into your house. I was watching from the open window when you walked into the living room with a phone in one hand and a steak knife in the other, telling him to get himself and his drugs out of there or you would call the police and get him locked up for life. I had my hand on my gun the entire time, ready to burst in and protect you if he tried anything. Luckily he ran out, but do you know how reckless that was? What if he'd had a gun?"

"I didn't think about that at the time," she said, although she'd realized later that she should have. "I just knew my mom had enough trouble with the alcohol, and no way in hell was I letting that loser turn her into a junkie, too. I wouldn't let her do that to my sisters."

"You never told them about that night, did you?"

"No," she said. "It was late when it happened. They were sleeping, and my mom had passed out, which I guess is why that loser came into the living room to get his fix. He just didn't expect me to still be awake. He actually had the nerve to ask if I wanted some." She scoffed. "What an idiot."

"He had no idea who he was dealing with," Jackson agreed, his eyes focused on hers, energy crackling between them. It was the way guys looked at her when they wanted to kiss her, and she leaned closer to him, letting him know he could. But he stepped away, and whatever had passed between them disappeared. "We're not supposed to talk like this, Peyton," he said. "I'm your bodyguard, nothing more."

"It's okay for you to talk to me," she said. "I won't tell on you to Adrian, I promise." She allowed her long hair to fall over her shoulder and turned her eyes up at him seductively. It was a look that any hot-blooded male couldn't refuse—and Peyton knew, because she'd used it before.

His eyebrows furrowed, as though he was conflicted, and he watched her so closely that Peyton thought he would open up to her to again. "This isn't appropriate," he finally replied. "You should be talking with kids your age, not with me."

She frowned and leaned back in her seat. When they were talking a minute ago, she'd felt a connection between them. But he really seemed to be turning her down. "Answer one more question, and then I'll leave you alone," she said, although she hoped she wouldn't have to follow through with that promise.

He remained silent, which Peyton took as a cue to continue.

"How old *are* you?" she asked.

"I'll be twenty-three in three months."

"So you're twenty-two," she said in victory. Only five years older than her—that wasn't bad at all. "How did you get to be a bodyguard when you're so young?"

"You said one question," he pointed out. "That's two."

"Fine." Peyton huffed and finished the rest of her drink. He might not budge right now, but she wouldn't give up on him. Not when he knew so much about her that she'd never told anyone else. "I'll leave you alone tonight, but don't expect me to pretend you don't exist just because you're supposed to give me privacy. I'm not going to ignore you in the elevator, or wherever else we see each other."

"Have a good night, Peyton," was Jackson's only reply.

Taking that as a hint to leave, she pushed her empty glass across the bar and walked to the balcony in the center of the club, watching the scene beneath her. The second floor was packed with people dancing so close that it was impossible to differentiate one person from the next. Everyone danced in time with the music, like a choreographed routine.

After that frustrating conversation with Jackson, Peyton itched to join the crowd below and get lost in the music. She walked downstairs and onto the dance floor, swept away in the heavy beat. Guys came up to dance with her, and she appeased them for a few minutes, switching to the next guy when the song changed. She hoped Jackson was enjoying the show. When he saw how his disinterest didn't bother her, he would think twice about dismissing her so quickly. He was simply a long-term goal. But in the meantime, Peyton would have fun tonight.

Then she spotted the dark-haired girl from the gym. Their eyes met, and the girl's face hardened. She was dancing with a guy a bit taller than she was, the two of them so close that their bodies melded into one. Peyton wished she could see his face. But his back was toward her, so she could only see his dark, shaggy hair.

The girl whispered something in his ear, and he swiveled his head, his gaze locking with Peyton's. There was something about his eyes that made her wonder what it would be like to dance with him—to get lost in the music, and each other. His face was soft, but his smirk gave Peyton the feeling he wasn't innocent in the slightest. He said something to the girl, and she marched to the stairs leading up to the VIP level, shooting Peyton a nasty glare on her way.

His eyes focused on Peyton, and he walked toward her. Her pulse raced at the intensity of his gaze, and she tuned in to the music to stay calm.

"Would you like to dance?" His voice was much smoother than Peyton had anticipated.

"Sure," she said steadily. This was the kind of greeting she was used to. Whoever this guy was, he made her feel wanted—which was a vast improvement from her conversation with Jackson.

He pulled her closer, his body moving with the music. The beat quickened, and Peyton kept in time with it, leaning into him so her cheek brushed against his. He smelled like alcohol and smoke, but whatever. She probably did, too.

"Which lovely Diamond sister are you?" he asked, his lips close to her ear.

"How do you know I'm one of the Diamond sisters?" She

leaned back and looked up at him, trying to sound mysterious. Word sure did travel fast around here.

"Lucky guess." He ran his thumb down her back, and she shivered at his touch. "Actually, I saw you walk in with Adrian earlier. Sort of gave it away."

"Oh," she said, although she was happy he'd noticed her. "I'm Peyton."

"Peyton," he repeated. "Pretty name. I like it."

"Thanks." She had never had anyone tell her that before. "And you are…"

"Oliver," he answered with a haughtiness that made her think he assumed most people already knew his name. "Oliver Prescott."

"Nice to meet you, Oliver," she said, smiling seductively up at him—the same look she'd given to Jackson earlier. But unlike with Jackson, it made Oliver move closer to her. The music changed to a remix of a popular song, and she wound her arms tighter around him. "Your girlfriend didn't look happy that you left her to dance with me."

"Girlfriend?" Oliver laughed. "Madison's just a friend."

"Good." Peyton had dated many guys, but the ones with girlfriends were out of the question. She refused to risk getting hurt, or make an enemy in the wrong place.

"Do I seem like the type of guy who would tell my girlfriend to disappear while I danced with another girl?" He looked amused, but Peyton believed he was serious.

"Going off the few minutes I've known you…?" She quirked an eyebrow. "It never hurts to check. But I believe you."

"And you would trust me that easily?"

"Mainly because Madison doesn't look like the sort of girl who would allow a boyfriend of hers to do that," Peyton said.

"You sure got that right." He trailed a finger down her arm, like he was taking in every inch of her. Peyton reveled in his touch. The back of his neck was moist with sweat, and she ran her fingers through his hair, enjoying the silkiness of it.

"Do you live in the hotel, too?" she asked.

"Not at the Diamond," he replied. "I live across the street at the Gates. My father owns it, along with a few other hotels on the Strip."

"Does that mean your family is in competition with mine?"

"Not in competition," he said, pulling her closer. "But our fathers' businesses aren't important right now."

"No," Peyton breathed. "They're not."

His lips were on hers a second later. He kissed her gently, like he was waiting to see her response. Her head felt light, and she tangled her fingers through his hair as she kissed him back. But as she kissed Oliver, she imagined what it would be like if Jackson were in his place, instead. The way his strong arms would feel wrapped around her waist, his full lips against her own. The thrill of capturing the attention of someone so forbidden made her blood pulse faster, and she pushed her body closer to his so there was no space left between them. Of course, she knew she was with Oliver—not Jackson—but Jackson had to be watching. She hoped she was giving him a good show.

Then an image of Mike flashed through her mind—his sweet blue eyes and the way he lit up when he saw her—and Peyton shut her eyes tighter, as though doing so could wipe away all thoughts of her sort-of boyfriend who she still had to officially break up with. It worked. She pressed her hips harder against Oliver's as they danced, wishing they were somewhere more private.

They continued like that through three more songs. Peyton

was about to suggest they get out of there, when the music softened and the announcer said that in five minutes, David Guetta would hit the stage and the fireworks show would begin. Peyton cursed under her breath. The moment—the very *long* moment—between her and Oliver had broken. His body was still touching hers, but neither of them danced as intensely as they had earlier.

He rested his forehead against hers, his skin hot and sweaty. "We should head back upstairs," he said. "We'll watch the fireworks from there. You can meet some of my friends, too."

"Okay," she said, although she really wanted to press her lips against his again and forget about his friends and the fireworks. "Let's do that."

He led her back upstairs, and when they reached the VIP floor she looked around for Jackson but couldn't find him. Maybe after she had approached him earlier, he was going to make more of an effort to remain concealed from her sight.

But she knew he would never be too far away.

Chapter 12: *Madison*

Madison couldn't believe Oliver had ditched her for the circus-freak Diamond girl. What the hell was he thinking?

Once upstairs, she tried to figure out how to get back to the table with her friends without bumping into Nick. She couldn't bear to have him ask her about their breakup again. Because she'd broken up with him for Brett, who wasn't interested in her as "more than a friend." It was pathetic. Madison knew it, and she hated it. No one could ever find out—not even Oliver. She normally told Oliver everything, but this would have to be an exception.

Not looking at where Nick had been sitting, Madison walked the long way around the club. She couldn't avoid him forever, but she could keep her distance before school started.

The Fourth of July was supposed to be one of the best nights of summer, but instead this whole day was pissing her off. The Diamond girls arriving in town, Damien talking about trying to make a move on one of them, Oliver making that stupid bet and then ditching her on the dance floor for another one of them, and Brett's rejection earlier.

Screw that it would put her well over her daily calorie limit—she needed another drink.

She sat down at the bar and ordered another Chardonnay, relishing the rich, smooth taste. Feeling better, she looked at the table where her friends were still sitting. Larissa sat close to Harrison, and Kaitlin, Tiffany and a few others were doing a round of shooters.

Damien was missing. She hadn't seen the other two Diamond sisters around, either. And Brett appeared to be gone, too.

What was going on?

She sighed. Part of her wanted to go up to her room and watch a movie, but being antisocial wasn't her style. She wanted to have fun tonight. Maybe she'd meet someone new who would make her forget about Brett.

"It looks like your night's going as great as mine," someone said from behind her.

Madison swirled in her seat. She'd thought this day couldn't get any worse, but of course Nick had to approach her. She took a good look at him, surprised by how stressed he seemed. While his bright blue eyes stood out in the dark lighting, she also noticed dark circles below them.

He sat on the stool next to her and managed a smile, which only made her feel worse.

"My night's going great," she lied. "I just came to the bar to get a quick drink—I'm about to go back over to my friends." She motioned to the table where Larissa was topping off everyone's glasses of champagne. She wished she had headed over there a minute earlier so she could have avoided this run-in with Nick. Hoping he would get the point, she picked up her glass of wine and stood up.

"Wait." He stopped her, his eyes begging her to stay. "I've been wanting to talk to you."

"There's nothing more to say." Madison cringed at the harshness of her words.

"Yes, there is." He looked so defeated, and Madison couldn't bring herself to walk away. "I've been thinking a lot about everything that happened between us, but none of it makes sense. You told me you'd never been happier with anyone in your life, but then you moved to the Diamond and everything changed. What happened, Mads? You know you can tell me anything, right? You don't have to push me away."

"I already told you." Madison hated that she had to go through this with him again. All he was doing was causing himself more pain.

"That you 'lost interest,' I know," Nick muttered. "But I don't buy it." He looked at her straight-on, and Madison jerked back, surprised at his determination. "I want you to tell me the truth. Whatever it is, I'll understand. I promise. Then we can go back to how we were and be happy again." Madison started to speak, but he stopped her. "And don't say that you're happy now, because I know that's a lie. Don't lie to me, Mads."

Nick looked so vulnerable, and Madison hated what she had to do next.

"Fine. You want to know the truth?"

His eyes widened in hope, and as much as she knew it would hurt him, Madison had to do this. A clean break was the only way he would be able to get on with his life. She wanted him to be happy, and it wasn't going to be with her. The kindest thing she could do now was be honest—even if that meant ripping his heart out.

"I was with someone else one night when we were together," she said, keeping her voice steady. The words were hers, but it felt like someone else was saying them, and she was watching from a distance.

Nick looked at her like he didn't recognize her. "What?" he finally said. "You *slept* with someone?"

"I didn't sleep with anyone—you know me better than that—but I did have feelings for someone else, and we kissed." Madison tried to block off her emotions, not wanting to think about how painful this must be for him to hear.

"I don't believe you." He shook his head, as if he couldn't bring himself to face it.

"It's true." She swirled her wine, feeling something inside her starting to crack. Nick looked so devastated. He was a good person, and she was breaking his heart. "I'm so sorry," she said, blinking back tears as she reminded herself she was doing the right thing.

Finally he asked, "Who was it?"

"It doesn't matter." Madison couldn't bring herself to say Brett's name out loud—it would make her cry. She wished she'd never had feelings for him. If she had never been assigned to be his biology student tutor, she wouldn't have ever *talked* to him. It would have made her life a lot easier. But that wouldn't have made her relationship with Nick any better. Nick was a great guy, but Madison believed in soul mates, and he wasn't "the one."

Nick slammed his hand down on the bar. "It matters to me," he said, his anger surprising her. "At least do me the decency of telling me who it was."

"It wasn't anyone important." She kept her voice steady so

she wouldn't lose her cool. "It was a one-time thing, and I feel awful, but I can't change what happened. I really am sorry." She started to walk away, but Nick wrapped his hand around her wrist, holding her in place.

"Was it Oliver?" He grimaced when he said his name.

"Oliver?" Madison laughed at the accusation. "Why would you think it was Oliver?"

"I saw the two of you together earlier," he said, loosening his grip. "You looked close."

"And what if it was Oliver?" Better for him to suspect Oliver than find out the truth. In the background she heard the announcement that David Guetta and the fireworks would be starting soon, and Madison yanked her wrist away, pulling her arm back to her side.

"Then you should know he was making out with that Diamond girl on the main dance floor," Nick said. "They were still at it when I walked over here."

Madison hated the image of Oliver with that circus-freak girl he'd left her for downstairs. Then she got annoyed at herself for getting jealous about one of Oliver's girls. The Diamond girl was only part of his dumb bet with Damien. He would ditch her after hooking up with her and find someone new. "Does everyone know about those Diamond girls already?" she asked.

"Word travels fast around here," Nick said.

"Well, it wasn't Oliver, so it doesn't matter. And do me a favor and give me some space." She wanted to tell him that she wanted to be friends when things returned to normal, but she couldn't bring herself to do it. Not when she was the one who'd cheated on him.

"Whatever." He threw his hands up in defeat. "I'm outta here. I guess I'll see you around."

Madison watched him walk away, her heart dropping as she replayed everything she'd said to him. The worst was that it was all the truth. She was a terrible person. And there was nothing she could do to make Nick feel better.

She rejoined her friends, pretending everything was normal as they went out to the balcony to watch the fireworks. Damien and Savannah appeared a few seconds later, followed by Oliver and Peyton. The sight of the two new happy couples made Madison's head pound, and she massaged her temples to try to relax. It didn't help.

Damien and Oliver tried to wave her over, but she ignored them, instead wedging herself between Larissa and Kaitlin. At least they could protect her for the time being.

She was so upset that she barely saw the fireworks. When they finally ended, she muttered something about not feeling well and went up to her room. She didn't want to think about anything that had happened that night—Brett, Nick or the Diamond sisters—so she took a sleeping pill and went to bed.

Maybe she'd feel better in the morning.

After all, tomorrow was another day.

www.campusbuzz.com

The Diamond Sisters
Posted on Tuesday 07/05 at 9:26 AM

The Diamond sisters showed up at Myst last night. Savannah, Courtney, and Peyton. The rumors are true. They're in town, and they're here to stay. Not only that, but they're going to Goodman in the fall. Should shake things up, don't you think?

Despite their unfortunate fashion choices (although the youngest one, Savannah, wasn't as bad as the others), they've inherited Adrian's good looks. (I know he's old, but his gorgeousness is undeniable). It looks like a certain reigning brunette at school—not gonna say names—is in for some serious competition.

1: Posted on Tuesday 07/05 at 9:40 AM

two of them are hot, but what's up with the girl with the blue streaks? with her heavy makeup, hooker outfit, and weird goth bracelets, she looks like a slutty tourist.

2: Posted on Tuesday 07/05 at 9:45 AM

oliver prescott didn't seem to think she was too weird. they were making out on the main dance floor all night. if you ignore the makeup and hair, she's for sure the hottest of the bunch. i wouldn't mind getting a piece of that, and we all know how fast he moves through his girls. i heard Oliver bet a friend he could sleep with all three

Diamond sisters by the end of summer. she'll be up for grabs any day now.

3: Posted on Tuesday 07/05 at 10:08 AM
oliver's always so fucked up, he'll get with anyone.

4: Posted on Tuesday 07/05 at 10:23 AM
I don't care if he IS a manwhore, he's still hot!

5: Posted on Tuesday 07/05 at 10:37 AM
You're only saying that about Oliver because you don't know him. You'd be lucky to get someone as great as Oliver. He's sweet and kind, and if you weren't a sad wannabe and actually knew him then you would know that.

6: Posted on Tuesday 07/05 at 10:46 AM
ohhh is that peyton diamond sticking up for her man? don't get too attached, but don't worry, i'll be there to ease your pain when he ditches you.

7: Posted on Tuesday 07/05 at 10:59 AM
it's probably damien sanders. i heard the reason he and oliver are such players is cause they're secretly sleeping together. too bad, since they're the hottest guys in school.

8: Posted on Tuesday 07/05 at 11:08 AM
Way to be an idiot. Damien and Oliver are best friends. Anyway, Damien was busy with Savannah Diamond all

night. I heard they went into the caves together, looking more than ready to get it on...

9: Posted on Tuesday 07/05 at 11:11 AM
I heard about that, too. One night in Vegas, and she's already had sex with Damien Sanders. What a slut-hoe.

10: Posted on Tuesday 07/05 at 11:24 AM
What about the other sister? Courtney. She was barely there for five minutes.

11: Posted on Tuesday 07/05 at 11:36 AM
who knows? and who cares? you all need to get off this message board and get a life.

12: Posted on Tuesday 07/05 at 11:50 AM
Aren't you the definition of hypocrite.

chapter 13: *Savannah*

Savannah checked her cell phone upon waking, excited to find one text message, but disappointed when she saw it was from Evie.

So glad you called last night even if it WAS super late (early?) and you woke me up…. I still can't believe ADRIAN DIA-MOND is your dad. Anyway, even though it's only been a day it's not the same here without you. Once you get an iPhone let me know and we can FACETIME! xxoo SEC 4 life! <3

Damien hadn't tried to contact her. He'd kissed her good-night when he'd dropped her off at her condo last night—and wow, it was amazing—and had told her he would text her in the morning. Now it was morning—well, almost afternoon, since she'd slept late—and he still hadn't texted her. Had she done something wrong?

Maybe he planned on doing that thing when guys waited three days after meeting a girl to contact them again. Savannah hated that rule. But at the same time, she didn't want to look desperate by texting him first.

Her best chance to see him today seemed to be by "accidentally" bumping into him. Where would he hang out?

Then the answer came to her—the gym. Savannah didn't work out regularly until a few weeks before volleyball season, but she could start now. Especially if it meant more time with Damien. And she had no idea what the competition was going to be like to get on the volleyball team at Goodman, so she should get back into shape as early as possible. If they even *had* a volleyball team. She'd been playing volleyball since sixth grade—if Goodman didn't have a team, what would she do? That could be a good conversation starter if she did run into Damien.

Anyway, there was no excuse for her not to work out now. At home she could only use the machines at school during the school year, since that was free for students at Fairfield High. She always stopped working out in the summer, because her only option was to run outside. It was too hot during the day, and her neighborhood wasn't safe at night. But now she had a gym down the hall.

Then there was the question of what to wear. She hadn't had time to go shopping in Vegas yet, but she *did* have some cute clothes from California. The black stretch shorts and spaghetti strap top she liked to work out in weren't expensive, but they showed off her slim body. Even though she wished she were tall and gorgeous like Courtney, or that she had curves and high cheekbones like Peyton, she knew how to work with what she had. She put her hair up and posed a few times in the mirror, smiling at her reflection. Her hair was limp from sleeping on it, and she wondered what the dark-blond color would look like if it were lighter. It would brighten her entire face, but she'd never had the money to color her hair. Now, with her new credit card, she could finally make the changes to her appearance that she wanted. To transform on the inside, it made sense to do so on the outside, too.

Curious about what the hotel salon had to offer, she walked over to her new MacBook Pro that Adrian had sent up to the condo last night while they were out. He'd sent ones for Peyton and Courtney as well, along with a note saying they would need the laptops when school began, and he was sorry he couldn't spend more time with them since he was busy with the grand opening, but hoped to make up for it soon. Savannah was grateful for the computer, since she'd never had a computer of her own before, but she was bummed Adrian wouldn't have much time for her and her sisters until after the grand opening. Hopefully he would follow through and make up for it once the opening was completed.

She did a search for the Diamond Hotel and found a list of services for the salon: hair extensions, highlights, manicures, pedicures, eyebrow waxing, eyelash tinting and eyelash extensions. They also had lessons on how to apply makeup, along with facials and massages. Everything was overpriced—a normal haircut was a hundred and twenty-five dollars!—but she didn't have to worry about money anymore. She wasn't sure how a haircut could be worth that much money, but she would find out.

It sounded like she could spend the entire day at the spa—hopefully they would have openings tomorrow. She made a list of everything she wanted done and picked up the phone.

"Diamond Spa and Salon," a friendly voice said on the other end of the line. "How may I help you today?"

"I'd like to make a few appointments for tomorrow." Savannah tried to speak steadily so the lady wouldn't realize this was her first time making her own spa appointments.

"Of course." The lady sounded overly perky. "What would you like to have done?"

Savannah read everything from her list.

A mouse clicked in the background. "I'm afraid we don't have enough room tomorrow to accommodate everything you'd like," she said. "Would you be available at 9:00 a.m. on Friday? You'll have to come in early so we have time to get everything done."

"Sure, that works." Savannah had wanted her transformation to happen tomorrow, but Friday would be fine.

"Great," the lady said. "May I please have your name, building and room number?"

"Savannah Diamond," she said. "I'm in the Residences, in room 7501."

"Ms. Diamond," the lady gasped. "I'm so sorry about the misunderstanding—of course I'll be able to make room for you tomorrow, and I'll book you with the best stylists we have on staff. Will 9:00 be all right?"

Savannah had been pacing around her room, but when the lady said that, she stopped in her tracks. Could she really rearrange an entire day of appointments because Adrian's daughter wanted a spa day? "Yes, that sounds perfect," she said, dumbfounded. "Thanks."

"Thank *you*," the lady said. "I'm Jessie, and if you need anything else, let me know."

Savannah placed the phone back in the cradle and smiled. She couldn't wait to see Evie's comments once she posted pictures of the "new her" on Facebook.

Savannah texted Evie back that she missed her, too, and of course they'd FaceTime once she got an iPhone. Now to focus on Project Find Damien. She put on music and sang into her hairbrush as if it were a microphone while applying her sheer pink lip gloss, concealer and waterproof mascara. If Damien was at the gym, she wanted to look presentable, but natural.

Luckily Peyton and Courtney weren't in the main living area. Peyton was most likely still sleeping, and Courtney was probably reading or studying for the SAT. She didn't want to face another inquisition like the one Courtney'd given her last night when she got back, so she left a note on the hall table so they wouldn't worry about where she'd gone. Savannah was old enough to make her own decisions. Yes, Damien had come on to her stronger than she'd expected, but that was because he was older and more experienced. He'd respected her when she'd said it was too much, and that was what mattered. Right?

She left the condo and found all three bodyguards waiting outside the door. Savannah understood that Adrian worried about their safety—especially after what he'd told them at dinner last night about Courtney being kidnapped as a baby—but were they really in such danger that they needed to be followed around the hotel? It seemed excessive, but whatever. At least her bodyguard, Carl, hadn't made himself known during her adventure with Damien last night. As long as he didn't interfere in her life, Savannah didn't mind. Having someone watch out for her all the time was a small price to pay for joining such an incredible world.

"Good morning, Savannah," Carl said.

"Morning," she replied. This was the first time they'd talked, and she liked him already. He was the oldest of the three and seemed like the grandfather-type. Savannah had never met either of her grandfathers. "I'm just going to the gym."

"Lead the way," he said. "I'll be waiting for you in the hall."

When she entered the gym, she spotted the dark-haired girl she'd seen yesterday on one of the ellipticals. Last night she'd learned the girl's name was Madison, although they hadn't officially met. Madison wore a black sports bra with yoga pants, the outfit showing off her perfectly toned body. At the sight of her, Savannah's confidence plummeted. Why would Damien go for her when he was friends with someone like *that*? And Damien wasn't even there. She was disappointed, but she couldn't leave. Madison would think it was weird if she walked into the gym and left a second later.

All the ellipticals except the one next to Madison were taken. Savannah liked the elliptical the best, but since she would feel awkward getting on the machine next to Madison, she headed to the stair steppers in the back.

She started the machine, and it wasn't long before she got lost in her iPod playlist. The iPod was old and cracked, since it was pre-owned, but Courtney and Peyton had gotten it for her for Christmas a few years ago and she loved it. When she listened to music, she imagined she was onstage performing. Maybe someday she would be—if she could beat her stage fright. She wasn't a master on the guitar, but she could accompany herself, and she had a good voice. Even so, the most she'd done with music was recording a few covers on her webcam and saving them onto her computer. Once she perfected the songs, she planned to make a YouTube account and upload the videos, and then maybe she'd get discovered.

Three songs later, Madison got off the elliptical and hopped onto the stair stepper next to Savannah. Sweat trickled down the side of Savannah's face. What was Madison doing? There was an unspoken rule at the gym that you left an empty machine between you and the other people working out—like how you leave a seat between yourself and people you don't know at the movie theater. Madison was breaking that rule right now.

Savannah wanted to switch machines, but moving less than a minute after Madison had come over would make it obvious that Madison was making her uncomfortable. She had no other option but to stay on for ten minutes longer.

Trying to stay calm, she listened to her music and looked straight ahead. But since she hadn't worked out in a few weeks, it was taking a toll on her now. Her legs burned, and her heart rate was already way up. Maybe it was good that Damien wasn't at the gym. Being sweaty and out of breath wasn't the most attractive way to run into the guy you were interested in.

"You're one of Adrian Diamond's daughters, right?" Madison asked as she started up the machine. Her voice was barely audible over Savannah's iPod.

Savannah removed an earbud and looked at Madison. Her eyes were blue like Savannah's, made more striking by the contrast of her dark hair, which was in a perfect ponytail. "Yeah," Savannah answered. "Savannah Diamond."

Madison nodded, and Savannah had a feeling that she already knew her name. "I'm Madison Lockhart," she introduced herself. "My parents are friends with Adrian, and he told them his daughters would be moving here. How are you liking Vegas so far?"

"I love it." Savannah didn't have to think about her answer. "I mean I've only been here for a day, but it's amazing."

"Where are you from, again?"

"Northern California." Savannah glanced at her iPod, hoping Madison wouldn't ask about her hometown. She doubted she'd heard of Fairfield, but she wanted to be safe. "Near San Francisco." Well, San Francisco was almost an hour away, but it was the closest major city to Fairfield.

"I love California," Madison said. "My grandparents live in Newport Beach, so I visit every year. It's beautiful. Very different from Vegas." She looked at her phone, which had buzzed with a text message, and texted the person back.

"Newport Beach is nice." Savannah hadn't been there, but she'd watched some old episodes of *The OC,* so she knew it was pretty. And full of people who were superrich.

"It is," Madison agreed. "You'll be at Goodman in the fall, right?"

"Yeah," Savannah replied. "I'm hoping it isn't too different from my school in California. The last thing I want is to have to do extra work to catch up."

Madison looked at her in a way that made Savannah think she would definitely have catching up to do at her new school. "What grade are you going into?" she asked, pressing a button on her machine to up the level of difficulty. Savannah would have done the same if the muscles in her legs weren't already burning.

"I'll be a sophomore," she replied.

"I'm a student tutor, so I can help you in math and science if you need it," Madison offered. "I'm going to be a junior, so everything from sophomore year is fresh in my mind."

"You're a tutor?" Savannah didn't realize how surprised she sounded until after she spoke. She hoped Madison wouldn't be offended. Madison just didn't strike her as the brainy, helpful type. Savannah thought tutors were more like Courtney—so focused on academics that they didn't have a social life. The academic people at Fairfield High weren't involved in the party scene. Madison, on the other hand, seemed popular, and like she partied a lot.

"Yeah," Madison said. "It looks good on college applications."

"Oh." Savannah hadn't thought about college applications yet. She secretly hoped she would do well enough with her music that she wouldn't have to go to college. If not, her grades were average, so she assumed she would go to the local community college or nearby beauty school, if she went at all. "Where do you want to go?"

"Stanford," Madison replied quickly.

"Wow." Savannah felt more intimidated by Madison than before. "My sister Courtney wants to go there, too. That's a good school."

"It is," Madison said, as though she had already been admitted. Then she brightened, her blue eyes sparkling. "Oh, look who's here."

Savannah looked to the front of the gym and saw Damien walking in as if he owned the place. She nearly lost her balance on the stair stepper. He grabbed a towel from the rack and swung it over his shoulders, walking toward Savannah and Madison. Savannah focused on breathing steadily so she wouldn't sound like she was gasping for air when she talked to him.

"Hi, girls," he said when he reached them. "Mind if I join you?"

"Not at all." Savannah tried to stay calm as he got onto the stair stepper on her other side. This was what she'd wanted—for him to show up at the gym. She had to relax. He liked her—he had made that clear last night. She just wished she didn't get so nervous and freeze up around him.

"You know how much I love your company," Madison purred.

"Not nearly as much as I love yours," Damien teased.

Was Madison flirting with Damien? And was he flirting

back? Savannah picked up the pace on her machine and focused on the screen.

"How did you meet Madison?" Damien asked Savannah. At least he was acknowledging her presence. "I was going to introduce you after the fireworks last night, but Madison disappeared before I had a chance." At that he refocused on Madison. "Where did you run off to, Mads?"

"I had a headache." She shrugged. "Called it an early night." She didn't elaborate, and the whirring of the machines was the only sound in the room for a few seconds.

"Madison and I just met," Savannah answered Damien's question. "A few minutes before you got here."

"Am I interrupting girl bonding time?"

"No." Savannah shook her head. "I'm glad you're here. I had fun with you last night." After she said it, she realized it might have been too forward. Madison probably thought she was a pathetic loser.

"Likewise." That was what she needed to hear. Savannah's hands shook, and she held tighter to the handles on the machine so she didn't lose her balance.

Madison pressed a button on her phone, looking bored, like she wanted to get out of there. Damien glanced at Madison, and he looked hurt for a second.

Was Damien interested in Madison and not Savannah? Had last night been a game to him—see how far he could get with the new girl?

Her lungs constricted, and she felt trapped, as if the walls of the gym were closing in on her. If Damien *was* interested in Madison, Savannah didn't stand a chance. This was going to be an Evie situation all over again, with Savannah doomed to be second best. It was so stupid of her to think she could remake her personality in less than a day.

"So, Savannah," Damien said. "What are you doing tomorrow night?"

"Tomorrow night?" She wished she had plans so he wouldn't think she was always available. "Not sure yet. Why?"

"I wondered if you were interested in going to Luxe at the Gates."

"Is that a club?"

"Yep. So, do you want to go?"

Was he asking her to go *with* him? As in, on a date? She wanted to ask, but she had to play it cool. "Sure." Her head spun as she thought about the awesome possibilities that could happen between her and Damien tomorrow night at Luxe. It sounded enchanting, full of magic and excitement, especially with Damien at her side. "I would like that."

"Good," he said. She must have been paranoid in suspecting he had feelings for Madison. If he did, he wouldn't have asked her out.

The three of them continued to talk while working out. Damien and Madison told her all about the places they frequented in Vegas—their favorite restaurants, lounges, hotels and clubs. They also told her about the people at Goodman, specifically their group of friends, so she would get an idea of who to hang out with once school started. Their group had been friends since elementary school, so Savannah imagined it would be hard to break in, but Damien seemed happy to help. It was sweet how willing he was to include her. She had obviously been overthinking things that morning when she'd worried about not hearing from him.

She had to find the perfect outfit to wear to Luxe. Damien was the hottest guy who'd ever noticed her, and after her transformation at the spa tomorrow, he wouldn't know what hit him when he saw her. It would be like an old nineties movie, when the girl walks down the steps after getting a makeover and the gorgeous, popular guy she's interested in falls instantly in love with her and realizes she's the only one for him.

One thing was for sure—after working out, it was time to do some serious shopping.

chapter 14: *Courtney*

The morning after the Fourth of July, Courtney woke up late—around 9:30 a.m. Savannah and Peyton were still sleeping, so she passed the time by reading. Once it was eleven-thirty—Grandma's lunch break—she called her, pacing around the room in anticipation of how this conversation would go. She picked up after the second ring.

"Hi, Grandma," Courtney said.

"Courtney." She could hear the smile in her grandma's voice, and Courtney's eyes prickled with tears at how she wouldn't be able to move back home for a year. "How are you and the girls settling in?"

"Everything here is very nice." Courtney's body tensed at the reminder of the secrets that had been kept from her, but she tried to remain calm. "As I'm sure you knew it would be. Why didn't you ever tell us who our father is?" Despite her best efforts, she couldn't stop the anger that leaked into her tone.

"I'm sorry, sweetie." She spoke slowly, and Courtney knew

she meant it. "But I had an obligation—to your mother and to the safety of you and your sisters—to keep quiet until your father decided he was ready to tell you. I'm just glad he was willing to have you live with him now, given the situation with your mom."

"How's Mom doing?" She pressed the phone closer to her ear, hoping for good news.

"Her doctors want her to have personal reflection time, so they're sticking with their decision that she's not allowed to communicate with anyone outside of the facility," Grandma said. "They told me she's not happy to be in rehab, but she's not trying to leave, either. I suppose it's a start."

"I suppose so." Courtney sighed. Her mom had always yelled at anyone who mentioned rehab in her presence, as if it was a dirty word. If the state hadn't threatened to punish her severely for drunk driving unless she went to rehab, she probably wouldn't be there now. But it was better than nothing, and for that Courtney was grateful. "Adrian told us he bought you a new place, so you'll be better able to take care of Aunt Sophie and have Mom move in with you when she's ready. We could have stayed with you, too, you know."

"Yes, he did." Grandma clucked her tongue in disapproval. "I don't like it, but I have to do what's best for Aunt Sophie and your mom. The move will be rough for Aunt Sophie, and I'm worried about how she'll adjust to your mom moving in with us." She said what Courtney knew was true. "But as much as I would love for you and your sisters to move in, I don't think Aunt Sophie would be able to handle it. I've been holding off telling you, because I didn't want to worry you, but her cancer is getting worse. The doctors predict she has a year, tops, if she's lucky."

"Oh, Grandma," Courtney said, the news not taking her by

surprise. Aunt Sophie's cancer was untreatable, but she hadn't realized it could progress so quickly. Courtney couldn't imagine what it would feel like to have a terminally ill sister, and Aunt Sophie was Grandma's twin. The bond the two must share was something Courtney would never be able to understand. "That's more reason why we should be home, or at least close enough to visit."

"I appreciate it, Courtney," Grandma said. "But I don't want to burden you girls. I'm tough, and I'll get through this. For now, your father wants to be in your lives, and I'm not going to take that opportunity away from you. You deserve the chance to explore other possibilities for your future. It's going to be hard to be far away from you all, but despite the possible dangers in Las Vegas, I know this is the right decision."

"Adrian talked with us last night about the kidnapping when I was a baby," Courtney said. "It's a lot to process."

Grandma gasped. "He told you everything?"

Courtney repeated what he had told them at dinner. When she finished, Grandma sighed in what Courtney thought was relief. As if she thought there would be more.

What had she expected Adrian to tell them?

"We're all grateful you were returned safely," Grandma said. "That's what's important. Now, I only have a few minutes left before I have to get back to work. Are Peyton and Savannah around?"

"Let me check." Courtney walked out of her room, trying to be quiet. Peyton's light was off, so she was still sleeping, and Savannah had left a note on the foyer table that she was at the gym. Strange, since Savannah usually didn't work out until she had to get ready for volleyball season.

Courtney returned to her room and relayed the information to Grandma. "I'll tell them to call when you get back home," she said. "I'm sorry to call while you're at work, but I needed to talk to someone."

"Don't apologize," Grandma said. "You know I always want to hear from you. I love you."

"Love you, too, Grandma." Her throat tightened with homesickness, and she hung up, staring at the phone in her hand for a few seconds.

With Savannah at the gym and Peyton sleeping, it was a good time for Courtney to go to the coffee shop downstairs and see if they were accepting job applications. She freshened up, threw on jeans and a T-shirt and headed out of the condo. Teddy and Jackson were standing outside keeping guard.

"Good morning, Ms. Diamond," Teddy greeted her. He had a funny name for a bodyguard, especially since, with his large frame, he reminded her more of a grizzly than a teddy bear.

"Good morning, Teddy," she said. "You can call me Courtney, you know."

He nodded, and Peyton's bodyguard—Jackson—flinched and shook his head, as if he disapproved of the informality.

"Were you out here all night?" Courtney asked Teddy as they walked down the hall. Surely he had to sleep at some point.

"No, I wasn't." He laughed. "The night guards take over while you and your sisters are asleep. I only returned to my post about an hour ago."

"That makes sense," Courtney said. Would he say anything about how she'd left the party last night to go with Brett to Red Rocks? She hoped not. They entered the elevator, and she pressed the floor for the lobby. "Would you mind leading me to the coffee shop? I saw it yesterday, but I don't quite remember how to get there."

"Of course, Ms. Courtney," he said, apparently not understanding that the "Ms." before her name was unnecessary. Courtney didn't bother correcting him.

The elevator dropped them off at the lobby, and he led her to the coffee shop, the Diamond Café. It was sleek—elegant light fixtures hung from the ceiling, and modern, colorful mosaics covered the walls, but it still had that familiar coffeehouse vibe. Courtney took a deep breath and smiled, the delicious smell of freshly roasted coffee beans making her feel at home.

"I trust you can take it from here," Teddy said. "The next you'll see of me will be the elevator ride back to the condo."

"Thanks, Teddy." It would be an adjustment to have him watching her all the time, but he seemed nice enough. Plus, he hadn't mentioned the journey to Red Rocks, which led Courtney to believe he really wasn't there to babysit.

She waited her turn in line and ordered a skinny vanilla latte. The girl at the cash register looked friendly—perhaps a year or two older than Courtney, although the freckles on her face and two short braids in her hair could make her look younger than her actual age.

"I know summer already started, but is there any way I could fill out a job application?" Courtney asked once she'd paid for her drink—with her own cash, not Adrian's fancy credit card. "I just moved here, and I worked at Starbucks in my old town, so I have experience."

"One of my coworkers just gave her notice, so you're in luck," the girl said with a smile. She removed a piece of paper from a drawer beneath the register and handed it to Courtney, along with a pen. "I'm Rachel. You can fill out the application at one of the tables and bring it back to me when you're done."

"Thanks, Rachel," Courtney said, returning her warm smile.

She filled out the application while enjoying her latte. The questions were straightforward, and she had no problem answering them. The only one she wasn't sure of was her address. They didn't want her address in California, and she hadn't paid attention to the address of the hotel, but Rachel could probably help her out with that.

After triple-checking her responses, she brought the application back to the counter. "All done," she told Rachel.

"Great," she said, smiling brightly. She leaned closer and lowered her voice. "I hope you get it. Most people here are in their mid- or upper-twenties, so it will be nice to have someone close to my age around."

"Thanks," Courtney said, hopeful for the first time that morning. Could she have just made her first friend in Vegas? "I hope I get it, too. The only thing I wasn't sure of is my address, since I moved here yesterday. What's the address for the Diamond Residences?"

Rachel leaned back, a skeptical look crossing her eyes. "You live in the Diamond Residences?"

"Yeah." Courtney bit at her thumbnail.

"You can't be…" Rachel didn't finish her sentence, instead looking down at Courtney's application. She sucked in a quick breath and looked up again, her eyes wide. "You are. You're one of Adrian Diamond's daughters."

Courtney nodded slowly and pushed her hair behind her ears. Rachel was looking at her like she was a celebrity, and her cheeks flushed at how conspicuous she felt. Maybe she should have applied somewhere else. But that would have been silly, since the Diamond Café was so conveniently located to her condo.

"Is this some kind of joke?" Rachel took a step back, hurt and confusion replacing the friendliness that had been in her eyes a minute before. "Like, *The Simple Life 7,* or whatever season they're on now? There are probably cameramen hidden around here. Or you're using the eyes in the sky. Well, you can forget it, because I'm not signing any releases."

"This isn't a joke." Courtney looked around, and wrapped her arms around herself. People were staring. She wanted to run out of there, but instead she swallowed, lowered her arms to her sides and pushed her shoulders back. She had to set Rachel straight. "Yes, Adrian Diamond is my father. I moved here yesterday from a small town in California." Rachel looked like she was about to interrupt, but Courtney continued, "I don't know what *The Simple Life* is. I was raised like everyone else, and I've always worked. That's not going to change now that I'm here." She pushed the application in Rachel's direction and looked at her straight-on. "I'm qualified, I'm a hard worker and I want this job. So I would appreciate it if you would consider my application."

Rachel studied her for a few seconds. Finally she nodded. "Okay. I suppose I believe you. I'll show your application to the manager. In the meantime, take this form and get it signed by a parent or legal guardian." She removed another piece of paper from under the register and handed it to Courtney. "It's a permission form. Since you're a minor you'll need it signed to work here."

Courtney folded the form and slid it into the back pocket of her jeans. Her mom had signed something similar for her when she'd gotten her first job. "Thanks, Rachel," she said. "And I meant what I said—I hope I get the job. At my old job everyone was older than me, too, so it would be nice to work with someone closer to my age."

"See you around, Courtney." Rachel wasn't as friendly as she'd been at first, but she didn't seem as suspicious, either.

When Courtney got back to the condo, Savannah was still

at the gym and Peyton was still sleeping, so she read some more. She loved having a room to herself. The white settee she sat on reminded her of the type ladies at court sat in centuries ago, and she was so comfortable she could stay there all day. Every so often she looked guiltily at the huge SAT prep book on her nightstand, but the book she was reading was so good that she needed to know what would happen next.

She finished a few more pages, and then the doorbell rang. She reluctantly slid her bookmark inside the book and went to see who was at the door. Peyton plodded behind her, looking hungover—her hair was a mess and she had bags under her eyes. What had happened to her last night? She would have to ask later.

Courtney opened the door, expecting to see the housekeeper with the huge cart of cleaning supplies, but it wasn't the housekeeper at the door.

It was her father.

"Good afternoon, girls," Adrian greeted them as he walked through the foyer, his hands clasped behind his back. The top two buttons on his white shirt were undone, giving him a more casual look than last night, and his pinstriped suit had obviously been tailored specifically for him.

"Hi." Courtney's throat went dry, and she looked down at her feet. She still had no idea what to say to him.

"I enjoyed spending time with the three of you at dinner," he said. Despite her mixed feelings about Adrian, Courtney was glad he thought their first dinner together had gone well. She supposed they had to start somewhere. "I trust you've gotten settled in?" His eyes were approving when they met Courtney's, but not so much for Peyton, who had mascara smeared under her eyes and looked like she was about to throw up.

"Yes," Courtney said, wanting to keep his attention away from Peyton. "Thank you for the computers. And the condo is beautiful."

That earned a smile. "I'm glad you like it. I figured you would need the computers once you started at Goodman." He glanced around the living room. "Is Savannah around?"

"She's at the gym," Courtney told him. "I don't know when she'll be back, but I can text her."

"I wanted to talk to the three of you together, but I have a meeting in thirty minutes, so you'll have to relay to her what I'm about to tell you," Adrian said. "Tomorrow night I have a dinner reservation with a colleague at one of his hotels. You three will come as well, and I expect you to be on your best behavior." He looked at Peyton as if she needed extra reminding.

"Of course," Courtney said before Peyton could think of a snarky remark—not like Peyton was alert enough to do so. "It sounds fun."

Peyton snorted softly. Adrian and Courtney ignored her.

"The reservation is at eight," Adrian told them. "We'll meet in the lobby at seven-thirty, where the car will pick us up." He glanced at his huge gold watch. "Once the grand opening is over I'll have more free time, and I want to spend it getting to know the three of you. In the meantime, if you have any questions, I hope you're not afraid to ask. I know this whole situation is rough, and I want you to be able to come to me."

"I've been thinking a lot about what you told us at dinner... about what happened to me when I was younger," Courtney said, playing with her hands. "Is that the whole reason you stayed out of our lives for so long? Or is there more?"

Adrian's eyes darkened, and Courtney wondered if she'd said something wrong. "What happened was hard on the whole family," he said, his voice rough. "Your mother and I agreed it would be safest for you and your sisters to live away from Las Vegas."

But "away from Las Vegas" didn't mean Adrian had to be absent from their entire lives, especially with bodyguards looking after them 24/7. Having the guards outside their condo all the time seemed excessive, and after Grandma had shied away from discussing the kidnapping, it felt like there was more to the story than Adrian was letting on.

What could be so horrible that he and her mom felt like they had to keep it a secret?

"That's the whole reason?" Courtney asked.

"Yes." Adrian nodded and moved closer to the door.

"One more thing." Courtney stepped forward and removed the parental approval form from her jean pocket. "I applied for a job at the Diamond Café this morning, and they need your signature before they can hire me."

Adrian took the paper from Courtney's hands, ripped it into two, and threw it into the nearest trash can.

Courtney's mouth dropped open. "What was that for?"

"I will not have one of my daughters brewing coffee for my guests," he said. "It's not appropriate, and frankly, it's insulting to the people who work there who need that money. The press would have a heyday wondering what kind of publicity stunt you're trying to pull by working for minimum wage."

"So you're not going to let me work?" Courtney couldn't believe this. "What am I going to do all summer? And how will I earn money?" She could only study for her SATs and read books for so long every day. She needed *something* else to occupy her time.

"Is there something wrong with your credit card?" Adrian asked, with a hint of a smile.

"No." Courtney's cheeks turned red. "But that's not my own money. It's yours. I didn't do anything to earn it."

"You are one of my daughters, so that money is yours, as well," he said, as if this was a simple fact. "As I thought I made clear last night, you earn it by not getting into trouble and by doing well in school. Your job is to be a student. Once school begins, that will include extracurricular activities, sports and whatever else your college guidance counselor recommends to bulk up your college application. In your free time, have fun with your friends. If you need something else to do, there are plenty of volunteer opportunities around the area. Rebecca is involved with charities, and I'm sure she will be happy to help you find a reputable charity to which you can donate your time."

"Okay." Courtney's head spun with everything Adrian had said. No one had ever forbidden her from working before. She would never feel right about spending money that wasn't hers, but apparently he wasn't giving her a choice. "I'll ask Rebecca for help, then."

"Now, if you'll excuse me, I have to head out. After my meeting I have my weekly golf game with my friend Garrett, but I'll be available by cell phone if you need to get in touch with me. I hope you have fun today."

They said short goodbyes, and then he was gone.

"Not exactly the loving father type," Peyton muttered.

Courtney bit her lower lip. "I still feel like he's keeping something from us."

"He's probably keeping a lot from us," Peyton said. "He doesn't even know us."

"It's strange, though," Courtney continued like she hadn't heard Peyton. "That I was kidnapped all those years ago. You think I would have known before now."

"How would you have known?" Peyton said. "You were an infant. I was a little older than one, and I don't remember. Even you don't have a memory *that* good."

"I guess so," Courtney said, although she couldn't shake the feeling that there was more to the story.

"I'm going to lie down some more." Peyton groaned and wrapped her arms around her stomach. "Remind me to never mix wine and vodka again." She trekked down the hallway to her room, shutting the door behind her.

Courtney had heard that one before—mainly from her mom, but sometimes Peyton mixed drinks that weren't supposed to go together and felt sick the next day, too. She went back to her room to continue reading, but couldn't focus on the book. Her mind was reeling after the chat with her father. It wasn't even the part about him not letting her work that upset her, because as much as she hated the idea of frivolously spending his money, she liked his suggestion about volunteering. It was that he didn't want to spend any quality time with her or her sisters. He'd mentioned being busy with the grand opening, but he *was* managing to squeeze in that golf game with his friend. The only times he wanted them around were at family dinners.

If the family dinner tonight was like the one last night, would Brett be there? Courtney brightened at the thought and picked up her phone to text him.

Are you going to the family dinner tomorrow night?

Her phone buzzed a minute later.

Yeah. What are you up to right now?

Nothing, she texted back. Why?

Wanna go to lunch?

Courtney's breath caught in her chest. Had Brett just asked her out? She reread the message, searching for a sign. But it could be a friend thing *or* a date thing. It was impossible to tell.

She wanted it to be a date thing.

Not that it could be. He was just reaching out to her because of the future step-sibling situation. No matter what, they could only be friends.

Sure, she replied. I'll be ready in 15 min.

Brett told her he would come by her room so they could walk down together. Courtney hurried to her closet and rummaged through it. She wanted something cute, but she didn't want to look like she was trying too hard to impress him. She settled on jean shorts and a white lace top that she borrowed from Savannah's room. She slid into her flip-flops, and since it tended to be cold indoors, she put on a lightweight peach jacket, pushing the sleeves up to her elbows.

She wasn't sure what Savannah would be more upset about—that she'd borrowed the top without asking or that she'd paired it with flip-flops.

She went natural with her makeup, using BB cream all over her face, neutrals for her eyes, peach blush on her cheeks, pink lip gloss and mascara. It was more than she usually wore during the day, but she wanted to look her best for Brett. She rubbed lotion onto her hands, since they felt like sandpaper in the Las Vegas desert, and ran a brush through her hair one last time.

Her phone buzzed on the countertop. She picked it up, her heart pounding in anticipation of what it could say. As she'd hoped, the text was from Brett.

Heading out. I'll be there in a second.

He lived across the hall, so it really would be a second. She examined her reflection again—she shouldn't be so nervous. It was unlike her to get bent up over her appearance. She'd had a great time with Brett at the fireworks last night. He enjoyed spending time with her because they had a lot in common, not because of how she looked. She shouldn't worry about a casual lunch.

So why wouldn't her pulse stop racing at the thought of seeing him? She didn't know many guys in California, beyond the ones who'd asked her for help with schoolwork, but she'd never wanted to spend time with a guy as much as she did with Brett. She wasn't even bothered by his interrupting her reading time.

The doorbell rang, and Courtney opened it, her breath catching in her chest when she saw Brett. His hair was messy, and he had on jeans and a forest-green T-shirt that matched his eyes. She was glad she'd gone for a casual outfit, too.

They greeted each other and were quiet when they walked to the elevator. Teddy followed them, along with another man in a matching suit whose short dark hair and thin face reminded her of the lead guy from *The Matrix*. She assumed he was Brett's bodyguard. As they walked, Courtney had a sinking feeling that the silence was uncomfortable. They'd had so much to discuss last night, but now she had no idea how to start a conversation. It was stranger knowing their bodyguards could hear everything they said. Luckily, they seemed to care only about doing their jobs. But still, it was superawkward.

"I had a great time last night," she said to Brett as she stepped into the elevator. "I've never watched fireworks in such a beautiful place before."

"I thought you would like it," he said.

"And your friends seem nice."

"They liked you."

"They said that?"

"They didn't have to." He gave her a shy smile. "Who wouldn't like you?"

Courtney paused, unsure how to reply. She was glad when the elevator arrived at the lobby. Their bodyguards allowed them to walk ahead, and she and Brett fell into step as they walked along the outskirts of the casino. An old lady whooped at one of the slot machines, the flashing lights signaling she'd won. Courtney didn't understand the point of slot machines. Mindlessly pushing buttons didn't look fun, but she supposed it felt good to win. The casino seemed to always be packed, no matter what time it was.

The people who say New York never sleeps must have never visited Las Vegas.

"Where are we going to lunch?" Courtney tried to keep the conversation casual, not wanting to clue Brett in to how being around him made her thoughts bounce crazily around in her head.

He took a moment to consider it. "Do you want to eat at the Diamond or somewhere else?"

"The Diamond," Courtney decided. "Since I'll be living here for the next year, I need to learn where everything is."

"Only for the next year?" Brett asked. "You're not considering staying longer?"

"I don't know yet," she said. "To be honest, I hadn't thought about it, but I'll give it time to see how it goes. Of course it matters what my sisters decide, too. Well, Peyton's graduating next year and will probably do her own thing, but I don't want to be somewhere different than Savannah. She needs someone to watch out for her." Plus, although Courtney was independent, she had always had her sisters. She couldn't imagine being alone.

"Savannah seems to like Vegas," he observed.

"She does," Courtney said. "She thinks it's Wonderland or something."

"Maybe it is." Brett stopped in front of a restaurant called the Grand Café. "Well, here we are. This is where you can get some of the best food in the Diamond, at any hour you want."

The café lived up to its name, although it looked more like a luxury lounge than a café. The ceiling had to be thirty feet high, with crystal chandeliers hanging from it. Wide white columns supported the archway in the entrance, with green-and-white striped curtains draping down from the sides, like something out of a palace. A man in a suit played a grand piano in the back corner—Courtney recognized the song "Memory" from *Cats*—and the mirror in the back of the restaurant made it look like it extended back for miles.

The restaurant was packed, but Brett showed the hostess his VIP card, and she got them a table instantly. Courtney scanned the menu—they served breakfast all day long. When she saw they had Frosted Flakes French toast, she had to try it. It didn't disappoint. She finished every last delicious bite.

The waiter placed the check on the table, and Brett put a black American Express on top of it.

"Adrian gave me a Blamex after he proposed to my mom," he explained when he caught her looking at it.

"A Blamex?" Courtney had no idea what that meant.

"A black American Express," he explained.

"We can split it." Courtney reached for her wallet, even though breakfast was expensive and she was running low on cash. She still didn't feel right using the credit card—"Blamex"—Adrian had given her. "I don't mind."

"Don't be ridiculous." Brett laughed. "Our cards both go to Adrian's bank account, so it doesn't matter."

"He really doesn't mind us spending his money so frivolously?" Courtney asked. "There must be some limit for how much we can spend per month."

"There is no limit," Brett said. "I wouldn't buy a plane or yacht or start a luxury car collection without asking him, but it's expected that you eat. I would hardly say eating is 'frivolous.'"

"Yes, but my breakfast cost twenty dollars," Courtney pointed out. "It was a special treat. Surely you can't eat like that all the time."

"Courtney," Brett started, seeming unsure of how to phrase what he wanted to say next. "My mom told me about how you grew up. It sounds rough, and I can't say that I'll ever fully understand it, but your life is different now. Adrian—your father—is one of the wealthiest men in America. You could eat out or order room service for every meal, and he wouldn't notice."

"But just because I can doesn't mean I should," she said. "It doesn't seem fair to do that when there are people who don't know where their next meal is coming from. I mean, back in Fairfield, we had enough food in the apartment for breakfast and dinner. My sisters and I had it good compared to some people in school. But there were times when my mom was in between jobs that the only real meal we had all day was our school lunch, and she was too busy drinking to notice how bad things were. Now I'm expected to eat expensive meals every day without thinking twice about it. I don't think I'll ever get used to this. It still doesn't feel like this is my real life."

"Wow." Brett looked down at the table. "I'm sorry. I didn't really realize what it was like for you."

"Don't be sorry," Courtney said. "It's not your fault. It's just a huge change for me. Adrian suggested that I talk with your mom about charities I can volunteer with, so I think I'll do that. With all of my good fortune recently, it's the least I can do to give back."

"My mom's really into volunteering, so I'm sure she would love to help," Brett said as he signed the check. "But anyway, are you ready to start our world traveling?"

"What do you mean?"

"When we were watching the fireworks last night you said you dreamed of traveling the world," he said. "There's no time to start like the present."

Was he serious? "Adrian might not have noticed our leaving Myst early last night, but I don't think he would be too happy about us leaving the country," she pointed out. "First of all, I don't have a passport. Secondly, I know Adrian hasn't spent tons of time with my sisters and me yet, but he might like to soon, and he won't be able to if I'm not here. Plus, can we really do that? Just take off without asking?"

"Calm down." Brett laughed. "We're not 'taking off.'"

"Then how are we traveling the world?" This was getting more confusing by the second.

"Trust me," Brett said. "Like you did with the fireworks. You had fun, right?"

"I think you know the answer to that."

"I know," he said. "I just wanted to hear you say it again."

"I had a *fantastic* time watching the fireworks with you," she said, smiling. "It was the best Fourth of July ever." Considering how every other year she'd watched fireworks on television with her sisters while her mom was out at a bar, it wasn't hard to beat. But even if Courtney had had fun Independence Days up until now, she still thought last night would be the best.

"Good." He looked to the exit of the restaurant, and then back at her with a smile that made her heart race. "Then let's get out of here."

"Welcome to Venice," Brett said as he pulled his car in front of a hotel called the Venetian. It wouldn't have been an impossible walk, but Vegas was so hot and dry in the summer that being outside felt like being in an oven. And the hotels were so huge that despite the Venetian being two hotels away, the walk still would have taken fifteen to twenty minutes.

Once inside, they took an escalator to the second floor, and Courtney gazed around in awe. It looked like they were on the streets of Venice. Of course Courtney had never been to Venice, so she didn't know how accurate it was, but it felt like she was in a different country. The ground was paved with cobblestones, and all around were wrought-iron street lamps and vendors selling Venetian masks, Murano glass and other trinkets. The ceiling was painted like the sky, bright blue with fluffy clouds, lit up to look like midday. Shops and restaurants lined the streets, looking like old Italian buildings, the marble and brick facades complete with columned archways and balconies. There was even a canal through the center of the streets with people going on gondola rides. The long black-and-red boats floated down the waterway, and arched bridges connected the "streets" on both sides.

"I'm guessing you like it?" Brett asked.

"Like it?" Courtney said, looking around in amazement. "I love it! It doesn't feel like we're in a hotel—it's like we're really in Italy. This is incredible."

"Themed hotels are fun," Brett agreed. "They were popular a few years ago, so there are a few on the Strip. The Venetian is the best, but there's also Paris, Caesars Palace, New York New York, and a few more. We'll get to them eventually. But for now…what do you say we go on a gondola ride along the Grand Canal?"

"I'd like that," she said, knowing that gondola rides were romantic—an activity people did on dates. She tried to find any hints implying he saw it like that, but he seemed relaxed, like it wasn't a big deal. Maybe she was overanalyzing the situation.

Brett helped her into a black gondola, which was really a lavish canoe. The man steering in the back wore a red sash, a black-and-white striped shirt and a straw hat with a red ribbon wrapped around the brim. Courtney sat on the velvet red bench facing forward, and Brett took the seat next to her. No one else joined them. Maybe Brett *did* see this as a date. Why else would he sit next to her instead of across?

Courtney had never been on a date, though, so she wouldn't know the difference. The only semidate she had ever been on was when Paulo Bernal, a boy in her English class, bought her a coffee after her shift at Starbucks. The only commonality she could find between them was their class, and he'd seemed bored discussing the characters in the novel they were reading at the time. Courtney didn't think he'd gotten past the first few pages of the book. Needless to say, he'd never bought her a latte again.

At least her conversations with Brett so far were going better than that.

Water lapped against the sides of the gondola as they floated by shops and under bridges, and Courtney was intensely aware of Brett's arm inches away from hers. The nervous energy coursing through her body made her want to fidget like crazy, but she focused on staying still, so he wouldn't notice his effect on her. He seemed so relaxed and comfortable—why couldn't she feel the same?

After the gondola ride they got gelato, which they ate with tiny plastic spoons. It was the most deliciously smooth ice cream Courtney had ever tasted. When they finished, Brett suggested exploring the rest of the hotel, and Courtney let him lead the way. Everywhere she went, she couldn't believe her eyes. The casino was beautiful—marble floors, hand-painted frescos on the ceiling and golden chandeliers that looked like they'd come straight from a palace.

They walked from one end of the casino to the other, arriving at a golden sign hanging from the ceiling that simply said Phantom. Below the sign, inlaid within the patterned marble floor, was an image of the white half mask from the famous musical.

"Is this *Phantom of the Opera?*" Courtney asked Brett. She'd watched it countless times on DVD and had memorized every song.

"*Phantom—the Las Vegas Spectacular,*" Brett corrected her. "It's been changed from the original. They cut out some of the dialogue, but kept all of the songs. They also added extra effects that you won't see in the Broadway version."

"How do you know that?" Courtney asked. "Have you seen both?"

"Yep. Hardcore fans would kill me for saying this, but the Vegas one is better."

"I've only seen the movie," Courtney said. "It's my favorite. I listen to the soundtrack all the time. It would be amazing to see it live."

"Then what are we waiting for? Let's get tickets." He strolled up to the ticket booth, and Courtney followed close behind. The only live musicals she'd seen were productions at school. She couldn't imagine what a professional one would be like. "Two tickets for tonight," Brett told the cashier. "Fifth row center, if they're available."

The cashier typed something in her computer. "That'll be one hundred and sixty-five dollars each," she said.

Brett reached for his wallet, but Courtney stepped forward to stop him.

"That's way too expensive," she insisted. "Why don't we get balcony seats instead? The price is much more reasonable, and it's still the same show."

Brett looked confused, but then he smiled, like he found what she'd said endearing. "Don't worry about it," he assured her. "Adrian won't notice the charge, I promise. He'll actually like that you're experiencing Las Vegas. And believe me when I tell you there's a reason these seats cost more. Sure, it's the same show, but it's much better when you're up close." He handed his Blamex to the cashier before Courtney could argue any more. Once the cashier gave him the tickets, he handed one to Courtney. "Nine-thirty tonight," he told her. "Let's meet at the Diamond lobby at eight forty-five and head over from there."

"Okay." She still felt bad about how much it cost, but she was excited to see the show. "Thank you so much. I didn't even know you liked theater."

"I appreciate music and production," he explained. "Andrew Lloyd Webber is a great composer. One of the best of all time."

"He is," Courtney said, impressed by Brett's knowledge on the subject. None of the guys in Fairfield would have known the composer of *Phantom of the Opera,* let alone have wanted to see the show with her.

It was official—Brett was perfect.

He was also the one guy she wasn't allowed to be with.

Her phone buzzed before she could think about it any longer. A text from Savannah.

"Savannah's begging me to go shopping with her and Peyton," she told Brett, disappointed she wouldn't be able to spend more time with him that afternoon. "I should go with them."

"You're not going to invite me to come with you?" he joked. "It'll be prefamily bonding time."

Courtney clammed up at his mention of their soon-to-be step-sibling situation. "It's a sister thing," she said, trying to play it off like what he'd said didn't bother her. "We didn't have the opportunity to buy much in California, and Savannah's really excited." She didn't say it, but she also wouldn't mind buying a dress for the show tonight. Reasonably priced, of course. She wasn't so oblivious that she didn't notice how the dress she wore to the Five Diamond Steakhouse and Myst last night didn't fit in with what everyone else was wearing. It would be embarrassing to be dressed inappropriately for her first live show.

"Don't worry about it," he said. "We'll see each other in a few hours. Think you can make it until then?"

"I'll do my best," she said. "Although I'm so excited for the show that I'm sure it will feel much longer."

And excited to see you, she thought. If this didn't qualify as a date, she didn't know what did. Maybe dinner beforehand, at a quiet, romantic restaurant...

Stop it, she told herself. Wishing for the impossible was pointless. Adrian had been clear about the rules. They were going to be family soon, and a romantic relationship with Brett was wrong.

But was it really? They weren't related by blood, and finding someone like him, who she was interested in getting to know and wanted to spend time with, was rare. There could be something special between them if she let it happen.

She was getting ahead of herself. She didn't know if Brett felt the same way about her, and she was afraid to ask. It would be embarrassing if she asked and he was confused, because he didn't see her that way at all. Maybe he was just spending time with her to get to know his future stepsister better.

She couldn't help but hope it was more than that.

Chapter 15: *Peyton*

The last place Peyton wanted to be was the mall. She'd never gone to the mall at home. She rarely had extra money from her job as a hostess at a nearby pub, since she had to make sure the bills were paid. Her mom valued drinking all night at a bar over paying for electricity, cell phone plans and internet. When Peyton did shop, she preferred finding original pieces at thrift stores. But Savannah had begged her to come shopping, and it was impossible to turn down Savannah when she asked for something—her huge blue eyes looked so upset if anyone said no to her. Peyton gave in to her little sister more than she cared to admit.

The plus about having a different style than her sisters was that they rarely tried to steal her clothes, so Savannah never yelled at Peyton the way she did Courtney when Courtney showed up wearing one of Savannah's shirts she'd borrowed without permission. But Savannah did get into Peyton's makeup a lot, so when they reached the Sephora in the Miracle Mile shops at the Planet Hollywood hotel, she hoped Savannah would get some of her own. She was sick of searching everywhere for her favorite lip gloss only to find that Savannah had taken it with her to school.

The products at Sephora were more expensive than those at the drugstore—palettes could cost anywhere from thirty to a hundred dollars—but Savannah bought enough makeup to last twenty years. The salespeople had the time of their lives helping her pick out what she wanted—brushes, eye shadow palettes, bronzer, foundation, powder, blush made from "Amazon clay," eyeliner, mascara, an eyelash curler that resembled a medieval torture device, lip glosses and lip conditioner, which the sales lady promised would keep lips from chapping in the dryness of Las Vegas.

Savannah rushed to where Peyton was getting her makeup done, an eye shadow palette in her hand. "You should get this," she said, shoving the palette in Peyton's face. "It's perfect for you."

Peyton took the little black box from Savannah—it was by some brand called Too Faced and it said Smokey Eye on the front. The colors were mainly blacks and grays, which Peyton liked. She swiped her finger over the darkest color, and when she checked out the swatch, she was amazed by the jet-black pigmentation. It was way better than her current eye shadows, and she was almost out of her favorite color in her smokey eye palette anyway.

"You like it, I know you do," Savannah said. "Want me to add it to our stash?"

Peyton had no idea how much it cost—probably too much for nine colors of eye shadow—but she did love it. It was best not to ask. Savannah was putting everything on her credit card, anyway, since Peyton had done what Adrian had said and tossed hers in the back of a drawer in her room. "Sure, go ahead," she said. "And I think I'll get that blush called 'Orgasm,' too."

"Ohh, that's the NARS one." Savannah literally jumped from excitement. "It's a total makeup classic—all the gurus on YouTube rave about it being a must-have. I have a decent dupe, but I've always wanted the real one, so I'll get it, too."

And here Peyton had only wanted it because the name was clever.

Once Peyton was finished getting her makeup done, she found Savannah and Courtney browsing one of the aisles.

"Is Savannah trying to convince you to buy something, too?" Peyton asked Courtney.

"This one." Courtney showed her a rectangular palette with the word *NAKED* in gold capital letters on the brown velvet cover. "I know I can find similar colors in the drugstore, but I have to admit I've heard of this before. I swatched the colors and they're very pretty."

"The neutrals will look amazing on you," Savannah chimed in. She was like a little devil on their shoulders, convincing them to buy makeup they didn't actually need. "Come on, Courtney. Just get *one* thing?"

"Fine," Courtney said, probably more for Savannah's benefit than her own. "But that's all I'm getting."

"I bet it won't be long until you're digging into Savannah's stash," Peyton joked. The three of them might not have had a ton in common, but they all did love makeup.

Courtney shrugged it off, but Savannah held her bags closer to her side.

They paid at the register—a huge amount of money, mostly from Savannah's stuff—and headed out of the store.

"I texted our driver while we were checking out and he's ready to take us to the Fashion Show Mall," Savannah said.

"We're going to another mall?" Peyton groaned. "Why don't we just stay at this one? We're already here."

"Because Fashion Show has department stores like Saks and Neiman Marcus, and Miracle Mile doesn't." Savannah clearly had done her research. "Come on, let's go." She led the way, not leaving room for debate. Peyton rolled her eyes at Courtney, but Courtney just shrugged and went along with Savannah. One thing was for sure—Savannah would owe her for this later.

Fashion Show Mall was only five minutes away. As they walked through it, Peyton discovered how the mall got its name when a runway rose out of the floor and shoppers gathered around. Lights beamed down on the models strutting down the runway to fast-paced music. The show was flashy, like everything else in Vegas.

"Can we stay and watch?" Savannah asked, looking wistfully at the models.

"We only have so much time," Courtney said. "Would you rather watch the fashion show, or go shopping?"

"Shopping, I guess," Savannah said with a small pout.

"So what did you do last night?" Courtney asked Peyton as they passed the show. "I didn't hear you get back."

"Just hung out with a friend." Peyton didn't want to go into detail, although she did replay the night in her mind. After the fireworks at Myst, Oliver had said he was sick of sneaking in drinks from his flask since his father was watching his every move, so they'd gone to a nightclub at another hotel. The drinks had flowed all night, so everything was hazy, but they couldn't keep their hands off each other. Since Oliver lived with his parents and Peyton lived with her sisters, Oliver had the brilliant idea of getting a room.

She smiled at the memory of what had happened once they got there. Neither of them had held back—and Oliver sure knew what he was doing.

What happens in Vegas stays in Vegas...but that doesn't matter when you live there.

Jackson hadn't been waiting in the hall when she'd left the hotel before dawn to return to the condo at the Diamond, and Peyton was glad about that. It would have been beyond awkward to do the walk of shame with the other guy she was eyeing by her side. If she hadn't drunk so much last night, she would have realized that *before* staying over with Oliver, but luck had been on her side since she and her sisters had different guards while their regular guards were sleeping. Her night guard wasn't nearly as cute—or as young—as Jackson. But Jackson had been there when she'd left the condo this afternoon with Savannah to go to the mall. Peyton wondered how much he knew about last night...and if he cared. He'd made no hint of it when he'd seen her.

"A friend?" Savannah asked. "We only moved here yesterday. Who was it?"

"A guy I met at the club."

"Aren't you still with Mike?" Courtney asked.

"I'm breaking up with him." Peyton didn't like how she'd cheated on him, but it was nothing that hadn't been done to her before. Mike might be getting with other girls, too. He didn't seem like the type to do that, and the texts he'd sent last night about missing her didn't indicate it, but guys could be deceiving. Even the nicest ones could end up being jerks.

"But you haven't broken up with him yet?"

"No," Peyton said. "But I will. In the meantime, I'm not

going to stop living because I haven't gotten around to it yet. I don't want to do it through a text, and everything's been so busy around here that I haven't had a chance to call him, but he knows it's coming." She also hated breaking up with guys, so she preferred to avoid thinking about it until she absolutely had to.

She checked out the stores they walked by, making it clear she was finished with the subject. Courtney was so judgmental of Peyton's love life, but really, it wouldn't hurt Courtney to learn from her. Courtney had never kissed a guy, and Peyton always got the guys she wanted. For the most part. There were always some like Jackson, who weren't interested in the first place.

Jackson wasn't Peyton's type, anyway. She liked guys who were adventurous and enjoyed breaking the rules. She didn't know much about Jackson, but he'd seemed set on following rules when they'd talked at Myst. As for the adventurous part...he had to have had *some* adventures as a bodyguard. She couldn't imagine the training he must have gone through to land his current position. Maybe she would ask him about it sometime. Hopefully he would be more receptive to her questions than he had been last night.

Curious, she glanced over her shoulder to see if she could spot him. Sure enough, he was off to the side at the end of the hall, walking with Carl and Teddy. She couldn't believe she had been oblivious to the guards when she'd lived in California. It was eerie that she had been followed everywhere and hadn't noticed. It also pissed her off that no one had told her and her sisters that three men were following them around everywhere they went. Shouldn't that be the sort of thing she should have known about?

To amuse herself, since the guards were supposed to stay inconspicuous in public, she gave Jackson a wave.

He didn't return it.

"Who are you waving to?" Savannah asked.

"Our bodyguards," Peyton said, her tone laced with mischief.

Courtney glanced over her shoulder. "I don't see them."

"Maybe they checked out a store." Peyton snickered, since the store closest to where they had been standing was Victoria's Secret. They would make quite the trio in there.

They arrived at one of the department stores Savannah had mentioned, and it was the most preposterous store Peyton had ever visited. T-shirts cost over a hundred dollars, because they were made by a fancy brand. She could get similar tops at Forever 21 for a tenth of the price. But Savannah wasn't having any problem buying as much as she wanted, and even Courtney tried on some dresses that Savannah threw her way.

The makeup was one thing, but Peyton refused to use money that wasn't hers to buy stuff that was so overpriced, so she watched as her sisters tried on clothes. After ringing up their items, the saleslady handed Savannah her business card, telling her she would let her know whenever they got in new arrivals she might like, as if she was Savannah's personal shopper. Savannah didn't hesitate to take the card and thank her.

"Where to now?" Peyton asked when Savannah finished up at the cash register. "Back to the Diamond?"

"The Gates Hotel," Savannah told her.

That was the newest hotel Oliver's dad owned, where he lived with his family. He'd mentioned it last night.

"Why the Gates?" Peyton tried to act nonchalant, but she hoped she would run into Oliver. She wasn't wearing anything particularly stunning—tiny jean shorts with a black tank top—

and she still felt hungover from last night, but whatever. The salespeople at Sephora had done a good job with her makeup, so she didn't look terrible.

"They've got great shopping—especially shoes," Savannah said, as if this should be common knowledge.

"And it's not too far from the Diamond," Courtney added, looking at her watch. "I need to be back soon."

"You're going somewhere?" Peyton didn't hide her surprise. Courtney was more likely to stay home to practice her SATs or read a book "for fun" than go out and enjoy herself. Peyton didn't understand the concept of reading for fun. If a book was good enough, it would become a movie, and she could see it that way.

Savannah looked at Courtney expectantly, apparently as confused about Courtney's sudden social life as Peyton.

"Brett and I are going to see *Phantom of the Opera,*" Courtney said quickly.

"Brett, as in our future stepbrother?" Peyton asked.

"Yeah," Courtney said. "You and Savannah were busy earlier, and I was hungry, so Brett and I got brunch. I mentioned how much I like the show, and he got us tickets. It was thoughtful of him."

She shrugged in a way that might have seemed casual to someone who didn't know her well, but then her eyes went distant. Something was up. Peyton had been forced to listen to Courtney and Brett's boring conversation last night at dinner, and they had a lot in common. Was something more going on between them?

If it were anyone else, Peyton would assume yes, but Courtney never broke rules. She must be hanging out with Brett because she didn't know anyone else. And Courtney was picky when it came to guys. She'd told Peyton that high school boys weren't worth the time or the drama.

The chance that her outlook had changed in one night was slim.

Their driver met them in front of the mall, and it didn't take long to get to the Gates. Peyton had talked enough to Oliver last night to know that if she was going to find him anywhere in the hotel, it would be at the casino, so she kept her eye out as they walked through it. Just like the mall gave Savannah energy, casinos did the same for Peyton. She loved the beeping of the slot machines, the sound of coins jingling whenever someone won and the constant chattering. It made her feel light and happy, as if she were walking on air.

Oliver was easy to spot in a red velvet smoking jacket that reminded Peyton of a fancy bathrobe, sitting at a blackjack table holding an amber drink. The sign on the card table said there was a twenty-dollar minimum—per hand. What a rip-off. Peyton doubted he was playing for the minimum, either.

He spotted her and put his remaining chips in his pocket—there weren't many left—and headed in their direction. She swung her hair in front of her shoulders and smiled. The smoking jacket was ridiculous, especially since it was late afternoon, but he managed to pull it off. Hopefully Jackson would recognize Oliver as the guy she'd hung out with last night. Once he saw how quickly Peyton had moved on, maybe he would regret dismissing her at the bar.

"Is it just me, or is that guy walking over to us?" Savannah whispered, moving closer to Peyton. "Do you know him?"

"Yep," Peyton said. "Let's say hi."

Her heart beat faster as they got closer to Oliver. Since when did she get so worked up around guys?

"Peyton Diamond," he greeted her. "What brings you here? Not that I'm disappointed to see you."

"We're shopping." She held up one of the bags she was holding for Savannah. "These are my sisters, Courtney and Savannah."

"Oliver Prescott," he said, holding out a hand to shake theirs. He paused when he got to Savannah. "Weren't you watching the fireworks with Damien at Myst last night?"

Savannah brightened at the mention of Damien. "I was," she said. "Are you two friends?"

"We've known each other for years."

"So did you win?" Peyton asked, referring to the game of blackjack he'd been playing.

"Pssh." He took out a pack of cigarettes and opened it. Peyton took that as a no. He removed one, lit it and inhaled deeply, watching the smoke swirl up in the air. "I was just occupying my time before meeting up with a friend."

Peyton wanted to ask who, but she held back. *Clingy is bad,* she told herself. No guy liked a girl who became attached after one night. Instead she looked around the casino as though she couldn't wait to continue shopping.

"You know about dinner tomorrow night, right?" Oliver asked.

"Dinner?" Peyton asked. Had Oliver asked her out to dinner last night? She'd had too much to drink, so she could have forgotten.

"Our dads organized a 'family dinner' for tomorrow night," Oliver explained, moving to an empty table to tap his cigarette over an ashtray. "We all have to go."

"Is your dad the business partner Adrian's been mentioning?" Peyton had hoped Oliver had asked her on a real date, but this was better than nothing.

"They're not partners yet, but that's the goal," he said. "They're trying to give off this family-man appearance to the public. It's lame if you ask me. But due to your dad's reputation…" He paused as though contemplating saying more, then continued, "My dad wants to make sure he's making a good decision in working with Adrian."

"Your dad doesn't like our dad's reputation?" Peyton asked. It didn't seem like big-time hotel owners cared about anything except money. Apparently she was wrong.

"*Didn't* like," Oliver corrected. "Adrian used to be notorious for jumping from woman to woman—supermodels and starlets half his age. But now he's moved in with his high-school sweetheart, and things are looking serious between them. There's talk they might be engaged. And now he's got the three of you. Don't you know how glad he was when you three decided you wanted to live with him, after all of those years that you chose to be with your mother instead? Apparently he cares about family more than most people knew. He surprised everyone. In a good way."

"*Choosing* to be with our mother?" The words tasted like rusted copper on Peyton's tongue. Oliver knew she and her sisters had never had a choice—she'd told him the story last night. Had he been so drunk that he didn't remember? "You know that's not what happened. And why does your dad care what our family does?"

"Isn't it obvious?" Oliver lifted his glass in the air and downed the rest of the drink. "As far as I know, this idea they've got works in both of their favor. Something about a mega-resort in Macau. But my family's got enough bad talk surrounding us as it is—thanks to me—" he smiled wickedly "—that any association with your father, who doesn't have the best reputation with all the women he's gone through in the past fifteen years, would have made things worse for mine. Now that your family's one happy little group, my father doesn't have to worry about that anymore."

"I'm glad our being here is so beneficial for him," Peyton said with so much sarcasm that no one could miss it. At least that explained why Adrian wanted them to live with him after all those years. She'd known something was up, and now Oliver had confirmed it. Adrian was using them to make more money.

"It was nice to meet you, but we have to get going." Courtney's sweet voice, always polite, interrupted Peyton's train of thought. "I'm meeting someone to see a show, and I don't want to be late."

"Yeah," Savannah said, backing away from him. "We'll see you at dinner tomorrow night."

"See you then," Oliver said.

Peyton could have sworn Oliver winked at her as they headed toward the shops.

He was a total jerk, but for some reason, she liked him even more than before.

Chapter 16: *Madison*

Madison threw her iPhone onto her queen-size canopy bed, creating an indentation in the fluffy white comforter. The text from her mom shouldn't have surprised her, but that didn't stop her from being irritated.

I know we had dinner plans for tonight, but there is an emergency at the hospital. Your father and I will have to work longer than expected. We will be home later tonight. Love, Mom.

As always, it was written perfectly—more like a work email than a text to a family member. And the news didn't surprise Madison. The only time both her parents were home was when they were sleeping. More often than not, she was left home alone. That's why her favorite times of the year were winter break and spring break—not because it was a break from school, but because her parents took her on vacation. Those were the only times she felt like she was part of a real family.

She paced around her room, the pointy heels of her stilettos messing up the thick, parallel lines the maid had left in the carpet with the vacuum cleaner. Her room in the Diamond, with floor-to-ceiling windows overlooking the Strip, was better fit for a movie star than a teenage girl. Meaning it was perfect for her.

Her parents' decision to move to the Diamond was the best one they'd made in years. Her mom had been friends with Adrian since he'd built his first hotel on the Strip way before Madison was born, and the deal he'd given them on the three-bedroom condo had been too good to pass up. They had debated over moving out of the suburbs for a while, and in the end, it was an offer they couldn't refuse.

Madison looked down at the glittering Strip, packed with tourists making their way from one hotel to the next. She checked her watch, surprised to see it was already 8:15 p.m. Dinner with her parents was supposed to have been at 8:45 p.m., so she was dressed and ready to go.

She'd spent a long time selecting the outfit she'd picked for tonight. The short Dolce & Gabbana black satin dress was stretchy, hugging her curves while still simple enough to wear to a classy dinner with her parents—and out with her friends later that night. Her dark brown hair was straight, no frizz in sight, thanks to her CHI straightening iron. The red Chanel lipstick made her look older than sixteen (Madison thought she could pull off eighteen or nineteen), and her favorite YSL mascara gave her lashes a false lash effect, without actually having to wear false eyelashes.

Now she had to figure out how to kill some time.

She picked up her iPhone and contemplated who to text. Brett was out of the question—for now. There was always Oliver, but he'd ditched her for the trashy Diamond girl last night. Larissa would be happy to hang out, but Madison wasn't in the mood to talk about boys with her, which was what they usually did when they were together. And all of the other girls in their group were probably with Larissa right now.

It came down to Damien. That wasn't a problem, since she enjoyed Damien's company, but she hated that he was getting involved with Savannah. And Damien had been acting strange around her lately. Their flirting had always been friendly, but he kept getting more serious about it. It made her uncomfortable. She valued their friendship, and she didn't want things to get awkward between them.

But she was antsy to get out of her empty condo.

Drinks at the lobby bar? she texted him.

Already there, he wrote back a few seconds later.

Madison wasn't surprised. Damien had been drinking more than usual lately—almost as much as Oliver. He was good at hiding it, but by the end of the night he was usually trashed. Hopefully it was a summer habit and would end when school started.

Be down in a min.

He responded a moment later. Looking forward to it ;)

Madison stopped in front of the mirror, studying her body from the side. The black dress was slimming, but she shouldn't have had that bagel and cream cheese after her workout. If she kept giving in to cravings, she would regain the twenty-five pounds she'd lost before eighth grade, and would go back to being the unnoticed chunky girl in her group of friends. She refused to let that happen. The only other food she'd eaten today was a salad with low-fat dressing, but she could practically see the carbs from the bagel on her hips already. She would have to stick with fruit, salad and lean meat for the next few days.

The Lobby Bar had the best view of the first floor, and Madison loved watching the tourists trying their luck in the casino. But her favorite part was the golden sculpture of a girl transforming into a tree in the center of the circular couch in the middle of the bar. Branches emerged from the top of her head and her hands, climbing toward the ceiling; roots came out of her feet; and the bottom half of her legs formed the trunk of a tree. It was some reference to Greek mythology. It captivated Madison, because she could never tell if the girl was happy or sad. Every time she walked by she reminded herself to Google the story, but she always forgot when she got home.

She spotted Damien at a love seat in the front.

"Looking gorgeous as always," Damien greeted her. His eyes roamed over her body, stopping when they met hers. "You look beautiful."

"You said that twice." Madison laughed. Then the strangest thing happened—redness crept onto Damien's cheeks. Was he nervous? No, she decided. It probably had more to do with how the clear drink in his hand—most likely vodka on the rocks—was already three-fourths finished.

She sat down next to him and studied the drink menu. Since she felt bloated from the bagel, she settled on Diet Coke instead of wine. No point in wasting calories this early in the night.

Then she spotted Brett Carmel standing in the lobby with Courtney Diamond, dressed up like they were going somewhere special. Madison clenched her jaw as she remembered the way Brett had looked at Courtney at Myst last night. To make the situation worse, the deep pink strapless dress Courtney was wearing looked perfect on her. Madison recognized the Aidan Mattox dress from her trip to Saks a few days ago. It had looked great on the mannequin, and terrible on her when she'd tried it on. But the belted waist showed off Courtney's disgustingly flawless model-tall body, the full skirt flouncing out above her knees like it was designed for her.

Madison's anger was further fueled by the way Brett was looking at Courtney as if she were the only person in the room. He said something to her, their heads close together, and she laughed in response. Madison felt sick. Luckily her soda arrived a second later. She took a sip, relaxing at the first taste of the cool drink.

"Madison?" Damien asked, concerned. "Is everything okay?" His arm rested on the back of the couch, and if he lowered it, it would be around her shoulders. She didn't mind. It felt good to be reminded that Damien was there for her. And at least if Brett saw them like this, he wouldn't think she was still pining for him.

"I'm fine," she told him, brightening as much as she could. "Why do you ask?"

"You looked upset," he said.

"I was thinking about stuff." She looked around the room again and pretended to notice Courtney and Brett for the first time. "That's one of the Diamond sisters, right?"

"The middle one. Speaking of which, way to text me to meet you at the gym earlier and *not* let me know you were with Savannah."

"I thought you would want to see her," she said sweetly, amused again by what she had done that morning. Once Savannah had walked into the gym, Madison had texted Damien asking him to come by. Damien would eventually get sick of Savannah—that happened with him with most girls—so it wouldn't hurt to speed along the process. Savannah was too clingy and desperate to hold his attention for long. Especially since rumors were already flying about how easy she was.

"Not as much as I wanted to see you," Damien said, serious now.

"You wanted to see me more than Savannah?" she teased.

He seemed hurt, but his expression turned into a smirk a moment later. "Would you be upset if I didn't?"

"Positively devastated." Madison lifted her hand to her forehead and pretended to swoon like women did in old movies.

Damien studied the glass in his hands. "I'm glad you texted me tonight," he said. "I've been thinking about a lot of stuff lately."

"What kind of stuff?" she asked. Damien rarely got so serious.

He took another sip of his drink, his forehead creasing as he swallowed. If Madison didn't know better, she would think he was scared to say what was on his mind.

"Savannah stuff?" she prompted. "Or about that redheaded cocktail waitress with the bad boob job who's been staring at you for the past five minutes?" She gave the waitress in question a less-than-friendly smile, and the woman ducked her head and scurried off to a group of older men gathered around a craps table. Madison made a face when one of the men—who must have been around seventy—squeezed the waitress's ass. Gross.

"Can you blame her for being ridiculously attracted to me?" Damien asked.

Madison rolled her eyes. "If your ego gets any bigger, it's going to explode."

"But really, Mads." He became serious again. "You've been acting differently since you moved into the Diamond. I wanted to make sure everything was okay."

Madison loved when people cared enough to ask her questions like that, wanting an honest answer. Not enough people did. They believed the great Madison Lockhart could handle anything. "I guess it has to do with the Nick situation," she said, hoping he would buy the excuse.

"Why *did* you break up with him?" Damien asked. "Everything was going great with you two, then suddenly it was over. Not that I mind that the hottest girl in Las Vegas is single." He smirked again, his dark eyes lighting up. "I know you said your feelings for him weren't as strong anymore, and you're happy you broke up with him, but you've seemed down lately. What really happened between you and Nick?"

"I don't want to talk about it right now," Madison said. "But is it really that obvious?"

"Only to me," Damien assured her. "And just so you know, Larissa mentioned that she feels like you don't want to spend as much time with her anymore. I told her it was because you're adjusting to living here, and she seemed to buy it."

"Thanks." Madison was glad he'd given her something to go on that didn't involve Brett. "You're right. Breaking up with Nick was hard. He's a great guy, but he just wasn't 'the one.'"

"Do you really believe in that?" he asked. "That there's someone perfect out there for everyone?"

"I do," she said. "Don't you?"

Damien shrugged. "I've never thought about it."

"Well, now that you're thinking about it, what *do* you think?"

He considered it. "I guess it would be nice, but I don't think it's real."

"Oh." Madison sighed. "Okay."

"Come on, Mads." His tone lightened. "This is me we're talking about. What did you expect?"

"I don't know." Madison shook her head. It was obvious that Damien had feelings for her, and maybe she secretly wanted him to think she was his soul mate, but she didn't feel the same way for him.

At least she didn't think she did. This was too confusing. She was starting to wish she hadn't met him here tonight.

Her phone buzzed, and she picked it up to read the text.

"Larissa and some of our friends are meeting at the Cosmopolitan for sushi soon and are hitting up Marquee later tonight," she told Damien. "You in?"

"If you're going, I'm going," he said, downing the rest of his drink. "But first I need another drink."

Madison laughed, glad Damien had returned to his lighthearted self. Tonight would be good for her—no Nick, no Brett—just the normal group having fun.

Still, she wondered where Brett and Courtney were heading, dressed up like they were going somewhere special. She wished he was taking her out instead. What was so great about that girl?

It would be so much easier if Damien was the one she wanted.

But no one ever said life was easy.

www.campusbuzz.com

High Schools > Nevada > Las Vegas > The Goodman School

Madison Lockhart
Posted on Wednesday 07/06 at 11:25 AM

Who else thinks Madison is the bitchiest girl in school? My question is, why do so many people put up with her? Isn't it enough that three of the hottest guys in school follow her around like she's Aphrodite come to life? Plus, she's a total skankho. I heard she slept with all three of them at once.

And she also lost like, ten pounds so far this summer. Which would be good if she *needed* to lose weight, but now she's so skinny that it's gross. Madison, if you're reading this, eat a French fry. You need it.

1: Posted on Wednesday 07/06 at 11:34 AM

I saw her at the Lobby Bar with Damien Sanders yesterday. She was practically on his lap, and he couldn't get his hands off her. PDA, much? No one wants to see that. They needed to get a room.

2: Posted on Wednesday 07/06 at 11:56 AM

madison's hot. whatever fat bitch posted this needs to shut up and go to the gym. you're just jealous of how you'll never be anywhere near as awesome as madison. and she's not a "skankho" at all. obviously you don't know her if you think that.

3: Posted on Wednesday 07/06 at 12:15 PM

i heard shes still got her v-card and thats why nick gordon dumped her.

4: Posted on Wednesday 07/06 at 12:31 PM

First off, Nick is too nice to dump someone for that reason. Secondly, Madison's the one who broke up with Nick. Thirdly, Madison looks amazing, and the only reason you would say otherwise is because you're jealous. So back off, and it sounds like you should consider staying *away* from the French fries.

5: Posted on Wednesday 07/06 at 12:49 PM

Well that was obviously Madison or one of her friends. Way to be subtle, girls.

6: Posted on Wednesday 07/06 at 1:10 PM

don't be an idiot. madison and her friends are too cool to bother with this site. girls like you hate madison cause you're jealous, and girls like madison don't notice, cause they don't care what you think.

chapter 17: *Savannah*

Savannah had had an amazing day at the spa. It had looked like a golden palace, and she'd been treated like royalty. The highlights and hair extensions had taken forever, but her golden hair now hung to midback, full and lustrous like those models in shampoo commercials. She couldn't stop touching it.

And that wasn't all. The gel nails she'd gotten made her stubby ones long and pretty, the French manicure with sparkly tips giving her a sophisticated look. She loved holding her hands out to admire it. She'd gotten a French pedicure, too. Her skin had become dry and flaky since arriving in Vegas, and the people who worked at the spa had given her the best facial and moisturizer to help. They'd also given her eyelash extensions, so her eyes had a dramatic flair they'd never had before. Well, they hadn't *given* it to her—they'd charged it to her dad's account—but that was pretty much the same thing. She did some poses in front of the mirror, imagining she was a famous pop star on a photo shoot. Savannah could get used to this.

Then the doorbell rang, and her heart jumped into her throat. Was it Adrian? She arranged her hair around her shoulders and walked out of her room, but Peyton had gotten to the door first. And she was standing not with Adrian, but with Rebecca.

"Hi, girls." Rebecca smiled and ran her hands over her pants. "How's it going getting ready?"

"Good." Savannah adjusted her extensions again, hoping Rebecca would notice.

"Did you do something different to your hair?" she asked.

"Yes." Savannah smiled. "I got extensions today. Do you like them?"

"I love them." Rebecca smiled back, and Savannah got a feeling the two of them might get along. "Is Courtney around? I was hoping to talk with all three of you."

"She's in the shower." Peyton placed her hands on her hips and narrowed her eyes at Rebecca, as if she'd done something wrong by stopping by.

"Oh, okay." Rebecca reached up to fix her hair, even though it was perfectly in place in a ponytail. "I'm going to start getting ready soon, but I know this is all new to you, so I wanted to stop by and see if the three of you wanted help choosing what to wear tonight."

Peyton pressed her lips together, her eyes hard. "Did Adrian put you up to this?"

"No." Rebecca swallowed, and Savannah felt bad for her having to deal with Peyton's attitude. "I just wanted to reach out to you girls and let you know I'm here if you needed help. And I know Adrian's been busy, but I don't want you to think he doesn't care about you. He does, trust me, but he has a lot on his plate with the grand opening approaching so soon. Once that's all over he can't wait to spend time with you. But I hope you know that I'm around whenever you need anything."

Savannah was about to say yes, she would love help choosing which dress to wear tonight, but Peyton spoke first.

"There's no need to bother. We can dress ourselves." She sent Savannah a look that meant *don't you dare contradict me,* and Savannah couldn't bring herself to meet either of their eyes. Rebecca seemed so shot down, and she wished she could say something to make her feel better. But she didn't want Peyton to feel like she was betraying her trust as a sister.

"Thanks, but I think we'll be okay," she said softly. "See you tonight."

"All right," Rebecca said. "Let me know if you change your mind."

Savannah nodded and didn't say anything else as Rebecca saw herself out.

"What was that about?" Savannah asked Peyton once the door was closed. "I would have liked Rebecca's help."

"She thinks she can replace our mom." Peyton sneered. "But I'm not going to let her, and I hope you won't, either. Don't be fooled by her acting all nice, okay?"

"I don't think she's trying to *replace* Mom," Savannah said. "No one could do that. But Rebecca's going to be around a lot, and she really sounded like she wanted to help. Maybe she just wants to get to know us."

"Maybe." Peyton shrugged. "But I don't care. I don't want to get to know her."

"I don't think it would be a bad thing if we gave her a chance."

"Whatever," Peyton said. "Do what you want. I'm going to

get ready, and I'll make sure to pick an outfit that definitely *wouldn't* have met Rebecca's approval."

Savannah knew she wasn't going to change Peyton's mind, so they both went back to their rooms, and she returned to admiring her makeover. For the first time, she looked in the mirror and felt good. Even if she was standing next to Courtney, someone might notice her first for a change.

Speaking of Courtney, she had to ask her what was going on with Brett. They seemed to have a lot in common, and even though Adrian had forbidden any of them from getting involved with Brett, Savannah would love to see Courtney find someone. After how much Courtney had worked in California, she deserved it. But breaking the rules would be hard for her. Savannah would help keep their relationship secret if it came to it, because she wanted to see Courtney happy. But would Courtney *really* be happy if she had to lie? It was a lot to consider, and Savannah worried she wouldn't be much help. Her sisters had always been the strong ones who would watch out for her, not the other way around.

She checked her new watch from Tiffany—it was 6:45 p.m. If she got ready fast, she would have time to talk to Courtney before their father picked them up for the big dinner—the one he'd invited them to so he could prove to Oliver's dad how he was a "family man" and worth doing business with.

Savannah stomped across her room at the memory of what Oliver had told them at the Gates. She'd thought Adrian cared about taking care of them now that their mom was in rehab, and she believed he was being honest when he'd told them it wasn't safe for them here when they were younger. After what he'd said about Courtney's kidnapping, Savannah understood that the Vegas Strip wasn't a place for children. But the three of them weren't children anymore—they were teenagers, and they could stay away from dangerous situations. Plus, they had their bodyguards. They would be fine.

But Savannah had other problems—like figuring out what to wear tonight. She opened the doors to her gigantic walk-in closet and surveyed the dresses she'd bought yesterday on her shopping spree. Tonight she wanted to sparkle. Her makeover would make her stand out from the crowd, and everyone who saw her would want to get to know Savannah Diamond. She still couldn't believe who her father was…and who *she* was. She also couldn't stop thinking about yesterday when Damien had asked her if she would be at Luxe. Her heart jumped at the memory—it meant he would be looking for her. She couldn't wait to see his reaction to the new Savannah.

Tonight would be the night that Damien Sanders realized that she, Savannah Diamond, was the perfect girl for him. Savannah wasn't sure if he was interested in Madison or if she was just being insecure at the gym, but if he *was* interested in Madison, he would forget all about her when he saw Savannah tonight. Maybe Savannah and Madison would even end up being friends. Madison seemed confident and popular, like the type of girl Savannah would want to be friends with once school started in the fall, and she had been welcoming when they were working out.

The moment Savannah stepped into her sapphire sequined Mark + James dress, she knew she'd made the right choice. The dress was short, giving her legs an illusion of length. It had thick straps, so it showed skin without showing *too* much, and the La Perla push-up lace bra made her barely-B cups look like full Cs.

Damien would certainly notice the difference there.

Silver Jimmy Choos with four-inch heels finalized her outfit. Flipping her hair over her shoulder and posing for the mir-

ror one more time, Savannah headed out of her room to go
talk to Courtney. Maybe Savannah was being dramatic, and
Courtney was hanging out with their future stepbrother because both she and Peyton had been busy, but she still wanted
details. And what if Courtney *was* involved with Brett? Would
that be future-incest?

But Adrian had been clear about Brett being off-limits,
and Courtney never broke the rules. Courtney was the angel
child that Savannah could never live up to. Even her teachers
had been disappointed when Savannah hadn't done as well as
Courtney on tests and papers, as if she were a huge letdown.

It wouldn't be an issue now, though, since Savannah looked
better than ever. Finally she would stand out. No longer would
she be the overlooked shadow to her sisters and her friends.
She brightened at the thought, and walked across the condo
to Courtney's room. The shower was running in Peyton's
room—leave it to Peyton to wait until the last minute to get
ready. Hopefully Peyton wouldn't wear something *too* out-
landish to dinner.

She knocked on Courtney's door, opening it when Courtney said she could come in. Courtney was sitting in front of
her vanity, wearing a purple bubble tube dress from BCBG
that Savannah had found for her at Saks. It made her willowy
frame appear more supermodel-esque than ever. Savannah
almost felt jealous, until she caught sight of her own reflection. She loved the glamorous version of herself staring back
at her. This was who she was meant to be. Now, if she could
act as cool and sophisticated as she looked, the transformation
would be complete.

"I love your dress," Courtney complimented her. "Twirl
so I can see."

Savannah obliged, her long hair spinning around her. She

felt more like a princess than she had when she'd first arrived in Vegas. "I love yours, too," she told Courtney, making herself comfortable on her bed. "Trying to impress anyone in particular?"

Courtney paused in the middle of applying her NARS lip gloss in Turkish Delight. Savannah had bought it for her at Sephora, and she was glad Courtney was using it. "No," she said, pressing her lips together to even out the gloss. "I haven't met anyone besides Damien and Oliver."

"And Brett," Savannah reminded her.

"Right. And Brett." Courtney's voice wavered, and she focused on putting concealer on a nonexistent pimple. As if Courtney ever broke out.

"You *did* go to the show with him last night," Savannah said. "By the way, how was it?"

"It was wonderful." Courtney swiveled in her chair to face Savannah. Her cheeks were pink, and she was smiling. This was the happiest Savannah had seen her since their arrival in Vegas. "The theater was designed to look like the Paris Opera House, and the performance was magical. Our seats were right under where the chandelier drops."

"The chandelier drops on the audience?" Savannah asked. Courtney had made her watch the movie a hundred times, so she knew the chandelier broke, but shouldn't that happen *on*stage?

"Yes." She placed her hands on her knees and leaned forward. "It falls from the ceiling, and stops right before hitting the audience. I think I screamed—it looked like it was about to fall on top of me. In the beginning the entire chandelier assembled above the audience—four pieces of it came together from different ends of the theatre, each one with blinking lights like flying spaceships—"

"Flying spaceships?" Savannah looked at Courtney like she'd gone crazy.

"Yes. And when the pieces came together, the curtains along the sides of the theater pulled away, and there were box seats full of people dressed in clothes straight out of the 1800s. They weren't real people—they were mannequins—but they looked so real, as if we had traveled back in time. You have to see it. We'll go together sometime."

"I'd like that," Savannah said. Seeing *Phantom* sounded exciting—Savannah loved music—but right now they had more important things to talk about. Things named Brett. "Did Brett like it?"

"He did." Courtney looked down to examine her nails. They were unpainted and short. Savannah *had* to take her to the spa.

"A guy who takes you to see *Phantom of the Opera*..." Savannah's lips curled into a knowing smile. "Sounds perfect for you, don't you think? And he's definitely cute."

Courtney's eyes lost the light they'd had while she was talking about the show. "He's going to be our stepbrother."

"But you wouldn't be blood-related," Savannah pointed out. "And how often is it that you meet a guy you're interested in?"

"I don't know." She played with her hands, which she only did while nervous.

"Never," Savannah answered for her. "You're never interested in anyone. Don't let Dad's stupid rule stop you."

Courtney raised an eyebrow. "Since when did you start calling him Dad?"

"Since now. It sounds better than calling him Adrian, doesn't it? He *is* our father." It felt strange to refer to anyone as Dad, since they'd been without a father for their entire lives, but Savannah hoped she would get used to it.

"It just sounds weird," Courtney said. "And moving away from me and Brett—because *nothing* is going on there—what happened with you and Damien at Myst? You never gave me the whole story."

"He just gave me a tour of the club." Savannah didn't like lying to her sister, and she wished she could tell her about what happened with Damien in the caves, but then Courtney would hate him more than she already did.

"That's all?" Courtney sounded surprised. "He didn't try anything funny?"

"That's all." Savannah looked down at her hands and played with her bracelets. She rarely lied to her sisters, but she didn't want to give Courtney another reason to dislike him. "He's really nice, and he asked if I would be at Luxe tonight."

"And you said yes?"

"Obviously." Savannah rolled her eyes. "Anyway, what do you think about what Oliver told us at Gates? About the reason he thinks we're here. It sounded shady."

"I don't know what to think," she said. "There must be more to it than what Oliver said, because I doubt Adrian lied about the safety issue. But I do feel like he's keeping something from us."

"What do you mean?"

"I'm not entirely sure." Courtney crossed her legs and balanced her chin on her hand. "It's just a vibe I get whenever he mentions it. Like there's more to the story than he let on. A secret he isn't telling us."

"Maybe," Savannah said. "Or maybe not. If you really think so, you should ask him." But she knew that was easier said than done. Their dad was intimidating. He was comfortable around adults, but around his own teenage daughters? He totally clammed up. She wanted him to warm up to them, so he could get to know them, but she wondered if it would ever happen.

"I'll think about it," Courtney said.

"So how do you think Mom's doing?" Savannah asked, her throat tightening. "When I called Grandma back yesterday, she said the doctors are sticking by their decision that she needs a break from the outside world. I can't help but worry if it means things are really bad for her there."

"It's what they think is best for her." Courtney's eyes glassed over, and she joined Savannah on the bed. "Adrian picked the facility, so we have to trust it's the best."

"I want to believe Mom will get better." Savannah swallowed, hating what she had to say next. "But what if she doesn't? What if she gets out and it gets bad again?"

"We can't think like that." Courtney wrapped her in a hug, and the doubt Savannah had been feeling began to melt away. "We have to believe the treatment's going to work. If we don't, and she senses that when she gets out, it's only going to hurt her. All we can do is support her when she's ready, okay?"

"Okay." Savannah nodded and blinked away tears. "Thanks for that. I don't know what came over me. I like being in Vegas and all, but…"

"It's a big change from home," Courtney finished. "I understand. I miss her, too. So does Peyton, even if she won't admit it. But we have each other, and that's what we have to remember."

"Thanks." Savannah's chest tightened, and she felt guiltier now about not telling Courtney everything that had happened with Damien. It was time to be honest.

She took a breath in preparation to spill the rest of the story, but before she got a chance, Courtney checked her watch and said they had to hurry up or they would be late for dinner.

With that reminder, Savannah rushed back to her room to do the final touches on her makeup. She would tell Courtney later.

This was her night to shine, and she wanted to make it perfect.

chapter 18: *Courtney*

The limo ride to the Gates couldn't have been more awkward. Savannah and Peyton sat in the seat facing backwards, which meant Courtney and Brett sat along the side, since it seemed polite to allow Adrian and Rebecca to face forward. Peyton's outfit was far from acceptable for a family dinner—the tight black skirt showed every curve of her butt, and the matching tank top was so sheer that her lacy push-up bra was visible underneath. Adrian complimented Courtney and Savannah on their dresses and said nothing to Peyton, but he didn't make her go change. He must be doing the *she'll stop rebelling if I pretend not to care* approach. Which probably *was* the best way to handle Peyton.

She wanted to tell everyone about seeing *Phantom* with Brett, but remembering Adrian's comment at dinner the first night, she stayed silent. It wasn't hard, since Savannah dominated the conversation by telling Rebecca the details of her grand makeover. Even Adrian complimented her on the changes.

The benefit of Savannah being so talkative was that Courtney never felt pressured to converse in stressful situations. The seating arrangement in the limo counted as one of those. She was trying not to look at Brett, but she couldn't help it, since he was sitting next to her. Then her arm brushed against his, and neither of them moved away from each other. Courtney froze, not knowing what to do, but then she readjusted in her seat to move her arm away from Brett's. She didn't want Adrian or Rebecca noticing whatever was going on between them.

The hardest part was that Courtney had no idea how Brett felt about her. After seeing *Phantom of the Opera* last night, they'd come straight back to the hotel, and Courtney had spent the rest of the night reading, trying to lose herself in fictional worlds and not overthink the real one.

But it was hard to relax after Savannah had asked about her night with him. She was clearly digging for information, and there was no way Courtney could admit her true feelings. She wasn't *allowed* to have those feelings. She would have to make them disappear.

Still, it hadn't stopped her from texting Brett when they were walking downstairs to clue him in that Savannah suspected something was going on. Courtney wasn't normally gossipy, but she didn't want to get in trouble her first week here, so it made sense for Brett to know that they might be overstepping their bounds. She'd wished she could take back the text message—Brett might think she was being dramatic— but she couldn't change it now.

Feeling Brett move beside her, Courtney checked out what he was doing. His iPhone was out, and he was typing something onto the keypad. She couldn't see who he was texting, but his fingers moved swiftly across the screen, as fast as Courtney could type on a computer.

He put his phone back in his pocket, and Courtney's purse vibrated. She itched to see what the text said. But instead of checking it, she crossed her legs away from Brett's and pulled her hand away from her bag.

It felt like forever until they reached the Gates Hotel, even though it couldn't have been more than five minutes. Courtney reached inside her purse when she got out of the limo, anxious to check her phone.

Happiness flooded her body when she confirmed the text message was from Brett. Then she read what it said, and the elation disappeared as quickly as it had arrived.

What's there to worry about? There's nothing going on between us that they wouldn't approve of. We both know that can't happen.

She read it over again to make sure she'd seen it right. She had. A lump formed in her throat, and she refused to look at Brett. Why had she been clueless enough to send the message in the first place?

She zipped her phone back into her purse without bothering to respond. What could she say? She didn't want to agree, but she didn't want to disagree, either. And she and Brett weren't going to argue via text message while they were around the rest of the family. It would be rude, and she didn't want Adrian or Rebecca to know how close they had grown after two days.

Realizing she had been so out of it that she was dragging behind the group, she hurried to catch up and followed them inside the hotel.

"Honey," Rebecca said to Adrian. "The girls really need new phones. The ones they have now look practically ancient."

"You're right." Adrian took his phone out of his pocket, typed something into it, and put it away. "I just told Bernard to send a staff member out to get them iPhones. They should be at the condo when we get back."

"iPhones?" Savannah bounced with excitement. "I've always wanted an iPhone. Thank you so much."

"I don't want one," Peyton said. "The phone I have now works fine."

"And you can continue to use it." Adrian didn't miss a beat. "But if you decide to switch to the iPhone, it'll be there waiting for you."

Courtney was still in a daze from Brett's text message, and while she'd never felt a need to have an iPhone, she thanked Adrian as well. If he was getting the phones for them no matter what, she might as well use it. It was most likely more reliable than the old flip phone she had now.

To distract herself from the sinking feeling in her stomach, she tried to look interested in the Gates Hotel, despite seeing it yesterday with Peyton and Savannah. It had a tropical country-club theme, with greenery all around—palm trees, flowers and huge leafy plants. She even heard birds chirping above.

She followed Adrian and Rebecca through the casino in silence, which was easy since casinos were so loud. Finally they arrived at a restaurant called Aqua. Like most everything in Vegas, the entrance to the restaurant was flashy. Light reflected off the marble tiles, and obsidian columns flanked the glass double-door entrance. They reached the hostess stand—which was, no surprise, lit up—and Courtney scanned the menu on display.

It was a Chinese seafood restaurant. They should have good

vegetarian options. Like all the restaurants she'd seen in Vegas so far, the food was ridiculously expensive, but at least she wasn't being dragged to another steakhouse.

She made an extra effort to avoid Brett as they walked inside. The hurtful text message kept repeating in her mind: *There's nothing going on between us.*

On one level that was what she wanted—for nothing to be going on between them, so she wouldn't get in trouble. But the thought of Brett saying it, and thinking it, made her want to vanish into a corner. Why were her feelings so irrational? She wanted to scream, or cry, or...throw her phone against a wall. Instead she looked around the restaurant to focus on something else; the tan marble floors, wooden tables and matching contemporary chairs in calming shades of brown. She blinked and took a few deep breaths, glad when the water that had pooled in her eyes disappeared. Hopefully no one had noticed her temporary loss of control.

The hostess told them they were the first in their party to arrive, and led them to a rectangular table in the back with nine empty chairs. Then Adrian began telling them all where to sit.

"Logan Prescott will be at the head of the table," he instructed. "I will sit next to him. Rebecca will sit next to me, then Oliver, and then Savannah. On the other side Logan's wife, Ellen, will sit next to him, Brett next to her, Courtney next to Brett, and Peyton next to Courtney." With that, he took his place at the table. The seating arrangements were not up for debate.

Next to Brett. The words echoed in Courtney's mind. She didn't look over at him as she took her seat, instead focusing straight ahead at where Oliver would sit across from her. She didn't know much about Oliver, but he'd seemed full of him-

THE SECRET DIAMOND SISTERS 239

self when they'd met at the casino yesterday. At least her sisters were near her, so she could talk with them if Oliver annoyed her and the conversation got awkward with Brett.

Courtney went to put her napkin in her lap, since that was the first thing Adrian and Rebecca did upon sitting down, but she stopped when she saw two napkins in front of her—one white and one black. Was she supposed to use one for the appetizer and one for the main course? Or one for dark foods and the other for light foods? She glanced at Adrian and Rebecca to follow their lead, but Adrian was using the black napkin and Rebecca was using the white. Not helpful.

"Why do I have two napkins?" she whispered to Brett.

"So you can pick which one matches your outfit better," he explained.

"Seriously?" The strange things rich people did astounded her.

"Yeah," he said. "You should go with the black one."

"Okay." She picked up the black napkin and placed it on her lap, leaving the white one where it was.

Adrian rose from his seat before Courtney could say anything more to Brett. "There you are," he said, smiling widely at someone behind her. He was back into Congenial Hotel Owner Mode, as opposed to Awkward Father Mode.

Courtney wondered if she should rise as well, but since no one else made an effort to stand, she turned to see who he was talking to. A short, dark-haired man wearing a gray suit was walking in their direction. Behind him was Oliver, more casual in a blue striped dress shirt with dark jeans. Next to Oliver was a woman who Courtney assumed was his mom, Ellen Prescott. She looked like the perfect high-society mother in an off-white pencil dress that hit her knees, her highlighted hair sprayed into a neat bob.

Once they'd finished with introductions, Logan Prescott ordered a bottle of champagne—with four glasses. Courtney was surprised. She hadn't expected to drink at a restaurant, or would even have done so if given the choice, but Adrian had made it clear he didn't mind if they had a glass of wine or champagne with dinner.

Apparently the rules were different with Logan around.

"How are you girls liking Vegas so far?" Logan asked, leaning forward in anticipation of their responses.

"It's nice," Courtney said. "Although it's very different from where we grew up in California."

"It's amazing!" Savannah gushed.

"It's okay." Peyton glanced at Logan's glass of champagne, as if she was jealous he had some and she didn't.

Logan continued asking them questions—what their hobbies were, what grades they were going into, et cetera, before the waiter took their order. Courtney settled on the vegetarian hot-and-sour soup and vegetable lo mein. She hadn't eaten meat since third grade when her class had gone on a field trip to a nearby farm to see how milk was produced. Once she'd looked into the cow's big brown eyes and realized eating red meat meant she was eating a dead cow, she'd decided she would never eat an animal again.

"You shouldn't have hidden your daughters away all these years," Logan said to Adrian once the waiter had left. "It's so nice to finally meet them."

"And I couldn't be happier that they've chosen to live with me," Adrian said. "Northern California was a wonderful place for them to grow up, but as mature young ladies I'm confident they can handle living here now."

Mature young ladies? Courtney bit the inside of her cheek to stop from laughing. Plenty of adults had called Courtney mature for her age, but never Peyton or Savannah. Peyton was still rebelling after the jerk boyfriend she'd had in ninth grade had ripped her heart out, and Savannah was… She didn't want to say oblivious, because Savannah was loving and sweet, but she had been a lot more sheltered than Peyton and Courtney.

"You made a smart choice." Ellen sighed. "Perhaps if we had done something similar…"

"It's all right." Logan placed his hand over his wife's. "We're all friends here. We can be honest with one another."

"Well," Ellen said, looking at Courtney and her sisters. "Oliver hasn't been as lucky as the three of you. Vegas has gotten to his head. Logan and I believe you will be a good influence on him."

It was strange how Ellen talked about Oliver like he wasn't there. That must make Oliver feel so belittled. And was it Courtney's imagination, or had Ellen focused on *her* when she'd said that last part about being a good influence?

Curious about his reaction, she looked at Oliver. His dark eyes were glazed over, as if he wasn't fully present. Courtney didn't blame him. She would hate it if anyone discussed her like she wasn't in the room.

"You don't have a date to the charity dinner I'm holding tomorrow night, do you?" Ellen asked Oliver. The tight skin over her cheekbones made it obvious she'd had a facelift. Or two.

"Nope." He gave her an annoyed look that said she already knew the answer. Courtney was surprised at his response. She got the impression that Oliver was the type of guy who never had trouble finding a date.

"It would be wonderful if you invited one of the girls," Ellen said brightly, looking pointedly at Courtney. "You're going to be a junior next year, right? The same year as Oliver."

"I am," Courtney said slowly, keeping her voice level. Was Ellen trying to set her up on a date with Oliver? Did parents even *do* that? This was real life—not a Jane Austen novel. But she had a sinking feeling that this was exactly what Ellen was doing, right here, at the dinner table. And there was no way to stop her.

Ellen turned back to Oliver, a fake smile on her bright red lips. "Since you and Courtney will be in the same grade, you should get to know each other before school starts up again. Don't you agree?"

Oliver focused on Courtney, appearing to notice her for the first time that night. "I do," he said, looking more engaged in the conversation than he had all evening. "Courtney, would you like to come with me to my mother's charity dinner tomorrow night?"

Everyone at the table looked at her, and her blood stilled. Why was this happening to her? Some girls might find Oliver's bad-boy act attractive, but Courtney just thought he was arrogant. She doubted they would have anything in common. Peyton related to a variety of guys—surely she would prefer to go with him.

Then she realized how she could use this situation to her advantage. She had made a fool of herself with the text to Brett, and things were bound to be awkward between them next time they were alone together. But if she said yes to this dinner invitation, it could send Brett the message that she was fine with just being friends. And she wasn't worried about hurting Oliver, since there was no way he was *actually* interested in her. His mom was pressuring him into this date and he was going along with it to avoid conflict. By accepting, both of them could please their parents and get something good out of it.

"You mentioned the event is for charity," Courtney said to Ellen. "What is it supporting?"

"Scholarship USA," Ellen said with pride. "We raise money to help American high school students get into and graduate college."

"That sounds like a great cause," Courtney said truthfully. It was something she would have benefitted from before, and she would like to find out how she could help. That solidified her decision, and she refocused on Oliver, who was still waiting for her response. "I would love to go with you."

"You won't regret it." He smirked, and a chill prickled through her spine. She hoped she was right about him not being interested in her. She didn't want him to try anything that would make her uncomfortable. If he did, she would just have to set him straight about how she'd only agreed to go with him to be polite.

Ellen beamed at her answer.

And Brett refused to look at her for the rest of the meal.

Chapter 19: *Peyton*

Peyton silently fumed through dinner. Oliver and *Courtney?* They had nothing in common. Yet Ellen Prescott seemed determined that Oliver take Courtney to her stupid charity dinner.

Maybe because Courtney reminded Ellen Prescott of herself.

She shuddered at the thought of her hardworking, down-to-earth sister turning into that fake woman who'd had too much cosmetic surgery. Every time Ellen lifted her fork to her mouth, Peyton wondered how much collagen would ooze out if she accidentally poked her ginormous lips. Courtney was nothing like that plastic monster.

The worst was that the pressure to ask Courtney to the event didn't faze Oliver. Shouldn't he have said he'd rather go with Peyton, since they'd already hung out? He didn't *know* Courtney. And Courtney wasn't Oliver's type. He gambled, drank a lot, did drugs on occasion—he was too wild for her.

Courtney would tell him to get lost the moment he tried to drag her into his partying ways.

To calm herself down, Peyton considered why Courtney would have agreed to go with Oliver. Courtney disliked conflict. It would have been rude to say no with both their families watching, and Courtney would never insult someone to their face. Plus, Courtney seemed more interested in the charity event than in Oliver. Maybe on their pseudo-date, Courtney would even talk up Peyton to him.

Perhaps this could work in Peyton's favor.

That's what Peyton wanted to think—until she caught Oliver checking Courtney out during the main course. He wasn't even being subtle about it.

What a jackass.

Peyton went from angry to seriously pissed off. She wasn't even emotionally attached to Oliver—she was keeping him at arm's length, just as she did with everyone. Except for that one time years ago, she was the one who ended things with guys, not the other way around. She refused to let Oliver pretend the night they'd spent together didn't happen. Tonight she would get his focus back where it belonged—on her.

No one noticed that she said nothing through dessert. Then there was the boring lingering over after-dinner drinks, and finally Logan handled the check. Everyone got up, and Oliver refused to look at her. What was wrong with him? They had *slept with each other,* for crying out loud. Now he was acting like she was invisible. He should at least give her some acknowledgment. Instead he headed to the other end of the table, where Ellen stopped him to exchange a few quiet words.

Peyton turned to Savannah, and she was taken aback by her youngest sister's transformation all over again. In her se-

quined blue dress, tall heels and hair extensions, Savannah
could pass as a celebrity.

"You're still coming to Luxe, right?" Savannah sounded so
eager, which reminded Peyton that no matter how sophisticated Savannah *looked,* she was still a naive fifteen-year-old
from Fairfield, California. She would have to do a better job
looking out for her tonight. She wasn't used to her sisters coming to clubs with her, since their social lives had been so different back home. She'd messed up on Fourth of July, when
she'd lost track of Savannah while she was dancing with Oliver, but luckily Savannah hadn't done anything stupid, like
leaving the club with Damien. She would watch to make sure
she also stayed out of trouble tonight.

"Of course I am," Peyton answered, using every ounce of
her will not to look at Oliver.

Savannah leaned closer to Peyton. "I still can't believe
Damien invited me tonight, and he did it in front of Madison. It was classic. I wish you'd been there to see it. Madison's
eyes looked like they were about to bulge out of her head. I
wonder if she's interested in him?" She lifted a hand to bite
her nails, but dropped it a second later. "Not that it matters,
because if he was interested in her, he would have asked her
and not me. Right?"

Wow—Savannah had it really bad for Damien. Unfortunately, Peyton had been through too much to believe it would
be all sunshine and rainbows for them. "Right," she assured
her, lowering her voice. "Although if he does end up hurting
you, tell me and I'll take care of it."

"Damien wouldn't do that," Savannah said, although she
played with the hem of her dress, which made Peyton think
she wasn't as confident as she was trying to sound. But at least
Savannah was talking, which was more than Peyton could

say for Courtney, who had been standing next to them playing on her cell phone. Normally Courtney was quiet, but not *this* quiet.

"Are you okay?" Peyton asked her.

"Me?" Courtney looked up from her phone. Her eyes were glassy, as if she were about to cry. "Yeah, I'm fine."

"No, you're not," she said. "Want to go to the bathroom and talk?"

Courtney bit her lip and shook her head. "I'm probably just homesick. It's no big deal."

"You're missing Mom?" Peyton had found these past few days of not having to clean up their mom's messes to be a relief, but there had been a time when their mom had been involved in their lives—she would take them to the pool, or to the zoo or the movies. Peyton had given up hope of seeing that version of her again. But now there was a chance, so she did worry about how their mom was doing in rehab.

"And Grandma," Courtney said. "But I'll feel better once I read and get some sleep."

Then Oliver approached them, looking confident as usual. "You girls are still coming to Luxe tonight, right?" he asked smoothly. Peyton didn't know whether to feel happy when his eyes met hers or pissed that he was looking at Savannah and Courtney in the same way.

"I think so." Peyton shrugged. No need to seem eager.

"You *think* so?" Savannah pouted and crossed her arms. "But a second ago you said you were definitely coming."

Damn it. This was why Peyton never hung out with Savannah in social situations back in California. She was too transparent.

Peyton turned to Courtney, determined to get the focus

away from how Savannah had called her out. "Are you coming to Luxe?"

"I don't think so." Courtney sighed and placed her hand on her forehead. "My head hurts a little. I'm going to take it easy tonight and go back to the condo."

"All right," Peyton said, although she was glad Courtney wouldn't be at the club. It would give her time to snatch back Oliver's attention and find out what the hell he had been thinking at dinner. "Call me if you need anything, okay?" She knew Courtney wouldn't, since she wouldn't want to be an imposition, but she liked to offer.

Outside the restaurant, the adults made a big deal of saying goodbye and how nice it was to meet everyone. The conversations felt so forced. Peyton hated it.

"Have you made up your mind if you'll be joining us at Luxe?" Oliver asked her with a smirk. He was full of himself, but he was so cute when he looked at her like that.

Peyton took a piece of gum out of her purse and popped it into her mouth. "I'm in," she said.

"Good." He smiled for real this time. Maybe Peyton was wrong in doubting his interest in her. He'd clearly only asked Courtney to the dinner because his mom had forced him.

"Are we just going to stand here, or are we going to the club?" Savannah crossed her arms and looked back and forth between Peyton and Oliver.

"I have to get something from my room first," Oliver said. "Meet up with you at Luxe?"

Peyton's chest panged. Did Oliver not want to show up at the club with her?

"See you there," she said calmly, not wanting to give away her irritation. Why did he have to be so confusing?

She didn't look back at him as she and Savannah made their way to the club.

★ ★ ★

Oliver had mentioned that Luxe was the second-most expensive club in Vegas—Myst coming in first—and Peyton didn't doubt it. The line to get in snaked around the hallway. Girls in short skirts and low-cut tops leaned over red velvet ropes, begging for attention from the bouncers so they could cut the line, but they were mostly ignored.

Once Peyton and Savannah found the VIP entrance, the bouncer pulled the rope aside to let them through. It didn't matter that they were underage since they were on Oliver's special list. Some of the girls who were almost to the front of the long line gave them nasty looks, but Peyton didn't care. She had once been one of those girls standing on the other side, watching the VIPs go ahead of her. The system wasn't fair, but it beat waiting in line for an hour.

A girl in her mid-twenties with long auburn hair and ivory skin met them at the entry, telling them that her name was Devan and she would escort them to their cabana. Luxe was smaller than Myst, but the rich browns and golds on the inside screamed extravagance. People in their twenties packed into cushy couches surrounding the tables, but every so often Peyton caught sight of groups who appeared to be around her age. The most striking part of the club was the colossal chandelier hanging above the dance floor. Of all the chandeliers Peyton had seen so far in Vegas, she had never seen one so enormous. It belonged in a giant's house. In the center of the club, beneath the chandelier, people raised their arms in the air as they danced to the thumping music, a sea of bodies moving to the beat.

They passed through massive gold curtains leading to an outside area where two-story cabanas circled around a gambling area. Everyone walking around had a drink in hand.

This was Peyton's sort of place.

Devan dropped them off at the central cabana—the one reserved for Oliver's group. The wooden building was airy, the large open windows making people inside feel included in what was happening in the rest of the club. People Peyton vaguely recognized from Myst surrounded the tables, and in the corner a spiral staircase led to a second-floor deck looking over the club.

"I see Damien on the second floor," Savannah said. "Let's go up and say hi."

Since Peyton didn't know anyone on the first floor well enough to sit down and join the conversation, she followed Savannah up the spiral staircase. Damien stood next to the balcony, talking with Madison and a petite blonde girl who Peyton remembered was named Larissa. Much to Peyton's irritation, Madison also wore black. But instead of being sheer, Madison's dress had large stripes of black sequins, and she had leggings on so she wasn't showing as much skin. Damien looked involved in talking to her, but her thoughts seemed somewhere else.

Savannah grabbed Peyton's hand and dragged her over to Damien and the girls. When Damien saw Savannah, his jaw literally dropped. He didn't even notice Peyton.

"You look…stunning," he finally said to Savannah.

"Thanks." Savannah played with her hair extensions, clearly not used to them yet.

"When did you get here?"

"Now," she answered. "This club is awesome."

"It is." He pulled her closer and draped his arm around her shoulder. Savannah's eyes lit up—she was clearly enamored with him—and while Peyton didn't like him being so grabby with her little sister, she didn't say anything because she didn't want to embarrass Savannah. It wasn't like he could do much with Peyton watching. "But I like Myst more," he said, his gaze locked with Savannah's. "There aren't any caves here, and with how hot you look right now, I wish there were."

Savannah's cheeks heated, and she mumbled a quick thanks, refusing to look at Peyton.

Peyton crossed her arms and stared down Damien. "What do you mean about caves?" She could think of many things he could mean—all of them R-rated and something Savannah would have mentioned.

"Relax," he said. "It's an inside joke."

"Yeah." Savannah looked at her in a way she knew meant "back off."

Damien whispered something to Savannah, and she giggled in response. Peyton would definitely make sure she didn't lose track of them tonight. But, not wanting Savannah to feel like she was hovering, she looked over the balcony at the people gambling, all focused on the cards in front of them.

Then she spotted Oliver. He sat at a poker table, pushing a pile of chips toward the center.

"I'm going to say hi to Oliver," she told Savannah, pointing to where he was sitting. "Promise you won't leave without letting me know, okay?" It was an assumed rule whenever they went somewhere together that they didn't leave without telling each other, but Peyton wanted to make sure Savannah knew how serious she was about it. Besides, how much trouble could Savannah get into when she was in the cabana surrounded by people, and with their bodyguards watching out for them, too?

"I promise," Savannah said. "Have fun!"

Peyton left the cabana, but she stopped in her tracks when she saw Jackson leaning against the wall next to the entrance. He was in a suit, as always, but other than that he looked…

relaxed. If Peyton didn't know better, and if he wasn't dressed like he was ten years older than his actual age, she might think he was here to have fun. Would Jackson even *go* to a club to have fun? She didn't know what he did in his free time, but he didn't strike her as the partying type. He was too serious for that.

She wasn't sure if she should speak to him, since he hadn't been receptive the last time she'd tried. But after a few seconds of them staring at each other, she had to say something to keep the encounter from being awkward.

"Aren't you supposed to remain inconspicuous?"

"You're interested in that Prescott kid, aren't you?" was all he replied.

Peyton's eyes narrowed, but she was inwardly amused that Jackson had asked. Looked like her flirting with Oliver had gotten his attention, after all. "What is it to you?"

"He's bad news," Jackson said. "You should stay away from him."

"Excuse me?" She crossed her arms and held her ground. "Who are you to tell me who I can and can't hang out with?"

"I'm supposed to keep you safe."

"From kidnappers and other…dangerous people!" she said. "Not from the son of Adrian's future business partner. And how do you know anything about Oliver? You've probably never talked to him."

"I looked him up on Google," Jackson said with a shrug.

Peyton laughed, pressing her lips together a second later to control herself. "And what did you find on Google that was so horrible?"

"He's not a nice guy, Peyton." His hazel eyes twisted with anger, as if he knew something she didn't. "He's a player, and he treats women like they're things for him to conquer instead of actual people. I don't want you to get hurt."

"Wow." She couldn't believe Jackson was getting so involved—he had to be jealous she'd hooked up with Oliver. "What exactly did you find?"

"I don't want to quote my sources, because I can't be positive they were accurate." His gaze was so intense she could feel the energy buzzing between them. "All I can recommend is that you look him up yourself."

"I'm not going to spy on him," she said. "He's grown up as the son of a major hotel owner, so there must be tons of rumors about him online."

"I don't think that would be a wise decision." He sighed and ran a hand through his short hair. "I wish you would trust me, Peyton. I'm only saying this to help you."

What the hell? A few nights ago Jackson had made it clear he couldn't get involved in her personal life, and now he cared about her feelings for Oliver? Peyton didn't know what game he was playing—if he meant to play a game at all—but his sudden interest was intriguing.

"If I didn't know better, I would say it sounds like you care about me." She stepped toward him so there was barely any space between them. "Did you change your mind about not wanting to be…friends?" She added extra emphasis on the final word to let him know she could see more than friendship between them. He knew so much about her, and from the way he was looking at her, he was attracted to her, too. The chemistry between them was undeniable.

He took a sharp breath inward, and backed away. "I didn't change my mind," he said. "You're only a kid, Peyton, and it would be unprofessional for us to be friends. I'm just doing my job to keep you from getting hurt."

"If you say so." Peyton raised an eyebrow and smiled knowingly. Jackson might have reined in his emotions, but the way he looked at her a minute ago made it clear he was attracted to her...maybe even *interested* in her. He might pull away now, but this wasn't over. "Thanks for the help, but I'm going to say hi to Oliver," she said, amusing herself by her blatant disregard for Jackson's advice. "Have a good night."

She shot him a killer smile, and added an extra sway to her hips as she sauntered toward the gambling area. She caught Oliver right when he was preparing to walk away from the table.

"Did you manage to strike it rich?" she asked playfully, motioning to the handful of chips he was shoving into his pocket.

"Not quite." He shrugged in mock disappointment. "Although I did donate around a grand to the casino. You'll be surprised to discover I'm quite charitable."

Peyton's eyebrows shot up in surprise. He'd wasted a thousand dollars playing cards?

"I need a drink," she said. "Come with me to the bar?"

He said okay, and once he bought their drinks (and slipped the bartender a hundred to serve him even though his parents forbade him to drink on their property), Peyton realized how nervous she was.

"So, you and Courtney..." she said, taking a large sip of her drink. The margarita—heavy on the tequila—burned down her throat.

"What about me and Courtney?"

"You're going with her to that dinner thing tomorrow night."

"I am," he said nonchalantly.

"You could have asked me."

"Aw, come on," he said. "You saw what happened. It's no big deal."

Peyton fumed at how blasé he was being about it. "It was to me."

"What happened to make you so messed up when it comes to relationships?"

The question took Peyton by surprise. "What do you mean?"

"I've seen your type," Oliver said. "You must have been burned real bad, and that's why you have this act going on now."

"Act?" Peyton balked. "I don't have an act."

"You mean pretending you don't care when you really do isn't an act?"

Peyton took a swig of her drink. "You don't want to know."

"Oh, I think I do." He scooted closer to her.

Peyton didn't know what inspired her to go on—maybe it was the alcohol, that she was in a new place far away from Fairfield or how Oliver seemed sincerely curious about what had happened—but she found herself spilling the entire story.

"It happened in the spring of ninth grade," she started. "I was dating this guy Vince for six months. I thought it was serious, and that he loved me."

"Love in ninth grade?" Oliver laughed. "That doesn't happen."

"I thought it did," Peyton snapped. "Now, do you want to hear the story or not?"

"Go on."

"He was in Model UN, and every spring they went to this big meeting in North Carolina."

"Sounds like trouble," he guessed.

"It was. There was this sophomore girl, and she was a total slut. They fooled around for the entire trip. When she got back, she wrote about it in her online diary that she thought no one knew about. But someone discovered it and emailed it to the whole school. There were pictures of the two of them together. The worst was this one part when she talked about how she was dancing with him, and he took an ice cube and put it near places I don't want to mention."

"Sounds kinky." Oliver laughed.

"It was disgusting," Peyton said. "Everyone at school knew, and he didn't even apologize. He just broke up with me, like I never mattered, and started dating her a few days later."

"That sucks," he said, and it sounded like he meant it.

"Yeah. And now here you are, ditching me for my sister. You know there's no way she'll go along with it once I tell her we hooked up, right?"

"Listen." He held his hands out, like he was telling her to calm down. "My mom thinks Courtney would be good for me, and if bringing her on this date gets my mom off my back, then whatever. It won't mean anything, so it's no big deal."

"Now you're calling it a *date?*" Peyton was getting angrier by the second.

"Yeah," he said. "What else would it be?"

Peyton couldn't believe it. What an arrogant jerk to say that after what she'd told him, and for him to assume Courtney would go along with his messed-up plan. "But what about us?"

"Courtney's more appropriate for me to publicly date," Oliver said. "It'll just be for my mom's sake. But we can still hook up. No one has to know about that." His fingers grazed Peyton's thigh, and she pulled away. She'd been an idiot to let her guard down with Oliver. It would never happen again.

"You've got to be kidding," she said. "Courtney's my *sister.* You're deluded if you think she'll go along with this after I tell her we hooked up, or that I would do that to her."

He leaned closer to her. "Is it any worse than what you're

doing right now? To your boyfriend? Unless you've broken up with him and haven't mentioned it."

"What happens between me and Mike is none of your business," she said. "You knew about him before we hooked up, and it didn't bother you then."

"And it still doesn't bother me," he said smugly. "I was just making a point."

"Your point sucks."

He brushed his finger across her cheek. "Relax," he said. "This is no big deal. You're freaking out over nothing."

Peyton wanted to believe him. But she didn't trust anyone that easily. She pulled away from his touch, and his hand dropped to his lap. The place where his fingers had been on her cheek felt cold. "It's not nothing," she said. "And you're stupid thinking Courtney would be interested in you. You're not her type."

"Her type?" Oliver raised an eyebrow. "I'm everybody's type."

Peyton was amazed at how full of himself he was. "Hate to break it to you, but not everybody likes conceited assholes."

"You seem to." He laughed.

"Courtney doesn't."

"We'll see about that." He didn't sound concerned. "And I hate to break it to *you,* but even though I'm your type, you're not mine. Sorry. I thought you understood that we were both having fun to pass time. But Courtney…" He paused, his eyes going distant before meeting Peyton's again. "Courtney *is* my type. She's sweet and innocent—qualities that are hard to find in Vegas, especially in my group of friends. Unlike I was with you, I'm actually interested in her."

Peyton couldn't believe he had the nerve to say that to her. "You're not interested in anyone," she spat, backing away from him. How had she been so dumb to allow herself to be interested in him? "All you care about is yourself."

"Aw, come on." His face twisted with arrogance. "Don't be like that. You threw yourself at me— What did you expect? For me to fall for you? If you want that, sweetheart, you've got to play harder to get. You were easy, so don't make me out to be the villain."

Peyton sat back, stunned. No one had ever said anything like that to her before.

Or maybe since Vince, she'd never let herself care enough about a guy to get to the point where they would. Vegas must be getting to her head. Or maybe she'd just never met anyone like Oliver before, since guys like him didn't live in Fairfield— or know that Fairfield existed. Then again, guys would be guys, whether they were from a run-down neighborhood in Fairfield or if they were hotel heirs in Las Vegas. She wouldn't allow herself to be blinded by the glitz of this city again.

"Whatever," Peyton said, trying to act unfazed. "Courtney's not going to be fooled by you."

"Are you sure about that?"

"Of course I'm sure." She glared at him. "She's my sister. I know her better than you do."

"So you're saying that Courtney would never be interested in me, even without you telling her that we hooked up, or about this conversation right now?"

Peyton fumed. "That's exactly what I'm saying."

"Fine," Oliver challenged. "Then prove it."

"What do I get when I'm right?"

"*If* you're right, you can ask me to do one thing—anything you want," Oliver proposed. "And if I'm right, I can ask you to do anything I want."

Then the last person Peyton thought she would be happy to see interrupted the conversation—Madison.

"How have you two been tonight?" Madison asked, resting her hand on Oliver's elbow. For being just friends, they sure were touchy with each other. She tossed her long hair over her shoulder and examined Peyton's outfit. "I like your top."

"Thanks," Peyton said, too pissed at Oliver to show surprise that Madison was faking nice.

"You won't mind if I steal Oliver for a minute, would you?" Her voice dripped with pretend sweetness.

Saved by Madison Lockhart. Who would've thought. "No problem," she said. "I'm getting a headache, so I was about to head out anyway."

"Too bad," Madison said, although she didn't sound concerned. "Feel better."

"And tell Courtney I'm looking forward to tomorrow night," Oliver added.

Peyton walked away, not bothering to respond. Oliver could go to hell for all she cared.

After texting Savannah that she wasn't feeling well and was leaving, she headed to the exit of the club, blinking away tears that were threatening to spill out of her eyes. She might feel like crap, but she didn't want other people to know. She just wanted to go back to the condo and lock herself away. Hopefully some late-night TV and sleep would make her feel better in the morning. Maybe she could find a good movie on-demand. Preferably an action or thriller with a kick-ass female heroine, so she wouldn't think about relationships and how guys sucked at life.

Of course when she reached the door to leave the club, Jackson was waiting for her. It was clear from the pity in his eyes that he had seen—and maybe heard—her conversation with Oliver. Peyton didn't want him to say that he'd told her so. He was only five years older than her; he had no right to tell her who she could and couldn't hook up with. His job was to keep her safe physically, not emotionally. Her personal life was none of his business.

He looked like he was about to say something, but Peyton cut him off. "Don't even think about it," she said, her voice full of daggers. "I don't want to talk to anyone else tonight. But if you want to do me a favor, you'll make sure Savannah's bodyguard doesn't let her leave with Damien."

He nodded, but kept his distance after that, not a word spoken between them.

Chapter 20: *Madison*

Madison slid into the seat vacated by Peyton, letting her fingers linger on Oliver's arm. She crossed her legs and rested an elbow on the bar, studying him.

"What was that about?" She motioned to Peyton stomping out of the club. "She seems a bit pissed off."

"A bit?" Oliver laughed. "She got obsessed with me after one night and freaked out when I asked her holier-than-thou sister to my mom's charity dinner instead of her."

"It must be difficult to be you." Madison shook her head in pretend sympathy. "So many girls obsessing over you. I don't know how you handle it."

"It's a hard life, but I manage." Oliver smirked. "What can I say? They can't resist my charm."

"It's your eyes," Madison said, surprised when the words came out of her mouth. "You do this thing with your eyes."

"This thing with my eyes?" He looked entertained.

"Yeah." She thought about how to clarify what she meant.

"When you look at someone, it's like they're the only person in the world. Like you're reaching out and really listening to what they're saying."

"And you're immune to it?"

"Apparently." Madison chuckled. "And judging from that little scene when I got here, Peyton Diamond definitely *isn't*."

"You're the only one who is," he said thoughtfully.

"But you don't try it on me."

Oliver took another sip of his drink, the conflicted look returning.

"So which sister did you ask to the dinner? Courtney or Savannah?" Madison asked, trying not to sound too interested.

"Courtney," he said. "You should've seen it. My mom practically forced me. Not that I mind—it gets me a step closer to winning the bet with Damien, and she's hot."

"She's okay," Madison said, hiding her hurt that Oliver hadn't asked *her* to go with him. His mom arranged these dinners regularly, and he always brought Madison. It would look bad if he showed up with a different girl every time, and Ellen Prescott liked her, so it made sense for him to bring her, since they were best friends.

The answer she came up with pissed her off. While Madison's parents were well-off, her family wasn't close to the same league as the Diamonds. Combined, her parents made almost a million dollars a year. Adrian Diamond had over a billion, as did Logan Prescott. Both of them were on the Forbes 400 list of the richest people in America.

In Ellen Prescott's eyes, Oliver and Courtney were a perfect match. And Madison was a pauper.

The thought made an angry heat shoot through her veins, and she leaned back in her chair, crossing her legs away from Oliver.

"Courtney's not my type, though," he said, playing with his lower lip as though he were in deep thought.

"Every girl's your type." Madison laughed.

He grew serious. "That's not true."

"Sure it's not." She wasn't convinced.

"If any girl was my type, I would be interested in Peyton as more than a one-time hookup," Oliver defended himself.

"The last time you seriously dated a girl was the beginning of seventh grade," she said. "Kaitlin. And you broke up with her after four months."

"I gave her a chance," he said. "But like I said, she wasn't my type."

Madison sighed. "And so we return to the original problem."

"It's harder than you think." He slammed his glass down on the bar. "They all just look at me as Logan Prescott's son. No one can see past my inheritance."

"I see past it."

"But we're not dating."

"Right." Madison suddenly wanted to escape. She'd never wanted to think of Oliver as anything more than a friend, but now that he mentioned it, she wondered if they would make a good couple.

She pushed the thought away. Oliver was a player. Maybe the Brett issue had messed with her head more than she realized. And now she had the Diamond girls screwing up her life.

Summer was supposed to be relaxing and fun, but this one was turning into a disaster.

"Anyway," Oliver said. "I heard you and Damien were getting awfully close at the Lobby Bar last night."

The Lobby Bar with Damien reminded Madison of seeing Brett with Courtney, and thinking about them together made her want to pick up Oliver's glass and throw it at the wall. What was so special about Courtney Diamond? First Brett was out with her last night, and now Oliver was bringing her to his mom's charity dinner tomorrow night. She was more of a problem than Madison had expected.

"Let's drink," Madison decided. She needed to forget about all this drama. She never drank away her problems, but then, her problems usually resolved themselves quickly. This time that wasn't the case, and it was making her head hurt. For once, she wanted to be like other girls and lose herself in semi-oblivion.

One night of drinking wouldn't be the end of the world, right?

Oliver sized her up. "Okay," he finally said. "What do you want?"

Madison racked her brain for what would get her drunk the fastest. "A Long Island Iced Tea," she decided. Not the classiest drink, but it would do the job.

"Are you sure?" He looked concerned. "We both know you're a lightweight."

"Are you worried about me?"

"I was just pointing it out." He finished his drink in one gulp. "But I know you can handle yourself. Two Long Island Iced Teas it is."

The bartender picked up a few bottles of liquor and dumped them into the glasses, topping them off with an inch of cola. It was practically all alcohol. Perfect.

Madison tried it, surprised by the sweet flavor. "I can barely taste the alcohol," she told Oliver, feeling giddy just knowing what was in the drink.

"Is that good?"

She leaned closer to him and whispered, "I don't like the taste of hard alcohol. Don't tell anyone."

"It'll be our secret." He took a long drink, his glass already half empty. Madison matched his pace, and it didn't take long before their drinks were gone.

"You ready for another?" she challenged.

"You sure about that?" he asked. "I don't want to be carrying you out of here at the end of the night."

"I'm sure," she said. "I don't even feel the first one." All right, that was a lie, but whatever. She felt it, but not enough to make her forget about Brett and the stupid Diamond sisters everyone loved so much.

She hated them.

"Okay." Oliver didn't look convinced, but he ordered the drinks anyway.

It didn't take long to finish their second round. Madison's head was spinning, and she couldn't focus on one thing without the world moving around her. The sucky part was that the drinks didn't make her problems disappear. Instead, everything crashed down on her at once. She hated how she'd strung Nick along for months, knowing the connection they'd felt in Deer Valley over spring break didn't exist in their real lives, and how she'd gone so low as to cheat on him. She'd never cheated on anyone before that, and it made her feel horrible. Then she was rejected by the guy she'd cheated on him with. It was pathetic.

The conversation she'd had with Nick when she'd admitted she had cheated on him flashed through her mind, the pain she'd seen in his eyes refusing to leave her thoughts. It was her fault she'd hurt him. She wished her feelings for Nick were as strong as his were for her. Why couldn't they be? It would be easier if she could feel the way she wanted to about Nick—the way she *should* feel about Nick.

And what was so great about those hick-town Diamond bitches? Oliver was *her* best friend, and he'd invited Courtney to go to the charity dinner with him. Madison had wanted to dance with Oliver at the Fourth of July party, but he'd ditched her for Peyton, an obsessive freak who should go back to the trailer she came from. Then there was Savannah, who thought her sweet, small-town smiles and Las Vegas make-over could make Damien fall for her. Damien didn't care about Savannah, and Madison wanted to throw it in her face for the world to see.

Madison looked at Damien and Savannah, leaning against the railing of the cabana, his arm draped around her like they were a real couple. He would eventually break her heart. She watched them for a few more seconds, disgust in the back of her throat. Then Savannah walked away from Damien and to the restrooms.

Now was Madison's chance. In the end, this would be a favor to Savannah. Maybe Savannah would thank her later.

"You look like you're up to something." Oliver drew her out of her thoughts.

"Wait and see." She smiled devilishly. "I'll be right back."

With that, she flipped her glossy hair over her shoulder and strutted toward the cabana. Keeping her balance was difficult in her four-inch heels, but she could manage. She felt eyes on her as she walked by—they all loved her, so why didn't Brett? Her jaw tightened at the thought of him. But now wasn't the time to mope. Now was the time to put Savannah Diamond in her place.

Madison marched up the cabana steps, glad the railing was there. She would have been in serious trouble otherwise.

She said hi to her friends as she walked across the second floor, making sure not to get her stilettos stuck in the wooden planks. Finally she found him—Damien Sanders standing at the railing, talking with Larissa. She walked toward him until she was right in front of him. Why hadn't she seen how sexy his eyes were until now? They were dark like she remembered, but now she noticed the golden flecks surrounding his pupils in an ethereal glow.

He didn't have time to say hi before she put her hand against his chest and pressed her lips against his.

He didn't respond for a second, but then he kissed her back—hard. The world disappeared around Madison. His hand caressed the back of her neck, and she pushed her body closer to his until there was no space between them. Heat emanated from his skin, warmth spreading from his body into hers.

Eventually he pulled away, cupping her cheek in his hand. "Mads," he said softly, his lips brushing against hers. His voice was full of wonder, like he wasn't sure if he was dreaming or not. "What's going on?"

"I kissed you." She tilted her head to look up at him, her eyelashes brushing his cheeks. "And you kissed me back."

"Of course I did," he replied, closing the space between their lips again. Madison wrapped her arms around him so she wouldn't lose her balance. The world was still spinning from the drinks, and the kiss grew more passionate, despite the audience around them. She felt like she could melt right into him. With all the years they'd been friends, it was hard to believe she hadn't known what an amazing kisser Damien Sanders was until now. She'd heard rumors, but it was different knowing they were true from a firsthand experience.

"Damien?" a soft voice asked from behind.

Madison broke away from him to look over her shoulder,

her eyes meeting the bright blue ones of Savannah Diamond. The hair extensions, highlights and new dress made a huge difference for her, but she was still no match for Madison.

Savannah blinked a few times, as if making sure what she was seeing was real. Her face scrunched up in horror. Then a single tear rolled down her cheek, and her chin quivered like she was about to break down sobbing.

Madison had expected Savannah to yell, get pissed off or pretend like she didn't care. What she hadn't expected was for her to cry. Despite the makeover, Savannah still looked young, and Madison felt like she'd kicked a puppy. But then she reminded herself that she was doing this for the greater good. Savannah would be more hurt if Damien ditched her after she had more time to get attached. It was better for her this way.

"Is there a problem?" Madison asked sweetly, trailing her manicured fingernails down Damien's arm.

Savannah opened her mouth to speak, but tears flowed down her cheeks instead. Then she gathered her dress and ran down the steps, hurrying out of the cabana like Cinderella after her stepsisters ruined her disguise at the prince's ball.

Damien stared at the place where Savannah had disappeared, and Madison worried that he might follow after her. Had she put too much faith into Damien's crush on her? Maybe he *did* care about Savannah. But it hadn't seemed like it when they'd talked in the Lobby Bar last night. Savannah had barely come up in conversation.

"She seemed…upset," Madison finally said, trying to downplay the situation. If Damien had planned on running after Savannah, he would have done it already. He looked surprised about what had happened, but Madison understood. Damien never humiliated girls in public. That was more Oliver's style.

Well, it was *Madison* who had humiliated Savannah in public, but whatever.

"She liked me a lot," Damien said, running a hand through his hair. Then he refocused on Madison, studying her like he was trying to figure her out. "Why now?" he asked, his voice soft and confused.

"What do you mean?" She widened her dark blue eyes in a way she hoped was the perfect impression of innocence.

"You know what I mean."

"I just…" Madison searched for a response, since she couldn't tell him the real reason. She decided to say what she knew he wanted to hear. "I saw you standing there, and it clicked. You get me, Damien. You always have. I was so stupid not to see it until now." She felt guilty for getting his hopes up, but the drinks were making her head buzz and say things without thinking them through. Hopefully he'd also had enough to drink that he wouldn't remember the details of this conversation.

"Yeah, you were," he said. "Not that you're stupid. You're really smart. But—"

"Are you nervous?" she asked.

"No." Damien laughed like that was the craziest idea in the world. "You're perfect."

Then he kissed her again, sweeter than the first time, like everything was coming together like he wanted. Which she supposed it was—for him. But if she wasn't into him, why had she responded when they'd kissed the first time?

Not wanting to think about it, she imagined Brett in his place, wrapping her arms around his neck and pulling him closer as if they could sink right into each other.

What had Madison gotten herself into?

There was one thing she knew for sure—she needed another drink.

www.campusbuzz.com

Hottest Guys?
Posted on Wednesday 07/06 at 4:27 PM
Let the games begin...who do you think is the hottest guy in school?

　1, 2, 3, GO!

1: Posted on Wednesday 07/06 at 4:39 PM
Nick Gordon for sure! Totally hot. Heard he and Madison broke up over the summer. Anyone got details?

2: Posted on Wednesday 07/06 at 5:03 PM
It doesn't count if you write about yourself, Nick.

3: Posted on Wednesday 07/06 at 5:56 PM
Oliver Prescott.

4: Posted on Wednesday 07/06 at 6:32 PM
i heard oliver slept with that diamond girl with the blue streaks in a hotel room the other night.

5: Posted on Wednesday 07/06 at 6:59 PM
what a slut she probably thinks he likes her too haha what a joke..

6: Posted on Wednesday 07/06 at 7:06 PM
Oliver spends a lot of time with Madison Lockhart, especially since Madison broke up with Nick. (And even though people are saying different things, I know for a fact that Madison broke up with Nick and not the other way around). Madison and Oliver have been best friends forever. But we all know it's impossible for girls to be friends with guys without one person falling for the other. It always ends badly. Maybe she broke up with Nick because she cheated on him with Oliver. It would make sense...

7: Posted on Wednesday 07/06 at 7:15 PM
It would "make sense" if you had any idea what you were talking about.

Back to the topic of hottest guy at school, my vote goes to Damien Sanders. He's got that dark and sexy thing going for him. I'd hit that any day.

8: Posted on Wednesday 07/06 at 8:38 PM
Damien Sanders = agreed. No contest.

9: Posted on Wednesday 07/06 at 9:58 PM
EDWARD CULLEN

10: Posted on Wednesday 07/06 at 10:34 PM
HAHAHAHA i wish.

chapter 21: *Savannah*

People stared at Savannah when she pushed past them, but she didn't care. All she cared about was getting that horrible image out of her mind. The one of Damien's arms wrapped around Madison Lockhart, the two of them making out in front of everyone in the club. Madison had acted so nice to Savannah at the gym, and Savannah had thought they could be friends. Then she had to do *that*. When Madison had turned around and seen Savannah, she'd looked so spiteful, as if she had been all over Damien to purposefully hurt her. What had she done to make Madison hate her so much?

Now Savannah understood how Peyton had felt when Vince had cheated on her and the whole school found out. She'd thought Peyton had overreacted—she'd shut herself in their room all weekend and listened to sad music while sobbing so loudly that Savannah and Courtney had heard her throughout the apartment—but now Savannah knew how awful it felt when something like that happened to you.

She had thought Damien was interested in her, but clearly she meant nothing to him. She felt gullible and used. Plus, the girls who went to Goodman had seen everything, so when she started school in the fall they would never accept her into their group. She would forever be known as the girl who stupidly fell for Damien over the summer and left Luxe in tears.

She hid her face in her hands as she left the club, not wanting anyone to see her cry. She had almost reached the exit when she crashed into someone.

"Whoa." The guy wrapped his hands around her arms to keep her from falling. He looked at her, and his face melted into concern. "Are you okay?"

Even through her tears she could tell he was cute. No, not just cute. Really, really hot. With his blond curly hair, deep blue eyes and glowing skin, he reminded her of an angel. He was the opposite of Damien.

Her eyes watered again.

"I'll take that as a no," he said.

"Yeah." Savannah wiped the tears from her eyes. It was good she was wearing waterproof mascara, or she would have had black streaks down her cheeks. "I mean, not yeah as in no. Yeah as in I'm fine."

He looked doubtful. "Are you sure about that?"

"Yes." She sniffed. "Well, no."

"You're new here, right?" he asked. "I think I saw you hanging out with some people I know on Fourth of July at Myst."

Fourth of July at Myst—she had hung out with Damien all night, and except for the minor incident in the caves, she'd had an amazing time with him. Savannah shook away the memory. "I just moved here," she told him. "Savannah Diamond."

His blue eyes twinkled, and Savannah sensed that he already knew who she was. "Nick Gordon."

The name sounded familiar. Then Savannah remembered where she'd heard it before. Damien had mentioned him in conversation.

Nick used to date Madison.

She shouldn't talk to him. Madison already hated her—why else would she make out with Damien when she knew Savannah was interested in him?—and she wouldn't be happy if she knew she was talking to her ex. Savannah didn't want to give the girls at Goodman *more* of a reason to make her a social outcast in the fall. So even though Nick was cute, she would have to get away from him before anyone saw them together.

"How are you liking Vegas so far?" he asked, as though she wasn't having a breakdown in the middle of the club.

"It's great." Savannah sniffed again. "Can't you tell?"

He stuffed his hands into the back pockets of his khaki pants. "Sorry. Stupid question."

"It's fine," Savannah said. "I'm just having a bad night. I was about to head back to my condo."

"Wanna talk about it?" he asked. "We can go somewhere else—I'm sick of this place, anyway. But only if you want to."

She should say no. But he seemed so nice, like he really cared about helping her. If they left the club, Madison and her friends wouldn't know Savannah was with him. "Sure," she said, since it was either hang out with him or cry alone, and the latter sounded too pathetic. "Thanks."

"No prob." He started toward the exit, motioning for Savannah to follow. She did.

The sounds of the slot machines in the lobby were more welcoming than the loud music in the club. Figuring Nick knew where to go, Savannah fell into step with him, neither

of them saying anything. At least he wasn't trying to make
small talk. When she was upset she liked to disappear into her
head. Nick seemed to get that.

Images of Madison and Damien kept popping into her
mind, and she tried to push them away. Instead, she thought
about what Evie would tell her to do. Evie liked having fun
with guys, but she never took them seriously. Sometimes Savannah thought guys fell for Evie *because* of that. And while
she would fall for them, too, she always moved on to the next
one quickly. Once Evie had ditched one guy at a party and
started dating his best friend in the same night. She'd bragged
about that "accomplishment" for days.

Evie would tell Savannah to stop sulking about Damien,
focus on the hot guy who wanted to spend time with her
right now and not worry about Madison and the rest of the
Goodman girls. *Live in the moment,* she could almost hear her
best friend whisper.

Savannah decided to do just that.

Nick found a table near the back of the bar and snagged it
before a middle-aged couple could get there. The table was
tall, and Savannah hopped onto the chair, her feet dangling
above the ground. It was nice to sit, since her high heels were
making the balls of her feet throb. Even high-end designers
couldn't make four-inch heels less of a torture device.

"You want a drink?" Nick asked, waving the waiter over
to their table.

"A Cherry Coke would be great." Savannah had had enough
alcohol for now. Plus, while the bars at the Diamond served
her because she was the owner's daughter, she doubted the
ones at the Gates would be so lenient.

Nick ordered water for himself, from the tap, not a bottle.

The waiter didn't look pleased—he probably thought it meant he wouldn't get as much of a tip.

"So who's the reason that you ran out of the club like that?" Nick asked.

"How do you know it's a who?"

"Because I've spent some time with that group," he said. "And knowing them, it's bound to be a *who*."

Savannah decided to go with her gut feeling and trust him. "Damien Sanders," she admitted.

Nick pressed the pads of his fingers together and grimaced.

"You know him?" It wasn't too far out of a guess, considering how close Damien was to Madison.

"Unfortunately," said Nick. "What'd he do?"

"It wasn't a big deal," Savannah said. She and Damien weren't an official couple, so it wasn't like he'd cheated on her. She also knew Evie's number-one piece of advice when it came to guys—they don't like drama queens and girls who talk badly about people. It might have become too late for that when Nick had caught her bawling her eyes out as she ran out of the club, but Savannah could try acting cool about it now.

"It looked like a big deal to me," he said. "Unless you like to pick up guys by crashing into them and pulling the damsel-in-distress routine. Then I guess you're right—no big deal."

Savannah laughed. "I thought he was interested in me," she started, trying to figure out how to phrase it. "We were talking, and I left to go to the restroom, and when I came back he was all over Madison."

"Damien's always all over Madison," Nick said bitterly. "But they're only friends. It didn't mean anything."

"By 'all over her' do you mean 'making out in front of everyone in the club?'" Savannah asked.

Nick sat back, shocked, and he took a drink of water to

compose himself. "No, not from what I know," he finally said. "They flirt a lot, but it's never serious. Then again, it seems like there's a lot about Madison that I didn't know until recently."

"You're friends with her?" Savannah might as well play innocent and pretend she didn't know he'd been in a relationship with her. She'd only been in Las Vegas for a few days. He couldn't expect her to know everything about everyone.

"Friends," Nick said in disgust. "More than that. We used to date."

"What happened?"

"I'm still not sure," he said.

"But you want her back?" It was a daring question, but she got the impression that Nick wasn't over Madison. She also couldn't figure out why he would be interested in Madison. Nick seemed so nice, and Madison…didn't.

As if Savannah knew what Nick was really like. She didn't *know* any of these people. Nick was acting friendly now, but it could be an act. After Damien, she wouldn't be surprised. But something about Nick felt…genuine.

She wanted to give him a chance.

"I shouldn't want her back," Nick said, his eyes hardening.

"But you do."

Nick nodded.

"I know what you mean," she said. "I mean, not that what happened with me and Damien was anything close to what you and Madison had, but I wish I could rewind time and stop Madison from making out with him at the club."

"And how would you do that?" Nick looked amused.

"Rewind time?" Savannah contemplated the question. "I guess I would have to have superpowers, but I don't know how I would get those, so maybe a DeLorean would work—"

"Not rewind time," Nick interrupted, laughing. "Change what happened with Damien and Madison. I know both of them, and if they want something, they're not going to let anyone stop them. No offense."

"Oh." Savannah realized how dumb she must have sounded, talking about time travel. "Maybe I could have gotten Damien to leave the club and go somewhere else?" she said, unable to come up with a better answer. "I don't know. I guess if they both want to be with each other, there's nothing I can do to change that." Her chest panged at the undeniable truth, and she looked down at the table, forcing away tears that were threatening to emerge again.

"Exactly," Nick said, his voice soft and understanding. "It's not your fault."

"Right." Savannah tried to smile, but it felt fake. Being around Nick was helping her feel better, but the hurt from what Damien had done made her feel empty inside. Damien hadn't even bothered getting to know her. Maybe if he had, he would like her more than Madison.

"So, tell me something about yourself," Nick said, yanking Savannah out of her thoughts.

"Like what?"

"Umm… What do you want to do when you 'grow up'?"

"I want to be a singer." Savannah didn't have to think about her response.

Nick's lips parted, and Savannah could tell that she'd caught him by surprise. "What kind of singer?"

"Pop songs," she said, brightening at the turn of the conversation. "The stuff that's on the Top 40 radio stations. I've written a few songs, but nothing too great. I was thinking about making a YouTube account and singing covers—some people get discovered that way—but I haven't done it yet. I will, though."

"What are you waiting for?"

"I don't know." She twirled her straw around in her soda. "I guess I don't want people to think I'm not good."

He studied her. "Have you ever sung for anyone before?"

"My sisters," she said. No way was she going to tell him about the talent show disaster in eighth grade. "And my best friend, Evie, from home."

"And what did they think?"

"They're my sisters and my best friend. They *have* to say I'm good."

"They don't *have* to say anything," he told her. "If they say you're good, then you're good."

"You're just saying that to be nice." She smiled. "You can't know that."

"Not yet," he said. "But I will."

"You will?" Savannah played with her bangle bracelets, jingling them on her wrist. "Why do you say that?"

"You'll see." He placed some cash on the table for her soda. "Come with me, and don't ask any questions. I promise it'll be fun."

The Imperial Palace Hotel and Casino was a complete dump. Squished between Harrah's and the Flamingo, it was a square white building with blue siding that reminded Savannah of a papier-maché Japanese house. The inside was no better. Dust layered on top of the aging carpet, and everything reeked of smoke, like it was permanently ingrained in the furniture.

A singer wearing a skimpy, sparkly outfit belted out Christina Aguilera songs on a platform in the center of the casino, but no one paid attention to her. Which was sad, because she had a great voice. Savannah hoped that her singing career—once it got started—took her farther than that.

"Why are we here?" she asked Nick. After saying it, she felt bad for sounding like a snob. If her mom had taken her and her sisters here before she'd known she was Adrian Diamond's daughter, she would have been impressed. Still, it didn't make sense to be at the Imperial Palace when there were much better hotels on the Strip. She couldn't imagine Damien and his friends hanging out at a place like this. But she was supposed to be enjoying her time with Nick and *not* thinking about Damien, so maybe being here was good.

"You'll see," he said, his tone final. "Just follow me."

Savannah skirted around a drunk college kid holding a Busch Light. "I mean, no offense, but this place is a dump."

"Three days here and you've already been corrupted by the Vegas elite." Nick shook his head in fake mockery. "You know, expensive decorations don't mean the most fun."

"But they don't hurt," she said.

Nick stepped onto the bottom of a narrow escalator, and Savannah joined him. That was when she saw the sign overhead.

"No way," she said, shaking her head for emphasis. She looked over her shoulder, wanting to run back down the escalator, but a few people had gotten on behind them. "That is so not happening."

"How do you know where we're going?" he teased.

She crossed her arms but managed a small smile to let him know she wasn't totally annoyed. "It's kind of obvious. And I can tell you already. So. Not. Happening."

"You already said that." He laughed. "Relax. Some people I know are hanging out here, and I thought it could be fun. No pressure."

Savannah reluctantly followed him around the corner, and groaned when she saw another lit-up sign:

The Imperial Palace Karaoke Club.

Great. And if by *great* she meant *totally not what she ever felt like doing,* then, yeah. It was one thing to put up videos on YouTube—or in her case, *talk* about putting up videos on You-Tube—and totally different to perform live. She would panic and make a mistake, if not humiliate herself like she had in eighth grade. If Nick and his friends saw her mess up onstage, they would make fun of her all night and maybe longer. She would never hear the end of it. Dread twisted in her stomach.

"You can memorialize your performance on DVD if you'd like," Nick said.

"I won't have to worry about that, because there won't *be* a performance," she insisted. "At least not by me." Still, she followed him, lagging behind as she looked around in horror.

The Karaoke Club was more like a bar than a club. People of all ages surrounded the tables, the majority with large glasses of beer in front of them. On the stage, a group of guys wearing shirts with matching Greek letters were singing a slurred, off-key rendition of "Sweet Caroline." The crowd contributed to the song with the necessary "ba ba ba!" and "so good, so good!," pumping their fists or beer glasses in the air for emphasis. A few people were dancing next to their tables, and one girl was dancing *on* a table. She was chunky, and her clothes were too tight, but she was smiling so radiantly that none of that mattered.

The frat boys surrounded two microphones on the small stage, reading the lyrics from a screen. Which meant the words were in front of them.

With the words in front of her, it would be impossible for Savannah to forget them and look stupid.

Maybe she would give karaoke a try.

"Let's find a table," Nick said. "My friends aren't here yet, so we should save one before it gets packed."

They secured a table in the middle that had just cleared out. The college guys finished their song, and the DJ, Rusty Varney, brought on the next act—an older couple in matching Hawaiian shirts who chose "I Got You, Babe" by Sonny and Cher. They weren't great, but the crowd sang and danced along anyway.

"Do you come here a lot?" Savannah asked Nick. This didn't look like a place where kids who went to Goodman would hang out. No one wore the expensive designer clothing she saw on the people at Myst and Luxe. It had a relaxed atmosphere, and Savannah felt overdressed in her sequined blue minidress and tall heels.

"My brother and some of his friends got me into it," Nick replied, glancing at his beat-up flip phone that reminded Savannah of her own. Well, the one that was hers until the iPhone Adrian had ordered arrived to replace it. Finally she wouldn't feel like an outcast because she couldn't Instagram or Snapchat. "They'll be here soon."

"Does your brother go to Goodman?" Savannah asked.

"He did," Nick replied. "He graduated last year. In the fall he'll be a sophomore at UNLV."

Savannah remembered seeing signs on the way in from the airport for the University of Nevada Las Vegas. Then she did some calculations in her head. If Nick's brother was going to be a sophomore in college, that meant he was around nineteen or twenty. Would he want to hang out with a fifteen-year-old girl?

Probably not, but she would try not to worry about it. Nick wouldn't have brought her if he thought it would be a problem.

"So, are you going to pick a song?" Nick asked. He looked at the couple on stage, who had gone horribly off-key. "I'm sure your singing is better than *that*."

He was right, but it didn't stop her chest from tightening and her hands from shaking at the prospect of going onstage. "I guess it can't hurt to check out the songbook," she said, worry bubbling in her stomach. Then she reminded herself about the words on the screen. There was no way she could forget them.

"Go get 'em!" Nick said as she walked to the booth where Rusty Varney sat with the songbooks. He watched her as she flipped through the book, which had a startling 15,000 songs listed. Her breathing quickened with the awareness she was being watched.

"You look like a talented one," he said, his voice traced with a Spanish accent.

"Why do you say that?" Savannah pushed her hair behind her ears. She still wasn't used to her extensions.

"I do this every night." He winked. "Trust me, I can tell this sort of thing."

Savannah found the song she was searching for, and her hands continued to shake as she wrote it and her name on the slip of paper. She couldn't believe she was going through with this. DJ Rusty took it from her and smiled.

"Good choice," he told her. Then he looked at the couple onstage, who were reaching the end of their song. "You wanna go next? I don't normally bump people in line, but we're desperately in need of some talent right now."

Savannah froze. Was he serious? But she apparently didn't have a choice, because he hopped onstage and announced, "Next we've got the one and only Savannah Diamond singing 'I Love Rock and Roll'! Get on up here, Savannah, and show them what you've got!"

Everyone looked at her expectantly, and Savannah heard clapping from a table in the middle. Nick. She groaned inwardly, took the microphone, and watched the television screen for the words.

The music started, and Savannah focused on holding the microphone steady. Then she took a deep breath and started to sing, her eyes glued to the screen. But she knew the song by heart—it was on the "getting ready" playlist on her iPod to listen to when she was preparing to go out. She always danced around her room when it came on, posing in front of her mirror and using her hairbrush as a microphone.

The crowd quieted after the first line, and then the cheering began. Savannah was too wrapped up in the music to catch what people shouted, but she knew it was positive. But what showed her that the crowd loved her was that no one sang along. Instead they listened to her, like she was a real performer. She absorbed the encouraging cheers, unable to believe it. Even the "Sweet Caroline" frat boys danced along, waving their arms in the air during the chorus. For the first time, the anxiety Savannah had felt when she'd stepped onstage was replaced by the rush of performing.

When the song finished, she thanked everyone and rejoined Nick at the table, where he was waiting with a huge smile. Two older boys and a girl had joined him while she was onstage. Savannah assumed one of them was Nick's brother.

"You were awesome!" Nick said, giving her a high five. "Your sisters and friends weren't giving you enough credit if they only said that you're 'good.' You're a star."

"Nick's right," said the guy sitting next to him, holding out a hand to introduce himself. "I'm Ben, Nick's brother. You were great up there."

The family resemblance between the brothers was obvious. Ben had the same athletic build as Nick, but unlike most jocks Savannah knew, he wore a T-shirt with the name of a band Savannah hadn't heard of on it. He introduced the two people with him—his girlfriend, Lexie, and his best friend, Xander. They didn't seem to mind hanging out with high-schoolers, but Savannah still felt young when they talked about college.

Xander went to the bar and brought back two pitchers of beer, filling up glasses and passing them around. Savannah tried not to look grossed out. She didn't like the taste of beer, but it was generous of Xander to buy it for everyone. She drank hers slowly, hoping they didn't notice.

She mostly listened to the conversation, but they were friendly, which was more relaxing than talking with Damien, Madison and the rest of that crew. Savannah deflated at the thought of Damien, but while the memory of him kissing Madison still hurt, she didn't feel as terrible as she had an hour ago. She was having fun listening to drunk people butcher karaoke songs as she and everyone around her danced and sang along.

After Nick had a few beers, he agreed to do a duet with her—"Summer Nights" from *Grease*. He wasn't good enough to take up singing as a career, but he was energetic onstage, and the crowd loved him. He grabbed Savannah's hand when they finished, holding it up in the air and thanking the crowd, repeating her name to make sure they didn't forget it.

"You're kind of awesome, Savannah Diamond," he whispered in her ear.

Savannah didn't know what to think. Was he interested in her as more than a friend? When they were talking about

Madison earlier it hadn't sounded like he was over her, but it was impossible to tell. And more important—was Savannah interested in Nick? He was a great guy, but while the hurt from Damien's actions had waned over the course of the night, it was still there. It would probably return full force the next time she saw him.

She wouldn't be able to avoid him forever.

chapter 22: *Courtney*

The charity dinner with Oliver didn't go as poorly as Courtney had anticipated. The coral cocktail dress that Savannah had insisted she buy received loads of compliments—even Ellen Prescott liked it. Many people offered her glasses of champagne throughout the night, but Courtney stuck to soda. Oliver ordered soda as well, since his parents were watching him, but he spiked it using the flask hidden in his jacket. He'd asked Courtney if she wanted some, and she'd declined.

In the beginning of the night everyone was mingling, and Courtney felt out of place, since she didn't know anyone. But Rebecca spent a lot of time with her, introducing her to so many people there was no way Courtney would be able to keep their names straight. It was a pleasant break when Ellen and some other women who had planned the event spoke after dinner, and Courtney was proud to support a good cause. But while she felt good being there, she also wanted a more hands-on way to contribute to the community. She would have to ask Rebecca about that later.

Oliver spent the night drinking and giving her the dirty details on everyone at the event. Half the women there were cheating on their husbands, and there were two politicians in attendance accused of accepting bribes from a strip club owner. Now they were both on the brink of impeachment. Courtney did her best to listen, but she didn't have much to add, and she found the gossip slightly mind-numbing.

Now she and Oliver were getting into the town car that would drop her back off at the Diamond, and she wondered how he could stand after all the drinks he'd had throughout the night. He had to be wasted, but she got the impression he drank so much that he either had a liver of steel or was a master at hiding it.

"You're not planning on going back to your condo, right?" Oliver asked.

"Where else would I go?" Courtney checked her watch. It was 11:00 p.m.—the time she started getting ready for bed at home.

"The rooftop club at the Palms." He looked at her like she should have already known this.

Courtney was exhausted—meeting so many people and listening to Oliver gossip about the scandals of the Vegas elite had tired her out more than she'd realized. "I'm just going to go back and get some sleep," she said, not caring if Oliver thought it sounded lame.

"Come on." He slung his arm around her shoulders, his brown eyes softening.

He must have taken her silence as a yes, because the next thing she knew he had smashed his lips to hers and was trying to force his tongue into her mouth. Courtney pulled back immediately. She didn't want her first kiss to be with Oliver, a guy she had nothing in common with and who reeked of alcohol. She'd thought he wasn't interested in her and had only invited her because his mom made him. Apparently she was wrong.

"What are you doing?" She wiped her mouth and leaned as far away from him as possible.

He looked distraught at her rejection, but he pulled himself together. "Sorry," he said. "I shouldn't have moved so fast. That was stupid of me. I thought you liked me…but I guess I was wrong. I promise it won't happen again."

Courtney scooted closer to the door. She had never had a guy come on to her so strongly before. At least he was apologetic, and he seemed genuinely sorry. He'd probably misread her signals because of how much he'd had to drink. "I really am tired," she said, praying he would get the point. "It's not that I don't like you… I'm just interested in someone else. Someone I can't be with."

Oliver's eyes flashed with understanding. "Someone from California?"

She nodded, feeling bad about the lie. But it seemed the safest route. She couldn't exactly admit to Oliver that she had feelings for Brett.

"Well, that sucks," he said.

"Yeah." Courtney agreed. "But thanks for inviting me to the dinner tonight."

"I had a great time with you," he said. "And I've been waiting to ask you… Do you want to go to the grand opening of the Diamond with me? Just as friends, of course. Our dads will be announcing their new hotel in Macau, so it will look good for the two of us to be there together. Plus, it would make our parents happy. I wasn't *that* bad of company tonight, right?"

Courtney hadn't seen that one coming. If Oliver hadn't apologized for making moves on her... But he had, and he did sound sorry. Plus, he had promised her it would only be as friends. Being seen with him would ensure that no one suspected her feelings for Brett. It was the perfect cover.

"Okay," she said tentatively. "That would be nice."

"I think so, too," he said as the chauffeur pulled the town car up to the Diamond Residences. "I'll see you tomorrow night?"

"See you then." Courtney stepped out of the car, shooting Oliver one last forced smile.

All she could think about was how she felt like she was betraying Brett. Which was silly, since nothing was going on between them. He had said so himself.

She walked toward the elevators, and then she saw him.

Brett was in the Lobby Bar, a bottle of beer on the table in front of him. It was in her best interest to avoid spending time with him—her feelings for him would grow if she did—but it would be rude if she didn't say hi.

Perhaps this was fate's way of intervening.

She pushed the thought from her mind. If fate wanted to be kind to her, she and Brett wouldn't be step-siblings in a matter of months.

"Hi," she said when she approached his table, playing with her hands in front of her. She didn't sit down—he was probably meeting someone there, and she didn't want to intrude.

She hoped it wasn't a girl.

"You look nice," he said. "Did you have fun with Oliver Prescott?" His bitterness took Courtney by surprise.

"It was okay." She shrugged and bit her lip.

He studied her as he took another swig of his beer. "You don't sound so sure about that."

"Oliver's nice," she said. "But I'm not interested in him as more than a friend."

Brett motioned her to sit in the chair next to him. She did. "It's rare that girls say that about Oliver," he said. "What kind of guys *are* you interested in, then?"

"Well…" Courtney crossed her legs, trying to figure out how to say this politely without insulting Oliver to Brett. "Oliver likes going to clubs and other places involving crowds of people and drinking. I prefer activities that are one-on-one, when I can have fun without being drunk." Brett chuckled, and she blushed. "Not that I've ever been drunk," she said. "But I like going to dinner and on walks and to the movies and things like that."

"And to shows?" he asked, watching her closer. "Like *Phantom of the Opera?*"

"Like that," she said. "I like people who I can talk to—people who have similar interests to mine."

"And Oliver doesn't," Brett concluded.

"Not from what I've seen of him so far."

He was quiet for a few seconds. "Do you want to get out of here?" he finally asked.

The change of conversation caught Courtney by surprise. "And go where?"

"Hmm. Have you ever been to Paris?"

"No." Courtney was confused. "But I've always wanted to go there."

"Well, we have a mini-Paris on the Strip," he said. "Are you ready to continue our world traveling?"

He sounded so excited—was she wrong that he wasn't interested in her? Because he was watching her like it would crush him if she said no. The thought that he might see her as more of a friend sent her heart racing, and the tiredness she'd felt in the car with Oliver evaporated. "Do you mind if I go upstairs and change first?" she asked. "These heels aren't meant to be worn for more than a few hours."

He told her he would wait there for her, and she headed to the elevators, stealing one last glance at Brett as she turned the corner.

This night was about to get way better than she'd anticipated.

Courtney was glad Peyton had her door closed and Savannah wasn't in the condo, so she could change as quickly as possible. She wouldn't want her sisters to ask where she was going, or worse, invite themselves along. Kicking the heels off, she happily changed into skinny jeans, a deep pink spaghetti-strap top and, of course, her flip-flops. Then she applied clear lip gloss and headed out the door.

She couldn't believe she'd said yes to Brett's invitation. It would have made more sense to tell him she was tired and wanted to go to sleep so she wasn't exhausted for the grand opening tomorrow night. But she couldn't bring herself to do it. She would regret it too much if she didn't go with him tonight.

Of course, going to Paris together didn't mean anything romantic would happen between her and Brett—even though it *was* the city of love. Still, there was no denying that she wanted something to happen. She couldn't ignore it for much longer.

But she would have to try.

She stepped out of the elevator and found Brett waiting for her.

"You couldn't wait to change out of that dress," he said when he saw her. "You look more comfortable now."

"I am," she said. "I've never been a big dress wearer. That's more Savannah. You should see how many she bought when we went to the mall…. She'll have a lifetime supply." She had also spent enough money to pay their rent in California for months, but Courtney didn't feel comfortable sharing that information.

"You act like the mall is torture." Brett laughed. "I'm sure your dad will be happy that Savannah's enjoying herself. Besides, I thought every girl liked buying new dresses."

"Trust me, no one needs as many as Savannah bought," Courtney said. "I gave in to a few because I didn't want to be underdressed for seeing *Phantom* and going to fancy dinners, but I would be happy wearing jeans and flip-flops everywhere."

"For the record, I think you look great in anything you wear." Brett held the door open, and she walked through, smiling at his comment.

The drive to Paris was short, and the hotel was hard to miss, with its blue chateau roof and replica Eiffel Tower in front. Courtney pressed her hand against the window and admired the tower. Bright lights glowed from the inside, and she craned her neck to look to the top.

"Is it an exact replica?" she asked Brett.

"It's smaller," he said. "And the real one looks bigger since it's not surrounded by huge hotels. They made a rule in Paris that no building is allowed to be taller than the Tower. You'll love it when you go."

"*When* I go," Courtney said in disbelief. She'd imagined days spent in the Louvre admiring timeless masterpieces, venturing inside the Paris Opera House that inspired *Phantom of the Opera* and going to the top of the Eiffel Tower, but it had always been a dream.

"What are you doing in August?" Brett asked as they drove

under a replica of the Arc de Triomphe. It looked more beautiful than in pictures, and this was only a copy. She couldn't imagine what it would be like to see the real one.

"I guess I'll be here," she said. She liked having an organized schedule, but she didn't plan *that* far in advance. "There are a few books I want to read this summer before I'm bogged down by homework in the fall. I also have to get in SAT practice. I've got the reading and vocab sections down pretty well, but I need to work on math. And I want to volunteer somewhere, since Adrian won't let me get a job, but I still need to figure out where. Why?"

"Set aside a week," he said, stopping the car in front of the hotel. "Because we're going to Paris."

"What do you mean, we're going to Paris?"

"You want to see Paris, so we should go to Paris. Bring your sisters, too."

"Just like that?"

"Just like that," he said. "But for now, we should enjoy the Paris we have here."

As in most of the hotels in Vegas, the main entrance of Paris led straight into the casino. This was the most original one Courtney had seen yet. Two of the legs of the Eiffel Tower sprawled from outside and into the center of the lobby, and wrought-iron street lamps displayed signs directing tourists around the hotel. The blue-cushioned chairs in front of the slot machines and game tables were in the traditional French style, the ceiling was painted like the daytime sky and a huge white stone bridge that Courtney recognized as Le Pont Alexandre III hung from the ceiling.

"You like it?" Brett asked.

"It's beautiful," she said, looking around in admiration.

"Before coming to Vegas, I never knew hotels could be like this. Each one is like its own city."

"Vegas is different from any other place in the world," he agreed. "So are you up for going to the top of the Eiffel Tower?"

"We can do that?" Courtney asked. "It's not only for decoration?"

"Of course we can," he said with a laugh. "Come on. It's this way."

Brett purchased their tickets from the counter, and they took the elevator ride up the Eiffel Tower.

"Wow." Courtney stepped up to the railing and admired the Las Vegas Strip. The hotels were all lit up, the screens blinking, the cars like organized fireflies as they drove down the street. The city was always in motion. "This is beautiful."

"The Bellagio fountain show is about to start," Brett said, leading her to the front of the observation room. "Let's watch."

Courtney looked at the Bellagio, a tall, wide hotel painted in crèmes with a large lake in front of it. The unmistakable first riffs of "My Heart Will Go On" from the movie *Titanic* played from speakers around the lake, and the surface lit up, coming to life. Water shot up from formations below—a long arc, a huge double-rimmed circle and smaller circles all around—dancing to the song. It was like magic.

Other couples watched from the observation deck, holding hands, leaning against each other, or touching in some way. Brett stood so close to her that his body heat radiated against her arm. If she moved the slightest bit, her skin would touch his.

She glanced away from the fountain to look at him. His eyes met hers, and her breath caught at the intensity of his gaze. Her cheeks heated, and she refocused on the fountains, her heart racing through the rest of the song. In the crescendo the water exploded high into the sky, to the rhythm of the music. Then the song ended, the water calming, and everyone clapped in appreciation.

"I never knew fountains could do that." Courtney broke the silence between her and Brett. "That was wonderful."

"I'm glad you liked it." He leaned his elbows on the railing and looked at her. "You know, I don't know what you were like in California, but you seem really happy here."

"I guess I am," Courtney said, surprised at the realization. "I miss my mom—and I definitely miss my grandma—but for the most part, living at home was hard. I know my mom is better off in rehab, and I'm starting to wonder if I might be happier here in Vegas."

"I can't imagine what it must have been like for you," Brett said. "Having to deal with your mom's situation."

"It got really bad a year ago, but the turning point was about two years ago," Courtney said, looking over at the lake where the fountains had danced minutes ago. "I remember the exact day when I realized she was only going to get worse."

"What happened?" he asked. "You don't have to tell me, but you can if you want to."

"This isn't a story I normally share, but I'll tell you." She took a deep breath and started. "It was the summer before my freshman year of high school. I was fourteen, Savannah was thirteen and Peyton was fifteen, so our mom had to drive us to Walmart to get school supplies. She spent more money than she intended to, and she was in an awful mood on the drive home. Then Savannah and Peyton started fighting over the radio station—Savannah wanted to listen to Top 40, and Peyton wanted rock. It blew up into a war between them.

"My mom got fed up with their yelling, and she pulled over

at a gas station, telling us to get out of the car for a thirty-minute time-out. She didn't notice that I wasn't involved in the fight, so I had to go with them. She told us to work it out, that she would be back soon, and she took off. At first Savannah and Peyton kept fighting. When almost an hour passed, we got worried about when Mom would come back. A few more hours passed without any sign of her, and it was starting to get dark. We discussed walking home, but we were afraid Mom would show up soon and when we weren't there we would be in more trouble for leaving. So the three of us were stuck at the gas station, sitting at a picnic table, hungry because we didn't have any money. Finally a nice man gave us sandwiches and soda for dinner. He called our grandma, and she picked us up. We found our mom at a nearby bar. She'd had so much to drink that she'd forgotten to come back and get us."

"Wow." Brett looked sad, like hearing the story had really upset him. "That sounds awful. I'm sorry you had to go through that. You deserve better."

"Thanks," she said. "I know our mom loves us, but she has a hard enough time taking care of herself, let alone three kids. Our grandma bought us cell phones the next day and paid for the monthly bill, because she didn't want us to be left alone like that again."

"It sounds like you get along well with your grandma."

"I do." Courtney smiled. "Grandma's told me—in secret, of course—that out of my sisters and me, I remind her the most of herself. She's hardworking and kind, so hearing that meant a lot."

"I hope she can visit you here soon," Brett said.

"I would love that, but her sister—they're twins—is really sick right now. Cancer," she explained. "It doesn't look good. Grandma's taking care of her, so I doubt she'll be able to visit until…" She shook her head, not wanting to say the only possible outcome out loud.

"I understand," he said. "I'm sorry I made you bring this all up."

"Don't be." Courtney smiled, attempting to lighten the conversation. "It feels good to talk about with someone. And this is going to sound awful, but I think it's been helpful for me to be here, in Vegas, where all of those problems feel so far away."

"That doesn't sound awful," Brett said. "It makes perfect sense."

"Thanks." For a moment neither of them spoke, their eyes locked on each other's. "So, what else is in the Paris Hotel?"

"How do you feel about strolling the streets?" he asked. "The ones inside, of course."

"I'd love to," Courtney said, intrigued.

They took the elevator back down, and walked through the hotel. It really felt like Paris—or at least how Courtney had pictured it. Three-story buildings lined the walls, with windows on the outside so it felt like walking down a winding street. Just like in the casino, the ceiling was painted like the daytime sky, and the floor was dark gray cobblestone, with wrought-iron street lamps down the center. Lining the "streets" were restaurants that looked like cute Parisian cafés with gated patios, giving the illusion of eating outside.

"Let's get drinks," Brett decided. "It's time for you to have a *real* Vegas drink."

"What do you mean?" Courtney asked.

"I mean we're playing tourist," he said, strolling up to a blue window with a wooden sign above it that said *Le Petit Bar.* "Two Eiffel Tower drinks, please," he ordered, pointing at the foot-tall plastic Eiffel Tower on display.

"You can't be serious." She stared at the plastic Eiffel Towers meant for *drinks*. No human being could finish that much liquid without feeling like they were about to explode.

"Strawberry daiquiri or piña colada?"

"Do those have alcohol?" she asked. "Because I don't drink—"

"We'll get virgin drinks," he said. "The point is for the souvenir glass. And to walk around Vegas with a super-tall drink. Come on, it'll be fun."

The glass *was* funny, in a ridiculous way. "Okay," she agreed. "I'll have a daiquiri."

Brett got a piña colada, and they walked down the cobblestone path, each holding an Eiffel Tower glass almost the length of Courtney's arm. It was heavy and hard to hold, but the sweet drink did taste good. They continued like that, looking into the shops and restaurants, until they stopped at a huge circular fountain with water flowing down three tiers of stone.

"A wishing fountain!" Courtney exclaimed, not caring that she sounded like a little kid. "Do you have a penny?"

Brett dug a coin out of his wallet. "No pennies, but I have a euro," he said, handing it to her. "Which means your wish will definitely come true."

"Are you sure you're okay getting rid of this?" Courtney had never seen a euro before. Silver inside and ringed with gold, it was prettier than any American coin. Surely he'd want to keep it.

"I'm positive," he told her, closing her fingers around the coin. "In fact, I'll be disappointed if you don't take it. Then your wish will be wasted, and that would be a tragedy."

"How do you know it would be a tragedy if you don't know what I'm going to wish for?" she asked, although all she could focus on was how warm his fingers felt around hers.

"Because any wish of yours is something you deserve."

Courtney studied the euro in her hand. One wish. Maybe this would be *the* magical wish—the one that would come true, like in a book or a movie. She knew that didn't happen in real life, but maybe this once it would be fun to pretend.

She never did things like this in Fairfield, but in Las Vegas with Brett, she felt like a different person. She didn't have to make sure her mom was sober when Savannah got home, help with the bills or worry that she wouldn't have enough time after work to do a good job with her homework. She felt...free.

And she loved it.

There were so many things Courtney could wish for, but she tossed the coin over her shoulder and thought, *I wish everything will work out between me and Brett.*

It couldn't hurt to dream.

Chapter 23: *Peyton*

Peyton's new iPhone ringing from her nightstand woke her up on Thursday morning. She hated the fancy new phone—it was pointless, especially since her flip phone worked fine. Why would she need to check her email or go online when she was out? But texting was easier with the keyboard, so she'd given in and was using it.

She checked the clock, surprised it was 9:30 a.m. Who was calling her so early? Plus, she felt awful. How come Courtney and Savannah had been out having fun last night in Vegas, but she'd been having the worst time ever? It had only been a few days, and her sisters were already changing from who they'd been in California. Peyton couldn't believe either of them. And after what Oliver had said to her last night at Luxe, she wanted to lie in bed with the lights off and never talk to anyone ever again.

Oliver hadn't even texted her to apologize. She'd just watched crappy television shows when she'd gotten home from the club, ordering room service when she got hungry. She wanted to stay in her room forever. Anything so she wouldn't have to face Oliver again. Or Jackson, who would probably say how he told her so the moment she left the condo.

She hadn't programmed the numbers from her old phone into her new phone yet, so she had no idea who was calling. All she recognized was the 707 Fairfield area code.

"Hello?" she mumbled into the phone, hoping it was someone she wanted to talk to.

"Peyton?" Mike. She cursed for picking up. "Did you get my calls last night? Or any of my texts?"

"My cell service is awful here," she lied. "Sorry about that. What's up?" She tried to sound perky, even though the last thing she wanted to do was talk to Mike. But since he had cornered her, she might as well get it over with and break up with him. He had to know it was coming.

"I was worried when I couldn't get ahold of you," he said. "So I caught the first flight this morning, and just landed in Vegas. I've been saving a lot from work this summer, and the flight was pretty cheap since it was so early. I wanted to see how you're doing."

Peyton wanted to throw her phone out the window. That was the last thing she expected him to say. He must have noticed she'd been avoiding him. Knowing Mike, he thought that any distance Peyton was feeling would go away the moment she saw him again. He *would* think a stupid romantic thing like that.

"Are you serious?" she asked, even though she knew he was. So much for breaking up over the phone.

"Of course I'm serious." He sounded less confident than he had before. "Is now a bad time?"

"No, it's fine," she lied. "Get a cab to the Diamond Residences. The driver will know where it is. I'll meet you in the lobby."

She pressed the end button, and walked to her full-length mirror to see how bad she looked. Her skin was dull and dry, and she had huge circles under her eyes from how terribly she'd slept last night.

Still, she should try to look decent. She took off her pajamas and changed into her favorite frayed jean shorts and a black tank top. She dabbed concealer under her eyes, brushed her hair and put on eyeliner, mascara and red lip gloss. Her hair still wasn't the greatest, but the airport was less than ten minutes away, so she couldn't shower before Mike arrived. She supposed she was going for the grunge look today.

She dragged herself out of the condo, and standing in the hall was the last person she wanted to see—Jackson. He had every right to be smug, since he had warned her away from Oliver and ended up being right about him—but she was *so* not in the mood for an "I told you so" right now.

"Leaving the condo so early?" he asked. Strangely enough, he looked…concerned. Did he actually care that Oliver had been a jerk to her?

"I didn't have a choice," Peyton said. "My boyfriend decided to show up. In Vegas. Right now." She ran her fingers through her hair. "I can't believe this is happening to me."

"You mean you haven't told Mike that it's over?" Jackson looked confused.

"How do you know about Mike?" she snapped.

He put his hands in the air and stepped backward. "I was your bodyguard for a few months before you moved to Vegas," he reminded her. "I wouldn't be doing my job if I didn't know about the guy you were seeing in California. And he never seemed right for you, so I assumed you had broken up with him already."

"I've been meaning to." Peyton examined her nails like they were the most fascinating things on the planet. "I just haven't gotten around to it yet."

"There's no time like the present," Jackson said with a chuckle.

"What's it to you?" she asked. "Don't you have more important things to worry about than my love life?"

"Actually, since a lot of the danger women today face is from the men they date, your love life is one of my prime concerns," Jackson said. Unfortunately, Peyton had a feeling he was only half kidding.

She glanced at her watch. Mike would be here any minute. "If you'll excuse me, I have some breaking up to do." She tried to act nonchalant, but she was fuming inside. What was Jackson's deal? One day he didn't want to be friends with her, the next she could have sworn there was something sparking between them and now he was acting like an annoying older brother. She wished he could decide what he wanted their relationship to be—if he wanted them to have one at all.

"Lead the way," Jackson said, motioning down the hall.

Peyton huffed and marched to the elevator. Of course, Jackson waited next to her, and stepped into it with her. She pressed the button for the lobby and was silent as the doors closed.

"Nervous about the big breakup?" he asked.

It took all of Peyton's effort not to hit him. Not like that would have been effective, since he was trained in self-defense.

"No," she said, keeping her eyes trained on the doors. Jackson didn't seem inclined to continue the conversation. That was fine with Peyton, because one major thought haunted her

mind: What was she going to say to Mike? She hated breaking up with guys, but it was a necessary evil of life.

She didn't have time to worry about it, because Mike
stepped into the lobby right after she got there. The awe on
his round face reminded Peyton of when Savannah had first
seen the hotel: like it was his first trip to Wonderland or Oz
or some other magical place.

He caught her eyes, and she waved, plastering a smile on
her face that she hoped was convincing. Jackson trailed far
behind her; no one watching would have any idea the two of
them knew each other.

"Is this for real?" Mike asked after greeting her.

"Vegas?" Peyton asked. "Yeah, it's real. The city is different from Fairfield, I know—"

"That's not what I mean," he interrupted. "But anyway, I
missed you." He said the last part more softly, and he really
meant it. Peyton wished she could honestly say the same in
return.

"Thanks," she said, and his eyes flashed with hurt. She
shoved her hands into her back pockets, unsure what to say
next.

With the jingling music of the slot machines behind them,
this should have been the perfect reunion. Instead, it was like
the machines were laughing at her, taunting her. Like they
knew what was coming, just as they knew the tourists who
gambled were probably going to lose. The coins jingling, chips
clacking and machines dinging swirled around in her mind
until she felt like her head was going to explode.

She needed a drink.

"Let's sit down," she said, motioning to the Lobby Bar.

He tensed up, like he realized what was about to happen.
"Sure," he said. "Sounds good."

The waitress walked up to them and smiled. "Good morning," she said. "Would you like to order some drinks?"

"I'll have a mimosa—light on the orange juice," Peyton said.

"Can I see some ID?" the waitress asked skeptically.

Peyton handed her the fake she'd gotten a few months ago—it had her picture but a different name—and sat back in her chair, trying to play it cool.

The waitress examined it for a few seconds longer than felt comfortable, and handed it back to her, her lips set in a line. "You can either order a soft drink, or I can bring that to the back, scan it and have to report you if the scan shows it's fake. Your call."

Peyton's throat constricted, and she took the ID back, shoving it into her pocket. It always worked at gas stations back home, but the gas stations at home never scanned. Looked like she would have to get a better ID. In the meantime, she ordered an orange juice. So much for that liquid confidence during the breakup.

"What do you want?" she asked Mike. "It's on me."

"Umm…" He looked uneasy. "A Sprite is fine."

The waitress walked away, and Peyton knew the questions were about to begin.

"Do you live here?" he asked, bewildered as he looked around. His eyes stopped at the statue in the center of the room—the golden one of the woman with tree branches coming out of her hands and head until they connected with the ceiling. Then he looked at Peyton again, waiting for her response.

"Yeah."

"Are you serious?"

"Yep." Peyton watched the waitress place her drink in front

of her, taking a long sip before turning her eyes back up to Mike's.

He looked like he was going to explode with curiosity, but he managed to calmly ask, "Is everything okay?"

Starting was the worst part about breaking up with someone. She would just have to numb her feelings and do it, like when ripping off a Band-Aid. "We can't see each other anymore," she blurted out.

He froze, his eyes wide. "Why not?"

"I don't want to do the long-distance thing," she explained. "I'm sorry."

"You can't mean that." He leaned forward and shook his head. "You're just worried about it, and with all of these changes in your life I can't blame you, but it'll be fine. I promise."

"I do mean it." Her voice was hard.

He was silent, and that hurt Peyton more than anything he could have said. "Did you cheat on me?" he finally asked, his voice wavering.

Peyton looked down and played with the frayed ends of her jean shorts.

His eyes hardened. "I'll take that as a yes."

"My life is different now," she said. "We have to move on. It wasn't going to work out between us, anyway."

"It could have worked out if you wanted it to."

"But I *didn't* want it to." It sounded mean, but she had to make him understand that he couldn't change her mind.

He let out a long breath. "I shouldn't have expected anything else from you," he said. "I was stupid to think you would be different with me."

"You're not stupid," Peyton said softly. "Things changed is all. If I hadn't moved here…"

"Then what?" he asked, his voice rising in anger. "Then we would still be together? Screw it, Peyton. If you wanted us to be together, we would have found a way to make it work, no matter where in the world we were."

"You're right," she admitted. "I'm sorry."

"Stop apologizing." He sighed and looked up at the ceiling. "I just wish you had let me know before now. Then I wouldn't have had to fly all the way out here. You didn't even let me know where you were—I had to ask your grandma. And don't give me that crap about not getting cell reception. I don't believe it."

"I know," she said, irritated. "But you should have waited for me to respond to your calls before coming out here."

"And you should have let me know you wanted to break up *before* you cheated on me!" He was practically screaming now, and people at other tables stared at him. "I should get going," he said, returning his voice to a normal volume. "And you're right, I *should* have expected this from you. Stupid to think you would be happy to see me when you've been too busy living it up in Vegas to remember my existence."

"It wasn't like that." Peyton shrank at how lame it sounded.

"Oh, yeah?" he challenged. "Then what *was* it like?"

She lowered her eyes, knowing he was right. "Let me buy you a plane ticket home," she offered, opening her wallet and handing him a few hundreds she had put in there before heading downstairs. She hated using Adrian's money, but this was an emergency. "This should be enough to cover your flight here and a ticket back to California."

"I don't want your money." He looked at the bills in distaste, but Peyton placed them on the table anyway. "It's not even yours. I never took you as one for charity, Peyton."

"It's not *charity,*" Peyton said, clenching her jaw in anger. "You would want me to take it if you were in my situation."

"But I'm not in your situation, am I? And if I were, I wouldn't have cheated on you with one of the other brats around here."

"You have no idea what you're talking about," Peyton said. "Just go home, okay?"

He shook his head, pushed the money away and walked out the doors. Peyton's heart sank as the hurt in his eyes played in her mind over and over again. It must have been the same way she'd looked when she'd found out about Vince cheating on her years ago. And here she was, doing the same thing to Mike. He didn't deserve it—no one did—but she couldn't change what she'd done. She'd thought building a tough skin and being the one who ended things before they got too serious would make her immune to feeling the pain of being dumped ever again. And sure, she didn't feel as low as she had after finding out about Vince, but she didn't feel happy, either.

Maybe with this fresh start in Vegas, it was time to make some changes.

Now she was left alone in the Lobby Bar, with a half-finished orange juice and Mike's empty Sprite. The waitress collected the glass, and Peyton asked for the check. She did an imaginary toast with the girl/tree statue and took a long sip of her drink. Then she spotted Jackson across the room, his hazel eyes watching her intently. Like he wanted to come over and talk to her.

She held his gaze for a few seconds, then motioned for him to join her. He didn't move, and she thought he would continue standing there, doing a crappy job of trying to ignore her. But then, after what appeared to be an intense emotional battle, he slowly walked toward her.

"I take from what I saw that you managed to get your point across?" he asked once he had arrived next to her chair.

"If you want to join me, you can," Peyton said. "You don't have to stand there awkwardly."

Jackson glanced around nervously, as if he could get in trouble for socializing with the daughter of his employer. Finally he sat down in the seat vacated by Mike. The waitress came over to see if he wanted anything, and he ordered a Mountain Dew. She guessed that his drinking alcohol on the job would be frowned upon—if he drank at all. He struck her as the straight-edge type.

"So you and Mike are over?" Jackson asked again. He must be really curious about what had happened. Peyton didn't know why he cared, but she wanted to talk with someone, and Jackson was here and listening. Why not talk to him?

She ran through the entire conversation with Mike. "It must sound like I've got serious commitment issues," she said when she finished, managing a small laugh even though it wasn't actually funny.

"I wouldn't say that," Jackson said.

"Then what *would* you say?"

"It sounds like you're a seventeen-year-old girl who's figuring out what she wants. Most seventeen-year-olds aren't in long-distance relationships, Peyton. It's normal for you to want to end things with Mike, especially since you weren't with him for a long time before you moved."

"At least when you say it that way I don't sound like a heartless bitch."

Jackson looked pissed. "Did Mike say that to you?"

"Not directly...but he implied it."

"You got hurt when you were younger," Jackson said. "It sucks, but you'll get past it."

Peyton clenched her fists and sipped her drink to cool down. "How do you know about Vince?" she asked. She never talked about Vince—except to Oliver at the club last night. Had Jackson listened to their conversation? He was supposed to watch out for her, but she didn't like the idea of *anyone* listening to her private conversations.

"I read your file," he said. She got angrier at the notion of having a file—*and* having someone read it—but he continued before she could speak. "I had to read your file before starting as your bodyguard, since knowing as much as possible about you helps me keep you safe."

"That's so...intrusive." She sat back, crossing her arms over her chest. "What sort of things are in my file?"

Jackson cleared his throat, looking guilty about bringing it up. "Normal things," he said. "Nothing too personal. It's an overview of your schedule, your personality, what to expect from you, and any past events that were important in your life. It helps us understand who we're protecting. But remember, it's all for your safety. Everything your father has done is because he can't stand the idea of you or your sisters getting hurt because of your connection to him."

"So he says." Peyton rolled her eyes. "Any chance I can see this file of mine?"

"I can't do that," he said. "Sorry. I wasn't even supposed to tell you about it."

"Figured as much," Peyton said. "But it couldn't hurt to ask." Still, she wouldn't forget she had a file. If there was any way for her to find it and read it, she would. But she had a feeling Jackson wouldn't budge right now, so she had to change tactics. "How did you get into being a bodyguard?" she asked. "No offense, but you seem young to be doing this."

"I've been doing martial arts since I was six," Jackson said proudly. "Became one of the best in the country by the time I was sixteen, won national awards and made it to international competitions. I could have competed professionally, but I wanted to use my skills to help others, so long story short, here I am."

"So if someone tried to hurt me, you could karate chop them to death?" Peyton did a fake karate move with her hand.

"Something like that," he said with a chuckle. "But hopefully you won't get into a situation where that would be necessary."

"And you're from Vegas?"

"Nope," Jackson said. "Omaha, Nebraska."

Peyton was mid-drink when he said that, and she laughed so hard that her juice went up her nose. "You really grew up in Nebraska?" she asked once she stopped choking. It was smack in the middle of the country, and the one place she and her sisters had always joked about probably being worse to live than Fairfield.

"Born and raised."

"Did you grow up on a farm?"

"For your information, Omaha is a real city. Tall buildings and all."

"So you lived in the city?"

"Well, my parents owned land nearby," he said sheepishly. "And we might have had some livestock. But we weren't *too* far from the city."

"And the truth comes out!" Peyton joked.

"Just don't tell anyone." He leaned back in his chair, looking more at ease than Peyton had seen him yet. "I wouldn't want you to ruin my reputation."

They chatted until they finished their drinks and Jackson had to return to his post. Peyton headed back up to the condo to watch a movie. She asked him to join her, but as she'd expected, he declined her offer. Still, after the Mike disaster it was nice to hang out with Jackson, talking like they were real friends. For the first time since arriving, she felt relaxed in Las Vegas.

Now all she had to worry about was what was going to happen with Oliver when she saw him at the grand opening. She had stupidly taken his bet and not told Courtney about what had happened between them. But she would win. She knew her sister, and Courtney would never be interested in Oliver.

She couldn't wait to shove it in his face tomorrow night.

Chapter 24: *Madison*

Madison woke up on Thursday morning with a pounding headache. Her mouth felt dry, and she could taste the alcohol from last night. Her stomach swirled from the reminder of how much she'd drunk. Her body felt like jelly, and she wanted to lay in bed forever until she felt better.

I'm never drinking again, she thought, rolling over and tossing her arm to the side of the bed.

That was when she hit something—some*one*—and memories from last night poured back to her. Damien, and how she'd kissed him in front of everyone at Luxe. How excited he was when he'd kissed her back, and how she might have liked it. The horrified look on Savannah Diamond's face as she saw them together, and how Madison saw Nick talking with Savannah as she ran out of the club, made worse by the way he looked *interested* in whatever she was saying and left with her. It made her hate Savannah even more.

After seeing that, she'd drunk more with Damien…and

the rest of the night was blank. She only knew she'd gotten a hotel room at the Gates with him later that night because she recognized the style of the room from after-parties Oliver had thrown last year.

What had she gotten herself into? Her lungs tightened, and the walls spun, like they were going to close in around her. She shut her eyes, as if doing so could make everything that had happened last night go away. If only she could teleport out of there and never see Damien again.

On top of it all, her parents were going to *kill* her for not coming home last night.

What had happened between her and Damien after they'd gone up to the hotel room? She would know if she'd lost her virginity to him—right? She would feel it? She'd heard the first time hurt, and she felt okay in that area. Also, Damien would want her to be sober before making a huge decision like that. Not like she would ever sleep with Damien in the first place.

Still, that didn't stop her from worrying.

She opened her eyes and saw Damien's sleeping face. His dark hair was matted to his forehead in a way he would never allow to happen in public, and he looked happy. More memories of kissing him passed through Madison's mind—he was a great kisser—and heat spread through her body. Which was absurd. She couldn't have feelings for Damien Sanders.

Now that they'd kissed, there was no way things between them would stay the same.

This was why she never allowed herself to get drunk. She had to take control of the situation—now. But first she had to brush her teeth. If she had to taste any more alcohol, she was going to throw up.

She slid out of the king-size bed and walked into the bathroom, shutting the door quietly behind her. The first thing she saw was the mirror, and luckily her reflection wasn't horrible. She'd taken her dress off before going to sleep, and she was glad she'd worn the Le Mystere black lace bra and underwear set she'd bought a few weeks ago. She placed her hands on her hips and posed like a model in an underwear catalog, giving a sultry smile to the mirror like it was a camera about to take her picture. Her makeup was slightly smudged, but it had survived the night pretty well. She dabbed a wet washcloth under her eyes to wipe away the flakes of mascara, ran her fingers through her hair and smiled at her reflection again. Perfect.

It wasn't like she *cared* about how she looked for Damien. But it was always good to look your best.

She didn't have a toothbrush or toothpaste, so the mouthwash next to the sink would have to do. She swished it, glad it was strong enough to dissolve the taste of sleep and alcohol.

She walked back into the room and was surprised to find Damien awake. He rested his chin in his hand, smiling lazily.

"Wow," he said, his eyes roaming her body.

The realization of what might have happened hit Madison all over again. If she'd had sex with Damien, that was it. Losing her virginity could only happen once. Her stomach rolled thinking it might have happened last night, and that if it had, she couldn't remember it.

She had to find out the truth before the possibilities drove her crazy.

She felt exposed in her underwear, even though Damien had seen her in a bathing suit plenty of times and it wasn't *that* much different, so she picked up her dress from the armchair and put it on. The short dress didn't cover much, and Madison yearned to snuggle into yoga pants and a tank top and go back to sleep.

She sat at the end of the bed, faced Damien and took a deep breath. It was now or never. "What happened last night?" she asked.

His eyes dimmed. "You don't remember?"

Madison was surprised at how upset he sounded. But it wasn't Damien's feelings she worried about—the question of her virtue was at stake here—so she regained her composure. "Of course I don't remember," she snapped. "Do you think this would have happened if I hadn't been completely wasted?"

He looked like he'd been slapped, and Madison wished she hadn't been so harsh. No matter what stupid decision she had made, Damien was her friend.

Well, maybe—it depended on how he answered the question.

"You kissed me," he said slowly, sitting up against the headboard. "In the club."

"I remember that," she said, not wanting to think about it any more than necessary. "Then we drank more. That's where the night gets hazy."

"Hazy?" he said. "It sounds like you blacked out."

She threw a pillow at his head, disappointed when he easily caught it. "I guess I did," she admitted. "So can you please explain how we got here?"

The smug look disappeared. "At the end of the night you were freaking out about your parents seeing you that drunk," he said. "You had no idea what to do. You said you couldn't go home like that. You could barely walk on your own, so you couldn't have hidden that you'd been drinking, and I know how your dad always wakes up when you get home to say good-night—"

"Get to the point," Madison interrupted, although flashes of what had happened were coming back to her. Like how she'd danced with Damien—really closely—in front of everyone for the majority of the night. But that still didn't explain how they'd woken up in the same bed this morning.

"It was your idea." He ran his hands through his already messy hair, sounding exasperated now. "You texted your parents that you were sleeping at Larissa's, but she had already left, so you had nowhere to go. You *wanted* me to stay with you so you didn't have to be alone. Plus, your parents would notice the charge on your credit card for a hotel room and mine wouldn't." He paused before continuing. "Listen, Mads, I don't know what you think happened here, but I would never let you do anything you weren't ready for. I thought you knew that about me. I...care about you, Mads. A lot."

His pained expression convinced her: despite his reputation, Damien would never take advantage of her like that. Plus, she remembered that once they'd gotten to the room, she'd collapsed into bed and passed out.

She also vaguely remembered her fingers being laced with Damien's as she'd slept, but she didn't want to think about that. Doing something while you slept was involuntary. It didn't count as real life.

"I know," she said softly. "I'm sorry."

"I'm not," he said, his dark eyes burning with intensity.

Madison had no idea what to say. Because she hadn't been so drunk that she didn't know what she was doing when she'd kissed Damien the first time. She'd known it would be leading him on, but she'd done it anyway. Had she been trying to prove she could steal him from Savannah? Was she that angry at Brett and Oliver for being interested in Courtney, and at Oliver for sleeping with Peyton?

Those girls were destroying Madison's life, and she hated all three of them for it.

"Listen, Damien," she started. "I never should have kissed you. I'd already drunk a lot by that point, and I wasn't thinking clearly. I did it because... Well, I don't know why I did it. But it was a mistake. I'm sorry." The apology sounded lame, but it wasn't like she could tell him the truth, and she couldn't come up with anything better. She hated that she'd let it get to this point.

"A mistake?" Damien's voice rose in anger. "Try telling that to Savannah Diamond. You destroyed that girl for a *mistake?*"

"Why are you bringing Savannah into this?" Madison snapped. "You think she had it so bad for you that seeing us together *destroyed* her? Please. You don't even like her."

"I never said that," he said. "Savannah's a sweet girl. She's different than most of the sluts around here. I was taking her more seriously than that."

"You were actually interested in her?" Madison doubted it.

"What I feel for Savannah is nothing compared to what I feel for you."

"And what exactly *do* you feel for me?"

"You're one of the most amazing girls I know," he said, his eyes serious. "Scratch that—you *are* the most amazing girl I know. And it's not just that you're hot, which you are, but you're smart and witty and fun, and you take action to get what you want. Whenever you're faced with something tough, you don't sit back and sulk, but you figure out a way to make things better and then you go do it. You're going to get into Stanford, then go to medical school and do something great with your life. I know you don't take me seriously or whatever, but if you're willing to give me a chance, I promise you won't be disappointed."

Madison sat back in surprise. She hadn't expected Damien to say that. It was kind of...sweet. Really sweet.

Maybe this could take her mind off Brett.

But the thought of Brett reminded Madison why she had never been fully attracted to Damien. Brett had goals, even if they were superartsy and not anything that interested her. He had direction, and he cared enough about school to voluntarily get tutored so he could catch up to the Goodman curriculum. That was worth something to Madison. Damien had no idea what he wanted to do with his life—he wasn't even sure where he wanted to apply to college, which was sad since he was going to be a senior in the fall and most applications were due in December. Madison, on the other hand, already knew that when she was a senior she was going to apply for early decision from Stanford—and that she would get in.

Okay, so she couldn't know that for sure, but Stanford had no reason *not* to want her.

Damien was right that she was going to do something with her life. The problem was that she couldn't say the same for him, and he deserved better than to be with someone who didn't 100 percent believe in him.

"This is when you say something in response," Damien interrupted her thoughts.

"Right." Madison snapped back into focus. Damien's hopeful expression made her feel terrible about what she had to say next. "That was sweet of you. Really. But you're my friend, Damien. And you're a great friend—one of my best—but there's nothing more than that between us. There's never going to *be* anything more than that between us. I'm sorry."

His eyes flashed with anger. "That wasn't what you were thinking when you kissed me last night."

"The problem was that I *wasn't* thinking," Madison said. "I had too much to drink."

"Too much to drink." He let out a small laugh that made

it clear he thought this was anything but funny. "Except you know what they say—it's not called truth juice for nothing."

"Whatever," Madison said, picking up her purse from the chair. "People do all kinds of stupid things when they're drunk. You of all people should know that."

He gasped in fake surprise. "Are you implying I drink too much?"

"Implying?" She raised an eyebrow. "More like pointing out the obvious."

"And now that you've so lovingly pointed out how much I drink, as an expert on the topic I can tell you that when you first came up to me you weren't drunk yet—just tipsy. You got drunk *after* we kissed. So you knew what you were doing when you first did it. Do you think I would have let you kiss me otherwise?"

"You would have let me kiss you no matter what," Madison said.

"Is that so?" He cocked his head to the side and smirked.

"You've never been subtle about your feelings for me."

"And I could say the same to you." His leisurely tone grated on Madison. "You don't exactly go light on the flirting whenever we're together."

"But you know it never *meant* anything," she said, exasperated. Damien's "logic" was driving her mental.

"Fine," he said. "You're right."

"So things between us can go back to normal?" she asked. Once he said yes, she could leave and pretend like last night—and this morning—had never happened.

He held his gaze steady with hers. "I never said that."

The ground wobbled beneath Madison's feet. "What do you mean?"

"I mean that sometimes you can't plan everything," he

said, angry now. "I can't say things between us will go back to 'normal,' because what happened happened. I can't erase my memory. And neither can Savannah, even though I wish she could."

"It was your choice to kiss me back knowing she would see," Madison pointed out. "Anyway, we both know that Savannah Diamond will always be your second choice. Don't lie and say you wouldn't ditch her in a second if I wanted to be with you."

He stared at her, hard, his eyes dark and full of anger. "You can be a real bitch, you know that?"

Deciding that didn't merit a response, Madison stomped to the door and slammed it behind her, not looking back. He might have a point, but he didn't have to be so cruel about it.

www.campusbuzz.com

High Schools > Nevada > Las Vegas > The Goodman School

The Diamond grand opening
Posted on Thursday 07/08 at 12:59 PM
We all know what tomorrow night is—the grand opening of the Diamond Hotel and Casino. And while hicks in small towns think homecoming and prom are the biggest events of the year, in Vegas we know nothing compares to a fabulous grand opening. Champagne will be flowing, appetizers will be anywhere you look, and does anyone else think the games are rigged so everyone wins a *little* more than on a normal night? Nothing ups the happiness in an atmosphere more than people thinking they're hitting it big in Vegas.

If you're in the know, then you're aware that the best part of a grand opening is the exclusive dinner beforehand and the busy VIP floor at the club after. Not like many of us get to go to the dinner, but if you're willing to pay (or if you call your Centurion card personal concierge), then you can try to get in and party with us in VIP. It doesn't mean we'll like you, but at least you'll get a chance.

But here's the biggest question—who will go with who? We all have an idea who the lucky few from school are who received invitations (with a plus one, of course) so post your best guesses here ☺

Have fun, and be safe! (In every way possible).

I'll see you all soon. Or at least those of you who matter!

1: Posted on Thursday 07/08 at 1:29 PM
whats a centurion card???

2: Posted on Thursday 07/08 at 1:40 PM
A Centurion card is a black American Express card, other-wise known as a Blamex. Something *you* clearly do not have.

3: Posted on Thursday 07/08 at 2:07 PM
i would kill to go with damien sanders. hes probably going with savannah diamond though. the two of them seem to be spending a LOT of time together recently.

4: Posted on Thursday 07/08 at 2:12 PM
Obviously you weren't at Luxe last night when Damien kissed Madison Lockhart in front of Savannah. Maybe Damien and Madison will go together. Courtney will prob-ably disappear in a corner, since she doesn't seem very social. As for Savannah, who knows? She's been ob-sessed with Damien since she got here, so maybe she *would* go with him after what happened. Or maybe she, Madison, and Damien will all go together...

5: Posted on Thursday 07/08 at 4:54 PM
savannah and madison at once? i'd take that ANY day!

6: Posted on Thursday 07/08 at 9:08 PM
I bet Oliver is going with Larissa. The two of them would make a cute couple. WHY aren't they dating already??

7: Posted on Friday 07/09 at 4:37 AM
because larissa is a sluthoe and theres no reason for oliver to date her when she sleeps with him whenever he wants. that way he can fuck all of the diamond sisters, and madison, too.

8: Posted on Friday 07/09 at 2:45 PM

Speaking of the Diamond sisters, has anyone seen THIS?
www.youtube.com/savannahdiamond

Savannah Diamond made a YouTube channel and there's a video of her singing karaoke at the Imperial Palace Karaoke Bar. It would be funny since that place is such a dump, but she's actually REALLY good...

chapter 25: *Savannah*

After the Imperial Palace, Nick and Savannah had split up to go home. But on Friday morning, they met up again for brunch at Zabu, the poolside restaurant in the Diamond Hotel. They had a cute table for two with wide wicker chairs, pushed up against the wrought-iron railing looking over the water. A huge umbrella shaded them from the hot desert sun. Savannah ordered pancakes, and they were delicious. Nick must not be a breakfast person, because even though it was a little after 10:00 a.m., he got a burger and fries.

"I'm worried about starting Goodman in the fall," Savannah admitted to Nick as she dug into her pancakes.

"Switching schools can be rough, especially coming into sophomore year," Nick said. "But you seem outgoing, so I'm sure you'll be fine. I'll introduce you to all my friends."

"That would be nice." Savannah smiled. "At first I was most worried because I know I'm going to be behind in the classes, since I'm coming from public school. But after what happened last night, it's pretty obvious that Madison doesn't like me. I have no idea what I did to her, and I don't want her telling her friends not to include me before they know me. It seems like she's one of those people who everyone loves and listens to."

"People do love Madison," Nick agreed. "But they're also kind of scared of her, too. She's confident and smart, and I think everyone is afraid of what she'll do to them if they get on her bad side."

"Like I've managed to do." Savannah stabbed a piece of pancake and ate it, even though it was soggy since she'd drenched it in syrup.

"Cheer up," he said. "Madison and I aren't on great terms either, so you're not alone. And I've been going to Goodman since first grade, so I've got a great group of friends there. Once I tell them how awesome you are, they'll all want to hang out with you."

"Why are you spending so much time with me when you have so many friends at Goodman?" she asked. "I mean, I'm glad we're hanging out, but why me?"

"I'm guessing your school in California was pretty big," Nick said.

"We had about 450 kids in my grade."

"That's huge," he said. "Each grade at Goodman has about 75 kids. I've been with the same people since I was five years old. They're my best friends, but when we get someone new like you and your sisters, it's a big deal."

"I would like to meet some of your friends," she said. "If you don't mind. It'll be easier to be somewhere new if I already have some friends when I start."

"If you're willing to come to house parties instead of clubs every night, you're more than welcome to join me," he said.

"Everyone at Goodman doesn't go to clubs all the time?"

"No." Nick laughed. "The people in the elite circle do—like Damien, Oliver, Madison and their friends—but most people at Goodman are pretty normal."

"But they still go to private school, which is way different from what I'm used to," Savannah said. "What's your definition of 'normal'?"

"Good point," he said. "Ask me some questions, and I'll let you know what's normal."

"Okay." She thought about her first question. "Where do most people live?"

"Not on the Strip," he said. "Most people live in gated communities nearby. St. Andrews Country Club, Woodfield Country Club and Long Lake Estates are the more popular ones."

"Hold up." Savannah nearly dropped her fork. "People live in country clubs? And that's considered *normal?*"

"Compared to living in a penthouse condo on the Strip." Nick shrugged. "It's not a far drive, so we still come to the Strip for events. But not everyone has a fake ID, a parent who owns a hotel or enough money to pay off the bouncers, so it's easier to have house parties."

"Damien mentioned that he and his friends have fake IDs," Savannah said.

"Yep." Nick nodded. "They're scannable and everything. Oliver knows some guy who makes them and hooked them all up. When Madison and I dated, she set me and my friends up with them, too. That's how we got into Myst and Luxe. The clubs are cool, but I like house parties more."

His mention of when he used to date Madison made Savannah feel awkward. She tried to think of another normal thing about Fairfield for her next question. "Does everyone take a bus to school?"

"We don't have buses," he said. "Our parents, siblings or neighbors take us to school until we're old enough to drive."

"So you all have cars?"

"Most everyone gets one for their sixteenth birthday," Nick said.

"I turn sixteen in December, so I guess I know what to ask for." Savannah sighed and buried her face in her hands. When she had imagined creating a "new Savannah" a few days ago she had felt so confident, but after what had happened with Madison and Damien, she wondered if she would always be on the outside looking in. "Your 'normal' sounds nothing like where I come from," she said. "I'm going to be so out of my element."

"Relax," Nick said. "You're Adrian Diamond's daughter, so it's a given that you'll be part of the elite. Don't let Madison get to you. My guess is she feels threatened by you and your sisters, and that's why she's acting like this."

"Madison doesn't seem like she would ever be threatened by anyone," Savannah said.

"Remember, I did date her for a few months," he said, finishing the last of his fries. "She seems confident, but she's no more perfect than anyone else. But enough about Madison. I promise everyone's going to be excited to meet you."

"You think so?"

"I know so."

The waitress dropped off the check, and Savannah reached for her bag to get her credit card.

"I've got this," Nick said, pulling the check to his end of the table and placing his credit card inside.

"Are you sure?" Savannah asked. "We can split it. Adrian pays for my card, and he doesn't mind."

"My dad pays for my card, too," he said. "Trust me, it's fine. My treat."

Savannah pulled her hand away from her bag. "Thanks," she said. Did Nick think this was a date? She had fun with him, but she didn't feel jittery and nervous around him like she did with Damien, whose slightest touch made her dizzy. She felt the same way around Nick that she did with her friends.

The waitress returned to the table and placed Nick's card in front of him. "Your credit card was declined," she said, sounding haughty and bored. "Is there another one you want to use?"

Nick examined his credit card, confused. "Did you try running it again?"

"Yes." She looked around at the other tables, as if she had somewhere else to be. "Twice, and I entered the numbers manually. It was declined every time."

"Take mine." Savannah thrust her Blamex at the waitress, wanting to save Nick the embarrassment. "I'm sure this one will be fine."

The waitress's mouth dropped open when she glanced at the credit card, and she straightened, her entire demeanor changed. "Of course, Ms. Diamond." She smiled, her eyes more awake than they'd been since Savannah and Nick had sat down. "I can charge your meal to your condo. I hope everything at Zabu was to your liking, and I apologize for the inconvenience. I'll be right back." She hurried to the kitchen, nearly knocking down a busboy in the process.

"Sorry about that." Nick played with a petal on the flower arrangement between them. "That's never happened before."

"Don't worry about it." Savannah felt awkward, and she didn't want to pry, so she tried to change subjects. "This hotel is so pretty," she said, looking out at the pool and the color-ful garden surrounding it. "I can't believe I live here now."

"It is nice," he agreed, the conversation now noticeably stilted. Luckily the waitress returned quickly, so they didn't have to continue it for long.

"I'm sorry again for the misunderstanding," she said, placing a huge slice of cheesecake and two forks on the table. "Here's Chef Bart's famous cheesecake, on the house. It was voted the best in Vegas. Enjoy, and please come back to Zabu soon."

"Thanks," Savannah said. She'd never gotten free food at a restaurant before. "This looks delicious."

That satisfied their waitress, who gave them another pageant-girl smile and hurried to another table.

"That was strange," Savannah said, taking a bite of the cheesecake. It was smooth and creamy and practically melted in her mouth. She would never be able to eat cheesecake from the grocery store again. "Omigod, this is amazing. You have to try it."

"She knows who you are," Nick said. "Or, more impor-tant, who your father is. She wanted to make sure you had a good time at the restaurant." He tried some of the cheesecake, and his eyes lit up. "This is really good," he agreed, taking another forkful.

Their conversation returned to normal as they enjoyed the cheesecake. Savannah didn't bring up Nick's credit card situ-ation again, but she wondered. Nick had said his father was a real estate developer in Vegas. It didn't make sense for him to have a problem with his credit card.

"I got something for you," he said once they finished eating. He pulled something out of his pocket, and with a dramatic flourish, placed a plastic flash drive on the table.

"A flash drive?" Savannah looked at him in confusion. "Um, thanks."

"Not the flash drive." He laughed. "But you can keep that. I got you what's *on* the flash drive. A recording of you singing karaoke last night."

"No way." She snatched it up and grasped it tightly to her chest. "You didn't show it to anyone, did you?"

"No," he said. "Relax. I just thought you would like to see it."

"Thanks." Savannah *was* curious about how she'd sounded last night. "Let's go watch it on my computer."

They went up to her room to watch it, and she was surprised that she sounded like a *real* singer. Judging by the crowd's reaction, they'd loved her. Maybe she had a shot at a singing career after all. Karaoke today, a record deal tomorrow.

She doubted that would happen, but it was nice to dream.

"Are you ready to make that YouTube channel now?" Nick asked once they finished watching.

"I don't know." Savannah sat back and wrung her hands together. "What if people watch, think I'm terrible and then write mean comments? I'm not sure I could handle seeing that."

"Did it sound like everyone at the bar thought you were terrible?"

"Well, no," she admitted.

"You told me last night that you wanted to make a YouTube channel," he said. "Now you have a great video of you singing. You can either do nothing with it and let it collect dust, or put it out there and see what happens. You're really talented, so I hope you choose the second option, but it's up to you."

She knew the right answer, but she wasn't sure if she was ready. Then again, wasn't this what she'd always wanted? If she didn't put herself out there, she would never know if she could make it. If she did put herself out there, she still might not make it, but at least she was giving herself a fair shot. "I'll do it," she finally agreed, unable to believe she was going through with it.

Nick sat by her side as she signed up for YouTube and up-loaded the video onto her channel. The only people she could think to add as friends were her sisters, her favorite musicians, Evie, some of the girls from the volleyball team, Brett, Nick, Nick's brother, Ben, and Ben's friends that she'd met last night.

It wasn't much, but at least it was a start.

"Do you live in one of those gated communities you men-tioned at brunch?" Savannah asked Nick while the video up-loaded. Maybe she'd have a few views next time she checked her account.

"I used to," he said, staring out of the floor-to-ceiling win-dows across from her bed. "My mom and I moved out in the beginning of summer to an apartment off the Strip. But it's only until she figures out where she wants to go more per-manently."

"Oh." Savannah felt bad about bringing it up. She assumed he and his mom had moved out from where they'd lived with his dad—meaning his parents had recently separated. "So you're close by, then?"

"You're happy about that?" Nick replied playfully, leaning back in the bed and smiling at her. It was impossible not to smile back—Nick radiated light.

"Of course I am," she said. "You're my first real friend here."

"Real friend? As opposed to your fake ones?"

"Yeah. Like Madison." Savannah wrinkled her nose as she said Madison's name. "Anyway," she said, changing the subject since she'd had enough talk of Madison for one day. "I still have no idea what to wear to the grand opening tomorrow night. I've never been to an event like this before."

"Your life is full of tough decisions," he joked.

"I know." Savannah laughed. "I have no idea how to choose."

"I'm sure you'll manage," he said. "Whoever you're going with is extremely lucky."

"About that…" she started, remembering the ominous "plus one" on her invitation. "I'm not going with anyone yet. Do you want to go with me? I understand if you're already going with someone, and I know it's last-minute—"

"Of course I'll go with you," Nick said before she could continue any more. Savannah was glad he'd interrupted her, since everything she'd said had come out in a jumbled rush, and she probably sounded like a complete spaz.

"Cool." She was relieved that was over with. "Thanks."

"Thanks?" Nick repeated. "I should be the one thanking you. I'll be going to the most exclusive event in the city with the most beautiful girl there."

Savannah's cheeks reddened. She wanted to point out that she wouldn't be the most beautiful girl there—that title would better fit Madison or Courtney—but she didn't. Also, Nick seemed to mean it.

Getting over Damien was *way* easier now that she was hanging out with Nick. He wasn't as drop-dead hot as Damien, but he had an angelic quality, and Savannah couldn't deny that she found him attractive. He was also nice, which was more than she could say for Damien.

After all, nice guys didn't make out with another girl in front of you if they were really interested in you.

Nick checked his watch, alarm crossing his eyes. "I'm actually late for something right now, so I gotta head out," he said. "I didn't realize what time it was. When should I be here to pick you up tomorrow night?"

Savannah thought back to the invitation. "Meet me at six. Dinner's at seven-thirty, but my father's having a reception at the pool first."

"Sounds good," he said. "I'll see you then."

She walked him to the door at the same time Courtney emerged from her room, still in her pajamas. Had Courtney just woken up? Savannah looked at her watch—it was 11:30 a.m. Courtney never slept past 9:00 a.m., and even that would be late for her.

"Hi," Nick said when he saw Courtney. "I'm Nick. One of Savannah's friends."

"Courtney," she introduced herself, looking stunned. "One of Savannah's sisters."

"I wish I could stay, but I have to be somewhere," he apologized. "I'm sure we'll meet again later."

"Bye." Courtney waved, and Nick headed out. The door shut, and she faced Savannah, looking seriously concerned. "Did he sleep here last night?"

"No!" Savannah laughed at how paranoid her sister could be. She gave Courtney the rundown on everything that had happened recently, up until Nick leaving this morning. "So you see," she said once she finished, "Nick's perfectly nice, and I promise nothing happened that you wouldn't approve of."

"Just wait until you tell Peyton," Courtney said.

"There's no way I'm going in there," Savannah said, pointing at Peyton's room. Peyton had been locked inside watching TV since yesterday morning and had refused to come out. "You know she's in one of her moods. I tried to go in there yesterday after you left for that dinner thing, and she growled at me. Literally. So I had to go shopping by myself and text Evie photos of outfits for her opinion. It was so pathetic."

Courtney took a deep breath and yelled, "Savannah had a boy in her room!" loud enough for the people at the opposite side of the building to hear.

"Shut up!" Savannah joked. What had gotten into Courtney? Savannah had never seen her so…giddy.

Peyton swung her door open and stomped into the living room. All she wore was an oversized T-shirt, and she looked like she hadn't showered in days. "Damien didn't sleep here, did he?" she asked.

"Not Damien," Savannah said, catching Peyton up on what she'd told Courtney. The only way to handle Peyton when she got like this was to ignore that she'd been moody to begin with. She would spill the story about why she was upset in her own time, but if you pushed her she clammed up.

"Wow," Peyton said once she finished. "You had quite the night."

"Yeah," Savannah agreed.

"And what about you?" Peyton asked Courtney. "How did it go with Oliver at that dinner event?"

"It was fine." Courtney shrugged.

Peyton's face hardened. "You're not interested in him, are you?"

"No!" Courtney shook her head so hard that her hair flew over her shoulders. "Not like that. There was an open bar at the event, and he got so drunk. Then he tried to kiss me in the car on the way home, and it was so… Ugh." She shuddered. "I pushed him away. But he apologized, and when I said I wasn't interested in him, he backed off. So we're going to the grand opening tomorrow night together—as friends—

because apparently our parents will be happy about it, but he knows nothing more will happen."

"But you stayed out late with him?" Savannah asked. "I've never seen you sleep past nine."

"I came back after the event," Courtney said quickly. "And I was up earlier this morning, but I was reading and didn't feel like changing."

"So you turned down Oliver?" Peyton looked pleased.

"Yeah," Courtney said. "I think I hurt his feelings, and I feel bad, but he's not my type and he seemed fine with being friends."

Peyton smiled. "I knew it wouldn't work out between you two."

"Do you guys want to go to the pool?" Savannah asked, not wanting to stay inside all day. "Nick and I overlooked it at the restaurant where we had brunch, and it's, like, the most amazing pool you'll ever see."

They both agreed. Just as they reached the doors of their rooms to change, Peyton yelled, "By the way, I broke up with Mike! You're going to love the story of how this went down."

Apparently they had a lot to discuss at the pool.

On the morning of the grand opening, Rebecca came by the condo and asked them to have a seat in the living room.

"Good morning, girls," she said once they had all gathered.

"Hi," Savannah said, wondering why Rebecca needed to talk to them. It felt so formal, and with the way Rebecca was pacing, she assumed there was a purpose to this visit.

Rebecca finally stopped walking around and sat down across from them. "How have you been doing getting settled in?" She fiddled with her pearl necklace, then seemed to realize what she was doing and dropped her hand back to her side.

"Good," Savannah said, and Courtney agreed. Peyton said nothing.

"It's strange not having our mom around," Courtney added, looking down at her lap and playing with her hands. "But we're managing."

"I'm glad to hear it," Rebecca said. "And I hope you know that if you ever need to talk, I'm happy to listen."

"Thanks." Savannah didn't see herself choosing to talk with Rebecca over her sisters, but it was kind of her to offer.

"As you know, today is an important day," Rebecca said, getting to what Savannah guessed was the point of her visit. "Your father is extremely busy making sure everything is ready for the grand opening, and he asked me to come over to talk to you about some things to keep in mind for tonight."

"What sort of 'things'?" Peyton looked skeptical.

"Just the basics of what to say when people ask you questions," she said. "Your father has been careful to keep your mother's situation away from the public eye, so he would like you to not mention it to any of his guests. Instead, he would prefer that you keep up his story about the three of you choosing to move to Vegas to get to know him better."

"Why should we keep up his lie?" Peyton asked.

"It will be better for your mother when she gets out of rehab," Rebecca said. "This way the press won't hound her and hurt her path to recovery. I'm not asking you to do this for Adrian. I'm asking you to do it for her."

Peyton sat back and crossed her legs, which was as much of an "okay" as Savannah knew Rebecca would get from her.

"He also would prefer that you not mention Fairfield specifically," Rebecca continued. "Just say you grew up outside of San Francisco and leave it at that. Again, this is all to keep your life before coming here as private as possible."

Savannah wasn't going to argue with her there. If any of Adrian's guests looked up Fairfield, it wouldn't take long for them to realize how different it was from life at the Diamond.

Rebecca went over a few more things—most consisting of them talking about their past as little as possible. They were supposed to keep conversation to general chitchat about the hotel, and make sure to ask the guests what they liked most about it so far. If Rebecca noticed any of them getting uncomfortable, she promised she would come over and rescue them.

"And before I head out to get ready myself, I want to discuss with each of you what you intend to wear," she said.

"Why?" Peyton laughed. "Was Adrian not happy about what I wore to the dinner at the Gates?"

"No, he wasn't." Rebecca held her gaze with Peyton's, surprisingly stern. "Mr. Prescott himself went out of his way to comment about his displeasure over your outfit."

"I didn't hear any comment," Peyton said.

"It was said in private to Adrian and myself." Rebecca shifted in her seat. "None of us want to tell you what to wear, Peyton, but we also don't want Mr. Prescott to have any reason to reconsider his deal with Adrian. I'm sure we can find something appropriate in your closet that you like."

"If you say so." Peyton yawned.

Savannah, on the other hand, was grateful for Rebecca's help. The two of them settled on a floral silk minidress by D&G with swirling colors of purple, turquoise, white and black. The thick black spaghetti straps gave it a sexy look, but it didn't plunge too low. With her black Jimmy Choo pumps, it would be perfect for the event.

But she had given herself too much time to get ready, so while she was waiting around, she Facetimed Evie.

Evie's face appeared on the screen, her strawberry-blond

hair ironed straight and her freckles covered with foundation. She must also be getting ready to go out. "Look who finally has time to talk," she said with a smile. "I'm getting ready for a party, but it won't matter if I'm a few minutes late."

"Good," Savannah said. "Because I'm in serious need of advice, and you're the only one I can ask."

"Ask away," Evie said, her light brown eyes glinting in anticipation.

And so Savannah spilled everything that had happened with Damien and Nick.

"I know I shouldn't have feelings for Damien, because he was a total asshole, but I can't help still liking him," she said when she was done. "I think about him all the time. What should I do?"

"I think it's obvious." Evie smiled.

"Maybe to you," Savannah said.

"Okay," Evie said, as if she had some sort of master plan. "You need to flirt with Nick, and make sure Damien sees. If Damien was ever interested in you in the slightest, he'll get jealous and stake his claim. From there, you should string him along—ignore him sometimes, and give him attention other times. After you have a good conversation with him, wait for him to reach out to you next. Whatever happens, don't reach out to him first unless he reached out to you the time before, because it will take away the chase. This way he won't think he can walk all over you."

"And what about Nick?" Savannah asked.

"What about him?" Evie said. "It seems like everything is going well with him. Besides, it's not like you have to pick either of them anytime soon."

"What do you mean?" Savannah asked. "Of course I have to choose between them."

Evie shook her head. "Are you dating either one of them?"

"No…" Savannah wondered where she was going with this.

"Then you don't have to choose either of them, at least not yet," Evie said confidently. "Trust me on this. Neither of them is your boyfriend, so if the plan works and Damien shows interest again, you're free to flirt with both of them until you come to your decision."

"You make it sound so easy." Savannah sighed.

"Because it is!" Evie said. "But anyway, I have to keep getting ready, or I'll be seriously late. Let me know how it goes, okay?"

"I will," Savannah promised, although she couldn't help feeling doubtful that this plan would work at all.

The poolside reception went well. Nick stayed by her side, and adults she didn't know—friends of Adrian—introduced themselves. Savannah felt like a shining star with how well the conversations went. She followed Rebecca's instructions and made it sound as if she'd lived in the high-end part of Northern California before coming to Vegas, and that she and her sisters had chosen to live with Adrian for the year so they could bond with their father. She pulled it off flawlessly. It was amazing how much could change in less than a week.

One thing that hadn't changed was Adrian's distance from them. Savannah remembered what Courtney had suggested— that he was hiding something from them, and that's why he hadn't talked with them much. But Savannah preferred to believe that Adrian was just busy. When the grand opening ended, he would get to know them. Right?

She tried not to overthink it at the party. When she introduced Nick to her sisters—for longer than thirty seconds this time—she could tell they liked him. But she also noticed how the adults asked Nick about his father, and how Nick grew tense whenever someone brought him up. Savannah suspected that something bad was going on with Nick's family, but she wasn't going to ask him about it in public. Maybe he would want to talk about it later. She liked Nick, and if something was bothering him, she wanted to give him whatever support she could.

It wasn't like she came from a perfect family, either.

At dinner, Courtney and Oliver sat next to each other. Courtney replied politely to his questions, although her answers were short and she didn't ask him anything in return. Savannah could tell she wasn't interested in him as more than a friend. Brett was there with a girl with stringy brown hair and bad skin named Dawn. Dawn went to a public school called Palo Verde, and Rebecca didn't seem thrilled that Brett had brought her to the grand opening. He also kept glancing at Courtney through the meal, and Courtney was looking at him, too. Savannah didn't want to think Courtney would lie to her about her feelings for Brett, but it seemed like they were into each other. She definitely planned on asking Courtney about it when they got home that night.

Peyton hadn't brought anyone, which surprised Savannah. Peyton *always* had a date. She had also worn an outfit that Rebecca hadn't approved that morning. The leather minidress wasn't formal enough, and she had on *way* too much black eyeliner. She looked like she was going to a rock concert in San Francisco instead of a grand opening of the most luxurious hotel in Vegas.

Adrian and Rebecca didn't join them for dinner, but they did stop by occasionally. As the hosts, they were making sure their guests were having a good time, and Rebecca kept her promise by checking on them to make sure they were doing all right. They would also be announcing their engagement during the ribbon-cutting in the casino at midnight. Savannah was nervous about the announcement. It wasn't that she didn't want Rebecca to be her stepmother—Rebecca seemed nice—but it was happening so fast.

Dinner ended, and since the ribbon-cutting wouldn't be until later, they all headed to Myst. The nightclub was packed.

"Drinks?" Nick asked Savannah, pointing to the bar in the back of the VIP section.

"Okay." She tried to be casual when she charged the drinks to her room, since she didn't want to embarrass Nick. Savannah had been poor her entire life. If Nick's family was having money problems, she was the last person who would judge him.

They sat close to each other at the bar, their foreheads nearly touching as they chatted about her new YouTube channel, which already had two hundred views and a few positive comments. Then she felt a tap on her shoulder.

She turned to see who it was—Damien. His hair had the "just rolled out of bed but still looks perfect" thing going on, and he wore midnight-blue jeans, a black top and a matching blazer. Somehow Damien managed to look badass-sexy while still dressing appropriately for the grand opening of the Diamond.

She stared up at him and swallowed. She should tell him to get lost. Pour her drink over his perfectly gelled hair. Let him know that she wanted nothing to do with him and his stupid games. Instead she sat there, unmoving, waiting for him to speak.

"Can I talk to you?" he asked. "Alone?"

Savannah knew the right answer—no. He'd embarrassed her more than anyone ever had, making her cry in public, and she shouldn't want anything to do with him. But simply being in his presence was making her heart beat so fast that she felt like it could fly out of her chest.

So she met his eyes and said, "Sure." The word surprised her the second it left her lips. Nick stiffened next to her. What was she getting herself into?

Then again, wasn't this how Evie had said it would play out? Maybe Damien realized what a mistake he'd made last night and was going to beg for her forgiveness. If so, Savannah wanted to hear it.

"Okay," Damien said. "The balcony?"

She mumbled to Nick that she would be back soon and followed Damien outside. The balcony was relatively empty because it was so hot out, and it looked out to where the Palazzo Hotel loomed next to the Diamond. She remembered her first night here, which felt so distant now, when she and Damien had watched fireworks from the same location. Could that really have only been six days ago? He had held her hand then. She flexed her right hand at the memory and placed it on the railing, waiting for him to speak.

"I'm glad I ran into you." He stepped forward so he was only inches away from her, the intense look in his eyes making her tremble.

She replayed the scene of him making out with Madison at Luxe. Despite how he made her feel when he looked at her like that, Damien was a total asshole. A complete jerk. Full of himself to no limit. She cursed herself for agreeing to go outside with him, but she was here now, and had to make the best of it.

Maybe he would even apologize.

"So what's up?" she asked, hoping he couldn't hear her voice shaking.

"You're hanging out with Nick Gordon now?" he said, ignoring her question.

So Evie's plan *was* working, but Savannah wasn't sure whether to feel happy about that or pissed at Damien. He'd humiliated her to the point where she'd run out of Luxe crying, and he hadn't brought her out here to say sorry? Her emotions felt like a jumbled mess inside her brain.

"Yeah, I'm hanging out with Nick," she replied, doing her best to remain calm. "Are you friends with him?"

"He's all right," Damien said. "But he doesn't seem like your type."

"My *type?*" Savannah was astonished he had the nerve to say that. "How do you know what my type is? You've known me for, like, six days."

"I have an instinct for these things," he said simply.

"Well, my 'instinct' tells me your type is Madison Lockhart." Savannah let out her feelings, done trying to contain her anger. "What are you doing out here with me when she's inside?"

"That's why I wanted to talk with you," he said softly. "What you saw at Luxe… It didn't mean anything. Madison was drunk, and she's had a crush on me forever, and she decided to walk up to me and kiss me. She took me by surprise. By the time I told her I was there with you it was too late— you had already left. I'm sorry. I wish you hadn't seen that."

Savannah wanted him to be telling the truth. He stepped closer, resting his hand on top of hers, and heat rushed up her arm. It would be easy to believe him and forget about the pain he'd caused her.

Instead, she pulled her hand away. He'd kissed Madison back for a long time—she'd seen the entire thing—and he'd enjoyed it. She refused to allow him to play with her emotions.

"If that's true, why didn't you call me?" she asked. "Or send me a text, or a Facebook message or something. You have my number, and it's been two days."

"I should have," he said. "But you were so upset. I thought you needed time to yourself." Savannah opened her mouth to speak, but he interrupted before she could say anything. "Listen, Savannah, I know we just met, and you have every right to never want to talk to me again, but I like you. I like you a lot. You're different from the other girls around here, and I've thought about you every day since meeting you that first time at your condo. You're sweet, and funny, and I like spending time with you. I want to get to know you better. I wish I could erase what you saw the other night, but I can't, and I want to start over. We can go out sometime—dinner, ice cream, a movie, whatever you want. Just tell me when, and I'll make it happen. I promise." His dark eyes looked so soft and…vulnerable. No guy had ever said something so sweet to her. It would be so easy to say yes. He'd said it had been a mistake—that Madison was the one who'd put the moves on him and he wasn't interested—and maybe he was telling the truth. She *wanted* him to be telling the truth.

Then she thought about Nick. With Damien it was all about attraction, with wanting to be close to him, and wondering why she—who had never stood out from the crowd—sparked his interest. With Nick, she had fun, and she enjoyed talk-ing with him. He cared enough about her dreams to help her make them come true, and being around him made her happy. There was potential there. She wasn't sure if she was inter-ested in Nick as more than a friend, but he deserved a chance.

Why did this have to be so confusing? She didn't know if she could choose between them. Instead, she thought about what Evie had told her to do: try to make both of them fall for her until she knew who she liked more and was ready to make the decision. Could she do that? It wasn't something she would have done in California, but she was supposed to be starting over and becoming a new person. A better, more confident person.

"I'll think about it," she finally said. Another piece of advice Evie would have given to her—don't be too eager. Savannah had been failing at that recently, but it was never too late to change.

Damien seemed taken aback—he must not be used to girls not jumping at the opportunity to go out with him. "So that's a yes?" he asked slowly.

She wanted to say yes, she'd go out with him, but she'd seen him respond to Madison when she'd kissed him. If Savannah wanted to be real competition, she would have to play hard to get.

"It's not a no," she said, running her hand through her extensions so they tumbled over her shoulders. "But after what happened at Luxe, I need to think about it."

"Okay," he said. "I can deal with that."

"Good." Savannah's voice was breathier than usual. Realizing that if she stayed out here with Damien for any longer he might kiss her—and that she wouldn't stop him—she looked at the French doors that led back into the club. "I should go back inside," she said quickly. "Nick's waiting for me."

"Right." Damien stepped back. "Let's go back inside, then."

Savannah made her way toward the bar, stopping when she saw Nick. Sitting next to him—so close that her long, dark hair fell against his arm—was Madison. She reached out to him, her hand brushing his, and he didn't back away.

The floor dropped out from under her. Why did Madison always have to mess up *everything*? Every time something good happened to Savannah, Madison showed up, dragging all of the attention back to herself. It wasn't fair.

"They're getting cozy," Damien said, resting his hand on Savannah's shoulder.

Savannah was too angry to respond—too angry to feel anything. Would she always be second best? At home the guys liked Evie better, and now it was the same thing again, but with Madison instead of Evie. The difference was that while Evie was Savannah's friend, Madison was a complete bitch.

Nick looked over his shoulder and saw her, and Savannah had no idea what to do. On one hand, going out to the balcony with Damien and walking back in with him made her look bad. On the other, Madison and Nick were sitting so close together that they passed as a couple. And Nick wanted to get back with Madison—he had all but outright said it the night they'd met.

"Come on," Savannah said, facing Damien. "Let's dance."

Damien took her hand and led her to the dance floor. It was packed. They got lost in the center, and Savannah kept Damien close. His hands traveled down her arms until he held her waist, and the two of them moved in time with the music. Savannah closed her eyes and rested her head on his shoulder, breathing in the fresh smell of his cologne. Maybe she could make herself forget about the past few days and return to how things had been between her and Damien before he'd made out with Madison at Luxe.

But while that would be simpler, it wasn't what Savannah wanted. She couldn't make herself forget. And she wasn't sure she wanted to.

Then someone's hand wrapped around her arm.

She slowly turned around, her eyes meeting Nick's. Damien stopped dancing, and if Savannah were living in a movie, this would be when the music stopped and everyone fell silent. But her life wasn't a movie, so the music continued and everyone kept dancing, oblivious to the three of them. What was she supposed to do? Here she was with the two guys she was interested in, both of whom viewed her as a second choice to Madison, and she was about to mess it all up.

"Hey," Nick said. He looked…guilty.

"Hey," Savannah answered back, pulling her hair over her shoulder. She was vaguely aware of Damien saying he would see her later and walking away, but Savannah would deal with him later. Wasn't this what she wanted—for Damien to see her as desirable to someone else? He looked upset, but if she gave in to him now, he would think she was weak. She couldn't have that.

"You didn't come back to the bar," Nick said.

"I was heading over there, but you seemed busy with Madison."

He was silent for a moment. "It's over between me and Madison. She wanted to get back together, but I told her no."

"You said no?" She had to make sure she'd heard him right.

"Yep," he said, his tone light. "You see, a few days ago I met someone else, and she's sweet, fun and she's an amazing singer. Who knows—maybe she'll be famous someday. No way am I messing that up now."

"And who is this 'someone'?" Savannah matched his playful tone.

"Come on," Nick said, running a hand through his golden curls. "Do I have to spell it out for you?"

"I guess not," Savannah said. "Do you really think I'm going to be famous?"

"I *know* you're going to be famous," he said. "No doubt about it."

He held out his hand, and Savannah took it, wrapping her arms around his neck as they started to dance. The thought of what Damien had done to her still made her heart hurt, but with Nick so close to her, she was already feeling better and more in control of her life than she had since arriving in Las Vegas.

chapter 26: *Courtney*

The dinner before the grand opening was the most awkward meal ever. Courtney sat across from Brett, and every time she caught his eye, she was reminded of the night at the Paris Hotel. It was hard to focus on being present when all she could do was replay the time she'd spent with him. She wished she could live in that night forever.

Whenever Oliver asked her a question, Brett stiffened and looked pissed. Peyton also tensed whenever Oliver spoke. Her older sister was in a sour mood—even worse than yesterday. It was probably because she had broken up with Mike and now she was the only one without a date. Courtney would try extra hard to include her when they went to Myst.

Unfortunately, everyone split up when they got to Myst— Savannah and Nick went to the bar, Brett and Dawn to a booth and Peyton to the second floor. Courtney had no choice but to follow Oliver to a VIP table with his friends, none of whom she knew. But the grand opening was a big deal, so for the one night, she could at least pretend not to be miserable.

The only other person Courtney recognized at the table was Madison, and while she didn't like Madison because of what she'd done to Savannah at Luxe, Courtney didn't want to cause a scene. It was difficult not to be intimidated by Madison's confidence. She looked like a fashion model in a short black flowing dress with silver sequins on the top. Then Courtney looked down at her own dress—an ocean-blue strapless that flowed from the empire waist to midway down her thighs—and reminded herself that she looked just as good. She never allowed herself to be intimidated by other girls at Fairfield High, since the only people she cared about impressing at school were her teachers, and she wasn't about to start now.

Everyone watched as she sat next to Oliver, and she was glad when a girl named Kaitlin started talking about the family vacation she was taking to Paris next week. It reminded her of Brett telling her they would go to Paris in August. Had he really meant it? She'd always wanted to go to Paris, but she'd imagined it would be on her terms, because she'd saved up enough to earn it. She hated the idea of Adrian paying for the trip, but she wanted to go so badly she wasn't sure she would have the strength to say no.

Throughout the conversation, a petite girl with short blond hair kept glaring at Courtney. She heard someone call the girl Larissa. And while it was hard to ignore Larissa's mean stares, it took all of Courtney's effort not to give Madison death glares of her own. She was glad Madison didn't try talking to her, because she might have said something mean about the way she had treated Savannah. But at least Savannah had met Nick. He seemed like a good guy—way better than Damien.

If only Courtney could meet someone like that—someone

whom she was allowed to be with. She kept peeking at Brett, who was chatting with Dawn in their booth across the room, his back toward her. She wished he would turn around. And then what? He would walk over and ask her if she wanted to get out of the club and go somewhere quieter like he had on the first night?

That wasn't even possible, since they both had to be at the ribbon-cutting at midnight.

"Do you want to dance?" Oliver's question jerked Courtney from her thoughts. He offered his hand to her, and she scooted away from him, bringing her arm to her side. His eyes crinkled in hurt, and Courtney felt bad. Oliver had been kind to her all night. And friends danced, right?

"Sure." Courtney forced a smile. "I'd like that."

He led her to the center of the packed dance floor, and she spotted Savannah and Nick nearby, their heads close together. At least one of her sisters was having a good time.

Courtney listened to the music and tried to move with it, wishing she were a natural dancer like Peyton. When Peyton danced, the music took over her body, and she was in another world. Courtney couldn't escape her thoughts that easily. Dancing made her feel awkward. She never felt like she was doing it right.

"Why so tense?" Oliver whispered in her ear. His breath smelled like alcohol, and his cheeks were flushed. Courtney hadn't counted how many drinks he'd had, but she suspected it was a lot.

"I'm not tense," she said, trying to relax her shoulders and neck.

"Yes, you are." Oliver wrapped his arms around her back, his hips pressing against hers in time with the music. All

Courtney could think about was that she wanted him to get off her.

She put some distance between them and did her best to relax for the rest of the song, since where else would she go? Over to Savannah and Nick, who were lost in their own world? Back to the table where Madison and Larissa were giving her death stares? Over to Brett, who was talking with Dawn at their table, and whom she wasn't allowed to be with?

None of those were good options. She also didn't want to strand Oliver. She *had* agreed to dance with him.

He pulled her closer, overwhelming Courtney with the smell of alcohol. Someone could get drunk just by being near him. "You look beautiful tonight," he said, brushing his thumb against her cheek.

"Thanks." Courtney swallowed and turned her eyes down to the floor. The way he was staring at her was not the way someone looks at a friend, and it was making her uncomfortable.

Suddenly he pressed his lips against hers. She jerked backward and pushed him off her, her eyes wide.

"What?" Oliver scrunched his forehead. "I thought you liked me."

"We agreed to come here tonight as friends," Courtney stammered, taking a step back.

He wrapped his hand around her elbow, and she tried to pull away, but he didn't loosen his grip. "If you only wanted to be friends, you wouldn't have danced with me," he said. "This is the perfect way for you to get over that guy you like in California."

"You're drunk," Courtney said, pulling away from him. "And we're in the middle of a dance floor."

"So?" He grinned and raised an eyebrow.

Courtney crossed her arms over her chest and stomped her foot. But she didn't get the chance to say anything back to him, because someone's hand clasped her shoulder, catching her by surprise. She turned around to see who it was.

Brett's jungle-green eyes stared back at her, fire raging within them. "Is he bothering you?" he asked, motioning to Oliver.

Courtney opened her mouth to speak, but closed it again. What was Brett doing? Electricity coursed between them, and she moved closer to him, trusting he would protect her from whatever Oliver would do next. She spotted Adrian, Rebecca, Logan and Ellen sitting in a booth with a perfect view of them, watching in concern. Brett's back was toward them, and Courtney had no idea if he knew they were there. Savannah and Nick continued to dance nearby, but then they noticed what was going on between Courtney, Oliver and Brett, and stopped to watch, too.

"What the hell is your problem?" Oliver said to him.

"Let her answer my question." Brett didn't budge from where he stood.

Oliver slung his arm around her shoulders. "Why don't you tell this loser to get lost, and we can get back to where we left off," he said. Courtney wondered if he'd put his arm around her out of affection or because he needed help standing. Probably the latter. She cringed, feeling suffocated by his touch.

Brett pushed Oliver to the side, stepped closer to Courtney and cupped her face with his hands. She barely had time to register that he was about to kiss her before he lowered his lips to hers. She kissed him back, as she'd longed to since their first night together at the fireworks. His lips were so soft, and everything she'd held inside for the past few days was set free. It was just her and Brett; no one else existed. She didn't care what anyone thought or said—being with Brett felt right. Courtney's emotions had always been controlled and steady, logical and levelheaded. But around Brett, it was like she was on a high-speed roller coaster with steep drops and corkscrew turns, and she never wanted to get off.

"I've been wanting to do that since we first met." Brett said exactly what she was thinking.

"Me, too." She looked into his eyes and smiled, unable to believe this was happening.

"Well, isn't this sweet," Oliver said, drawing her out of her Brett-induced trance. "I guess this is what you meant when you said you were interested in someone you couldn't be with. Clearly you've been bonding with your soon-to-be stepbrother." His eyes shone with malice, and Courtney's happiness transformed into dread at the truth of his words. At least he'd said it quietly, and the music was loud enough that no one else had heard. Adrian would *not* be happy if Oliver had ruined the surprise about his engagement to Rebecca.

Courtney's cheeks flushed in shame. The kiss with Brett couldn't have been more public. How could she have been so irresponsible? Now everyone would know about them. And if anyone didn't, Oliver would probably change that.

She checked Adrian's table to make sure he hadn't seen, but the livid look in his eyes made it clear he had. He walked over to them, his lips set in a firm line. This was a disaster. Courtney's head spun, and Savannah hurried to her side, holding her hand in solidarity. Her throat tightened as Adrian got closer to them, and she swallowed to force herself to relax.

"It's almost midnight," Adrian said when he reached them. His voice was tight, like he was trying to stop himself from screaming. "Rebecca and I are going into the casino for the ribbon-cutting. Get Peyton and meet us there."

Courtney nodded, her mouth dry. Adrian hadn't had time to get to know her yet, and she'd already let him down. She was a terrible daughter. Her stomach swirled, a lump formed in her throat and she felt like she was about to cry. This must be how other people felt when they broke the rules and got caught. It was positively awful. Why would anyone break rules a second time after feeling like this?

But she wouldn't take back Brett's kissing her, or kissing him back. Maybe the euro he'd given her to throw into the fountain at Paris really had been magical. Her wish had come true.

It also didn't lack complications.

One thing was for sure—things were only going to get harder from here.

Chapter 27: *Peyton*

Peyton hated Las Vegas, with its too-bright lights, phony smiles and noise blaring from every direction. She missed her friends in San Francisco and wanted to go home. At least at Myst she could lose herself in the music alongside the drunk tourists or locals who weren't "good" enough to get onto the VIP level. She lost count of how many guys she danced with, the minutes an endless blur.

Her phone buzzed in her purse, and she ignored it. Whoever it was could wait. But by the third time they tried to call, Peyton pulled it out to check who it was.

Courtney. With a giant sigh, she clicked the answer button, lifted the phone to her ear and waited for her sister to speak.

"Where are you?" Courtney's voice was barely audible over the loud music.

"The second floor," Peyton said, cupping her hand around her mouth to direct her voice into the speaker. "Why?"

"It's almost midnight," Courtney said. "We have to go to

the ribbon-cutting. We're waiting by the steps on the third floor. Come up and we'll walk over to the casino together."

"Fine." Peyton didn't hide the bitterness from her tone.

She took another sip from the fruity cocktail some guy she'd danced with had bought her and walked to the spiral staircase, heading up to the VIP floor. She took a deep breath, listening to the clanking of her stilettos as she made her way up. At least the drinks had made her tipsy enough to handle seeing Oliver and Courtney together. When Courtney had said yesterday that she wasn't interested in Oliver, Peyton thought she had won the bet. But after seeing them together at dinner tonight, she wasn't so sure. Could Oliver have won over Courtney? Peyton shook away the thought. They would make a terrible couple. Plus, he was way too wild for her.

She met up with her sisters, and the walk to the casino was silent. Savannah wasn't even trying to talk about something trivial, like who was wearing what at Myst and if it looked good on them or not. Courtney couldn't stop fidgeting with her dress, and Oliver's face was hard, his hands curled into fists by his sides. Peyton walked as far behind him as possible. He kept glaring at Brett, getting angrier every time. Courtney walked between them like she was trying to stop a massive war from breaking out.

Something big had gone down while Peyton was gone, and she wanted to find out what it was.

Peyton shot Savannah a questioning look, and her younger sister let her eyes roam to Courtney before looking over at Peyton again. She knew something. Peyton checked her watch. Eleven-forty. She still had time to get some info on whatever was going on.

"I'm stopping at the restroom," Peyton announced, spotting one and giving Savannah a "you're coming with me" look.

She got the hint and followed her inside. Courtney rushed in after them, and Brett said something about him and Oliver waiting for them in the hall.

The restrooms in the Diamond were top-notch. The stalls had floor-to-ceiling wooden doors leading to little "toilet rooms," the counter was granite and modern-looking chandeliers hung from the ceiling. A staff member even stood at the end of the sinks to pump the soap dispensers and provide people with cloth towels after they washed their hands.

"What's going on?" Peyton looked back and forth between Savannah and Courtney. "And don't say 'nothing,' because I'll know you're lying."

"Brett kissed Courtney," Savannah said, clamping her hands over her mouth after speaking. "In the middle of the dance floor. With Adrian, Rebecca, Logan and Ellen watching."

Peyton looked at Courtney for verification. Courtney nodded, her eyes focused on the floor.

"You and Brett?" Peyton repeated, astonished. Had the rule-following Courtney she'd always known been abducted by aliens and replaced by a rebellious pod person? "So there's no chance of anything happening between you and Oliver?"

"There was never a chance of anything happening between me and Oliver." Courtney scoffed. "And let me tell you, he was pissed I told him no. I get the impression that girls don't turn him down often."

Peyton couldn't have felt more relieved. Not only had she been right that Courtney wouldn't be interested in Oliver, but she'd won their bet. Oliver was *not* going to be happy. And after the cruel way he'd spoken to her at Luxe, she would have to get back at him somehow. With the bet won, she could tell him to do one thing, and he would have to do it. This would be fun.

Then Savannah's phone buzzed with a text message, and her mouth dropped open as she read it.

"What?" Peyton asked.

"Evie's having a sleepover with some of the volleyball girls, and they looked us up online," Savannah said slowly, as if she couldn't believe the rest of it. "They found this website where apparently people are talking about us a lot...." She shook her head, reading over the text again.

"Let me see it." Peyton grabbed the phone out of Savannah's hands. She scanned through Evie's gossip, her eyes finally finding the one line Savannah must have freaked out about:

i heard Oliver bet a friend he could sleep with all three Diamond sisters by the end of summer.

Peyton cursed and read it again. "What a douchebag," she said, handing the phone back to Savannah.

"Are the two of you going to tell me what's going on?" Courtney looked over Savannah's shoulder so she could see the screen, and she took a sharp breath inward. "I'm so glad I told that jerk to back off," she said.

"But we don't know if it's true or not," Savannah said. "It's from some stupid gossip site. It could be made up."

"There's only one way to find out." Peyton flipped her hair and strutted out of the bathroom, her sisters' footsteps pattering behind. Oliver and Brett were waiting where they'd left them.

"How did the sister meeting go?" Oliver smirked.

"I'm sure you would love to know." Peyton sneered. "Or better yet, join us so you could try hooking up with the three of us at once to win your little bet."

Panic crossed his eyes, and he took a step back. "What are you talking about?"

"The bet you made to sleep with the three of us before the end of summer," Peyton said steadily, not believing his innocent act for a second.

Brett's fist tightened, and he glared at Oliver. "Is that true?"

Oliver paused to think, and that must have been enough of an answer for Brett, who lunged and punched him in the eye. Oliver's hands went to his face and he fell back into the wall. Brett pulled back his fist to strike again, but his bodyguard was on him before he had a chance. Oliver pushed himself off the wall and rushed at Brett, but suddenly Jackson was there, his arms wrapped around Oliver to hold him in place. Teddy and Carl surrounded them, too, looking ready to jump in if necessary.

"You boys need to cut it out," Jackson said through gritted teeth. "The ceremony is in ten minutes, and your families are counting on you to be there."

"He punched me first." Oliver glared at Brett, his eye red where Brett had hit him.

"And it sounds like you deserved it." Jackson tightened his hold on Oliver, his voice eerily calm.

"Oh, really?" Oliver smirked. "I'm sure your boss would love to hear about how you're harassing his future partner's son."

"As much as he would love hearing about the bet you made involving his daughters?"

"Whatever, man." Oliver pulled at Jackson's arms, but he didn't budge. Oliver was built, but next to Jackson, he looked small. "Just let me go. Like you said, we have to be in the casino soon."

Jackson looked at Brett, who was still being held in place by his bodyguard. "If we let go, do you guys promise to act civil?"

"Yes," Brett agreed, flexing his fist. "I'm feeling much better now."

"I didn't want to fight with that loser in the first place," Oliver said.

Jackson looked at Brett's guard, who nodded, and they both let up their hold on the guys.

Courtney rushed to Brett to check on his hand, and Peyton turned to Jackson. "You didn't have to get involved, you know," she said. "I wouldn't have minded seeing Brett kick Oliver's ass."

"I would have enjoyed it, too." Jackson laughed. "But if I don't get you to that ribbon-cutting ceremony in time, I'll have to answer to your dad. Let's go."

When they arrived at the casino, Adrian was standing on a raised platform with a thick gold ribbon strung in front of it, Rebecca on one side and Logan and Ellen on the other. A crowd had gathered around them, and Peyton had to push her way through to the platform. Adrian smiled and motioned for her and the rest of the group to join him.

She hiked up the three steps to the platform, Savannah, Courtney, Brett and Oliver following behind her. Nick stood nearby to watch. Logan frowned when he saw Oliver, and the two of them stepped to the side to talk quietly. Peyton wondered if the tension between the group was as noticeable to the people watching as it was to her. It seemed impossible that it wasn't. When Logan and Oliver stepped back to the front, Peyton swore she saw a fire brewing in the older man's eyes, but it disappeared a moment later.

Adrian cleared his throat, and the crowd went silent. "Welcome to the grand opening of the Diamond Hotel and Casino, and the Diamond Residences!" he said, which was met with applause from the audience. "But before we begin, I want to make a very special announcement." He turned to Rebecca with a knowing look in his eyes. Peyton thought he would be angry about what had just happened with Courtney and Brett, but he looked so happy, gazing at Rebecca with what Peyton could tell was true love. Peyton had never believed true love existed, but seeing Adrian looking at Rebecca, she thought it might be possible.

He was clearly capable of love, so why was he so distant with his daughters?

He turned back to the crowd. "As of tonight, I am officially engaged to the woman I've loved since we dated in high school, Rebecca Carmel." He held Rebecca's hands in his, both of them beaming at each other as the crowd erupted into clapping and cheers of congratulations. "We're very excited about this, as is Rebecca's son, Brett, and my daughters, Peyton, Courtney and Savannah, who have made the decision to move to Las Vegas so our family can be together." The crowd cheered again, this time their attention on Peyton and her sisters. Peyton looked out at everyone, amazed that they cared about her life. There had to be hundreds of people out there.

Adrian lowered his hands, and everyone quieted. "I'm going to hand over the stage to my friend and colleague Logan Prescott, the owner of the well-known Gates Hotel among many others, for a few minutes."

"Thank you, Adrian," Logan said, taking the microphone and clearing his throat. He took a long pause, and started, "I would first like to offer my warm congratulations to both you and Rebecca, and for the opening of this magnificent hotel and condominium complex. You've outdone yourself this time." He continued for a few more minutes, talking about how difficult hotel openings were to accomplish and

how this would go down as one of the best in history, and
handed the microphone back to Adrian so that he could take
the stage once again.

Peyton was confused. Wasn't Logan supposed to have announced the collaboration for the new hotel and casino in
Macau? Adrian looked as puzzled as Peyton felt, but just for a
second. She doubted anyone in the crowd noticed.

"Thank you, Logan," he said, strong and steady. He thanked
a bunch of people Peyton had never heard of, and she tried to
remain as still as possible, despite having no idea what to do
with her hands. Finally, Adrian said, "And now, for the moment we've all been waiting for!"

A staff member handed Adrian a giant pair of scissors covered in crystals that glittered like diamonds. He posed for an
in-action photo, then cut the gold ribbon. Cameras flashed,
and the crowd cheered again, louder than before. Champagne
popped as cocktail waitresses dressed in tiny outfits uncorked
bottles around the room, and a jazz band played "Diamonds
Are a Girl's Best Friend." People gravitated toward the slot machines and green felt tables, and once more, the games began.

But Peyton had one thought on her mind—she wanted to
talk to Oliver. She spotted him at the circular bar in the center of the lobby. The bar was elevated with three steps leading up to it, and wrought-iron rails lined the edges, making it
feel private while still in the middle of the action. Oliver was
chatting with the bartender, a woman in her upper twenties.
She was too old to consider hooking up with a high-schooler,
right? Peyton didn't want to know.

She slid into the seat next to him, and he looked over at
her in surprise. "Hey," she said, trying to act nonchalant.
His eye was already swollen, and the bruise around it looked

painful. Thinking about how Brett had punched him made Peyton smile.

"Hey." He took out his cell phone and texted someone, apparently not thrilled to see her.

Peyton ordered a soda—she didn't want to get called out for her shoddy fake ID again—and looked at Oliver. "I heard about what happened earlier," she said. "With Courtney and Brett. It's kinda messed up, since they're going to be step-siblings and everything."

"Yeah." He shook his head and took a gulp of what looked like vodka on the rocks. "That's an understatement."

She figured she should get to the point. "Now that Courtney's made it clear she's not interested in you, without my telling her we hooked up and advising her away from you, I've won our bet."

"Right. The bet." Oliver leaned back in his chair and looked at her in challenge. "What do you want me to do? Have sex with you again?"

She rolled her eyes. Was he really that arrogant? "If we have sex again, it won't be because I won a bet," she said. Oliver made a face that implied that would never happen again, but Peyton ignored him. "Not like you'll have a chance with me again, since I know about the disgusting bet you made about me and my sisters. Luck isn't on your side this week, is it? Anyway," she continued, not giving him time to respond, "I'm not sure what I want you to do yet. But eventually I'll think of something, and when I do, I'll tell you."

"You do that." His phone buzzed again, and he texted someone back. "I gotta go," he said, barely looking at her as he shoved his cell into his pocket. "Have fun tonight."

He headed out of the bar, leaving Peyton alone. Restless, she got up and searched for the nearest restroom. The drinks were catching up with her. But she must have made a wrong turn, because she found herself in an unfamiliar hall lined with doors for hotel personnel only. She was about to turn around when she heard yelling coming from a slightly propped-open door—the voice sounded like Adrian's. She shouldn't eavesdrop, but unable to resist, she tiptoed closer to listen, hugging the wall so she wouldn't get caught.

"Why didn't you announce the deal, Logan?" The voice was unmistakably Adrian's, and he sounded pissed. "You know how important it is we get started in Macau as soon as we can."

"After what I've witnessed this week, I'm not sure there's going to be a deal," a low male voice that must be Logan Prescott replied.

"And why's that?" Adrian's ability to stay calm in any situation baffled Peyton.

"I have my reasons," he said. "Four of them, specifically."

"Oh?" Adrian asked. "Would you care to explain?"

"Of course," he said. "Savannah is the least concerning of them all, but there's been talk about her promiscuity since she got here. I don't see it as much as I do with the eldest, though—Peyton."

Peyton gasped and scooted closer to the door.

"You let her run around town dressed like a prostitute instead of the daughter of one of the biggest hotel owners in this city," Logan said. "Not only is she embarrassing herself, but everyone associated with her."

"I think you're being too harsh on them," Adrian interrupted. "They're teenagers. Don't you remember what it was like for you when you were their age?"

"They're not just any teenagers," he said. "They're teenagers in the public eye, and with their privilege comes a responsibility to behave in certain ways. Now, let's move on to

Courtney. I thought she was the best of the bunch—classy, composed—but she squashed that when she made out with her future stepbrother in the middle of the dance floor for everyone to see. Can you imagine what the press will think when they hear about that? It'll be all over the place in no time."

"I did forbid my girls from getting involved with Brett, and I'll talk to Courtney about how it's unwise to do so, but you have to remember that they're not genetically related," Adrian said. "The press will have a field day with it, sure, but it's not incest we're talking about. It will blow over. But still, I don't see how any of this could take precedence over our securing the biggest partnership Macau has seen yet. Are you forgetting how well both of us can do if it all goes to plan?"

"My decision became final when your future stepson *punched my son in the eye.*" The harshness in Logan's tone raised goose bumps across Peyton's arms. "That is physical assault, Adrian, and I won't stand for it. There are many others in this city who want to break into Macau, and while your name is one of the best-known, it won't be difficult for me to find another partner."

Peyton felt like a hole had formed in her chest. Not wanting to get caught listening, she ran back down the hall and eventually found the restroom. By dressing the way she did, she'd hoped to prove to Adrian that he didn't get to tell her what to do after being uninvolved in her life until now. She'd never intended to ruin an important business deal. She ran the water in the sink and splashed some onto her forehead. This had gotten way out of control.

She left the restroom in time to see Adrian and Logan walking back to the casino, neither of them looking happy.

"Adrian?" she called out when she saw him. "Can I talk to you for a second?"

"Sure," he said, although he did glance at his watch, the ever-present reminder that he had somewhere important to be.

"I know you're busy, so this will be quick," Peyton promised.

Logan continued to the casino, leaving Peyton alone for the first time with her father. She wrapped her arms around herself, unsure how to start. "So, I didn't mean to, but I accidentally heard some of what you and Logan were talking about a few minutes ago," she started. "I was looking for the restroom and took a wrong turn." She didn't want him to think she'd been purposefully eavesdropping.

Adrian frowned and scratched the back of his neck. "What did you hear?"

"I heard what Logan said, about me and my sisters." She looked at the ground and shifted uncomfortably, her chest tightening at what she had to say next. "And I just wanted to say…well, I'm sorry. I mean, I still don't understand why you haven't been involved in our lives until now—it pisses me off and I'm not okay with it—but I didn't mean for it to get that out of control. I'll talk to Courtney and Savannah, if you want."

Then Adrian did something unexpected—he stepped forward and hugged her. It was an awkward hug, and it only lasted for a second, but it was the most contact he'd had with any of them since they'd arrived.

He stepped back and straightened his tie. Peyton had no idea what to say.

"My guests are probably wondering where I am," Adrian said. "Are you ready to go back?"

"I'm actually going to stay here for a few more minutes, to think some things through," Peyton said. "I'll see you later."

He said goodbye and strolled back into the casino. Peyton stared after him, astonished. She wouldn't go so far as to say they were starting to have a father-daughter relationship, or that she *wanted* a father-daughter relationship with him, but it was certainly the closest they'd come to one yet.

She needed to talk to someone, but Savannah was busy talking to Nick, and Courtney had enough going on with Brett. She scanned the hall for Jackson, who must have been hiding himself well. But she knew how to force alone time with him, so she headed to the private elevators that went to the top floors. She pressed the button and waited.

"Leaving already?" Jackson asked from behind her.

"These shoes are killing my feet." Peyton said the first idea that came to her about why she would need to go to her room. It wasn't a lie—the strappy stilettos Savannah had convinced her to wear were giving her blisters. She'd only given in because the pool party earlier was outside and it was too hot for closed-toe shoes, but she missed her comfortable black boots. "I need a different pair."

"Good," he said. "Your father would be unhappy if you left the party this early."

"What are you, my babysitter?"

Jackson followed her into the elevator. "Just trying to be helpful."

Peyton narrowed her eyes and pressed the button for her floor. "I can do what I want. If I wanted to leave now, I would do it, whether Adrian would be unhappy about it or not."

"I've gotten that impression about you," Jackson said with a hint of a smile, and it took her breath away. She leaned against the wall of the elevator, trying to breathe steadily so she wouldn't feel so light-headed. She felt like a little girl with a crush. What was Jackson doing to her?

The doors to the elevator closed, the two of them the only ones inside. Peyton focused her eyes on Jackson, making them as smoldering as she could. "You were right about Oliver, you know. I should have listened to you at Luxe. I would have had much more fun with you than with him."

Without giving him a chance to reply, she stepped forward and pressed her lips to his. For a second he responded to her kiss, but he pushed her away so quickly that it could have been in her imagination. She looked up at him in question, and he backed away, his hazel eyes hard.

"You can never do that again," he said, his voice haunted, as if kissing her disgusted him.

"Because you work for Adrian?" That had to be the reason. Otherwise he had a problem with *her,* and that hurt too much to consider.

"That, and because you're a minor. I know I'm only five years older than you, but people change a lot in those five years. They grow up, and realize who they are and who they're meant to be. You're just a kid, Peyton. Do you know how much trouble I could get in if anyone saw what just happened?"

She couldn't believe that was how he thought of her. Sure, she was five years younger than him, but she wasn't an average seventeen-year-old. She'd been through too much with her mother to be as childlike as Jackson believed. "You don't have to worry about that, because no one saw," she said.

He looked baffled by her comment. "This is a casino in Las Vegas." He pointed at a small black dome in the top corner of the elevator. "There are cameras *everywhere*. They're always watching you, always recording you."

"That's what those black things are?" Peyton looked at it and tilted her head.

"Yes." Jackson didn't find her ignorance funny. "What did you think they were?"

"I don't know," Peyton said. "I never thought about it."

"Well, now you know," he said. "Let's just hope that no one who knows either of us ever sees the footage of what just happened here tonight."

The elevator doors opened, and they headed down the hall. "Go change your shoes," Jackson said when they arrived at the door to her condo. "I'm suddenly not feeling well. I'll get the night guard to cover the rest of my shift. Don't go back downstairs until he's here."

Peyton didn't see Jackson again for the rest of the night. But despite everything he'd told her, she didn't regret what she'd done. He'd kissed her back, even if it was only for a fraction of a second.

She didn't plan on forgetting that.

Chapter 28: *Madison*

Madison's phone chimed from her nightstand, and she picked it up to see who had texted her. She hoped it wasn't Larissa or Damien. She wasn't in the mood for either of them bugging her about her "headache" and asking her to come back to the party. After seeing Brett kiss Courtney, she'd wanted to change into her pajamas and watch *Moulin Rouge,* her favorite movie to put on when she was upset. So she did just that. She was at the part where Satine and Christian were standing on top of the elephant singing about how much they loved each other. She didn't want Larissa or Damien's nagging to ruin the perfection of the scene.

Madison wished her life was as simple as a musical. Not like *Moulin Rouge,* since Satine died at the end, but something happier—maybe a Disney classic like *Aladdin* or *The Little Mermaid.* Where the girl gets the guy and they live happily ever after.

But Madison wouldn't mope for long. When the movie ended she would take a sleeping pill, wake up in the morning and snap back into reality, all wishes of fairy-tale life aside. Because Madison knew that in order to get what she wanted, she had to *make* it happen. She had to forget about Brett Carmel. There were other guys out there, and so many of them wanted a chance with her.

The challenge was finding the one she was interested in back.

Realizing she had gotten lost in thought, she checked her cell phone. She breathed a sigh of relief when she saw it was Oliver who had texted her. He wanted to know where she was.

Went back up to my room, she texted him back. Tonight sucked and I didn't feel like staying any longer.

There was no point lying to Oliver and saying she had a headache. He knew that's what she did whenever she felt like leaving somewhere she didn't want to be anymore.

Her phone chimed again.

I agree with you there. Can I come up?

Madison paused. She wanted time to herself. Then again, this was Oliver, her best friend. She didn't have to pretend around him.

Only if you're in the mood to watch Moulin Rouge.

He replied a second later. It's better than dealing with Peyton Diamond. The girl won't leave me alone.

Madison laughed. There always was a girl who wouldn't leave Oliver alone. He brought it upon himself by leading them on and ditching them, but who was she to judge? As long as he didn't treat *her* like crap—which he never had—Madison didn't mind. He had more respect for her than that.

However, she was glad he'd ditched Peyton Diamond. She'd also done a fantastic job getting Damien away from Savannah. The problem now was that Nick seemed to be interested in Savannah, and he deserved better than that.

They wouldn't last long. If they did…Madison would find a way to intervene.

The "Elephant Love Medley" scene ended, and the doorbell rang. Madison's parents were still at the party, so she got out of bed to answer it, examining her reflection in the mirror. The black yoga pants from Victoria's Secret and matching tank weren't the sexiest pajamas on the planet, but Madison made them look good.

Not like she was trying to impress Oliver.

"Hey," he said when she answered the door. "Your night going as great as mine?"

"Oh, yeah," Madison said sarcastically, stopping when she saw the bruise around Oliver's eye. She reached to touch it, but held back, not wanting to hurt him. "What happened? Do you want me to get you an ice pack?"

"You should see the other guy," Oliver joked. "But sure, an ice pack would be nice."

She got one from the freezer, handed it to him, and they walked to her room. She wanted to know what happened, but knew he would tell her eventually if she didn't push him.

"So why'd you bail?" He kicked his shoes off and jumped onto her bed. He looked at the place where the movie had paused—when the camera was panning out on the giant elephant in the middle of the Moulin Rouge—and sank into the mountain of pillows at the head of the bed. "Just missed my favorite part," he said in mock disappointment.

"I can rewind it for you." Madison laughed and reached for the remote control.

Oliver cracked a smile, bringing out the dimple on his cheek. "I think I'll live. But why'd you leave early? I thought big parties like this were your thing."

"They are," Madison said, leaning back in the pillows. Should she tell him the *real* reason she'd left early? Keeping it secret was driving her crazy, and she trusted Oliver not to tell anyone. "But I just found out that the guy I like—or thought I liked—is into someone else. It's stupid, but I didn't feel like being there anymore."

"Understandable." He studied her with more intensity than normal. "If it helps, whoever he is, he's a total idiot."

"It's Brett Carmel," Madison confessed.

"That loser whose mom is marrying Adrian Diamond?" Oliver looked genuinely shocked.

"They're engaged?"

"They made the announcement at midnight."

"Huh," Madison said. If Courtney and Brett were going to be step-siblings, that could put a damper on their relationship. Maybe it could work in Madison's favor. "And, yes, that's Brett."

"That's one of the more random things I've heard tonight."

"Not that random," she defended herself. "I tutored him in bio last year."

"So he's a loser *and* stupid," Oliver joked, although Madison sensed a trace of bitterness in his tone.

"Hey." She gave his arm a playful punch. "Just because someone needs tutoring doesn't mean they're stupid."

"But it *does* mean you're smarter than him," he said. "You can do better." His lips twisted into a scowl, reminding Madison that he'd been having a bad night, too.

"Why'd you leave?" she asked.

"Because Courtney ditched me for Brett," Oliver said, confirming her suspicions. "Then Peyton somehow found out about that stupid bet I made with Damien, asked me about it in front of her sisters and Brett, and Brett clocked me in the eye. I was about to take him down, but their bodyguards held both of us back. He would have been toast otherwise."

"Sure," Madison said. She didn't think Oliver had been in a physical fight in his life.

"But you should have seen the look on my dad's face when he saw Brett and Courtney together," he continued. "Then I told him about how Brett was the one who punched me, and he held off on the announcement about the Macau hotel. It was priceless. But it messed up my game with Courtney. If Brett wasn't an issue, I would have easily been able to get with her."

"I didn't think you liked Courtney that much." Madison's voice was more bitter than she'd intended.

"She's okay," Oliver said.

Madison raised an eyebrow. "You can do better than the Diamond girls."

"I know," he said. Madison wondered what he meant by that, but he continued before she could ask. "Anyway, are we gonna watch the movie or what?"

She picked up the remote and pressed Play. The movie resumed, and she tried to relax as she watched, but she kept glancing at Oliver. Luckily he didn't notice. It wasn't like she was *interested* in him. He was her best friend. Whatever small interest she was feeling for him was a strange reaction to the Brett/Courtney situation.

All she knew for sure was that the Diamond sisters were causing some serious drama, and she had to put an end to it before it got worse. They weren't anything special.

The solution was simple: Madison would have to put them back on the sidelines, which was exactly where they belonged.

www.campusbuzz.com

WTF
Posted on Sunday 07/10 at 11:15 AM

Who else saw that Brett guy making out with Courtney Diamond in the middle of Myst last night? He came outta nowhere. Not gonna lie, he's a complete hottie, but as everyone who was there last night knows, their parents are *engaged*. To *each other.* WTF doesn't even cover it. Not that they're related or anything, but still. It's weird.

1: Posted on Sunday 07/10 at 11:49 AM

I never noticed Brett before, but you're right, he's super hot! Apparently he went to Palo and transferred to Goodman in the middle of last year. When he's done hooking up with his future stepsister (and I agree, definite weirdness), I'll be waiting...

2: Posted on Sunday 07/10 at 12:53 PM

those diamond girls are pretty hot, too. hopefully i'll have a few classes with them in the fall. maybe they'll need help catching up on the goodman curriculum...

3: Posted on Sunday 07/10 at 1:13 PM

School? We've still got a month and a half left of summer! Who wants to think about school?

4: Posted on Sunday 07/10 at 1:48 PM

You've got a point. But I think we can all agree on one thing—judging from the past week, there are gonna be major changes around school with the Diamond girls in town. I'm interested in what those changes will be. Guess we'll have to wait and see ☺

Cya around! And remember—what happens in Vegas stays in Vegas...but that doesn't matter when you live there ;)

★ ★ ★ ★ ★

Acknowledgments

Five years ago, I was a junior in college and decided to write my first novel for the goal of publication. I can't believe that dream has become a reality, and it definitely didn't happen without the help of some incredibly supportive people along the way, who never stopped believing in me.

Brent Taylor—you believed in *The Secret Diamond Sisters* from the very first draft, and that means so much to me. Your never-ending enthusiasm and advice showed me that this book deserved to be read by the world. Whenever I doubted myself, I thought of that and it helped me through!

My editor, Natashya Wilson—ever since we first met at Book Expo America, I knew I wanted to work with you, and I am honored to join your talented group of authors at MIRA Ink. Your insight and ideas have helped this book become so much more than I ever imagined it could be. You pushed me to dig deeper into the characters and the story, and without you, this book wouldn't be *close* to what it is today. I am a better writer because of you. Thank you a million times for taking a chance on me and believing in me!

My agent, Molly Ker Hawn—you are such an incredible person and agent, and I will never forget that day when I was in Nebraska and got the call from you that you wanted to take on *The Secret Diamond Sisters*! You helped me polish my writing, and pushed me to bring these characters to life. You are so organized, prompt, kind, fun and amazing at what you do, and I am so grateful that you believed in this story and took a chance on me.

Lisa Wray—it was so great meeting you at BEA last year, and thank you for your enthusiasm for *The Secret Diamond Sisters*! I loved hanging out with you, and I know that with you, this book is in perfect hands to get out into the world.

Erin Craig, and the cover design team—thank you for bringing the spirit of the story alive in your amazing cover art. The cover is beautiful (I literally stared at it for hours in awe of your work), and while I knew my cover art was in fantastic hands at MIRA Ink, it still exceeded all of my expectations!

My mom, Anne Madow—you have done *everything* for me to help ensure my dream of publication became a reality. Thank you for reading through hundreds of drafts, figuring out the details of the business side of writing when it became too much for me to handle on my own, scheduling all of my events, keeping me organized and for always, always believing in me!

My dad, Richard Madow—thank you for being patient with me, and for believing in me even when it might have felt like reaching this goal would be impossible. I know you worried about my plunging headfirst into such an eccentric career choice, but through it all you never gave up on me and were always proud of me, and that means so much.

My brother, Steven Madow—every time I meet a friend of yours, they tell me how you talk about my writing all the time and how proud you are of what I'm doing. Thank you for reading my books, giving your opinions, coming to my events and your never-ending enthusiasm! I hope you enjoy the inside jokes added for your amusement. :)

My grandparents, Phyllis and Paul Lichtenstein, and Lois and Selvin Madow—the four of you are such smart, hardworking individuals, and are fantastic examples to all your grandchildren. You are always enthusiastic, proud and supportive. Thank you!

Aunt Barbara, Uncle Jeffrey, Uncle Dave, Aunt Yoko, Uncle Marshall, Lauren Setzer, Michael Setzer, Evan Madow, Sandy Lichtenstein, Jackie Lichtenstein, Michael Lichtenstein, Kandy Scherr, Sam Scherr, Ben Scherr and the rest of my amazing family—thank you for the interest, support and questions about my writing whenever we get together. Your genuine interest and belief in what I'm doing means so much.

My college best friends and sorority sisters: Kaitlin, Tiffany, Devan, Alicia and Amy—you are all amazing people, and I'm so grateful that we shared an incredible (crazy, fun, emotional) four years together. You all know me better than anyone else. Thank you for believing in me from the first draft of my first book, for being my cheerleaders, for always being there to talk to and for your great advice. Even though we all live far apart, whenever we see each other it's like no time has passed, and I know with the group of you I have friends for life.

Everyone who picked up this book at a bookstore or down-loaded it to their e-reader—THANK YOU! I hope you enjoyed the story of the Diamond sisters, and that you continue to enjoy it, as there is more to come!

The fans who have been there since *Remembrance*—thank you for taking a chance on an unknown author, believing in me and supporting me from the beginning of my career.

My college writing professors from Rollins College: Twila Papay, Phillip Deaver and Bruce Aufhammer—you saw something special in my writing before I realized it myself. Thank you for guiding me and helping me grow to become a published author.

My classmates in my Fall 2008 Intro to Creative Writing class—I will never forget the first time I shared my writing with you, and the positive feedback you gave me. You made me believe that other people might care about the stories I'm always creating in my head. You may not know it, but you changed my life. Thank you!

The Secret Diamond Sisters
Playlist

Most of these songs don't have scenes they correlate to in the book, but they generally remind me of the vibe of the story. I listen to this playlist whenever I want to imagine the Diamond sisters having adventures in Vegas!

"Waking Up in Vegas" by Katy Perry
"Diamonds" by Rihanna
"I Like It" (feat. Pitbull) by Enrique Iglesias
"Vegas Girl" by Conor Maynard
"Don't Stop the Party" (feat. TJR) by Pitbull
"International Love" (feat. Chris Brown) by Pitbull
"We Run the Night" (feat. Pitbull) by Havana Brown
"Don't You Worry Child" (feat. John Martin) by Swedish House Mafia
"Va Va Voom" by Nicki Minaj
"Pound the Alarm" by Nicki Minaj
"Last Friday Night" (T.G.I.F.) by Katy Perry
"Gold" by Britt Nicole

"Party Rock Anthem" by LMFAO
"Raise Your Glass" by P!nk
"I Love It" (feat. Charli XCX) by Icona Pop
"Get Lucky" (feat. Pharrell Williams) by Daft Punk
"Crazy Kids" by Ke$ha
"Poker Face" by Lady Gaga
"My Heart Will Go On" by Mariah Carey

Q&A with
Michelle Madow

Tell us a little about yourself and how you became a writer.

I've always loved writing—in second grade, I was "that kid" who on free-write journal day would write long stories and share them with the class. In high school I wrote an (embellished) online journal about my life, and my classmates loved reading it. Then my parents discovered the journal (I talked about some things I did that they weren't aware of...) and I got in major trouble and stopped journaling. In college I discovered the world of fan fiction, and for two years I wrote a ton of it, mainly in the worlds of Twilight and Harry Potter. I didn't realize it at the time, but fan fiction was great practice for honing the craft of writing for later down the road.
In my junior year of college, I signed up for an Intro to Creative Writing course. Our first homework assignment was to turn in any piece of writing we wanted—it could be a poem, a short story or a first chapter of a novel. I wrote the first chapter of a novel. It

was the first time I shared my original fiction with anyone, and I was nervous about what people would think. To my surprise, my teacher and classmates loved it and said I had to continue writing the story because they needed to know what happened next. Hearing such positive feedback brought tears to my eyes. I had always been scared to try writing a novel because I doubted I would be able to finish it, or that the stories in my mind would be long enough to take up all those pages. But in that moment I realized I would never know if I could do it if I didn't try, and by the end of my junior year, my first novel, Remembrance, was completed.

You clearly have an inside knowledge of Las Vegas and what makes it unique. What do you love about the city, and where would you recommend visitors go to have the Diamond experience?

I've been to Las Vegas every year since I was fifteen, and I love how the city bursts with magic and excitement. Vegas does everything as big as possible, so being there is like entering a fantasyland.

As mentioned in The Secret Diamond Sisters, many hotels on the Strip have a unique theme, and one of my favorite activities to do in Las Vegas is visit the hotels and explore. Some of my favorite hotels are: Venetian, Paris, Bellagio, Caesars Palace, Mirage and my number one favorite, the Wynn.

I also love the shows in Vegas. In The Secret Diamond Sisters, Courtney and Brett see Phantom, which was my favorite show there. Unfortunately it has since closed, but the theatre where it played in the Venetian was built to resemble the Paris Opera House, so I recommend seeing whatever is playing there at the time you visit. I also love Beatles Love, which is playing in the Mirage, and Le Reve, which is playing in the Wynn.

Another great part of Vegas is the shopping. There are stores everywhere, and some of my favorite places to shop are: the Forum Shops at Caesars Palace, the Grand Canal Shoppes at the Venetian, the Miracle Mile Shops at Planet Hollywood and the major department stores (Saks, Neiman's, Nordstrom) at the Fashion Show Mall. Fashion Show Mall also has a huge Forever 21 if you're looking for more budget-friendly shopping.

What inspired *The Secret Diamond Sisters*? How did you create the sisters' different personalities?

I was inspired to write The Secret Diamond Sisters *while walking through my favorite hotel in Las Vegas. I thought, "What would it be like to live here?" and the story grew from there.*
As for the four main characters, there are pieces of me within each of them. Savannah, with her dreaming, optimism and desire to fit in, has bits of my high school self in her. Courtney, who is self-aware and happy to be who she is without needing the approval of her peers, has a lot of my current-day self, and she's what I wish I had been like in high school. Peyton is the most different from me of the four, but she has my dislike of following arbitrary rules and my desire for individuality. Madison has my confidence and ambition, along with my tastes in clothes and food. From there, I took those qualities and built each character into their own person.

Time to fess up—do you have a favorite sister? How about a favorite potential hero?

Out of the four main characters, I would most like to be friends with Courtney. But the ones I have the most fun writing are Savannah and Madison. Out of the guys, Brett is definitely the one who

I would most want to date. You know all of Courtney's reasons for liking him? Well, those would be mine, too.

You've given those heroes a lot of room to grow. Can you spill any secrets or give us a hint of what's to come for any of the guys?

At the end of The Secret Diamond Sisters, *none of the guys are where they want to be, as they're all trying to figure out what they want—either in life, or in their relationships. As the story continues, more secrets will be revealed that will challenge everyone, and will push them to think about where they're going in life and with whom their loyalties lie.*

What's in store for the Diamond sisters in book 2, *Diamonds in the Rough*?

In Diamonds in the Rough, *major secrets will be uncovered that will change everything. I don't want to give anything away, but I hope you end up feeling completely differently about certain characters by the end of* Diamonds in the Rough *than you did at the end of* The Secret Diamond Sisters!

What advice do you have for aspiring authors?

A writer I know once told me, "You have to write one million bad words before you write anything others want to read," and that is so true. Writing is a skill, and like any other skill, it takes practice to improve. Experiment with different approaches to writing a novel so you can find what works best for you. I can't write a book without outlining it in detail first, but some people like to let the story come to them as they write. There is no right or wrong way—only the right way for you.

Most importantly, above anything else, you have to write. Know what time of day you get your best writing done, and force yourself to write during that time, even if you're not feeling "inspired." Writing is work, and it's not going to be fun all the time. There will be parts you will struggle with, that will frustrate you to no end and make you want to hit your keyboard, but you need to keep your end goal in mind. Set a minimum goal of how many words you can comfortably write per day, and reach that minimum five days a week. Make sure your goal per day is attainable for you—if it's too high, it will be frustrating and will make you want to quit. And remember that even if you're having a rough writing day, force yourself to reach that minimum. First drafts don't need to be perfect, since you will edit it afterward. Once you draft and edit your first book until you can't edit it any further, write and edit a second. Your second book should be the first in a new series and not a continuation of the first book you wrote, because this will improve your chances of one of your books getting picked up by an agent. Then do the same with a third, and so on. During this time, do your research on the publishing world and submit your books to agents. If you continue to do this, if you believe in yourself and if you want it badly enough, you are giving yourself the best chance for success. Remember: the people who make it are the ones who never gave up!

xoxo,
Michelle

Rose Zarelli, self-proclaimed word geek and angry girl, has some CONFESSIONS to make...

No.1: I'm livid all the time. Why? My dad died. My mum barely talks. My brother abandoned us.

No.2: I make people furious regularly. Want an example? I kissed gorgeous Jamie Forta, boyfriend of the coolest cheerleader in the school. Now she's out for blood. Mine.

No.3: But, most of all, high school might as well be Mars. My best friend has been replaced by an alien...and now it's a case of survival of the coolest.

www.miraink.co.uk

They say be a good girl, get good grades, be popular. They know nothing about me

I can't remember the night that changed my life. The night I went from the top of the pyramid to loner freak.

They said therapy was supposed to help.

They didn't expect Noah.

Noah is the dangerous boy my parents warned me about.

Every kiss, every promise, every touch is forbidden.

But he's the only one who'll help me find the truth.

Are you walking in a dead girl's shoes?

It's hard fitting in as the new girl among the rich elite at Manderley Academy, especially when you're assigned to the old room of the perfect, popular Becca—who's disappeared.

Everyone acts like it's your fault—and you can't leave the mystery alone. What really happened to Becca? And what other sinister secrets have been kept hidden in the school's dark hallways?

www.miraink.co.uk

SHE WON'T REST UNTIL SHE'S SENT EVERY WALKING CORPSE BACK TO ITS GRAVE. FOREVER.

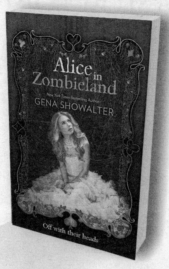

Had anyone told Alice Bell that her entire life would change course between one heartbeat and the next, she would have laughed. But that's all it took. One heartbeat, and everything she knew and loved was gone.

Her father was right. The monsters are real.

To survive, Ali must learn to fight the undead and trust the baddest of the bad boys, Cole Holland. But Cole has secrets of his own and those secrets might just prove to be more dangerous than the zombies.

www.miraink.co.uk

M290_AIZ

Read Me. Love Me. Share Me.

Did you love this book? Want to read other amazing teen books for free online and have your voice heard as a reviewer, trend-spotter and all-round expert?

Then join us at **facebook.com/MIRAink** and chat with authors, watch trailers, WIN books, share reviews and help us to create the kind of books that you'll want to carry on reading forever!

Romance. Horror. Paranormal. Dystopia. Fantasy.

Whatever you're in the mood for, we've got it covered.

Don't miss a single word

 twitter.com/MIRAink

let's be friends

 facebook.com/MIRAink

Scan me with your smart phone

 to go straight to our
facebook page

MIRAINK_SM